Penguin Books
Bloodfather

Born in Sydney, David Ireland now lives in a cottage in the hills outside a NSW country town and spends his days writing and planting trees.

Three of his novels have won the prestigious Miles Franklin Award: *The Unknown Industrial Prisoner* in 1971, *The Glass Canoe* in 1976 and *A Woman of the Future* in 1980. In 1985 *Archimedes and the Seagle*, his eighth novel, won the Gold Medal of the Australian Literature Society.

By the same author

The Chantic Bird
The Unknown Industrial Prisoner
Burn
The Flesheaters
The Glass Canoe
A Woman of the Future
City of Women
Archimedes and the Seagle

Bloodfather

David Ireland

Penguin Books
Published with the assistance of the Literature Board
of the Australia Council

Penguin Books Australia Ltd
487 Maroondah Highway, PO Box 257
Ringwood, Victoria, 3134, Australia
Penguin Books Ltd
Harmondsworth, Middlesex, England
Viking Penguin Inc.
40 West 23rd Street, New York, NY 10010, USA
Penguin Books Canada Limited
2801 John Street, Markham, Ontario, Canada, L3R 1B4
Penguin Books (N.Z.) Ltd
182-190 Wairau Road, Auckland 10, New Zealand

First published by Viking Australia, 1987
Published by Penguin Books Australia, 1989
Copyright© David Ireland, 1987

All Rights Reserved. Without limiting the rights under copyright
reserved above, no part of this publication may be reproduced,
stored in or introduced into a retrieval system, or transmitted,
in any form or by any means (electronic, mechanical, photocopying,
recording or otherwise), without the prior written permission
of both the copyright owner and the above publisher of this book.

Typeset in Australia.
Made and printed in Australia by the Australian Print Group, Maryborough, Victoria.

Ireland, David, 1927 –
Bloodfather.
ISBN 0 14 011630 3.

I. Title.

A823'.3

Creative writing program assisted by the Literature Board of the Australia Council, the Federal Government's arts funding and advisory body.

Bloodfather

To the liberation of God

The Month of Golden Wattle

Midwife Althea Chappell hurried to Legge's Butcher Shop at Bellbird Corner, part of that strange land between city and country called 'outer suburbs'; belonging to neither. She asked for several traditional items to help her deliver the woman lying on the butcher's block, which had been covered with a blanket and some spare aprons. The steel counter was too cold in August.

'It's either very big, or twins,' she said when she felt the abdomen of Lillian Blood, who knew it was twins. She was a good midwife, and liked to be in charge; glad no doctor was present. The mother had collapsed in the shop with her meat order incomplete. After the whole rump and the dogs' meat she gave a terrifyingly loud sneeze, and doubled up with pain. Jim Legge decently put up a Closed sign. It was Wednesday morning.

On the butcher's block the mother writhed. Once she gritted out between pain-locked jaws:

> '*God is my refuge and strength*
> *A very present help in time of trouble.*'

She also sang, a little later:

> '*O love that will not let me go*
> *I hide my helpless soul in you.*'

The butcher didn't hear. Religion was OK for women. He fetched what he was told to fetch by Althea, of the female race who know life, death, birth, and superintend all three.

When the baby boy emerged from the darkness of his mother into the light of common humanity, they cleared his mouth, washed his eyes and face, and tried to get him to cry. He wouldn't.

His new-washed face was contented.

The moment he opened his eyes he looked relaxed and pleased, as if he liked what he saw. The family story grew, despite occasional evidence to the contrary, that he came into the world happy, and stayed that way.

'There's another one, dear,' said midwife Althea. 'But it's dead.' They put it beside the live one. 'No wonder you were big.'

The living baby touched the dead brother. The family said, 'His twin was death, but he was born laughing. He'll die that way.'

It was that day of the year when volcanic ash buried Pompeii, and on which, over three centuries later, Alaric began the sack of Rome; but these details neither helped nor hindered. It was that time of year when the wattles in the valley were splendid, covered in fluffy golden balls of blossom.

Lillian picked up the new life and pressed him to her face. His unsteady sight was filled with glowing brown eyes that seemed to cover him, and also to look into him, meeting the self inside.

God is a Baby

*H*e was a human baby, all powerful, a tyrant who expected and got the best his mother could provide. A dictator, he bent the world to his wish. I am, therefore I will, was his starting point; it became his song, that refrain which sang itself just underneath his everyday actions.

He was the leader, she the led. He ruled with a toothless grin, she followed and loved with warm eyes. He held her with eyes intense and bright as hers. He looked her down and she retreated. He was lord of her universe, she made him believe.

So she installed him, a recumbent, helpless god; a new power in the house, new spring of family action.

Aunt Ursula Blood said, from her shining, elaborate wheelchair: 'A lord of the atmosphere has taken up residence.' Aunt Mira Mitchell, dressed as always in her pink outfit, croaked from her corner of the kitchen: 'Who's a bornless boy, then? Here's a fine kettle of kitsch! What'll he be when he grows up? A gifted busdriver with a stern view of things? Sticks and stones will break his bones but gnomes will never hurt him. Mind his genials now! Guard his decretals! Careful of his little tap and bells!'

The family shut her up with a limp drink of sherry and water.

Nevertheless, god or not, at six days he was baptised in the bath, totally immersed by one of seven Independent Dissenting Brethren. At eight days his foreskin was snipped off, as the Bible ordained.

He didn't miss it, didn't complain. A look of surprise accompanied the immersion, a frown followed the circumcision.

The seven Dissenters present at the baptism were Mr Halliday, Mr House, Mr Fowler, Mr Gardiner, Mrs Rokeby, Mrs Lichfield, and one only recently admitted to the inner fellowship circle, Mr Fox. They made a crowd in the modest bathroom of the old house in Country Road.

Mr Halliday prayed. The first song was:

> 'When I survey the wondrous cross
> On which the prince of glory died,
> My richest gain I count but loss
> And pour contempt on all my pride.'

Mr House spoke, then the little baptism ended with,

'Love divine, all loves excelling.'

sung, as before, without accompaniment. The visitors left a smell of discreet perfume, together with a faint aroma of expensive woollen winter suits. The Lord prospered the Dissenting Brethren. As they left, Aunt Ursula observed that a little of some people goes a long way.

Their sect had been formed in the early years of the nineteenth century, having found much to dissent from in the forms of the day. They had no hierarchy, no ministers, no bosses, no front men, but tried to be as like the early Church as they could. Each brother and sister was face to face with God, conscience, judgment, eternity. There was a ranking of spirituality, insight, eloquence and preaching ability — no formal system seems able to shut out individual force — but this wasn't allowed to disturb the equality of opportunity and responsibility of all members, within the confines of their customs. They made no attempt to go out into the highways and byways to evangelise or proselytise. 'Whosoever will, let him come' was their motto.

Adam in the Garden

The yard backed on to typical Sydney bush: plenty of undergrowth, steep gullies, trees in all stages of growth, rocks everywhere, wildflowers in profusion.

After he began to walk, around ten months, he discovered in the unkept part of the backyard, near where the back fence would be if there'd been a fence, that in this forest he was lord. If he saw an ant he trod on it, killed it, mashing its body, separating its parts. No voices were raised in blame or reproof. If he killed a cicada in December — a Greengrocer, Yellow Monday, Pisser or Black Prince, a Christmas beetle, caterpillar, praying mantis, stick insect, grasshopper, cricket, black and shining millipede — it wasn't as if he had trod on Crippen the cat, or fallen on him, pretending to slip; which he had done once or twice, to prove something to the cat.

It was not as if he had put a hand in the canary's cage and squeezed it dead, or poked Sarah the cockatoo with a stick. It was not as if he hit the dogs Glandular or Lautenbacher with a piece of wood to make them yelp so he could study the yelps.

There were no crimes in the forest, no justice. He was king, with power of life and death over all he encountered. The conqueror has no rules to keep. I am, therefore I can, he congratulated himself in the words of his song. Adult laws didn't run everywhere.

A month older, he ventured into the real bush down past Brown Rock. As he walked between the rough, prickly shrubs, he received from the aboriginal air intimations of a long ago frightening forest where huge fierce creatures raged, of serpents that uncoiled from trees and embraced the soft bodies of humans, crushing life from other life that their own might continue. A green treesnake, a blue-tongued lizard, or, further along the valley, a deadly brown snake, were all that remained of the terrifying past.

By way of stories, he was introduced to Adam and Eve.

GARDEN OF EDEN
When Adam and Eve inhabited their garden
it was full of vegetables, and other things.
There was fruit to be picked, from the tree of knowledge,
the plant of forgetfulness, the bush of courage,
the herb of invulnerability
the grove of immortality

the shrub of safety, the branch of hope.
There were serpents, of course, in the grass, but also
in this garden of lush fears and undying enmities
were huge fierce creatures. God said
they wouldn't bite, but Adam and Eve
took a look at their teeth and forgot God.
As well, their one-time cousins who hadn't changed
were beginning to look askance at them,
to poke fun at their hairlessness.
It was a frightening forest, nothing lovable
about it. The fruits of the herb of invulnerability
and the grove of immortality took
too long to have an effect. The branches
of the shrub of safety were too thin.
Adam and Eve left their so-called garden, scared stiff.
It was beautiful. But everything can be beautiful:
lies, ugliness, violence. Beauty
is no guide to what's good, or safe.
'You can keep your garden, God.' they said.
'We're off.' Embraced
the dangers of hunger and thirst
heat and cold, rather than the ease
of picking fruit; with, in the background
the horror of waiting to be picked like fruit
in turn by some larger animal.
'Let's stand up in our own strength
And die with courage, if we must.'

Davis Blood had no such terrors, the world he inhabited was tamed. The monsters, the huge and terrifying beasts, were gone. Only other humans remained to terrify.

Perhaps mankind is all ages at once:
childlike, curious, beautiful;
headstrong, foolish, energetic;
mature, competent, strong;
older, wise and tired;
foolish, incontinent, worn out.
Often a small child tasted
each age briefly every day.

Lillian

The baby's mother, a Stroud, had emigrated from England two years before she met Jackson Blood. She was a gentle, decisive woman. Her husband noticed her slight eye movement when she first met Aunt Olivine, one of Jackson's sisters, and saw a typical episode of indecisiveness. Olivine could be undecided before and after a decision was made, after action had been taken, and for years after that. As with philosophy down the ages, nothing was ever finally put to rest.

Lillian loved green things and all that was growing, from plump babies to fat radish, glossy spinach and vigorous roses. Her flowers in the front garden made a fine show, and when her husband had a job and she wasn't working, she worked in the backyard garden among the vegetables and herbs. Her succulents and ferns she kept under a half-shade of fine mesh on the eastern side of the house.

She helped people she met up the street; crying children, bag-snatched women, dog-bitten postmen. She listened to the woes of anyone who wanted to talk.

'I'd prefer to risk their ingratitude, rather than refuse to help,' she said once when Ursula gently mocked.

If she had a vice, it was to want her brood, and perhaps herself, not to be too anything: not too clever, not too rich, not too strong, not too good, not too ambitious, noisy, proud; not too quiet. But when they were very young, she encouraged them all, just in case any of them had anything worth bringing out.

She was an Anglican, and brought with her, among her, things, a small book, 'The Earnest Communicant'. Jackson Blood, to tease her, referred to it as The Earnest Communist.

She walked with a long stride and always seemed to be doing something; matters Davis Blood soon noticed. She also sang. Sometimes aloud, other times under her breath, or silently, in the privacy of her own head.

Jackson Blood prized her for her steadiness under pressure, her modesty, nobility, goodness; none of which qualities descended into pigheadedness, vanity, pettiness or hypocrisy, which he thought was an enviable record: but most of all for the fact that whatever the crisis, the disappointment, she remained in good heart.

He tried as best he could to live a Christian life, but often enough the passions and frustrations of daily life, the deceits and bloodymindedness of others, produced crises in him that could be relieved only by violent anger or loud shouts. Lillian seemed not to notice or be upset by what disturbed her Jack. Her wisdom was of a different kind.

The House at Bellbird Corner

Beside the door was a framed and glass-covered sign, 'Casuarina Cottage'. The letters were in gold on a brown background, and were beginning to peel.

The blue ridge of mountain country parallel to the eastern seaboard, the blue ridge that ran from North Queensland to Victoria, could be clearly seen from the western verandah of the old iron-roofed house in Country Road. The house was not far from where Country Road started in dense Sydney bush and only a few kilometres from the northern beaches, the nearest of which was Driftwood Beach, to the north of what locals called the Bay of Solids — because of the obtrusive nature of the outfall from the stark concrete sewage treatment works that scarred Windy Cliffs.

Bread and Butter Creek ran down in Kookaburra Valley behind the house, flowing into Spectacle Creek, then Spectacle Lake nearer the coast, after which it ran through flats into the lagoon, which in turn, when the sea was high and made a channel in the sand, was refreshed by the salt of the Tasman Sea.

It was a noisy house, always someone singing or yelling, dogs barking, fowls squabbling, ducks explaining loudly, Aunt Mira giving someone the rounds of the kitchen or arguing with the radio; or the boys' rock music would be on, or Danielle's New Music playing.

Surfboards and wetsuits littered the space under the house, together with fishing rods and other water gear. Randal's surf ski and paddle had a rack to themselves. Preston, the eldest, had bought it for him. Randal was everyone's favourite.

A short way along Country Road, Big Hill ascended to Anzac Street, which strolled along an east-west ridge past the shops to the railway station. Over the other side of the railway line and into the bush, Billabong Fields began. Further north Currawong Heights, a tiny place of a few dozen houses and two shops, was covered in trees.

It was some time since bellbirds were heard in any number round Bellbird Corner, though people at Honeysuckle Bend said they still had one pair. A new cutting had been blasted in a hill a little to the north-east, to take the new Koala Parkway, bypassing a congested stretch of two converging north-south highways which met to form an A shape. Honeysuckle had been encouraged on wire over the face of the exposed rock; the bellbirds were said to be in the tall trees above the bend, higher up the hill.

Every now and then a local paper would print a rumour that bellbirds were coming back to Bellbird Corner; years came and went but the birds were still coming.

The house itself appeared to be surrounded on three sides by bush. There were two fences defining the width of the block — the bottom fence had gone — but they were of the post and wire variety and gave no hindrance to the view or to animals.

Country Road, where it passed the house, was cut into a

steep hill. The few houses near the Bloods' house were on the low side, on a level with the ground at their fronts, and supported on brick piles at the back. There was room under number twenty for brick piles three metres high on the south-western corner, and two metres on the south-east.

A rope swing hung from the floor joists and swung between two rows of piles. A rock ledge began just past the extent of the swing's back-swing, and curved round to the laundry, making two levels under the house: one where everyone could stand up and the higher level where only kids could comfortably go. It was the house with the highest verandah in that part of Country Road.

Under the house was where you went during temporary disfavour, if you wanted to be alone or think or dream, or if you had some prize you wanted to examine and pore over and make yours.

Country Road, starting near the coast, ran west towards the blue ridge of the Great Dividing Range in the distance, cutting, at Bellbird Corner, the highway that insisted all heavy traffic go north and south along the coast, and also the railway which ran north and south, too.

Going west, Country Road linked up with every sort of road on the way, big and small, and went therefore everywhere and nowhere in particular. It tried hard to get to the blue ridge, but ran into bushland in the west long before it reached the hills, and broke down into dirt roads, access roads, tracks, and finally lost its way among fences and dams.

From the house, the ground fell away to the west and south, but rose again in hills as steep as Big Hill. Due west it rose to the ridge that carried the railway and highway; but in that ridge nature had cut a V through which, as through a gunsight, the deep blue of Blue Ridge could be seen in a closed V shape. That was Gunsight Hill. Lumps could be seen on the distant ridge of blue, like spaced vertebrae along a spine.

By contrast, the streets nearer the station and the shopping centre were shorter and more purposeful: they led somewhere. The better streets had the feel of competition about them; lawns carefully shaved, gardens of a regulation prettiness. If there was a steep slope, a rockery was demanded.

Jackson Blood had no taste for flowers, but liked shrubs and trees, trees more than shrubs, and didn't bother much about the trees. He loved to grow vegetables.

Honeysuckle shaded the front verandah, passionfruit vines masked the piles and spaces at the side of the house between verandah and the ground sloping away down towards Bread and Butter Creek.

It was a small valley, a fold between two ridges. Both slopes of Kookaburra Valley were covered in gum trees, except for the banks of the creek, where black sassafras abounded, lilly pilly sheltered, and coachwood trees grew from moist banks. At sunset galahs screamed and argued. Before sunset, kookaburras laughed their comments on the world and existence.

From September on, the new-born gumtips in the valley shone in the sunshine and flashed in the wind. The little valley was the only catchment for Bread and Butter Creek; in a dry spell the water shrank to a trickle or went underground a way. When the sun dropped over Gunsight Hill rays of golden dust spread out over the tree tops, and little by little the valley filled with darkness.

West from Gunsight Hill, you looked down on more bush, which was largely Crown land and unused, but further west towards the blue ridge the patchwork started, the cultivated fields of good soil where vegetables were grown for the Sydney markets. Suburbs were beginning to encroach, carpeting the best growing land with lawns, pools, roads and houses, but there was still some left for food, though not enough.

I See, Therefore I Can

It was the last day of his first July, a sunny winter's day. His mother sat in the kitchen of Aunt Olivine McGowan's house at Thripdale, further up the coast, talking to Aunt Olivine and Nanna. The burden of their conversation, as so often with Olivine, was the human desire to have nice things without debt and enjoy a long life without wrinkles. Inside the fly-wire screens two flies were dying with occasional bursts of energy. The boy was left alone upstairs. He'd been walking unsteadily for some weeks. Eventually he discovered the landing at the top of the staircase.

In his own head he had a picture of being able to walk as well as any big person, but he sat there at the top of the stairs in a fresh nappy and pilchers, under a blue suit that fitted his feet, covered his legs and went right up to zip at the back of his neck. It was the one with the red and white fancywork figures of two dogs on the chest. He would have to climb down the stairs in a sitting position.

His head leaped the sixteen steps; in that leap he flew down to the carpet runner that led to the front door, through which the light of the bright day shone, and beyond that the sea. That light gleamed on the brass strips that edged each step. Farther on, the light touched the varnished boards on either side of the carpet, and lit the red, blue, green and gold panes of glass that framed the doorway. The door was open, light streamed into the hall, illuminating the oak-framed text on the wall over the hallstand:

> *'The Eternal God is our refuge*
> *And underneath are the everlasting arms.'*

The concrete path to the front gate was white under the sun. He saw himself down there, walking unsteadily, but walking; in joy hurrying towards the front door.

I see, therefore I will — sentiments he couldn't yet express in words — sang inside him. He would have to ease himself down each step on his bottom. Then he was falling.

He noticed, in surprise, that the edges of the stairs detained him with prods and reminders as he passed them. Nothing could stop him now. The light was ahead, that was heart-filling and full of promise; soon he would touch the sun that splashed on the carpet and climbed up the door frame. The treads of the stairs that seemed so soft were bumpy and much harder, though not painful. They hit him in odd places.

As he turned over and over, many places on his body, his fat legs and knees, his soft shoulders, were contacted by those shiny brass stair edges before at last he was left to himself, upside down at the bottom. Slowly he overbalanced from his shoulder on to his back. He stopped to consider, sat up, but didn't complain, since he'd done what he wanted to do.

He stood, shook his head at the way the stairs had used him, then made for the front door, where he stopped and surveyed the brilliant world, the hedge, the white picket fence, the trees either side of the white path, the grey paling fences separating the houses, the electric light poles in the street.

There were interruptions. His mother ran to him with alarming sounds. He looked at her face to see if she was in control of herself. He wished she didn't need attention. He looked round her at the vista of sunny grass, the houses opposite, the gentle curve of the powerlines, the birds that came, sat, flew off. A truck with red sides passed, a yellow car. Yellow! Such a yellow he'd never seen before, it filled the eyes, made you wish it would come back and stay. It was more yellow than Sarah the cockatoo's crest.

He was picked up, his scalp at the side of his head patted with cottonwool soaked in brown stuff, though it felt better without a touch of any kind. He was nursed, enfolded and given something to drink. He was talked to and shown to Nanna and Aunt Olivine — again — but he regretted he was no longer at the front door. He could feel his mother's need to be near him, and touching, and didn't push her away. He would have to be patient. But hadn't he learned, in his three hundred-odd days, to be content with waiting?

Once his mother sneezed, interrupting her ministrations. Her sneeze was renowned in the Blood family and in the local shops and streets. It was so sudden, so cataclysmically loud, that people in crowds stopped stock still. Aunt Olivine and grandma flinched; they always did.

He'd forgotten his wound by teatime, and after the family had eaten resumed his nightly rounds, trotting and lurching from knee to knee round the circle of the family, as if keeping each in touch with the rest.

Warnings and Other Family Members

*H*is father issued warnings, intended to keep him safe.

'Mind the gate, now. Watch it doesn't pinch your finger. If you catch it in the gate, it'll give you curry!' Curry wasn't seen outside the house, so this curry must mean some sort of pain. But how could a gate pinch your finger?

His mother gave warnings, but these were of a different sort. Perhaps she warned him of things she was afraid of. Mothers were different, obviously: their fears weren't yours. As gently and kindly as possible, and without saying so and thus throwing her advice back at her, he let it wash over him with the classic defence of 'Yes, mum.' He knew she cared about everything that happened to him, but most of the things she feared, didn't happen.

'The Lord is my sheriff,' said Aunt Mira Mitchell

sarcastically when a warning was being issued. 'I shall not do what I want.'

The adults shushed her, but no one could keep her quiet when the words wanted to come out.

'You show 'em, bub! Happiness is a sloshy nappy! Oh, Christmas is coming, the ducks are getting fat; cats don't attack reindeer when they can eat rat! All power to the nuclear family! These are the blest years of your life, kid, so eschew respectomania and live with neither malice nor forethought! Above all, run for your life from the three great Australian evils: Wasgunna, Wouldabin, and Deference!

> 'Oh once upon a time when birds ate lime
> And monkeys chewed tobacco leaves
> Cats took snuff to make 'em tough
> And dogs built nests in poplar trees!'

'Hey, kid! The cat's washing itself — look out for visitors! Come on — what has fingers but can't use 'em?'

The little boy looked gravely up at her. He didn't know the answer, but knew by this time someone would be happy to supply it.

'Gloves, of course! What has four legs, a head, and can't walk? A bed. What has teeth but can't bite? A comb, silly! What has a neck but can't swallow? A bottle! Didn't you even know that? Or can't you talk?

> 'Ask no questions, tell no lies,
> Shut your mouth, you'll catch no flies!'

'Oh well, it'll all be the same in a hundred years,' she said, suddenly weary. 'The boneyard gets us all, after the doctor's sucked us dry.' She began to mumble a rhyme.

> 'Phoned for the doctor,
> The doctor couldn't come
> Because he has a pimple
> On his big fat bum.'

and fell asleep, her head falling on her chest, a little to one side.

Aunt Mira Mitchell was alone in the world. She'd lost her mate of many years, the Major, to a Kenworth rig on the Newell Highway south of Jerilderie twenty-five years before. Then, the two of them had been alone in the world.

Uncle Hector had picked her up by the side of the road, distraught after the accident, while Major Mitchell lay dead and bloody on the pink clay among tufts of straw-coloured grass. All Mira could think of was how he'd loved thick scrub country, and mallee best of all. Mallee was his favourite word.

Hector stopped long enough to see to the Major's interment. Mira was no help, poor thing. He was on his way up to Sydney to see his brother Jack, and that seemed the place to take Mira.

Hector was a solid, brown-faced, red-cheeked man on the land, his forehead pale from wearing a hat, his arms red-brown up a little beyond the elbows, where they turned milk-white from working always with a shirt. He'd been in sugar up north at Tyndale until he noticed that the desire for greater economic development had caused many other countries to think of sugar as a crop. He saw prices would drop, and got out.

He moved to Blighty — so far from England on the Riverina Highway — midway between Finley and Deniliquin, where he ran sheep, grew wheat, and kept bees. He had fruit trees and garden vegetables, and each year the story was of more trees. When he visited Bellbird Corner he was always on the point of getting into cattle, fattening steers, and planting more trees. His brother listened, and marvelled that a boy who ran away to sea should become a man who would take so well to the land and come to love it. He regretted that the land had been so ruthlessly cleared, and over the years had even begun to look sideways at books, whose existence necessitated the felling of trees. He read the financial papers, which he didn't understand; he kept up a gentle worried attitude towards the world and what people were doing to it.

When standing talking one to one, he would advance on

his audience, getting closer and closer until it became embarrassing. The family wisely saw to it that he had a chair, to prevent him. He loved machinery of all sorts, and oiled everything made of metal.

His brother said he'd altered the old services saying to:

>*If it doesn't move, paint it,*
>*If it moves, oil it.*

To which Ursula added 'If it's alive, feed it.' for he was a compulsive feeder of the dogs and cats.

The family sometimes wondered why Hector had never married. He was the soul of kindness, even-tempered, not a drinker, and owned his own farm. He was so straight that even when he lied he spoke the truth.

Once, on a visit, he said to his brother, 'With a woman round the place you have to listen to the truth about yourself all the time. And it hurts. But why does a man never tell them the truth about them? Vengeance, that's why. Fear. Stark, staring fear.'

Jackson Blood tried gently to prod for more information, but it didn't come. Whatever experiences or disappointments gave rise to Hector's complaint would go with him to the grave.

Jackson Blood mentioned the incident, as is the way in families, several times, and once Aunt Ursula remarked at the end of the story, in a tone of regret, 'Social intercourse is a delusion.'

This was received in silence; it too was a mystery. Ursula knew she was often not understood, and one of her sayings was 'Some are silent because others are ignorant.' but never said it at home, keeping it for those of her many friends who needed a firm put-down now and then.

With each visit Uncle Hector brought tubs of honey. The little boy looked at him in wonder, never more so than when, before answering a question, he stopped, looked at the questioner, looked out of the window into the distance; all this before he collected an answer, took a breath, and delivered it.

He smelled of a certain type of eucalypt that grew on his

property, whose long, pendulous leaves retain their fragrant smell for months after they've died and dropped.

In nothing he said when he visited the city did he ever show himself aware of the basic Australian class conflict: rural versus urban. Yet the rural districts where he lived were alive with it.

Aunt Mira grieved for years over her mate, covering her grief with an intense interest in spoken language, perhaps searching for words to make her loss understandable, or at least bearable.

For some reason the garrulous old bird would never talk in her lively fashion in front of Hector when he visited. Perhaps she thought he might see her as interesting company and take her back to the empty past.

She loved being in her corner in the kitchen, and rarely left it. She hated people coming up behind her. She was messy with her food. Also she hated Wednesdays, the day the Major was killed. She was modest by necessity. 'I know I lack great gifts,' she would say. 'But the great are simple, and so am I.'

The Major disliked words, except one. At one stage she accused him of learning sign language in order to avoid using words. She seemed intent on amassing a huge stock of words, like bits of scrabble, saying, 'Words can unlock, words are keys. New ideas can be created by new juxtapositions.'

Mostly she used words as mockery, as display, as little hooks or arms to reach out and hold the busier members of her adopted household. As when, in talking of Father Champion, a parish priest who visited the Thorolds and Wellers up the street, she said, 'He's got the local agency in the forgiveness business, holds a franchise from God.' Danielle, or Orville, when they were younger, and now Davis, would listen in a puzzled way, having been caught by one of the little hooks — perhaps the word God.

Hers was a lonely corner. So that when she said the rhyme about the doctor, and fell asleep, the small boy smiled up at her with a clear bright face and quick eyes. Intelligence can't be hidden. And went outside.

In the front yard he discovered spiders in curled leaves, and when he saw one retreating from the centre of its web to its brown house, he marvelled at its quiet legs, for though he bent right down and listened intently, he couldn't hear its footsteps. At nightfall, he was told, spiders began to repair their webs, and therefore all of them were on deck, so watch out if you go near them at night.

He was warned about spiders.

When Randal came home one windy day, on edge and aggressive from the dry abrasive westerlies and with a few drinks aboard, and made lots of noise, the little boy observed, 'Randal's much worse than one person!' Meaning bad enough for two. And on seeing Lillian wary of his mood, went over and gave his big brother some hits. His little fist reached just above Randal's knee.

'You're not hitting me?' Randal said. 'Are you?'

The little chap took that as another kind of warning and said: 'Just patting you — hard.'

He was warned about eating chocolates and too many sweet things. His defence took some words from a television advertisement. 'Lollies clean my skin deep down,' he countered.

A more delicate warning was conveyed to him when Lillian reproved Orville for a careless and ill-advised fart. The small boy thought for a while after Orville had apologised, then delivered himself of a theory on the subject.

'When your boppom goes Boomp! — that's your poohies bumping together.'

He was pleased at the laughter that followed, and that the awkwardness he detected in the atmosphere had dissipated. Yet he ran into warning frowns again when at the table he accepted his little dessert of apple charlotte and ice-cream and pronounced the words he'd heard Randal say, 'Yum, yum, pig's bum!'

The rules were puzzling.

One night, just before he went to bed, Lillian taught him his first prayer. It was not her choice, but Jackson Blood thought simplest and shortest was best. They knelt together, she with her arm round him, he able to reach the flat of his cot with his hands. He repeated each line after her.

> *'Gentle Jesus, meek and mild,*
> *Look upon a little child,*
> *Remember my simplicity,*
> *Let me always come to you.'*

The little boy liked this ritual, which made going to bed important and official, and a clear ending to the day.

But there was a question.

'Why are we saying this, Mummy?'

'We're talking to God. We're praying.'

'What will happen?'

'God hears us when we pray. God keeps us safe.'

'Why?'

'God loves us.'

'Why?'

'Because we're all little children to God. He's our heavenly father.'

There was a pause, then 'Oh.' Another pause, then, 'Is anyone else talking to God?'

'Yes. Lots and lots, all over the world.'

'At the same time?'

'Yes, all together.'

'How does he hear us as well?'

'He can do everything,' she said, and tucked him in, then gave him several goodnight kisses. He kissed her, partly on the side of her mouth, partly on her cheek. The child's kiss was wet. The mother put the light out, shut the door and went back to the rest of the family, feeling the wet on her face. As far as anyone could know, without access to the inside of her head, she was oblivious of the fact that her little family was a bastion against the state, and against state-imitating institutions.

In the morning, Aunt Mira mocked the evening prayer.

> 'Jesus loves me, I don't think
> Makes me wash up at the sink.
> He drinks whisky, I drink wine,
> Jesus loves me, but I'm lying.'

Aunt took no notice of warnings or frowns, the boy observed. When Lillian said something about prayers and children, Mira cheekily replied in song:

> 'Hark the jelly babies sing
> Beecham's pills are just the thing
> They are gentle, meek and mild
> Two for adult, one for child.'

Lillian ignored her pointedly, and set about getting breakfast ready, but Aunt Mira couldn't be snubbed.

> 'The sausage is a clever fish
> With fins both long and wavy
> It swims around the butter dish
> Homesick for thick gravy.'

Other warnings floated about in the warm air of the house, not directed at him, but detectable in the general conversation.

> Don't let the moon shine on your face, asleep.
> Don't break a mirror.
> There'll be a death if an owl screeches at night, or if a dog scratches the floor inside the house.
> Vinegar stunts your growth.

Never take a stone off a grave.
Tread on a crack, break your mother's back.
If a passing bird gets you, it's lucky.

When these things were said, there was something about the way the speaker looked that made the child doubt their truth. Something slightly out of line. He didn't know what it was, but it was a bit like the way his mother said, 'Yes, there's a Santa Claus,' at his first Christmas. Like a warning of another kind.

The Well of Fury

In the next visit to Aunt Olivine's, he negotiated the stairs, walked to the front door, crossed the verandah, got to the bottom of the front steps and with a feeling of triumph put his right foot, then his left on the first stone slab of the front path that led between aunt's borders of alyssum and petunias to the fence with the old gate which opened outwards to the street. I am, I can, I do, his inner song went.

The white picket fence invited him to walk, the hydrangeas beside the front steps urged him to stay, to go on the grass and stay near the house. He knew flowers and shrubs were like that, and said no. He said yes to the fence and set course by the gate.

His trusty pink hands pushed together at the stuck gate, then protected him as he fell forward when the gate gave way.

He'd been told many times in his first four hundred days to close the door, shut the cupboard, leave things as he found them. He shut the gate. It bit his finger and wouldn't let go. To raise the alarm would be silly — all that would achieve would be attention to his presence outside the fence, where he was not to go. His index finger was jammed between two wooden posts, one of which moved. Perhaps it would move again, with a pull.

It was so. Soon his finger was throbbing safely, enclosed in his other fingers. But the gate was open. He rested one hand against the gatepost and slammed the gate violently shut with the hurt hand, keeping the insulted finger out of the way, curled warm and throbbing. He hadn't foreseen that the resting hand was in danger. One finger of that hand had crept between the gatepost and the first picket of the fence, and when the gate shut it bit him again.

He should have learned from these happenings, and gone quietly on his way, exploring. What he did was different. A cold mask of something covered his face. He wrenched the gate open with the hand first hurt, removed the second injured finger, then without blinking or taking his eyes from the gate timbers that he now wholeheartedly hated, put both hands in a safe position on the outside of the gate and slammed it forwards, away from him, shut tight, smash! He put his hands again in places where they couldn't be hurt, pinched, hit, jammed or crushed, and wrenched the gate open towards him. He crashed it shut, wrenched it open, crashed shut, wrenched open, crashed, wrenched, shut, open, shut — and didn't stop. His face was pink, but felt cold. He puffed a little, but felt no fatigue.

He was borne upward on a tide of anger, away from petty tiredness, away from any need to slow down, and kept at it: crash, wrench, crash.

A neighbour reported over the fence to Olivine, and Lillian found him like that. After she undid his fingers from the gate she lifted the furious little body off the ground, still full of blind rage that dumb objects of this new world could treat him so badly when he had no such intentions towards them.

The thought that, under it all, everything was his fault simply for wanting something, and that once hurt he had failed to foresee the second hurt, was at the bottom of his anger. He was angry at himself.

Sometimes he wondered where the place was in which

that cold mask originated, that wellspring of blind anger, of cold, omnipotent fury; but always he stopped short of pursuing it. He didn't really want to know.

Checking

It was a bright, still Spring day. The little boy watched his mother's face.

'Oh dear, where have those matches gone? Has Jack taken the matches again? Naughty Daddy!'

Davis toddled out of the kitchen, full of concern for that look of worry on his mother's face. There was his father, down in the yard. He called out, his forehead wrinkled with what he felt was a facsimile of his mother's frown, 'Naughty Daddy!' And shook his head reprovingly. 'Take-it Mummy's matchits!'

The father looked up, cigarette in his mouth. He grinned tolerantly and looked back to his spinach plants. He was out of a job and no longer the provider as he was when the boys were little, and Danielle. Some men don't mind so much, or get used to it, but it shook Jackson Blood and never let go of him.

In the kitchen that night, the father finished his cigarette before the meal began. He gazed out of the window, looking at his past through the leaves of the camphor laurel. None of his sons smoked. On the other hand, he didn't drink. All the boys drank.

The little boy came into the kitchen, dropped his rubber play-ball, close to the wood stove.

'Hullo, hullo,' said Aunt Mira. 'Here's the future in miniature. His ball's on the ground. Silence in court, the monkey wants to talk! Mind your fingers, the future has a bite like a hyperpotamus! Pass me the machos, the machos quick!'

Jackson Blood looked round.

'Watch the stove, son. Burny!' he said with a note of urgency.

In bending to pick up the coloured ball, the boy's forehead came down close to the black cast-iron stove top. The skin of his forehead felt the intense heat. His father was right: it was hot. But how hot?

He examined the ball, turning it over in his fingers. He also examined the room, to see who was looking. Jackson Blood was gazing steadily out of the window, entertained by his own thoughts. Lillian was busy at the sink, humming a tune he didn't yet recognise. Aunt Mira was looking the other way, muttering. Ursula was out, visiting old girlfriends at Lavender Bay in Sydney.

He held the ball in one hand, and slowly advanced his right forefinger to the stove edge. He felt warmth on all his hand. A fingerbreadth away, the tip of his finger felt much warmer. He put his finger right up close to the black iron, then quickly touched it and pulled away in the same instant. That was hot!

His father watched his past parade outside the window, through the cloud of leaves. He smiled. Without moving his head he had seen very well the little checking experiment that had taken place. The boy was OK: not careless, not hasty, nor was he too fearful. He might make a man some day.

Jackson Blood

Jackson Blood went back to his past, which was in two places: in his head, and at the same time just outside the kitchen window. The chemicals sprayed in combat zones during his term overseas in the Army sometimes left a burning sensation, sometimes made you choke. The eyes copped it most, but how much did you breathe into your lungs? He shook his head. Governments and armies don't care for their own people.

He knew his constant going over the past was no different from millions of other lifelong conversations with the past by men who'd fought for their countries, on whatever sides; conversations that sought to bandage the sores of the past, though they could never be healed.

He'd been a Sydney boy, growing up on the south side of the Harbour close to the water at Haberfield. His father was a wharf-builder with the Maritime Services, once a cabinet-maker, and a leading member of the Dissenting Brethren; a hard man on his sons, an angel to his daughters. Both sons ran away: Hector to sea, Jackson to the Queensland Darling Downs to work with horses.

Jackson Blood boxed, and for a time worked as a chopping block — sparring partner — to some of the best lightweights of the time. There followed a number of years as horse trainer with a circus, a spell in the Army with a free holiday to the Asian continent; then back to horse-breaking, later a commercial traveller in the country, finally an insurance salesman and marriage.

He left insurance when he could no longer stomach having to tell weeping mothers of families, in a recession, that they must surrender their policies for a fraction of what they'd paid in. After that it was a succession of poor and irregular jobs, for times were hard and unemployment figures rising.

He'd never become what he originally wanted to be; leaving home for the Darling Downs to get away from

James Blood prevented that. As a boy he yearned to be a champion cyclist. He loved and was well adapted to explosive effort over short periods of time. His movements were quick, he was a natural sprinter; he swam a length of the pool like a seal, but that finished him, he was no good over a longer distance.

In himself he was strong. Nothing could shake his adherence to the faith of his fathers, even though the Dissenters didn't accept him; ostensibly by reason of his smoking. With them, by some quirk of dogma, drinking was fine but smoking not. He was a slave to nicotine but alcohol didn't suit him.

He had no pretence in him, treated all people the same, and lost jobs because of it. He wouldn't say to the boss what he wouldn't say to the cleaner, and wouldn't lie for anyone. He was anguished by some moral questions, such as capital punishment. 'Vengeance is mine, I will repay, says the Lord.' He knew that, but he'd seen things that almost convinced him that they deserved a life. He was most content when poring over his New Testament, usually Paul's letters.

His tolerance was often of the gritted-teeth sort. For instance, when well-meaning relatives would say to the little boy when the sun came out after a shower: 'Look, God's smiling!' Or, on a sunny day: 'See, that's God laughing and the whole world laughing too!' Or when aunts harped on whose eyes the child had, or whose nature. The extravagance of such sentiments were foreign to him; he suited the Independent Dissenters, with their seriousness and lack of ornamentation.

Jackson Blood had fierce angers. Sometimes it seemed to his youngest son that Dad was so angry that grass and flowers, all the trees and bush around, would have to die. His anger seemed so final. There was something electric about him. Even when he stood still, things near him seemed to sway.

He was a word person. After the evening meal and before his private reading, he would read to Aunt Mira. When Davis was older, he'd read to him, too. Once he read to Preston, Randal, Danielle and Orville from the Bible, but they'd grown out of being prepared to sit still for it. Even Orville, a pale heavy boy who hadn't walked till he was two, went the way of the rest.

When he'd finished reading, he put the radio by Aunt Mira and found the music programme she wanted. He adjusted the volume in the earphones and carefully put it by her head. She leaned close and listened, closing her eyes. It was her Mozart.

As for Davis Blood

As for Davis Blood, he was standing near the kitchen window, the coloured ball in his left hand by his side, his right hand raised near his cheek, standing quite still. He wasn't exactly looking out of the window, nor was he exactly gazing at the window frame. He was in one of his states of stillness when he seemed to be arrested between one step and the next, immobile in a dream.

When he came out of it, he turned abruptly to his mother and said, 'I wish I was grown up.'

'Why?'

'So I can wipe my own boppom.'

When he held up his very first essay in drawing with a pencil and said, 'Mum, look at it!' she asked, understandably, 'What is it?'

The little chap replied, 'You just have to look at it and you'll see what it is.'

He referred to the British anthem as 'God save our gravy Queen', to the trees in the bush as 'Lub in the bush'. When asked why love, explained that the trees kissed each other at their topmost crowns of leaves.

He liked the word 'lump'. When he was taken in his

stroller down near Spectacle Lake he commented, 'What a big lump of water!'

'My heart wants to cough,' he said as anxious faces watched him lean forward and appear to hold his breath.

Pestered by kisses he said, 'No, I don't want a kiss. I want something real.' And again, when Lillian detained him for a hug or perhaps a short, sharp cuddle and an 'I love you!' he said, anxious to get away, 'I do too! Keep well! Bye bye!' And escaped barefoot.

His first attack of pins and needles he described as 'My foot is starving.'

The Two States

His mother noticed Davis Blood's dreaming state from his earliest months. At such times an inward look spread round his face, his little body relaxed completely; he became a dead weight in her arms, loose and pliable, and stayed that way for minutes as if occupied with deep and pleasant meditation.

Coming out of that phase he blinked, stared, blinked rapidly, began to look round; then suddenly came alive, making his usual cheerful noises and moving his arms and legs with great energy, all the more for his time away from the world. As if his absence was a holiday, and his energy re-created.

The talkative, bright side alternated with the withdrawn, meditative one. The bright stage was marked by quick talk and fun-loving chat with Lillian and with the things around him: high chair, toys, the brown bear, the bits of wood and odd metal things he treasured, the shiny old tobacco tin of his father's from which the paint had long since been worn away, which he would touch, examine, turn over and over as if seeking a secret on its surface or an emanation from it that might still be part of his father.

Aunt Ursula

At one such time his aunt Ursula from her lifelong wheelchair said to him: 'Play, little boy, as long as you can. Never lose the child in you, or you'll stiffen and wither and stop growing.'

He smiled back at her serious, twisted face. Auntie was always nice to him.

Ursula had been taken at sixteen with a degeneration of motor nerve tissue which put her into a wheelchair and twisted her spine. Her arms described erratic movements, her neck bent sideways to the right and her legs were useless. When she spoke, her mouth grinned, gasped, opened sideways and down, and words eventually twisted their way out.

She'd played tennis at school, and was in the cricket team, with prospects as a spin bowler and a handy, though temperamental bat. She was in a swimming club, and had the odd ear infection, but her family was never able to establish how she came to be disabled.

Lillian, and sometimes her husband, lifted Ursula on to the wooden contraption that enabled her to go to the toilet and have a bath. Because of her daylong sedentary posture, she had to be washed with methylated spirit to prevent sores, and had an array of bewitching perfumes, talcs, toilet waters and soaps to fight the methylated smell.

Sometimes carbolic was necessary, for reasons she discussed with Lillian. Her clothes were stored in soaps and washed in aromatic preparations, but not all of them together could defeat a certain faint smell that lingered, or that vague odour that clings to polyester underclothes.

Once the little boy innocently sprayed her with Mount Fuji, one of her perfumes. Some years later, when he was reminded of it, he'd forgotten, but when the story was repeated to him a number of times, he remembered. Gradually he reconstructed every detail of the spraying, and it became fixed in him for the rest of his life as a memory of his own. As if he had never forgotten.

The scent of Aunt's toilet water and perfumes pervaded her books: Spanish Sun, Managua Silk, Flannel Flower, Mountains of the Moon, Passionflower, White Linen, Orange Petal, Crystal Fingers, Green Stems, Red Cotton, Pampas Grass and the rest impregnated her Rabelais, Dickens, Montaigne, Shakespeare, Chekhov, Turgenev, Dostoyevsky, Sterne.

Jackson Blood was so taken with this variety of names, particularly White Linen, that he referred to his sister's perfumes under the one heading of Brown Canvas.

When she went out, which was often, and dressed up, her bosom was high; around the house its size and heaviness made it hang down. The boy noticed, and on the clothesline he saw the reason why: her bosom-holders for official occasions were big and pointy, like casts from a well-endowed statue.

He liked her much more than Grandma, who in hot weather often wore dresses with horrible patterns. She made it clear she didn't take to happy, red-cheeked little boys. She liked males to be aggressive, quick to quarrel, unpredictable, headstrong.

Aunt Ursula had given herself a good education, and through her adult life never stopped learning. She was alert, articulate, busy; a lively woman who inhabited a grotesque body as if it were a cumbersome shell. Always at the back of her mind, though, however confident she was, lurked the thought that her nerve and muscular disability might be reflected in a similar disability of memory.

'There's something in me,' she mused aloud to the small child, who she was sure couldn't understand, 'that's all the time thinking, looking at things in me that I've forgotten. I worry that one day I'll lose it and be empty and not know.'

She accompanied this with a smile of such tenderness that no amount of muscular twitching or lopsidedness could obscure it.

Ursula got out of the house as often as she could. Her pension could stand taxis, and the good offices of friends brought abundant lifts. Often when she returned from galleries, meetings, lunches, exhibitions, afternoon teas, she would have another potted plant with her. There were dozens on the front verandah and in the garden. She loved living things, and managed slowly, laboriously, to water some of them herself. If she didn't, Lillian was backstop here, as in so many other things.

'There's nice big lumps of room here, isn't there, Auntie?' the child said. 'Big lumps of room to play in.'

'Yes, Davie, there are.'

He stopped what he was doing, and looked up at her looking at him. To his childish perception, Aunt was a great woman, there was no one in the world like her. The methylated spirit smell was almost vanquished by the smell of Helen Sarkissian's Yokohama Coffee talc.

'Why you always loving me, Auntie?' he said.

Aunt Ursula was temporarily unable to answer.

Widow of Major Mitchell

She was rescued by an outburst from Mira's corner of the kitchen.

'There is a happy land, far, far away.'

she sang loudly. For once, Ursula didn't say shut up.

> *'Where all the piglets run, three times a day.*
> *Oh how they squeal and run*
> *When they hear the butcher come*
> *Three slices off their bum, three times a day!'*

And watched them expressionlessly, with bright unblinking eyes. The little boy watched, fascinated.

> *'Stare, stare, like a bear,*
> *'Then you'll know me anywhere!'*

she screeched. It was she who'd been staring, he thought.

'Why did the hen run? Eh?'

He said nothing. He could think of nothing to say.

'Because it heard the tree bark, of course!' she said with an air of great cleverness.

Aunt Mira wore her pinky-white outfit, with something on her head that in colour was between orange and tangerine. Discarded food lay round her on her tray. Her arms were useless for holding things.

She groaned loudly, to get attention.

'Getting old,' she said tragically, 'is fulltime horror until you stop struggling.' And ended on a cheerful note, 'Then it's delightful.'

When she had no one to read to her and no one to annoy, she used to go over the names and sometimes the stories of the books she knew well. As the years passed, and she despaired of ever having someone read *War and Peace* to her, she said, accommodating herself to her fortune, 'Ah well, the greatest books are those that don't need to be read. It's enough to know that they exist.'

No one believed she'd give up trying to find a reader, till the trees in the yard buckled and the rocks melted.

Visions on Guringai Bay

While parents and aunts — Ursula and Olivine — sat on the Harbour beach at Guringai, Davis Blood was possessed by visions he had no words for, though if he'd tried hard he might have remembered stories his aunt had read aloud while Lillian was out periodically to work at the tent-making factory. Sometimes the picture in his head was a word, for which he had no regular sort of image. He sat in the summer shade of a Norfolk pine.

In his head he fought in a rocky place, killing a child-lion his own age. He slit the child-lion's skin with his sword, and walked away wearing the lion's skin as clothes, the lion's head as a helmet.

A little distance away in his head he fought a beast with many heads. No matter how fast he cut them off, more grew, until a kind of inspiration told him to set fire to the beast and bury the carcass under a rock, first opening its body to get its poison to tip his arrows. Then sallying forth to meet the next enemy.

He fought more heroic battles, until he noticed the adults were beginning to lie back and doze.

Without feeling any responsibility to them to be on hand, he listened to his legs when they commanded him to stand up, and he stood up. Walk, they said, and he walked. I can, therefore I will, his song said.

The Lost World

In the first moments of walking up Guringai Sands away from the waters of the Harbour and the picnic, he didn't give himself a chance of making it to the roadway; he hardly dared breathe, but crept up the slope, away.

On the path of cement slabs, he looked back and felt the joy of being away, being alone to do as he liked, free and unbound. He stepped off the gutter to the road. The heat of the bitumen persuaded him to walk faster across the road, up the opposite gutter and along the concrete path. He headed towards the shops, where crowds of people swirled and eddied. Perhaps he'd get as far as Guringai Ocean Beach.

He looked back. His mother and father were asleep on beach towels amid many-coloured food and drink things. They were a unit; they held together in moments of threat and when frightening things happened, but now he was having a holiday from the family. He wanted to be where crowds of people were; he loved lots of voices, faces, noise.

He made brief acquaintance with a Labrador, who walked part of the way with him, then stopped off outside a kebab shop, keeping watch with a Samoyed on the slowly turning vertical slab of meat; sniffing the air and finding it good, never taking his eyes off the beef or the man with the long knife.

There were many things to see along the Concourse. People of his own size glanced at him and he stood still to watch them go by, to see how they were dressed, to listen to how they spoke and were spoken to. He saw many things to be complacent about.

For a start, the boys and girls of his own age were often clamorous for food and drink. In the Blood family this didn't happen. Perhaps it was due to his own temperament, for if mealtimes were still a way off, he waited, he didn't try to hurry them up. If he saw something he could have wanted, but knew he had no chance of getting it, he didn't ask, didn't even begin to want it. The bounds of permissible wants, actions, ways of speaking were pretty clear by now, and it was no trouble to stay within those bounds.

Out here in the world he saw that other people his own age often accepted no rules, no customs, no verdicts, and were turned aside by no amount of harsh words and punishment, and yet they still were refused. Their efforts came to nothing.

It didn't escape him, though, that some parents, after having forbidden something, would, on repeated urging and complaint, give in and go back on all they had said. In the Blood family this didn't happen. Once a verdict had been given, that was that. It became incorporated in daily customs and rules and, certainly for him, had the force of the law of the Medes and Persians.

His father noticed his way of accommodating to family law, and found him lacking in the opposition and wilfulness, aggressiveness and readiness to quarrel that he privately thought were proper to boys. He seemed to lack the opposition to orders, the bloodymindedness that opposes for the sake of opposing, that disobeys for the sake of conflict. Jackson Blood was uncomfortable with a child that neither cried nor complained. This one even used a certain kindness and tact in pulling away from enveloping females, in that distancing that boys must do in order to breathe freely and have their own space clear, and room to move.

Outside a gaudy chemist's shop racks of brightly coloured sun-hats and eyeshades attracted him. He walked up and searched the display, turning it round to see everything. The woman serving in the shop smiled at him and he at her. She looked round for an adult and he recognised the look and its purpose. He left the place and kept on walking towards the ocean, which he couldn't yet see, but which he knew was there in that gap of blue sky at the end of the Concourse, where the only traffic was people.

He watched people playing chess, sitting at tables, kids riding bikes, people his own age climbing the sides of the embankments round trees, playing in the kids' pit, and everywhere people eating.

There was a narrow street to cross at the end of the Concourse, and when he crossed it he was on a broad paved promenade. The ocean spread wide in front of his delighted eyes. Several cargo ships stood off shore, waiting for docking space in Sydney Harbour. People lay on the beach, walked, ran, swam — it was a wonderful confusion of shapes, colours, movement.

He walked till he found steps and descended to the sunlit sand. His shoes filled at the first few steps, but he didn't mind. He trudged slowly, sniffed at the beach smells, and sat down when he got tired.

Two policemen, after asking where his Mummy was, and not being put off by the answer, kindly asked him to give them a hand each, and he went willingly.

They bought him an ice cream when they got near the station, and sat him at one of the shiny desks. Afternoon sun came through the frosted windows and lit the desk tops. It was hot in there, but he managed to finish the ice cream before it melted over his hand.

To give him something to do, when they thought he might cry at being alone, one officer emptied the shells from a spare pistol and gave the gun to the boy to play with. He needed both hands to hold it up and both hands to pull the trigger, even when it wasn't cocked.

When his father appeared at the desk, the officer asked for the weapon. The boy gave it back with regret. There was something beautiful about that blued barrel and brown stock: hard, full of purpose.

'Thanks, officer,' Jackson Blood said.
'All in a day's work. Found him on the beach.'
'Say thank you to the policeman, now.'
'Thanks, police-im.'
'Say thanks for finding me.'

'Thanks for finding me. My head was going to sleep there, on the sand,' he explained.

'You're welcome, son.'

As they were leaving, hand in hand, the boy looked round and announced, 'This is a quaint little house-building. They all like me here, Daddy. Can we come back again next time and I can hold the gun?'

'We'll see.'

Outside, walking back to Guringai Sands, he said, 'Why are those men police-im, Daddy?'

'Police-men. You shorten it to policem'n.'

'Policem'n.'

'Right.'

'Why are they?'

'It's a good job.'

'Why aren't you a policem'n, Daddy?'

'Me? Never in a million years! Risk your life for a weekly pay packet? Never!'

Yet he'd volunteered for the Army. He thought he'd better say more.

'Policemen are good men. Women too. They have to be very careful, dealing with the public, and criminals. The public has a lot of very funny fish in it, very difficult people, and criminals don't care for anything or anyone, and often not even for themselves — don't care if they die next minute and proud of it. The police have to be decent people, with a respect for the truth, and kind to people that need kindness. Have to obey orders, protect property, catch criminals.'

'Baddies?'

'Yes, baddies.'

'How do they catch baddies?'

'Well, mostly the baddies' mates or girlfriends ring the police and dob 'em in. Other times they leave clues or get caught red-handed. Don't have to be bright to be a crim, just lazy.'

That night Jackson Blood asked that the boy remember his rescue in his evening prayer. Lillian took the opportunity to teach him another child's prayer.

'Jesus, tender shepherd, hear me
Bless your little lamb tonight
Through the darkness please be near me
Keep me safe till morning light.'

Stories from a Wheelchair

Aunt Ursula not only read to him, but told the child stories. She got him to climb up into his high chair, with the tray to rest his arms, and she alongside in her wheelchair, sitting slightly lower than his head was. The difference in height gave him a magisterial look as he listened, head on one hand. The smell of methylated spirit was overlaid with apple blossom.

She told him of a place where ducks don't fly, but walk around giving orders and pecking people to get them to take notice; where rivers change course in the night, trees move off down the street, mountains move closer or retreat until one morning they're far away on the horizon; a place where dogs don't run but sit motionless, rusting, and kookaburras laugh backwards.

This place was called Sagrada, the Sacred City; its chief industry cascara, the sacred bark.

'In Sagrada, people go to sleep over here on this lawn, and wake up in the morning over there on that hill,' Ursula indicated her lap as the lawn and her left-hand armrest as the hill.

'Thought carries them.' She made the familiar jerky

movement of her wandering right arm up to her head, to indicate thought.

'I think, therefore I move,' she added. 'Or, if you like: I think, therefore I have a wheelchair.'

The boy changed hands to support his head, his unwavering eyes fixed on her.

'In Sagrada, words are visible. You can see what you say. As they are spoken, they come from your mouth, and change colour. If you were speaking green thoughts, they might come out into the world as red words. If we were sitting at the window and looking out —' they both looked out across the valley — 'You could see my words, and your words, when you say something, travelling at the speed of breath, which isn't fast, modified a little by the resistance of the air, and weighed down a bit by the pull of gravity.' Here she got both her hands to point their fingers upwards, which was difficult for her, to show the downward weight of that mysterious attraction. 'But still going across the valley, still travelling. There they go, my words, out the window, there, floating up, the wind is pushing them, they're blue and yellow, they're coming down, Oooh!'

She tried to rise in her wheelchair: it was impossible, her muscles wouldn't answer. All that happened was that her head rose a little and her eyes signalled that she was taller.

'They're coming down! They went down straight, on the other hill, like spears. Some of my consonants — they're very sharp — speared right into the ground!'

The boy watched. It seemed his eyes were opaque in that central black inlet to the brain, aptly called the pupil, as if his head were sucking at and ingesting her words; as if the brain behind those warm eyes were a gentle predator, consuming everything, covering all with a form of mental saliva of attention and dissolving it into components suitable for digestion. I hear, I have, I hold, his silent song said.

Sagrada was a wonderful place, and it was all around. Long after Ursula had stopped speaking, her voice talked to him in the words she had used, in her noddings and helpless arm movements, in the ways her mouth twisted as she tried to get words out past her lips, in the rolling of her eyes.

Above her wheelchair, hanging on the wall of the big room, was a black-framed text:

> 'In all you do acknowledge God,
> and He will make your path straight.'

It was worked in golden thread on white cloth, with coloured capitals: red for the I, blue for the G, and orange for the H.

Aunt taught him a rhyme she'd taught to his brothers and Danielle before him.

> *'There was a crooked aunt and she walked a crooked mile*
> *Found a crooked wheelchair against a crooked stile*
> *Bought a crooked cat, which caught a crooked mouse*
> *And they all lived together in a little crooked house.'*

He repeated it line for line after her, till he could say it through. She referred to it as *her* nursery rhyme. When he could say it perfectly he asked, 'Why do we live in a crooked house?'

'It's what we've got,' Aunt replied.

'Are we poor?' he followed up.

'Yes.'

'Why?'

'We don't have as much money as some do.'

'Is that 'portant?'

'Not very.'

'What's 'portant?'

'What you've got in your head.'

'Why?'

'Because that's what sort of person you are, inside.'

He thought about it.

'Does God and the Bible get in your head?'

'Certainly.'

'Then Daddy has God in his head, doesn't he?'

'He has.'
'And the Bible too?'
'Indeed he has.'
'What sort of person is Daddy?'
There was a pause. 'A good man.'
'Did God make him good?'
'Maybe, but I think it's mostly him,' she said drily.
'Is he brave and strong, as well as good?'
'Oh, yes.'
'But how do you know he's good?'
'He just is.'
There was a long pause. Then a question.
'Auntie.'
'Yes.'
'Do you ever make mistakes?'
She laughed as best she could, given her disability.
'Everyone does. It's a poor auntie that's never wrong and can't bear to be wrong,' she said generously.

Next time she clapped eyes on him he was trying to work an old yo-yo of Orville's, that he'd found in the toy box.
'It'll yo down but it won't yo up,' he reported.
'Then the string's loose at the bottom,' she said. 'Let it all out, down, then twist it round to tighten it.' Aunt had watched these manipulations and others like it, at least four times before.
He was successful, after a fashion, but a minute's playing was enough, given the repetitious nature of the game.
'Tell me another rhyme, Auntie.'
'Certainly, little man.'
He said carefully, 'I not a man, Auntie. I'm a boy.'
'OK, a fine big boy.'
'A little boy, Auntie,' he corrected gently. Everything in his world — people, furniture, dogs — shouted at him that he wasn't big.
'I stand corrected,' she said. 'OK, here's one:

> *'The hart he loves the high wood*
> *The hare she loves the hill*
> *The knight he loves his knighthood*
> *The lady loves her will.'*

'Another one, Auntie!'
'All right, then:

> *'The greedy boy is he who sits*
> *And bites bits out of plates*
> *Or else picks up the calendar*
> *And gobbles all the dates.'*

'More, Auntie!' he said, excitedly. Auntie was like a tap, and taps were magic.

> *'If all the world was paper*
> *And all the sea was ink*
> *If all the trees were bread and cheese*
> *What would we have to drink?'*

Ursula dealt heroically with the next request. It was: what is a hart? The little fellow remembered back to the first rhyme, and took her steadily through the things he hadn't understood, to 'the lady loves her will'. He didn't ask about the second and third rhymes.

I Feel, Therefore I Know

Coming out of the shade of the verandah, he felt the sunlight bite into the skin of his forehead and cheeks. He moved back into the shade; the heat was gone. Forward into the sun; there it was again. He put his arm out so the sun bathed his arm and wrist, and felt the cool start where the shade started. Heat and coolness shut off sharply, then. He moved his arm slowly up and down, keeping the sunlight on the same part of his arm. Yes, the edge of the heat and cold was sharp. If he moved his arm slowly back and forth, the edge of the cold and warm travelled up and down his arm.

He withdrew from the sun and stood. He could feel still the warmth of the sun on his face, but dimly; he could feel the band of warmth moving up and down his arm. But he wasn't in the sun. The warmth he felt was in the I part of him, the part inside where he remembered. Where was that? Somewhere behind his eyes, he felt. In his head.

As he went back inside the house for a drink of water he remembered a phrase he'd heard: the glare of the sun. From an aunt story. Yes, it was a glare.

He said to the kitchen at large: 'The sun glared at me!'

His father answered, 'But you weren't afraid, were you?' The fact that his father commented made the subject important.

Of course not. The sun was a friend. Why had his father said that? Was it bad to be afraid?

'Scaredy cat! Chased by a rat,' commented Aunt Mira.

'Shut up, Mira,' Jackson Blood advised.

The boy was puzzled. He'd never felt afraid, so far.

> *'When your life is up to putty,'* sang Mira,
> *'And you feel you can't go on,*
> *Laugh, clone, laugh!'*

'What are you going on about, Mira?' asked Lillian.

'Modern chain gangs of America,' answered Aunt darkly. 'As presented by the *Washington Toast*, in an admirable article on the sadistics of pain.'

'Chain gangs?' said Lillian absently. 'Surely not in these times.'

'As the man said to the bridge,' said Jackson Blood, 'we've both passed a lot of water since.'

'Since they stopped?' Lillian asked.

'Since they began,' said Jackson Blood. There was a lot of information about the world that Lillian didn't have.

'Don't pinch that kid's options!' called Mira, as they moved out of the kitchen.

'What options?' said Lillian.

'His soft options,' cackled Mira sleepily. 'Don't let his genials fall out, either. Or let his decretals dangle in the dirt.'

The boy had been silent. He heard it all, but his unspoken questions hadn't been answered, and his original perception about the glaring sun had been smothered. Why was being afraid so important? Fear seemed to come up often in their talk. Were people afraid of being afraid?

He would have to find out the answer, perhaps by listening and watching rather than asking. If he'd asked he'd probably get the comments he got when he put his jellybeans out of the car window to get the wind on them, or when he noticed that Webster's Labrador had wise eyes: gentle and benign answers, but without information. Maybe if he could put the question in the same way as when he asked where the shop people get new things from to sell, he'd get a better result, but what was the corresponding way to phrase a question about being afraid? They were different kinds of things: no one got intense and definite about shop goods, but they did about being afraid.

Another thing against direct questions was that they seemed to put people on the spot. He could feel their unease. So often the answers to direct questions were fine, strong, worthy answers, which were contradicted later by other words and actions when the mood was relaxed and easy.

He smiled to himself at the thought that people were difficult. After all, he himself was just as difficult: none of his family, not even Lillian, understood him, or not all the time. He knew that from the way he could feel their eyes on him after he'd said things.

Boysie

Preston, the eldest son at eighteen, came home one night with a bag of boysenberries. The beauty of the name struck the small boy, who repeated it many times.

'Boysieberries, boysieberries, boysieberries! We've got some boysieberries!'

After that, his brothers called him Boysenberry, Boysie for short. Lillian and Ursula stayed with Davie. Men's sudden crazes came and went, as they'd done for all of history, but didn't disturb what women had done for ever.

They were amused again when the boy touched his first grape, seeing how his forefinger disturbed its bloom; and again when he bit into his first peach, then quickly wiped its fine prickly nap off his lips.

On his father's shoulders, Boysie detected that his father rather looked down on him for clinging, as if afraid to fall. He *was* afraid to fall. Here it was again, but this time he shared the fear.

Yet he wasn't worried that he was afraid, he felt it was perfectly natural, and he'd own up to it any time, without shame.

His father, a man who prided himself on not being 'demonstrative', as he put it, was nevertheless pleased to see his son wearing his felt hat and trudging absurdly round the back yard in his heavy old gardening boots.

Unanswered Questions

Answers to some of the questions the boy asked needed long explanations or were thought to involve references to things he couldn't know, so they often went unanswered. He played a game, repeating the unanswered questions to Sarah the cockatoo, or to the cats, or whichever dog happened to be handy.

'Where does the fire go when the water gets on it?' he asked Crippen, the cat.

'Mister Crippen, wake up! Hey! What holds the ground up?'

Crippen the cat never once made an answer.

He asked Glandular the dog what stops people growing, why do people have to die, what does the government look like, why is red the danger when it's only a colour, what sort of towel can wipe water off another towel. Glandular usually barked an answer, but since he only barked at members of the family, his answer was by no means clear.

Some questions got answers. When this happened, he often had another question to ask, or a further response to give.

'Mum,' he said, 'you get a cold when it's cold, don't you?'

'Sometimes. Though you can get a cold in warm weather.'

'Then,' triumphantly, 'why don't we get a warm cough when it's warm, instead of a cold?'

'What do you mean?' She was cutting onion and garlic on the cutting board.

'Why don't we call it a warm, not a cold?'

She had no convincing answer. She began to cut up chillies.

'Mum,' the voice came again, 'were we always us?'

'From the time we were born.'

'What was before that?'

'Well, we were sort of bits, then, of the people we became later.'

'Where did the bits come from?'

'Some from our mothers, some from our fathers, and their bits came from their mothers and fathers and so on, back.'

That ought to be enough for him to go on with. Lillian went down into the yard with the clothes basket, and the peg holder.

He found Aunt Ursula, and asked: 'Why do people have to think?' He was often urged to think.

'So you'll know what to do.'

'Why can't people know what to do, and not have to think?'

'Lots of people think they do.'

But he'd meant something else.

During a calm lunch on the verandah with Aunt, he said: 'Do people have to eat every day?'

'Yes, if they're lucky.'

He wasn't a big eater, but nevertheless attacked his little sandwich with gusto, and announced, 'Then I'm going to eat every day till the days stop.'

'I'm sure you will,' said Aunt supportively.

'Can I have another rhyme, please, Auntie?'

'Would you like a funny one?'

'Yes, please.'

> 'Mary had a little lamb
> Her father shot it dead
> And now it goes to school with her
> Between two hunks of bread.'

The boy laughed delightedly. 'What's a hunk?'
'Something thick. Like a lump,' she said, remembering his liking for the word.
'Oh. Another one?'
'Certainly.'

> 'Little Davie's dead
> In the coffin, quick!
> Jam the lid down tight
> Cause funerals make him sick!'

'Can I have a puzzle, Auntie?'
'Right. What runs uphill and downhill and never moves?'
Little Davis Blood thought hard. No.
'A road. See it in your head? Up, down, round a curve, but the road just lies there, still.'
That was it, he thought. He hadn't pictured the puzzle, he'd tried to find inspiration in the words, without pictures. He would try both, next time.
'Another one?'
'What has an eye but can't see?'
No.
'A needle.'
Of course.
'What goes up, never down?'
He thought. The valley out there. Fires, smoke.
'Smoke?'
'Well, yes, I suppose so. My answer was: your age. But I think smoke could come down, in a wind.'
'Another?'
'What has a head, a tail, and feet like a cat, but isn't a cat?'
No.

'A kitten.'

But that was a cat, wasn't it? He didn't feel she was right.

'Another one!'

'If you went over a cliff, what would you do?'

He pictured it. Hurt yourself? But no, there might be a ledge. Yell out? You might not yell. If it was a high cliff, you'd fall a long way. You'd fall!

'Fall!'

'Yes! Well done! Did you guess or did you know?'

'I guessed.'

'Why?'

'There seemed lots of answers. It was the first one after I got the picture in my head.'

'Good boy,' said Aunt, and opened her book.

The little boy looked out over Kookaburra Valley, which consisted mainly of the tops of trees. Yes, the pictures he had of things were in his head, just behind his eyes, he thought. There must be room in there for lots of things. It was an effort, sometimes, to remember that others couldn't see in there: they could see only in their own heads.

Crippen the Cat

Crippen loved water, and would willingly take a bath. He got his name from his desperate hurry to get into the water, as, Ursula pointed out, the original Doctor Crippen tried to flee his crimes by an ocean voyage. Before the weekly bathing operation, the small boy ritually held him and recited:

'I love little pussy her coat is so warm—'

'But she's a he,' he protested.
'Never mind, say the poem,' he was told. But he had to change it.

> 'And if I don't hurt him he'll do me no harm
> So I won't pull his tail or drive him away
> And pussy and I so gently will play.
> He'll sit by my side and I'll give him some food
> And pussy will love me because I am good.'

Pussy was impatient with words. He struggled and twisted to get to the luke-warm water, the only cat who hadn't fought like seven yellow-eyed devils to stay clear of it.

Crippen was on the back step, the top step of fourteen, every morning. Jackson Blood said he wanted to know, first thing, if the family slept well.

The old house was rich in cats. The dogs were more of a floating population. There were never less than two, but some came and went, and some went missing for months, then came back, said hello, looked around, and settled back in without a word of explanation, as if they'd never been gone, and looked for dinner at the usual time.

Ursula noticed what they did that was clever, and commented, 'Insects, birds, animals, even the fish in the pond: they may or may not have intelligence, but so many of the things they do to catch food or stay out of trouble are things they would do if they did have intelligence.'

It was a pet subject of hers, like all the other subjects she was interested in.

'Another thing, they appear to need a certain amount of freedom. That means a lot to me, since I believe mindless things need no freedom.'

What irritated Aunt, and amused the rest of the family in varying degrees, was that she knew she couldn't begin to demonstrate the things about the inner lives of animals that she herself was sure of, until they could give an account of themselves. And so far, that hadn't happened.

Poor cats. If they were female, they had to get used to their new kittens being drowned, and, male or female, to being locked out at night. In return, they killed and ate pretty birds as well as ordinary old Indian mynahs, peewits and pigeons. They got few sparrows: sparrows were too wary, too quick.

When a spare cat was offered to the Bloods, one of the women checked the giver for the cat's tendency to caterwaul at night; whether it had teeth, eyes, ears, claws; whether it was a ratter and mouser; and if female whether it would eat its kittens or not.

When the cats got used to the place — and it was a paradise for animals — that is, when they had licked the butter off their paws — Lillian insisted that was the way to keep a cat — they surveyed the whole domain, got to know the other cats, and the dogs, distantly, and then began to fish in the pond when the netting wasn't secured, and make life even more dangerous for any mouse that peered out of the long grass down the back and was inexperienced enough to make a movement.

Preston — nineteen and ambitious in his job as office manager for a venetian blind manufacturer — had covered the fishpond with narrow birdwire, to keep out small thieves with wings, but often the fourfooted kind lifted the edge of the wire.

Lillian had a prayer for the various cats, and recited it while the little boy sat on her lap:

> 'O Lord, consider this cat
> That we serve
> For the affection it gives
> Small though it is
> And intermittent.
> For its loyalty
> Such that it is
> To us who feed it.

Grant that it may share
All we have of food
And some of our time
Until its life runs out
Or ours. And then
Whatever your will for us
Let it share too.'

Dogs were a different matter. They got prayers too, but because they gave more, there was more to know about them, and the prayers were different.

Glandular

They called him that because nothing else could account for his size. He was rather Newfoundland, but it would be a mistake not to mention spaniel. A diplomatic dog, he always preferred to negotiate rather than fight. He was a poor fighter: he'd never thought to fall on his opponent. There are in existence, unfortunately, dogs who have never heard of nor entertained the idea of negotiation, but always go straight in, fighting. There was a scar on his left rear flank testifying to a meeting with one such dog, and to his attempt to say goodbye.

He was a good watchdog, though often proving it when there was no one about, not a blind soul along Country Road as far as the eye could see. His bark was deep and fearsome, and acted as a protective screen against other dogs and any sort of confrontation.

'Every boy must have a dog,' the boy's father exclaimed when he appeared with the dog in tow. It was smaller then. 'A dog for every boy!'

'For boys that are fathers,' remarked Ursula drily.

'Think of it,' the father went on, by no means stopped. 'All other animals are enemies, or indifferent to us. The dog is the only one to have a pact with us.'

'Except cats,' Aunt said. 'Horses.'

'Horses are always looking to get over the top of us. Cats keep to a sort of pact, but they look down on us.'

Even then, sitting there for the introductions, Glandular was dreaming. His eyes kept closing. You could see the movement of eyeballs under the eyelids.

'Look at him. Dreaming of meaty bones falling from the sky,' said Aunt.

When he was awake he would sometimes look out at the world, then along Country Road, then in the most pointed way look straight at whoever was with him. It was his way of asking to go out. It didn't often happen, for he was lazy.

So lazy, in fact, that he sometimes leaned his head against the front step to bark. If he found himself elsewhere he might use a tree, a fence, or rock for this purpose. Once he used the laundry wall, since that was nearest, and went round for a day or two with a purple right side, since some small person had done drawings on the fibro sheet and it came off on the dog.

The thing about his watchdog duties was that the barking he did was most often directed at the family, not at strangers. Maybe it was a form of conversation. He wagged his tail and smiled at strangers.

His gait was a sort of waddle, his run a very slightly quicker waddle. He slept for so long that in winter the household cats slept on him, using him as a kind of lumpy rug with central heating.

He knocked into people. His steering was slow to react to inner commands — assuming he heard them — and once he was waddling along Anzac Street up near the shops outside old Jack Morris' house when he fell off the footpath, down a steep rockery, and came to rest in a flower garden, among cinerarias, stocks, delphiniums, and a row of Sweet Alice planted as a border.

Danielle, who was with him at the time, said that when he looked round and found himself surrounded by flowers, he almost decided to stay there.

When Glandular died, the boy watched while his father buried him near the self-sown pittosporum, past the bottom terrace wall. He needed a big hole, and the boy helped dig it there where the soil was moist and deep and nearly black, and alive with long, pink, vigorous worms.

Preston

Preston came down the yard to see the excavation, and remarked that people who made friends of animals love agreement and the absence of spoken criticism. None of the animals took to him. Danielle called him a sourpuss, but her voice, the boy noticed, retained its awe. She respected things and people that were bigger and older, and in Preston's case, oriented towards money and success. He had turned twenty and been newly made company secretary, even though he hadn't completed his course. He had loads of ability and was a fanatical worker.

Aunt Ursula called him pompous, and he didn't like that very much, but he didn't hate it, either. He couldn't see what was so bad in being pompous. Pomposity seemed a fine cloak for a managing director, as he hoped to be. He rather admired the robber barons, and the comfortably infamous.

He had opinions which, he felt, marked him as a thinker. Women, for instance, were those 'people who stand unsure, tentative, expectant, puzzled, with their purses shut while you find the money and pay.'

When Danielle played her New Music, he referred to it as 'the sound of curses. The twelve tone method isn't a language, it's like speaking in tongues.'

On the other hand he disliked Randal and Orville's rock

groups: Coffee Coloured Blood, Paper Staircase, Pneumatic Tools, Bald Bodies, Suburbs of Hell.

'He doesn't know what he likes,' Ursula said. 'As for me, I like music tough enough to last, to withstand people and fashion and all the seasons in between.' She meant Bach and Haydn, Mozart, Beethoven.

Preston helped pat down the soil on the grave and smiled derisively as the small boy said goodbye to the dead dog. His mind ran on lightning audits, catastrophic takeovers, market crashes, bank collapses, insider trading, the tides in economic affairs; not on pets.

Hammering

A pile of odd plates, five odd cups and a yellow butterdish with cerise flowers stood on the sink recess. They attracted Davis Blood for they were remnants of old dinner sets that Lillian had often turned her nose up at, wishing they'd go away because she was sick of looking at them.

He approached the sink, his eyes below the stainless steel edge. He went busily away and came back armed with a hammer. He busily pulled up a kitchen chair, climbed up laboriously — since he still held the hammer — and stood over the sink with its fragile burden. Considerately, he moved the crockery into the recessed sink.

Above the sink, on the wall facing the doorway, hung a framed text:

'The earth is the Lord's, and the fullness thereof.'

He glanced up at it, but it didn't stop him.

He raised the hammer, then brought it down on the

largest pieces first. At each blow he crunched the largest pieces remaining, until all were greatly reduced. Finally he was happily hitting a shifting pile of fragments, with Aunt Mira venting primal screams amid the din. The old despised plates, cups and butterdish were no more.

'A satisfying autistic achievement,' cackled Mira when Ursula wheeled in to see what the noise was. 'Talk about laugh!'

'It's no laughing matter,' said Ursula quietly.

'No, that's why I only talked about it. Let's get out of here, let's travel! Go to grey Paree, Trashville Tennessee, the Land of Ire! Anywhere! Oh hey little children, can you milk a cow?

> *Just grab on to the titties and go Pow! Pow! Pow!'*
> *'Oh! 'Twas in the month of Sydney*
> *In the city of July*
> *The snow was raining heavily*
> *The streets were still bone-dry*
> *The flowers were sweetly singing*
> *The birds were in full bloom*
> *As . . .'*

No one was listening.

Davis Blood had stopped being busy, and rather dreamily got down off the chair. His face was relaxed, limp, as if all interest had drained away. He was contained within himself. He went outside to the yard and poked around near the big tree, and came in under the house and sat on the swing Jackson Blood had made sixteen years before, for Preston.

After some silent meditation he went out into the backyard again and picked up a thin stick, now and then poking its end into insect holes in the big gum tree, or under loose bark and watching with interest as assorted insects ran for their lives from the dangers of daylight.

He supposed he would have to listen to some talk later about the plates and cups and things, but without being told, he knew no one had power over that part in him where he was really himself, where his life was lived, where he could say, 'No, I won't,' or 'Yes, I will.'

He knew he had helped Lillian get plates and cups she liked, and told her so that evening. Which was perhaps why she decided it was time for him to learn a second verse to his nightly prayer.

> *'Let my sins be all forgiven*
> *Bless the friends I love so well*
> *Take me, when I die, to heaven*
> *Happy there with you to dwell.'*

It's Secret in Your Head

Truth was foremost, his father said. Decency, honesty, kindness, cleanliness, cheerfulness, directness, came next. And not backing off.

'Never take a backward step, or do anything that would cause you to run for cover. Do the right thing and your heart will be strong. Bow to no one and let no one bow to you. Lie to no one. Respect people for what they are, not what they've got.'

When his father said these things, he felt they were so obvious, reasonable, right, that they needed no further comment. He put them in his head, where they were safe. His father's words.

But sometimes a lot of seriousness in one hit made the boy crave something to laugh at. One way he found of turning seriousness aside was by making original observations.

'Sometimes when Auntie talks it's like crying,' he said of Ursula.

'Randy,' he said to Randal. 'Every time you want to do something, you do it.' Which summed up Randal.

Seeing the wrinkles on his own heel, he said sadly, 'Look, Mum, afraid I'm getting old.'

When he said, 'Bugger,' imitating Orville, and was asked why, he answered guiltily: 'I'm not saying it to people, I just want to see if I can say the word.'

He was aware that his mother sang most of the time, usually just below the level of what was plainly audible. Sometimes she burst out with a line or two in full voice. When she was alone in the house she let the reins go.

If the boy half-caught some words, he would ask, 'What's that song, Mum?' She'd tell him the words, privately sensing his dawning feeling of proprietorship over his mother, needing to know more about her, needing to know what she was up to, who she was.

The first time he asked her what she was singing, she said, 'Oh, that's "Take my life".' They were in the kitchen.

He looked at her, at a loss. She lifted her head from what she was doing.

'I'll sing it for you, darling.'

> *'Take my life, and let it be,*
> *Consecrated, Lord, to you.'*

'Who's you?'
'God.'
'What's cons'crated?'
'Consecrated. Say it: con-se-crated.'
'Con-se-crated.'
'Good boy. It means given up to, giving your life to.'
'Oh.' He had to let that settle in his head, and didn't ask any more then.

Later, fresh from playing in the front yard, among her flower borders, he heard her almost-singing again.

'What's that one, Mum?'

Instead of talking she sang it:

> *'Pass me not, oh loving Saviour*
> *Hear my humble cry*
> *And while you are blessing others*
> *Do not pass me by.'*

'Is that God again?'
'Yes, darling.'
'Like on the text?' The text: 'Jesus Christ, the same yesterday, today and forever', hung on the wall above his parents' bed.
'Yes.'
'Do you talk to God a lot?'
'Most of the time, Davie.'
'Is God always listening?'
'God is everywhere, always there. He can hear what you say in your head, even if no one else can hear a word, and no matter how many people talk to him.' She recited:

> *'. . . to whom all hearts are open*
> *all desires known*
> *from whom no secrets are hidden.'*

He thought a bit. It must be so. When he said some things in his own head, like why does Randal come home loud sometimes and bang things around, no one else heard him say it. He'd found he could say lots of things with no one else hearing, or even knowing he was talking. It was secret. No one else knew what you said to yourself. No one could check what was said or not said in your head.
'Does God talk to you, Mum?'
'Yes, God does.'
'Where? Can I hear it?'
'Inside me.' She gestured with both hands, fingers spread, somewhere between her head and her breast. 'In the inmost parts of me. Where I am most myself, where I can't lie to myself because I know.'
It was mysterious inside your mother. Perhaps it was wonderful in there. He'd been in there once, he'd been told. He couldn't imagine it. How could you breathe?
'Will I ever hear it?'

'If you want to hear, you'll hear.'
He thought a bit.
'Do you ask God for things, like I ask you for things?'
'Yes.'
'Does God know everything?'
'Everything. Our inmost thoughts. Every secret.'
'Why do you have to ask, if he knows what you want?'
'To show him I know what I need, and that I wouldn't ask for anything selfish or silly.'
He digested that.
'When I was little, did I know I was me?'
'I don't know. I think so. Perhaps not when you were just born, but later.'
'How does God know he's God?'
'Oh dear. I don't know. I'm only a mother, God's God, eternal. He was before everything, and continues after everything. That's all I know.'
He was silent a while. Then delicately, with a softer voice, as if he wasn't really doing anything as pushy as putting a question, he asked, 'How do you know, Mum?'
'I believe. That's the way I know. Goodness, this is a big talk.'
'Is it making you tired?'
'No. I thought you might be.'
'I'm not. God talk is interesting.' His thoughts rested a bit, then he said, 'Mum, does it hurt when you're dead?'
'No. Nothing hurts in heaven.'
'Your bones don't hurt?'
'No, darling.'
'Not even with all the meat off?'
She hesitated. He'd watched often as she sliced the meat, and loved to gnaw the bits left on the bone after a roast leg had been devoured by the family.
'No, but you're not meat, your bones won't have the meat off.'
'Not even when I'm dead?'
Ah, he must have seen something on television, perhaps in a wildlife film showing predator and prey. Or had he seen human bones in an educational excerpt on extermination camps?

'When you're dead you won't need this sort of body. You and I will be in heaven.'

He was silent. He could tell she had no more to say on the question that interested him most just then: his own death. She had dodged answering what he had asked. It didn't occur to him that she might not know. There must be a good reason why she wouldn't say more.

Something was unfinished. Oh yes.

'Mum, what do you mean God was here before everything?'

'God is eternal. Forever. God always existed, and always will. God said, Before the universe was, I am!'

'Before Grandma?' She was very old, he knew. He didn't go into it, but his first impression of her was of a person always looking down. The first few times he saw her, he looked down to see what was there. He didn't realise age had bent her, he thought the bend was deliberate.

'Yes, before Grandma.'

'Before the world?'

'Yes. God called the universe into existence. The world is a small part of the universe.'

He felt he could follow that. But eternal?

'What does eternal mean again?'

'No beginning, no end.'

He thought a bit, then said, 'Mum?'

'Yes, darling.'

'Can I have a drink? This talk makes me thirsty.'

As he drank, a strange bird called loudly down in the valley.

'Caprigel! Caprigel!' It was a sad call.

'Caprigel!' it said again, sad and loud.

All That Exists, Plus

Tendrils of the honeysuckle vine twisted around the verandah posts and in and out of the wire netting placed there to give it support; night and day reaching for something to hold tight to. He loved to bite the green end of the honeysuckle blossom and suck the nectar.

'It suits me,' he said by way of explanation to Randal, as he watched his big brother, sitting on the front steps in the sun, getting out his boots ready for the first game of the football season.

Randal sat surrounded by shoulder pads, hip inserts for his shorts, pairs of new white laces, team socks and jumpers and training jumpers of all designs. The most loving care went into his boots. He was replacing the studs, unscrewing the old and worn and screwing in the new. The little boy watched, fascinated by such care and devotion.

To amuse his brother, Randal sang the one dressing room song that he judged fit for a little kid. None of that 'Twas on the good ship Venus' stuff.

> *'After the ball was over*
> *She lay on the sofa and sighed*
> *She put her false teeth in salt water*
> *And took out her lovely glass eye.*
> *She kicked her cork leg in the corner*
> *And hung up her wig on the wall.*
> *The rest of her went to bye-byes*
> *After the ball.'*

Davis Blood had noticed that, unlike him, his big brothers never asked questions. Well, hardly ever. As if they knew everything. So he was a big boy, and didn't ask what a ball was. He regretted it later, it nagged at him, so he asked Aunt Mira when he went into the kitchen.

She cackled savagely, and replied:

> *'Tiddly Winks the barber*
> *Tried to shave his father*
> *Razor falls*
> *Cuts his balls*
> *Tiddly Winks the barber.'*

That wasn't what he wanted. He knew Aunt was being rude, but he didn't know what was meant. He found a lost biscuit, all by itself in the jar on the kitchen table, and thought he'd ask Aunt Ursula later. But Mira had an audience, so she performed.

> *'Jesu lover of my soul*
> *Point me to the sugar bowl*
> *If the sugar bowl is empty*
> *Fill it from your mother's pantry.'*

'Hey, what goes up a chimney down but can't come down a chimney up?'

The boy shook his head. She wanted to trick him, then laugh.

'Umbrella, you dill! Umbrella!' The pinky-orangey-tangeriney thing on her head tufted up into full view, as it did when she was excited or enquiring. He caught a kind of garden smell from her direction.

She asked in a suspiciously sweet tone, 'Are you a stupid boy?'

Seriously he answered, 'Yes, sometimes.'

'Ah, don't give me that! Trying to make out you're the truth boy, are you?'

He looked at her sarcastic face and big tongue. He did tell the truth. Things were simple that way, and plain. He'd noticed Orville and Randal watch him with a sort of concealed, sideways look when he confessed to little accidents he'd had, that made a mess. Was he unusual? But no, his mother always admitted clumsy things she did, so it must be a good thing to do.

He wondered what it meant when he heard Aunt Ursula

say Mira was out of her mind — she'd lost what kept her together.

What keeps people together? But he took the opportunity to tell Ursula that they, Lillian and he, had been talking about God. He hoped Aunt might say something. She had words, marvellous words, lots and lots.

'God, eh? Good old God!'

'Who is God, Auntie?'

'God is all that exists, plus all that doesn't; all we know, plus all we don't know; all we see, plus all we can't see.'

So that, after all, a boy of three was no farther forward.

'God is alive, isn't he, Auntie?'

'Nothing's actually alive. This —' She swept her jerking hand around to indicate the world, or even the universe. 'This is all illusion. Life is merely organisation, and electro-chemical interaction. Apparently-living things are mechanisms by which life itself can be mobile, compressed, accessible to more connections, more possibilities of survival.'

He said nothing. She immediately apologised.

'Strike that, little man! Didn't mean it. Just slipped out. Let me tell you about the time I played cricket for the Australian Schoolgirls' team against the UK.'

She'd hardly begun when Randal came in loaded with polished boots, football jumpers, and lots of pairs of long white laces. He'd remembered another song:

> 'As I sat under the apple tree
> A birdie sent his love to me
> And as I wiped it from my eye
> I said thank goodness cows can't fly.'

The puzzle was, that after all, the valley was full of trees and wisdom, putting out shoots of eternity. Randal was a leaf.

Climbing the Box Tree

Often he had looked up at the shaded spaces in the box tree that stood out the front of the house, seen the comfortable branches and handholds evenly spaced. He'd seen the Campbell kids along the road climbing their old camphor laurel that they used as a swing — two ropes knotted to a motor tyre.

The lowest branch was more than a metre high. He tried his father's drums of oil and kerosene, to find one he could use, and was lucky. The mower petrol tin was just right. He rolled it to the base of the tree, and set it upright. He climbed on it and stood up. The branch was only a step up. With joy, he took the first step. His arms went round the tree and he stood there feeling the round trunk against his chest. It was neither cold nor warm, just warmer than the boards of the verandah.

His foot, on the rounded branch, soon tired. The best relief was to climb to the next branch, slightly further round the trunk. It was a big step and he pulled himself up with both arms. He climbed the next three branches and stopped to look. The view from here was like nothing he had seen before. He could see over the roof of number twenty, to the houses on the other side of the valley, surrounded by trees. Far away to the south-east he saw the cluster of ghostly, hazy towers of Sydney.

There was another branch as high as his chest. Too high.

Perhaps it wasn't. On the fourth try he got his knee in the crook of the branch, and put his hands high on the trunk to pull himself up. It worked. He could do it easily. He clambered up on his knee, took a higher grip, and shifted sideways to get both feet planted on the branch. He stood, and surveyed the world again. The branches above him were too high and the laterals too thin, to think of going higher. He gave himself up to the view.

There were so many things to look at in the world; the higher you got the more you could see. So many distant houses. He'd heard that buildings live longer than people. The sea, to the east, was a blue strip of royal blue meeting the pale sky of the horizon. Gunsight Hill to the west showed more of the blue ridge of mountains in its big V. The moon was riding high and white. You could almost see through it. And the birds: their territory was all round him. How easy it was to get to places if you could fly.

Somewhere in the house his mother called: 'Davie! Davie!' Soon she would be outside looking for him. He'd better think about getting down, in a minute.

One more big look. If you kept still and allowed the whole slice of world to be still, it was funny how flat it seemed, like a big painting pasted on the sky. Some moments all was still, just like a picture. Until a leaf moved or a car in the distance. Even then it was just a movement within a picture.

He thought about getting down, without taking his eyes from the pasted-on landscape. Could he trust his hands? He had a feeling he might let go. He had to pull his eyes away from the view, they wouldn't have left it without force. He shook his head, to clear it of thoughts of letting go. Getting down was real, he must take it seriously.

Even so, another look down past the end of Country Road yielded a sight of the first line of trees. That was as far as the last bushfire came before it was stopped. The bark on those trees was black near the ground.

Two crows passed overhead, flapping their wings strongly, making loud cries and delighting him. He was too young to realise he was learning to love the world and what it contained. The 'Ka!' of the crows sounded rather like an aggrieved baby's cry. He looked down.

It seemed a long way, but if he'd got up, there must be a way down. Though perhaps you could do things you couldn't undo.

It was frustrating being four. So much you'd never thought of, never seen, never heard of. He waited. His mother came to the back door, but since he didn't move, she didn't see him. He experimented with putting one leg down. His mother saw the leg and let out a loud 'Davis!'

It didn't help. The sudden piercing sound hit him like a blast and unsteadied him. Would his hands hold on?

'Come down out of that tree, Davis! This instant!' Then she sneezed, a real explosion. Her concern was obvious, but the electrifying sneeze was an extra hurdle. He would have to resist her, ignore what she said and how she said it, in order to keep his head free and muscles obedient to do what needed to be done. They both wanted him to come down, but her anxiety could disable him.

He carefully let down his left leg again, bending his right knee further into his chest, taking a lower grip with his hands, until the toe of his left shoe touched something. He watched and guided his foot to a foothold on the branch and let his weight settle on to that foot. He was standing, he'd made it, his hands hadn't let go. He took the other branches carefully until he was on the petrol drum.

His mother had her arms around him. He waited till her desire for contact had been satisfied and she began to take him to task. To do this she had to move slightly away; this was enough to give him room to get down off the drum. Despite her admonitions he had to concentrate on getting that drum back where it belonged. His father had an eye for things out of place.

When she was calmer, her song resumed. When he'd finished with the drum he asked her what the song was.

'Oh, for a closer walk with God,' she said.

He had climbed the box tree. He was a different boy.

When he was about to go to bed that night he felt so new, so complacent about his exploit that even after his prayers he didn't feel he ought to be going to sleep.

'I can't sleep, Mum,' he said.
'But you've got into bed.'
'I know. But I can't sleep.'
'Give it time. Just close your eyes.'
'But I've got nothing to dream about.'
'Dream about what you saw from the tree.'

'Right, Mum. Good idea.' Then he thought of something. 'Mum!'

'Yes?'

'Why doesn't our grass grow short to the ground like Mister Carroll's? Is it different grass?'

'Not different grass, Davie. Different people.'

He began to think about that, and was halfway into it when he fell asleep. As she tiptoed away in the darkness she found herself singing the last line of the song she knew as, 'If ever I loved you, my Saviour, it's now', and as she looked back for a last glimpse of the sleeping face, she smiled at her timing of those words. Yes, his life would always be another reason for her to love the Saviour.

Something New

When it was in season, his father tried him on a small piece of quince. The boy held it up, looked at it, smelled it, rubbed it cautiously near his top lip.

'Try it,' his father suggested.

The boy put it on his tongue. The family watched. It tasted bitter. He shuddered, then carefully brought his jaws together. His teeth touched the sliver gently, just enough to get some juice out of it. He tasted the juice, then suddenly spat the lot out. It seemed to rob all his mouth's moisture, and leave bitterness.

His father smiled, shook his head, 'Perhaps you'll like it some day.'

'When I'm big?'

'When you're bigger,' Randal said.

'Can he say quince?' said Preston.

'Say quince,' said Lillian.

'Quince.'

'Good boy,' said Jackson Blood.

'He's got a good ear,' said Ursula.

'He's an all right kid, that one,' said Preston, who was twenty.

'He'll pass, with a push,' said Orville, winking at him.

The family laughed as little Davis tried to wink. Lillian resumed her communing song, 'Oh, love divine, how sweet you are', at the level of a melodious humming. Now and then a word or two would break through the humming and sound clearly.

'Mm-m-m-m stronger your love than death, m-m-m-m!'

Danielle didn't join in, being full of silence. Anguish over her latest relationship was growing bigger in her; soon it would be the size of a bomb. Then there would be an explosion, then no relationship, only pieces to be picked up or discarded.

The little boy took the word 'quince' away with him and ran it over his tongue in much the same way as he had with the sliver of fruit. It was a bitter word, that made your tongue curl up. It was a white, pulpy word, yet hard. It was a word big and furry with quince-down, pale green as well as white; it had corners and lumpy things at one end, it smelled furry, tart, antagonistic.

He tasted and held the word. The contact of his own touch made it appear to him to have some warmth of its own.

He tasted again the smell of the piece he bit out of the sliver. In his mouth the flesh of the fruit left tracks of bitterness that made him smile with pleasure.

Years later, he had forgotten the exact moment when he discovered that a word is an object, with its own mass and qualities, its own weight and shape, its smell, taste and sound, and above all its colour; but the discovery was with him always.

Family Secret

After a silence at the dinner table one evening he asked, 'What's my little brother's name?'

The family was taken by surprise. Randal spoke first.

'You don't have a little brother. You would've had a brother, if he'd lived. But that was four years ago.'

'What was his name?' the boy persisted. All looked at Jackson Blood, then Lillian. No one spoke.

'Was it the same as mine? Would there be two of us?' he said anxiously.

'We didn't give names until after you were born,' Lillian said carefully. She had prepared names beforehand. She knew that there were two babies inside her, and in the case of boys, the first would be Davis and the next Jackson, after her husband. But she knew of the slight feeling of rejection this little boy sensed from his father, and whether the feeling was illusory or not she decided it would be more hurtful to tell him his twin would have had his father's name, than to keep silence.

The little chap knew the question hadn't been answered, but said nothing. The family was collectively uncomfortable that this part of the past had been brought out into the light.

Lillian, in particular, suffered each time this slight deception came to the surface in her head.

The little boy, though, thought further. If his brother had lived, he, Davis Blood, might be the dead one. In a way, his being here was perhaps accidental. Not absolutely necessary.

He shivered. What might have been was something you could never know.

In the valley an owl screeched.

Orville's Tree

Next afternoon, Orville called him when he got home from school and took him down the backyard, to the bottom terrace where the soil was deep and soft. He had a green whippy stick in his hand. He'd used it on the way home to slash at several trees, used it like a whip to scare a dog or two and had been about to throw it away when he thought of a use for it.

'It's for you. I'll show you,' he said. The boy watched. Orville pushed the thicker end of the stick into the moist black-brown earth, then closed the hole round its base when it was far enough in. A soldier bird flew up into a nearby blossom tree.

'That'll grow now. You'll see.'

It was an ordinary green stick, as far as the boy could see. How could a stick grow? Near the top, where it was about half a metre out of the ground, there was a bump on one side, the smallest lump.

Orville lifted his young brother up, mainly so the walk together up to the house would be quicker, but also for a bit of contact. The boy's face was turned to where the willow stick now pointed upright. The lump faced over where the sun came up each day.

It was also to give the kid something. They all felt the little chap had been cheated, somehow, when his twin was born dead.

On Orville's shoulder, the boy thought of the willow stick stuck in the ground, and of his brother who didn't survive birth. From all he'd been told, he was set apart, he was no accident; set apart by having a purpose.

Orville carried him right up the back steps, and shared a slice of bread and blackberry jam with him. Blackberry was Orville's favourite, which Davis Blood knew.

Lots of things died, it seemed. He was sorry about them all. Perhaps each dead thing lived again a little when you thought of it. Death was inescapable, though, from everything he'd heard. It was annoying. Why couldn't he live through to the end to see everything that happened?

Pushing God Out

One Monday morning the words of the Sunday night address came back to him. He asked his father a question as he came into the kitchen for breakfast.

'Dad, what's God?'

'God made everything. God is life. God is love. He's present everywhere, he knows us inside out. God's a spirit.'

'What's a spirit?'

'You can't touch a spirit, or feel it, or see it. You pass right through it.'

'Is God in here?'

'Yes.'

'If I've just come in here, then I'm not crowding him?'

'Crowding him?'

'Pushing him out a bit?'

'No. No more than you gave him more room in the bathroom by leaving it. He's a spirit. He's everywhere. Passes through all things, all things pass through him.'

'Oh,' the little boy said, but didn't understand. He tried to get a picture of such a being in his head.

When his father had left the kitchen, he heard Aunt Mira calling, 'Psst! Hey!'

'Yes, Aunt Mira?'

'What did one wall say to the other?'

'I don't know.'

'Meet you at the corner!' She cackled at the boy's puzzled face. 'Keep it under your hat!'

But he didn't have a hat.

'What does a diamond become when you put it in water, eh?'

The boy shrugged. This was trivial compared to his talk with Jackson Blood.

'Wet, silly! Would you rather be a bigger fool than you look or look a bigger fool than you are?'

He was getting annoyed. He made no answer.

'What smells most, in all the world?'

'Oh, I don't know, Aunt Mira, it's silly!'

'Nose, nose, nose! There! You don't know anything! Talking about noses, what did the big rose say to the little rose?'

'I don't know! Go away!'

'Hiya, bud! Do you underconstumble that, eh?'

'Go to sleep, you silly old thing! You're a pest!' He made for the door.

'You might be a rose,' she grumbled. 'You're prickly enough. I'm only a poor old thing, trying to get a bit of interest out of life.'

She said this so sadly that he looked back at her, but her pale bent head and downcast expression was betrayed by a bright, shrewd, unblinking eye. It was useless being sorry for her.

He thought about God. How could anyone be right inside you and know what you thought, and your secrets?

I don't have any secrets, he thought, do I? I wish I had a secret. But why? If it was a secret, no one would know. There seemed no point in it, unless people knew.

There was one secret. That was when he said things in his head, and could hear his own inner voice talking — to himself and to others — and no one knew, or could ever check on, what he said or what he heard.

Nothing in the World was Flat

The boy had climbed onto a chair on the verandah, which ran in a square U-shape round three sides of the house. Standing up, he could see out of the glass Jackson Blood had put up to keep the weather off part of the verandah. It was ordinary glass, smooth and shiny, like in the mirrors inside the house; so flat and slippery that no lumps or roughnesses stood up from it. If anything was flat, glass was.

He had his face close to the glass and watched as his breath clouded the surface. He looked to the right, up Big Hill, and left, down the valley. Something caught his attention. As he got his left eye close against the plate glass and looked up the hill he noticed, when he moved slightly, that a wave of something passed over road and trees and the house up the hill. What was it?

He moved his head again. Parallel waves distorted a section of the view. Just then, he caught his foot against something, and nearly fell. It was a tack that had worked loose in the seat of the chair. Tacks were supposed to be flat, when Randal or his father hammered them. Flat as a tack, he'd heard Randal say, though he wasn't sure that he knew all that was meant. He could tell there'd been big people's meanings along with it, things they knew went with it but didn't explain to those who didn't already know.

Flat as a tack. What was the other one? Flat out like a lizard drinking. Yes. There was a fish called flathead, too. There was 'Knocked him flat', another thing Randal said once. There was 'flat feet', a phrase his father used in talking of the Army.

He looked at the other tacks in the chair. Some were knocked in below the surface of the wood, others raised a tiny bit. He stooped close, and saw that none of them was flat.

Perhaps the glass he'd looked through wasn't flat, either. He knew the crazy shapes of the family faces when he lifted his glass of water and looked at them through the bottom of his glass, which was definitely not flat. When he looked through Aunt Ursula's spectacles the view was blurred in one and funny in the other, but the rest of the view just outside the edge of the glass lens was out of line, seriously out of line. Her glasses were rounded outwards, definitely not flat.

Then the verandah glass probably was uneven, and that unevenness made the band of distortion appear. But the glass looked so flat. He'd have sworn it was flat, yet obviously it wasn't. And all the other things people called flat were nothing like flat.

Lizards were bumpy, feet were lumpy, a flathead fish was rounded. Perhaps nothing people said about ordinary objects was accurate.

He stood again, and looked out at the world, going through the list of things he saw, for flatness. Leaves weren't flat, the road wasn't flat, neither were the rocks at the road's edge, nor grass blades, not the sides of electricity poles, nor the petals of flowers, nor Hansen's dogs, Challoner's cow, McCarthy's fruit trees, or their own fowls down at the bottom of the backyard; nor were any of their parts — beaks, combs, feathers, claws, tails, hooves, paws, or any other part.

He frowned. As far as he could see, nothing was flat. Why have the word, if there's no flatness? If everything was lumpy and bumpy, then flatness was the strange thing, not lack of flatness.

He sighed.

Over against the front fence, Stockhausen the cat was lying on his side, legs extended in opposite directions, trying to be flat. His coat was thin over his ribs, his chest heaved with the effort of his asthmatic breathing. He'd never been a well cat.

The boy got down off the chair and went looking for a drink. He was always drinking something.

Stockhausen

That cat could make music out of anything, even his asthma. Sometimes the spasms shook his body so as to outline the alarming shape of ribs, and he would wheeze for minutes after. When it was over he would stalk off with a miaow or two. The whole thing was like a performance. He was eleven years of age, his face grey. He'd always had a rattly chest.

The Blood family got him on loan from the Jessups, who went away on holiday and never came back. Husband and wife were drowned on Applegreen Water when the southerly came up in the late afternoon, while they were fishing for sand bream.

Danielle christened him after his first coughing fit. He was a mess of a cat, everyone said so. It was uncharitable, but honesty and accuracy have no compulsion to be pleasant.

'I think he's happy with his congestion,' she said. 'It's like a friend to him. There's always something there, he's never alone. And when he coughs and rattles it's like a conversation. In a way, you know, it's like Lillian, with her constant singing to God.' This wasn't meant disrespectfully. Lillian's sincerity was crystal clear; her wholehearted love for God couldn't be doubted for a second or mistaken for anything else.

'He certainly seems to enjoy bad health,' Ursula said.

'A case for cynical psychology,' said Aunt Mira. 'Worthy of a poem:

'The cough that tolls the knell of passing cats
And leaves the world to darkness and to rats.

'Gray's Allergy, that's it. With the music of Pan and the Sacred Bark Soloists. Dancers sacred and profane. Andante déshabillé. Have a toccata! Don't mind if I do! Nail down his decretals! This is farce becoming tragedy!'

'For heaven's sake, Mira, shut up that nonsense!' called Ursula.

'Careful, or I'll call down on you the Busonic plague!' Mira intoned in a high voice. 'Look at me. My name is Too Late. So much for fame, then.'

'Quiet, or we'll get the doctor to examine you again,' Danielle said. This was a dire threat. Aunt Mira hated being prodded and poked. She was quieter, her voice falling.

'Incisions, incisions. Demanding money with medicines,' she grumbled, then was silent, her head falling on her chest.

'Poor Stockhausen,' Danielle said. 'I suppose no one's so sick that they can't be sicker.' She thought with relief of her own good health, shaded only by such things as the odd fat attack, or its alternative, an attack of the thins. Or the occasional siege of sadness at the thought that nothing is perfect.

'What's fame, Auntie?' the boy said to Ursula.

'Fame is when you don't know the people who know you, and the good part is they don't really know you. But the best part is you never have to get to know them,' said Aunt.

Danielle thought it a bit much to be saying to a child.

'There's no such thing as Kant!' shouted Mira, waking up. 'Even if they put Descartes before the horse!'

'There's one sure cure for civilisation,' said Ursula grimly. 'And for people who talk nonsense.'

'You have no desideratum for others,' Mira replied.

Danielle

She was fond enough of her little brother, but too old to feel close to him. If she'd been in her early teens, she could have cuddled him like a doll, or a pet, but she was a young working woman now and just that little bit out of step with the generation represented by kids of four.

'Would you like the television on?' she asked.

'No thanks, Danielle.'

'It's Prince Galaxy, fighting for decency and justice.'

'He won't win.'

'Really!' she laughed. 'How do you know?'

'I'm not interested, they're silly pictures. Will you come outside with me?'

'When?'

'Now?'

She didn't spend much time with the boy. She was busy enough. Perhaps she should.

'All right!' She took his small warm hand; they walked out into the open air.

'Oh! I see a blue dog in the sky!' Pointing up at one of the thin clouds in the blue sky.

'So it is! What a clever boy!'

'Why don't green and blue go together, Dany?'

'I don't know. They clash, sometimes. How did you know?'

'I heard you say it. About your pants and shirt.'

She remembered and shrugged.

'I didn't like the way they looked, that's all.'

'Then why did God make trees green and the sky blue?'

'Oh heavens, I don't know!'

'Don't they go together?'

'Yes, I suppose so. No, they don't really. But I guess they are beautiful, so I suppose they do.'

'Danielle, why is the wind sour?'

'Is it?'

'On the weather —' he meant the television bulletin — 'It is.'

She thought a bit.

'Oh, you mean the sou-westerlies?'

'Yes, why are they sour?'

'That's bad pronunciation. They mean south-westerlies.'

'Danielle.' Now he had her for a while, he would hang on. 'Do you get hungry at night?'

'Sometimes. Do you?'

'Very.'

'In the middle of the night?'

'Yes, in mid-night.'

'Why don't you come and tell me? Or Mum?'

'I couldn't just leave my dreams.'

'Oh, of course not,' she agreed, then went on, 'do you have dreams in the day too?'

'No. No dreams, only little pictures that float in the air. They're so quick I can't catch them.'

'That's interesting. Well, I have to go inside now and wash up the lunch things.'

'I'll wash up!' he announced, and marched up the steps and through the front door that was always open.

'You can't wash up, you're only four.'

He turned grandly, 'Come and watch, then.'

She followed him, watched as he climbed a chair, tried not to make tentative grabs as she thought he was about to drop things. Like a thousand generations of women before her, she watched from a great height the stumbling efforts of a young male eager to show what he could do before he was competent to do it; and, like all her predecessors, failed to recognise the value of that impulse.

Finally, it was done, after a fashion.

'See?' he said, turning to her. 'Perfect!'

She laughed. 'Have you done it before?' Pretty sure he hadn't.

'No.'

'How did you know you could?'

'I have to look at things, then I can imagine it. I can't imagine it if I don't see it: I don't know what to imagine.'

'But you imagined doing the washing up?' What he'd said wasn't clear to her.

'Yes, Danielle,' he said with irritation. Wasn't that what he'd said?

'Can you imagine lots of things?'

'Yes.'

'Can you imagine being a bird?'

'Oh yes! I'd love to be able to fly. As long as I could become me again, after.'

'Can you imagine being a tiny baby?'

'Well, I can imagine a baby, and being born, but I can't see myself in the imaginaise.'

Danielle smiled. What a strange little fellow he was. Perhaps she ought to make more time free for him.

Ought to. She knew she wouldn't, but was still smiling as she went to her room, remembering the very hot day when he turned all the beds down so the family would be cool at night, and the time she came clumping home wearing those awful court shoes and he called everyone's attention to 'Dany's loud shoes'.

Funny how little boys so often looked like solemn old men. Poor things. Old men were so empty, somehow, as if they'd used up all their surplus energy years before, and now could barely hang on to life, where old women were still pushing still active, still looking at the world with interest. She knew, though, that she had no idea why the men were like that, or what they thought of the world and of themselves.

So there, she was left with nothing. How often she started off a thought and only followed it a short way before she found she had nothing left; it had melted away. Her English teacher's remark came back to her, as it increasingly did now, the cutting remark that followed one of her essays. 'On the surface it's got an appearance of depth but deep down it's really rather shallow.'

When I'm old, she asked herself, will I still remember every embarrassment in the clearest, most minute detail?

The Bursting Man

Orville was eleven and loved Steamrollers, a peppermint sweet. The little boy liked them, too, and Orville often slipped the coloured sleeve off his silver-paper-covered roll of round white lollies and gave it to his little brother, to look at, in lieu of another Steamroller to eat. But one summer day, when the old green kitchen linoleum was lifted in a combined painting and renovating operation, an ancient Steamroller packet was found underneath, among the elderly newspaper sheets used as floor packing. On this packet a fat man lay on his back. He wore a red and white checked waistcoat; a steamroller had run over his legs, flattening them, and was travelling up over his flattened body, puffing out the man's stomach like a balloon.

The five-year-old looked at the picture with delight and often went to bed with it in his hand. He was so fond of it that Orville glued it to thicker paper, for longer wearing.

'What's going to happen to the man?' his question was.

'He's been run over.'

'What happens then?'

'He'll burst,' said Randal, as they sat round after dinner.

'Ssh, don't say things like that to a child,' Lillian said.

'And when he bursts, will all the things inside him come out?'

'Davie, what a thing to say.'

Davis smiled, but had to know.

'Will they fly out and get on to things? Will bits of him stick on people?'

'There'll be a hell of a mess when he blows up,' Randal said, putting a piece of steak in his mouth. It was underdone, juicy to chew.

'All over people?'

'A frightful mess,' repeated Randal, grinning.

'Can you get it off, or will it be stuck there, on you?'

'It'll come off with a scrub. Everything washes off.'

'What's inside people?'

'Guts.'

'Yes, but what things? Is it blood? Will the bones come out? What do bones look like, before they're cooked, I mean.' He'd seen the cooked ones when the weekend roast was done.

'They're all shiny and dripping with blood. Bits of stuff hang off them.'

'Randal!' protested Lillian.

'What stuff? Skin?'

'No, that's outside. Messy bits, torn stuff, shreds, long red bits and green bits and yucky bits.' He chewed his steak contentedly.

Lillian looked from one to the other.

'Davis, please get on with your dinner.'

'Yes, Mum. And will bits hit people in the face?'

'A few.'

'And will bones stick in you?'

'Only if they're sharp.'

'How do they get sharp?'

'If they splinter, and there's long splintery bits, all sharp and ready to go in you.'

'Can you get them out?'

'Easy. Just give a sharp pull, you'll be right.'

'If bits of another person get on you, will you get like that person?'

'I don't know. What a question.'

'If you see the bits inside someone, will they be angry with you?' He knew his sister and mother dressed and undressed with the door closed, and that only involved, as far as he knew, the outside bits.

'Mum, this kid's got some weird questions. Where'd you get him?'

Davis stopped and waited for her to answer. Where he was got was important. No answer came. He would have to wait.

'Can you put the man together if you get all the bits and put them in?'

'Maybe, but why bother, he'd be dead then.'

'When he blows up and the bits fly out, what will he look like?'

'Flat.'

'Thank goodness your father's here most of the time. You don't talk to the boy like that when he's here, none of you.' Jackson Blood often gave the impression that his patience and good humour were held on a tight rein.

'He's got to learn the facts of life, Mum. Life's messy.' He was fourteen.

'Let's do it!' interrupted Aunt Mira, singing. 'Let's do it! If it ought to be done, let's do it!' Then sweetly, 'Go north for the rest of your life!'

'Where does she get it all?' asked Randal of the aunt they'd taken in. No one knew how to explain her. Ursula thought her habit of sleeping a lot accounted for her long life, but even that was a guess.

'Goodness knows,' Lillian said. 'Your father says she's well-read, but she can't even pick up a book. As you know, he reads a lot to her when he's off work, but not enough to account for it. She's picked up an education somewhere. Quite an achievement, really. Very likely she's some sort of genius.'

'Who laughs lasts!' shouted Mira.

'How would you know?' Randal said. But she would. She was old as the hills already.

'Rome wasn't burned in a day. Oh what a droll sense of hernia I have!' she added in a self-congratulatory way.

'How old do you think she is?' asked Randal.

'Seventy, eighty perhaps,' Lillian answered.

'Older than dreamtime, am I,' Mira sang. Then in her speaking voice declaimed dramatically: 'Hold me close to your ego. There's the scene of the grime!'

'She must be very old. Older than anyone I know,' Lillian said absently. 'And with a lot more cheek,' she added pointedly.

'Just a standard deviation,' Mira said. 'The state of nature is a dirty bum,' and fell asleep.

The boy wandered out the front in the sun, found nothing to do and continued on down the side of the house into the backyard. He felt more like being with the trees and plants, and the clothes drying on the hoist, than up in the house with people. Along the valley, a brush cuckoo sang its half-dozen mournful notes. He looked up, attentively. It stopped.

He wandered, in his few-steps-this-way, few-steps-that-way pattern, down the terraces near Orville's tree, which now had a small crown of leaves supported on two twiggy branches that grew from its very top. Another branch, that faced east, stuck out from below the top, and had its own colony of leaves.

Orville was right. It had grown. And the little bump that faced the morning sun was now a branch. If it had become a tree, it must have roots, but how did roots grow from a stick? He'd like to have pulled up the willow to check the roots.

Instead, he watched a spider who lived in a curled leaf strung between branches of a small tree called the finger-leaf tree because each bract of leaves was in the form of three fingers. He stood still, waiting till the spider came out.

The distant cuckoo called at intervals.

No matter how he tried, how close he got, he could never hear the spider feet on the leaf as they probed forward for safe footing outside the leaf-curl.

When the spider was right outside, there was a wary joy in its tread, as it made its web rock slightly.

Yes, I like going outside my house, too, the little boy said silently.

As afternoon cooled towards evening, sugar ants came out, ready for their nightly activities; guarding and guiding caterpillars up their favourite trees, or milling around, worrying. Campanotus can cope, was their motto, as they made for the red gums, hoping.

Soon bandicoots would be out under cover of darkness, digging little holes under plants; the possum in the ceiling would wake up and come noisily down off the iron roof on to the post on the back landing, then down the yard into the bush to begin the day. Davis Blood had never been awake between three and four in the morning to hear the return journey.

There was a soft westerly breeze bringing the smell of mown grass from the playing fields at Blackman's Flat and the smell of the bush from the far side of the railway line. When the wind was from the south and east, the open windows received the salt smell of the Tasman.

Thinking of Others

His mother's most frequent exclamation, unless you count an heroic sneeze as an exclamation, was 'Think of others! Put yourself in their place!' And she did put herself in others' places.

Davis Blood didn't copy her, but he seemed to know how others felt about many things. When he surprised himself by knowing what others around him hadn't observed, he tried to explain it to himself. I watch the way they move, when they speak and what they say, when they don't speak, how they put their faces and voices. Then I put myself in their frames and feel how they feel.

His empathy was to do with knowing: it had nothing to do with behaviour, at least in the kitchen. He loved to pick.

'Why do I have to keep telling you to leave the apple pie alone?' his mother asked.

'I always love the things you say to leave alone,' he said reasonably.

'Well, put yourself in my place,' she began. He knew what was coming, and tuned out. He spied the cut apple peel and grabbed a handful of the curls with the most apple on them, and disappeared.

On an impulse he came back and listened at the kitchen

door, just out of sight. Sure enough, the sound of her singing began, gradually gaining in volume.

'*Master speak, your servant hears,*' then a few lines he couldn't make out. She lifted her voice for the last two lines, as he ate the peel, and he heard them clearly.

> '*I am listening, Lord, for you;*
> *What have you to say to me?*'

He smiled with satisfaction and went out into the yard. His mother's life seemed one continuous song, interrupted briefly by the happenings of daily life, such as working in the house, in the flower garden out front, or now and then working in the city for the tent-making company. Other mothers he knew weren't a patch on his. Lillian was something: not weak and wavery and nothing in particular, like some. She knew what she thought, she knew what she was.

Underneath Lillian's song was a feeling for the passing of time, especially as it affected the growing of her children. Here was the last one, already five, and in him she detected the efforts at thinking that would take him out of childhood and away from her forever. The ability to think leads to sadness, she felt. It leads to many other things, naturally, but she feared above all the thinking which in so many people searches for unbelief, for a way out of commitment to the heavenly Father; for a way out of trust, towards complete freedom, aimless and ungrounded, anchored to nothing.

We Stay in the Universe

Aunt Ursula kept an exercise book in which the boy's little sayings, that came out unexpectedly, were noted. She'd done the same for the other children, from Preston down to Orville, but if anything, got more pleasure from the task than ever.

The boy Davis was sitting at the kitchen table with a pencil and pile of copy paper that Danielle had brought home from Merry-go-round TV Productions. She worked as secretary to the production manager, with ambitions to become a script assistant.

He lifted the pencil from the drawings he was making, put the used sheets with the other used sheets, looked up at Ursula and said, 'I wish I knew everyone in Australia, and they could just drop in.'

The methylated smell lurked in the shade of some generous pats of cologne.

Aunt smiled at him with her violently twisted mouth, her eyes bright, unconquered by decades of deformity and pain. 'Good boy,' she added, and added his words to her exercise book. The operation took several minutes. Her crazily angled elbows and wrists allowed her only to attack the paper in swoops. When she missed, the letters went all over the place. She held her arm back, aimed, and made a mark where the stroke had to go, or as near as possible.

The boy worked away on a fresh sheet of paper, drawing crowds of elongated human figures.

'Is the world like a piece of paper, Auntie?' he asked, pencil raised. He held up his head to show Ursula that he'd wait for an answer. Her whole tortured body grappled with the effort of speaking. Her mouth worked sideways, her head nodded, arms jerked; she began to make sounds.

'I've never thought of that, Davie. But what if it was like a sheet of paper?'

He held his rubber over some of the rows of figures.

'People who are nasty to people could be rubbed out,' he

said. 'At once,' suiting the action to the word and rubbing out.

She looked at him. If the world were a sheet of paper and could be made neater by a little rubbing out, would there be more goodness in the world? Ursula thought not. Children arrive, their natures unpredictable, they usually make a point of not being like their parents. There was a blessed non-uniformity about progeny. After all, biological variability works against exactness of detail. If some were rubbed out, others worthy of rubbing out would be sired and mothered by parents who were harmless. No animal breeds like a cutting, she thought, looking out of the window at the hypericum near the fence and the new weigela, struck only a short while before by Lillian. But how do I know plants are exact copies, she thought wryly.

The boy ran in to the bathroom then — he'd held it till he could hold it no longer — and stood at the toilet bowl looking up at 'The Lord is my Shepherd', lovingly printed in old script on white cardboard by Danielle when she was eight. The strait-jacket of need loosened quickly, as his water flowed. He ran back into the kitchen.

'Did Jesus say that?' he asked.

'Say what?'

'The Lord is my Shepherd.'

'No. King David did. Jesus, eh? A psychological genius, that one; a pointer towards a master therapy of inwardness, of psychological self-sufficiency, wholeness. Far greater than your poor little Freuds and Jungs.' The boy listened wide-eyed. 'But what a magnificent failure. His major insight was God is love, but he failed to develop it. He didn't see that love doesn't have to suffer for others, or that the good don't have to be poor. He took too much notice, in his formative years, of ideas from the East.'

The boy thought about it.

'Why did he?' he asked, though he didn't quite take in the rest of it.

'They lived right near a major trade route from the East to Damascus. Couldn't help being influenced. And another thing: they believed in sacrifice in those days. Sacrifice, to get good results, to keep in good with God and the unknown.'

'Did it work?'

'Sometimes. If it didn't, they'd say they'd missed another factor. They could get out of any bother that way. Either there were sins they hadn't noticed, or God's purposes were different. They could explain anything,' she said with a faint smear of derision over her voice.

'Is that why you don't agree with it?' he asked shrewdly.

'Yes!' she exclaimed in surprise. 'Yes, that's the weakness of belief! What a clever chap you are! Yes, belief systems stop you thinking, you just lapse into logic and apply ready-made answers from within the system to patch up the holes as they appear. That's why I don't believe in belief.'

The boy made no pretence of understanding this, but listened carefully to every word, each tone of voice. There was a great difference between what his mother and father said and sang and what Aunt thought. He was too young to ask Aunt about the strengths of belief.

Instead, he asked, 'What is believing, Aunt?'

'It means having faith in, being sure of.'

'Does it make you good?'

'It might. It might not.'

'Are you good?'

'Davie, what I should be but am not, haunts me night and day.'

'Auntie,' he said again, 'what's God?'

'God is a theory, a sort of hypothesis to try to account for all the things that are and that can't be explained. Like — how did it all begin and how will it end?' She waved her jerky arms, describing angles, but meaning the universe. 'Under everything the scientists imagine, beyond all the guesses, it seems reasonable that there has to be something before the big bang, if there was one, or before the earlier first states of the universe. It may be a force, a life principle, attraction and repulsion, mixing and change, an infinite intelligence — any name you care to give to the processes — but, in short, you can call it God.'

'What do you call it, Auntie?'

'Well, I call it God, myself. But mind you,' she added quickly, 'my sort of God just started everything, but isn't interested in little humans like us, what we do and what we don't do.'

'You understand things, Auntie, don't you?' he said after a while. He didn't, he knew, but he would remember the words.

'Nothing can be understood,' admitted Aunt Ursula. 'In full.'

Something surfaced in his mind. It was about the planted stick that had become Orville's tree, and its roots growing in the soil, underground in darkness.

'Auntie, where do we go when we die?' He knew of funerals, and people being buried in the ground, like dead pets were in the backyard.

'We get buried,' she said.

'No, we! Where do we go?' He tapped on his chest with both hands. 'The inside bits!'

'We don't go anywhere. We stay here, in the universe,' she replied.

He stood, puzzled. That wasn't the answer he wanted. He turned to go into the kitchen for a drink of water, but as he looked back to check on her expression, he saw she was smiling.

It was more puzzling than when he learned from Orville that the world was round, and people who stood on the other side of the world thought we were upside down, and people a quarter way round were standing out sideways like spikes; and the clouds and air above us were spherical envelopes for a near-spherical planet, above which was no air at all, but space.

A Difficult Child

First day at school he was told to sit on one of the low children's chairs. At home a chair was comfortingly big and solid, something you climbed up on. These looked ridiculous.

He sat. He got up and looked down at that chair.

'Sit down! Didn't you hear me tell you?' he heard.

That chair had lumps on it, he was sure. He ran his hands over it; the lumps sidestepped.

'What did I tell you?' the voice bellowed in his ear. He tried the chair again. A great face came down crossways over his field of forward vision, the bellowing continued. A hot breath that smelled of tea and recent food rushed over his face. He stopped breathing: he didn't intend to have that smell in him. He looked at the face. It was shouting at him. He'd heard one of the kids say this teacher was scotty.

'You'll do what you're told when you're told!'

He held his breath until the face went away, then released it. The chair was lumpy.

When he got home he gave the note to Ursula. She was nearest.

Before dinner that night he asked to be allowed to say the grace since he was now a schoolboy. The family ate at the kitchen table unless it was a special occasion with visitors, when they used the dining room, which was also called the lounge room, also the big room. The television was in there, and the big table.

> *'Thank you for the world so sweet*
> *Thank you for the food we eat*
> *Thank you for the days so fine*
> *Thank you God for everything.*

*Now don't just stand there, God, do something!
Amen!'*

The women smiled, the father frowned, the boys grinned, and Danielle laughed aloud joyously. The boy looked at her. He'd never heard that tone in her voice before.

'That was a high tinkle,' he said.

'Sorry, young man,' she said with mock gravity.

'Don't be sorry, I liked it. Will you laugh lovely like that every day?'

'I'll try. Just for you. But why?'

'Then no one will ever be unhappy,' he said seriously.

Danielle got on with her dinner, wishing the men she knew would say things like that to her. Or, better still, think them if they couldn't say them. It seemed that, apart from her father, the only male in the world who valued her for herself was five years of age. Some of her friends had joined the women's movement, but she referred to it derisively as Women's Lip. She thought the output of the movement had the effect of telegraphing punches, or notifying the presence of terrorist bombs. The war of the sexes, to her, was guerilla warfare, alone behind enemy lines, its victories individual ones.

The trouble with me, she thought as she ate, is that I forget that men don't see women as people. They don't see us as flowers, either. They see us as meals. Perhaps they're warped ever since that first babyhood sight of the breast. She regarded her small brother steadily.

'Dany's got thinking all over her face!' he said loudly.

No one spoke. Lillian and Ursula knew Danielle wasn't easy with her present life, though her job was interesting. The older boys knew it was no time for comment: one word out of place here and that would be it; words like flaming branches shoved down your throat before you even knew what was happening.

The little boy lifted some food to his mouth, and spoke through the food, 'But she's not happy.'

'Oh!' said Danielle, about to say 'Leave me alone!' But he

was only a small boy, and looked up to her, so she controlled herself.

'What a pity,' said Aunt Ursula softly. 'We grow up and think we've come a long way, only to find it's better back there,' pointing to Davis Blood happily eating his little portion of food — he was a finicky eater — in the eye of the family.

When he was lying in bed in the dark and the lights on in the rest of the house, it seemed that the gaps in the talk that came to his ear were lumps of silence coloured black, while the talk itself was like a lamp in the night, flickering when the voices paused.

Next morning he was handed a note to take to school. The reply note said it was no wonder he'd taken no notice of sharp correction or of a loud voice, since he'd never had to be corrected at home, nor had anyone ever shouted at him, and he could sit where he liked. He was no more nor less fidgety than Preston, Randal and Orville had been at that age, and all had been active boys; and to this day weren't noted for sitting still long.

The teacher, on the second day feeling more resigned to the start of term, put him among the difficult ones.

Making Friends

The first thing he noticed in the playground among the other boys was that each one he met was greatly unlike him. He'd wrongly expected that since all were 'little boys', with the same label, they would be somehow the same. He'd have liked that.

The second thing was that most of them tried to use

him, to put one over, to conquer and get above him, to trick him, to make him feel small and themselves correspondingly bigger. It seemed to him, by contrast, that when another was brought down and made to feel small, he felt smaller too, as if he was humbled along with anyone who'd been humbled.

As lunchtime raged in the schoolyard, he stood back and watched what they did.

One boy seemed as reserved as he was. Perhaps here was someone like himself. He was bigger and heftier, dressed much as he was, but there was something about him that Davis Blood felt he liked; a feeling that this boy knew the rules that he, Davis Blood, had been given to live by. But how could he know that? His eyes were clear and quick and he didn't look dopey. Perhaps they could be friends. He advanced in a kind of sideways motion on the other boy, so as not to scare him off.

'You live over that side of the creek?' he asked. A neutral sort of question, he thought. The boy didn't answer. His head was down slightly, as if he studied the paspalum clump between his feet. Davis waited a bit, then said, 'Are you new too?' No answer. Not even the courtesy of a glance.

There was something in the boy's stillness that stirred something in the Blood boy. He wanted to knock against this boy with his body; perhaps his shoulder, and make him take notice. The boy said nothing, and didn't look up. What can you do with someone like that? The Blood boy had only the friendliest intentions, and here he was, ignored. He'd been taught to speak when spoken to. The boy should have been polite, and answered, even if the answer was unfriendly, or he should have been outright insolent or nasty, not just silent.

There was something very wrong here. This boy was different from every other boy he'd met. It wasn't right to act so differently, to be so contemptuous of the rules. If most had to follow them, all should.

Suddenly he boiled. He pushed against the boy with his shoulder, knocking him over. The big quiet boy lay on the ground, curled up slightly, looking straight ahead between his knees at his shoes. Why didn't he fight? You had to fight back when attacked. You didn't just take it.

This boy betrayed the common imperatives of humankind. Besides, he was bigger, he had nothing to fear.

He was impelled to kick the unresisting boy, but his father's and brothers' teaching stopped him. 'That's no way to fight; that's for mongrels, kicking. Only the gutless kick.'

He didn't kick. Instead, he felt a great pity for the boy, mixed with distaste, as if he were a sick person.

Walking away, he expected the authorities would take revenge on him, but in the crowded playground no one noticed.

Next day he heard a teacher call the silent boy Adrian. He had a name all right.

Next time he saw the quiet boy he was jammed up against him in a crowd of kids milling round the wash taps just after the first bell went. When the crowd pushed him against the silent boy, the boy didn't push back, just went limply with whatever pushed him, like a bag of something soft. Davis got angry immediately. He felt restless and fidgety. He felt hot. He found he couldn't smell anything, his breathing seemed to have a blockage.

The crowd cleared the moment the second bell went. He had to go to the place where his class gathered before going in to school. He'd missed having a drink and a quick wash. It was that Adrian's fault.

Next time he was close to Adrian he didn't notice a breathing restriction. What he did notice was such an aversion to him that he tried not to breathe, in case he drew into himself something of that boy's person, his essence.

The fourth time he had to put up with being near the detestable silent boy, all the children were crowding down into the grassy part of the playground bordering on the oval where the big kids played cricket. In a while the Principal would be down there addressing them.

He spoke to Adrian as they walked in the mass of kids. Adrian didn't even look at him, just walked straight on. The fury came instantly. Davis Blood was all over Adrian, punching, kneeing, elbowing, his fingers in the boy's eyes. Adrian was down, Davis Blood on top, still going.

Two kids from the class above pulled him off Adrian.

'Cut it out. You'll get dobbed in. Save it for after school.' They pushed the furious Blood boy away.

Davis looked back at prone Adrian. His breathing came much easier when that boy was down.

A teacher came along and rebuked the silent boy for lying down and getting dirt over his school clothes.

The fifth encounter was in the wash sheds. Only a few kids were around. He quickly pinned the boy's hands up on either side of his head, in the surrender position.

'Why won't you say something?' he said in a low voice, soft enough not to be heard round about, but urgent enough to show the silent boy he was fierce and serious.

The boy looked up at him for the first time. His eyes were a clear pale grey round pinpoint pupils that widened as he gave a small secretive smile.

'I'll burn you to death,' he whispered.

'What?' was all Davis Blood could say.

'I'm going to burn everyone to death,' the boy said softly. 'I want to see them sizzle and curl up.'

'You're not going to burn me!'

'I'll burn you,' he said. 'To death,' and smiled that closed-in smile.

The smile stayed on the once-silent boy's face while Davis Blood released his arms, turned and went out of the wash sheds. He never again hit the big quiet boy. He figured that what he'd said was as good as fighting back, and was satisfied.

So much for trying to be friends. He went over to the fence and picked a plant of shivery-grass that had escaped the mower and went round blowing it and watching it shiver, until the bell went.

Around the classroom, at the height of the picture rail, were portraits of Ned Kelly, William Dampier, Captain Phillip, Dirk Hartog, Abel Tasman. There was a coloured poster showing the ruins of the prison at Port Arthur for early involuntary migrants to Australia. Old drawings of Chinese on the gold fields, the pathos of the Eureka Stockade, black-birding of Kanakas in Queensland, a picture of the man Bennelong alongside an enlarged photograph of the Opera House on Bennelong Point, gold mining scenes in Ballarat, Bendigo, Castlemaine, dire photographs of drought-paralysed farmland and enormous tracts of floodwater, extended the panorama almost to the edge of the large blackboard, leaving room only for a large drawing of a swagman with his bedroll on his back, an imaginative poster of a bunyip, and an all too accurate representation of destitute Aboriginals in the streets of early Sydney.

The Empty Shell

When he brought into the house a brown, transparent and empty cicada shell he'd picked off a tree on the way home from school, his father dipped it in varnish, dried it, and set it up on the insect screen over the kitchen window, hooking its claws into the mesh, where it clung, still as a fossil. In Summer the drumming of the cicadas went on into the night. Kids like Moey Larter always had either a Black Prince or a Yellow Monday at school, and loved to show the girls a Pisser and what it could do, getting a great kick out of their squeals.

Some girls never squealed, Davis Blood noticed. They wouldn't give boys the satisfaction they craved, but sometimes sang at him:

> 'Moey Larter is no good
> Chop him up for firewood
> If he is no good for that
> Give him to the old tom cat.'

Or said words that Davis Blood didn't bother to ask the meaning of, when he got home.

It seemed to him, years later, that like most days when he was young, these were glorious. The grass breathed, all the birds and insects breathed, the ground beneath him breathed.

He put his arms round the citriodora, the lemon-scented gum, felt it tremble at his touch and go on breathing. High in the sky forming and dissolving cloudlets breathed. He felt their shapes inside him, their movements and brief existence, and when they died to nothing, he felt a sadness without pain. Time, like a solar wind, touched him and he felt nothing.

The Confidence Boy

On Saturday, as the five-year-old and his mother went past Continental Beef and Sunseeker Fashions towards the supermarket, a big boy of eleven from Verdun Street, whose father worked for Monaco Investment Systems, caught sight of them, and began to idle outside the wide entrance of the supermarket.

Davis Blood knew him from school as a bully of young kids. He'd heard of Ritcho, and what he'd do to you if he caught you. What was he to do? You couldn't tell your Mum you were scared, men weren't supposed to be scared, they were fighters and protectors. He was scared. He kept close to Mum, and she must have felt his uneasiness, without knowing it was fear, because she pushed him away a little impatiently to give her arms freedom of movement.

She noticed several panels of Specials ads stuck up inside the windows and stopped to look. The big boy sidled up and said something to Mrs Blood. She felt her boy pull away slightly.

'You're looking well, Mrs Blood,' the big boy said with what Davis Blood saw as a greasy gloating smile. Ritcho knew that Mums weren't clued in to the facts of street life.

Mum looked him over, noticed the smile, oblivious of her son's terror. She decided this was a nice polite boy, even though a bit rough at the edges, and thought her Davis would be quite all right left to play or whatever boys did when you weren't there. Yes, it would be better, specially as she had to call in on the first floor to the toilet.

When she came back her youngest son was scratched and grubby, his top shirt button ripped off. He was holding himself in places where the big boy had hit him.

'Davis!' his mother said faintly, 'Your button!'

He put his hand on his shirt, felt where the threads were torn, and felt guilty.

'He got me,' he said helplessly.

'What have you been doing?' His mother wasn't with it at all. In her world there were no such things as people who'll get you if you come too near them or even arrange it so you are too near them. She had about her that air of silently humming a tune. It was 'Love is the key of life and death'. She listened, gently, to her little son.

'That big boy Ritcho got me. I wanted to come with you into the shop.'

She hugged him to her wide front. He had both arms round her hips, his face buried in the soft of her stomach. Her warm smell had never been more reassuring, the expanse of her motherly bottom had never been more comforting.

'There. There. Don't cry.' She couldn't remember if the others used to cry at that age. She supposed they did.

He knew she hadn't registered what had happened to him. Nor had he cried one single tear. As they walked together to the next shop, he wondered if his mother's affection for him was separate from her knowledge of him. Was that affection a thing natural to her? Only that? Or did she perceive things in him worth loving?

If she was so vague about the natural world of bullies, was her love worth less?

He didn't let go of her hand.

How marvellous it would be to be big.

Questions and Answers

The little fellow had forgotten his fright by the time they'd returned home, and looked for a game to play on the verandah. He began to sing, in his clear boy's voice as he went in to the kitchen for something to eat.

> *'Diddly diddly dum-tee*
> *The cat ran up the gum tree*
> *Throw a ball*
> *To make him fall*
> *Just like Humpty-Dumpty.'*

Randal had taught him the words.

Aunt Mira lifted her head from the radio earphones. The Mozart programme was over. Her quick eyes darted from the boy to Ursula, who was reading over by the window.

> *'Genital gee-gees, fierce and wild*
> *Don't do it on a little child,'* she sang.
> *'Watch out for my Auntie too*
> *Or I'll smear your face with —'*

'Mira!' said Ursula, at once.

'Guilty,' answered Mira, her beady eyes gleaming in their surround of pale wrinkled skin. When she spoke, her thick clumpy tongue was visible. It seemed to fill her mouth. The boy wondered how she got any food in there.

'Think of the boy,' Ursula said.

'I was.'

'You don't want him to be old before he's young, do you?'

'I don't want him to be a verbal quadriplegic,' said Mira firmly. Neither did Ursula.

Aunt Mira rolled on; nothing could stop her. 'The day's past when happiness for that boy was a sloshy nappy. He's ready for the ceremony of rhubarb. Ready to understand his place in the ego-system, ready to play Mozart and win.'

'Not Mozart?' said Aunt Ursula incredulously.

'Well — no. Rossini, Puccini, Peducci, whoever! The heart has reasons — the nose has tears unpremeditated. At this moment dark-eyed men in fancy dress are publicly tormenting cattle for money and applause.'

'Wandering again,' said Aunt Ursula. 'Like a Mongolian drover.'

'Ah, cow country,' sighed Mira in her cracked and edgy voice.

'Temora and Temora and Temora. Each town in its petty pace, crawling with marvellous obscenery, creaky with scenic retractions, lighting each tourist the way to dusty deserts and big bald rocks. Watch out for the jaws of the Madonna, beware the vibes of Marx. Here we go, gathering nuts in play,' she mumbled inaudibly, then, 'all on a mundane night.' And was asleep, her head on her chest, breathing regularly. Her pinky-white dress was ruffled in spots.

'Is she really asleep, Aunt?'

'Impossible to tell, Davie,' said Ursula. 'But there's one way to find out: talk about her.'

'What will we say?'

'Something nasty.'

'She might hear me.'

'Not if she's asleep.'

That was reasonable. He thought a bit, then recited:

> *'Aunt Mira is a tell-tale tit*
> *Hold her while her tongue is slit*
> *Chop it with a knife and fork*
> *Give each pussy cat a bit.'*

They watched the sleeping head. No movement.

'Or we can steal some of her sayings,' suggested Ursula.

> *'We three kings of Orient are*
> *One in a taxi, one in a car*
> *One on a scooter blowing his hooter*
> *Following that star.'* she sang in her stop-start voice.

The boy crept round the other side of Aunt Mira, looking for the glint of an open eye.

'Why is it unsafe to sleep in a train?' Ursula said.

'Because trains run over sleepers,' he replied.

'What turns without moving?'

'Milk!' he answered.

'How deep is the ocean?'

'Just a stone's throw,' he said triumphantly. Aunt Mira had got him with these, many times.

He caught the flash of light on a glittering eye.

'She's awake!'

'Yes, I'm awake! Why did the fly fly?'

'Because the spider spied her!' said the boy quickly.

'Why did the ear hear?'

'Only the nose nose!' His words began before hers finished.

'Whoa! Give me a chance to get out the question! Why did the window box?'

'Because it saw the garden fence!'

'Why did the jam roll?'

'Because it saw the apple turnover!' he said excitedly, then took the questions as well. 'Why did the lobster blush? Because it saw the salad dressing! Can the orange box? No, but the tomato can!'

'You'll need a bigger repertoire, Mira,' said Aunt Ursula.

'I bet he doesn't know the ballad of Daisy Crockett,' said Aunt Mira Mitchell.

'No,' said Davis Blood, 'Tell us, Auntie.'

'Oh,

> *'Reared on a paddle pop in Joe's cafe*
> *Dirtiest dump in the U S A*
> *Shot her Dad with a 3-0-3*
> *Poisoned her Mum with D D T*
> *Daisy Crockett, Daisy Crockett*
> *The girl who was no good.'*

A lull followed. He headed for the door.

Aunt Mira tried to keep her audience.

'What container has no top, no bottom, yet it holds flesh and blood?' she said.

The boy stopped, thought, looked about for inspiration. He thought of the old Pride Without Vanity headstone down the backyard, memorial to Lautenbacher, one of the dogs of the past. Dogs, dog collar.

'A dog collar!'

'Yes!' exclaimed Aunt Ursula.

'Oh,' said Aunt Mira, 'I wanted ring for an answer.'

'But dog collar fits the question. Good answer, Davie! How'd you think of it?'

'Old Lautenbacher's grave, down the backyard. It just came into my head.'

Aunt Mira subsided, grumbling.

At sunset, the squawking sociable rosellas were flying overhead, in groups leaving the valleys and bush to the north-west, and flying to the pines of Guringai Beach to spend their night.

Lautenbacher's Death

The boy hardly remembered the labrador retriever apart from its gravestone. The old dog was still alive at the time of the boy's first trip to the shops with his mother, under his own steam. He was then two, proud of making it 'by mineself'.

For a long time his eyes had been cloudy. Gradually he went off his food, but would take a little wine towards the end. Never red, and it had to be sweet. Preston provided the wine. Gradually he became an old feeble dog, given, apparently, to prayer and deafness.

When he came to die, Lautenbacher had been right off his food for days. His stomach was blown up and he looked in pain: you could tell when he caught his breath, and saw his lips drawn in and the anxious expression in his eyes. When he was spoken to, the old tail would thump a couple of times on the floor and he'd look interested for a second or two, then the blank turned-in look came back.

There was a big swelling you could feel through the tired old muscles over his flanks.

'Is he going to die?' said the boy.

No one answered, but Preston picked him up carefully and took him right the way down the backyard into the bush. Randal followed with Preston's rifle.

'It's better to put him to sleep,' said Aunt Ursula, and Lillian's arms went round the boy, pulling his face into her stomach for protection. He hardly heard the shot.

On Lautenbacher's headstone, under the flowering cherry, they put in white paint the words:

LAUTENBACHER
HE HAD PRIDE WITHOUT VANITY
THIS DOG WAS OK.

Danielle wrote the first sentence. Randal the second.

At the meeting next Sunday, when it was time, during the last song, for anyone who wanted prayer or help with a problem to go out the front and be prayed for or listened to, he thought he ought to go out and ask for a prayer for Lautenbacher, but he wasn't sure if it was the right thing to do. He knew some people thought of dogs, and cats — and birds — as no better than weeds.

The World was Never Like That

Father and son walked up Big Hill onto the flat, going to the meeting in Alamein Street. This was an 'Including' branch of the Independent Dissenting Brethren, where everyone was welcome and doctrinal matters not bolted down so tightly. He'd been baptised in the Occlusive branch, and later would go back there to Anzio Street, Ashwood. But while he was small, Jackson Blood felt that the more cheerful, free and easy atmosphere of the Includings was better for him. The Occlusives made no concessions to the young in their meetings and Ashwood was some distance away.

It hadn't begun properly to be night, but one star was glowing and fat in the eastern sky. Two the boy could see now, as he looked further. His father saw him looking.

'The evening star,' he said. 'Venus. It's actually a planet, but they call it the evening star.'

'Are stars round?' asked the little boy.

'Sort of round.'

'Like those little lights?'

'That's a star. Huge. Bigger than the Sun. Even though it looks tiny. Millions of them go to make our galaxy; and there are millions of galaxies. The whole lot is called the Universe.'

The boy tried to grasp that. Bigger than the Sun? Millions? Universe? His father looked down briefly, as if he heard him thinking.

'The Sun's a star, too. Stars are burning, like lights. The Sun is burning. There's no atmosphere between it and us to absorb the heat: that's how it's warm on us every day.'

The boy tried to take it in. His warm friendly Sun just a star, not something special? Well, it must be right. He'd have to leave the millions and the universe for thinking about later.

'Big and round?' For some reason he found himself thinking of his father's head, and the clearings he'd discovered in his hair.

'Sort of round. Nothing's perfectly round. Perfectly round is in the mind — something to think of, but nothing's actually round. Even a round billiard ball, when you look at it with a microscope, is rough and lumpy, not smooth. In the same way, there's no such thing as a straight line. Close up, it's bumpy like a mountain range, just like a razor blade under a microscope.'

The little chap walked along, in wonder. But it did seem reasonable. Things he'd seen in the distance as neat and straight were rough and lumpy when he got close up. Was smooth the same?

'And smooth?' he asked. 'Like the windows? Like a mirror?' Remembering his experience with the glass on the verandah.

'Nothing's smooth, when you get right down to it. Everything's rough and bumpy.' They walked together to the meeting, place of spiritual certitude for the man, the certitude of faith and belief. As they walked, he continued the thoughts he'd started.

'Yes. Nothing's smooth, nothing's round, nothing's flat, nothing's straight. They're all words for the way people wanted to think the world was, but the world was never like that.'

'Didn't anyone know?'

'Always some people, just a few, knew that. No,' he went on, 'nothing's ever finished. Nothing's ever exactly now. Nothing's not made of other things — everything's made of something else. And nothing is nothing: but I don't expect you to understand that.'

The boy felt he didn't understand it at all — that is, what it meant — but he heard what his father said and he would never forget it. Some words were wrong, apparently: the words themselves. There was nothing in the world to fit them, only in imagination; you had to bend the world to make it fit such words.

But why didn't people throw out the wrong words and find better ones?

His father went on, almost in a chant, 'Nothing's the same as anything else, nothing's entirely one thing and not another, nothing's separate from other things.'

At the age of five the boy knew that nothing is what it seems; anything may happen at any time; all things depend on all other things; nothing lasts forever.

'And nothing's certain,' his father added with a certainty the little boy didn't draw attention to.

They walked on in silence. The boy had suspected something was wrong with things called certain. In the privacy of his head he thought that if some things are uncertain, many might be; and if many, then perhaps all. But now here was his father confirming that all things were uncertain. He felt closer to his father then than at any time before, but it wasn't a physical closeness: his father rarely touched him. On the other hand there was no evidence that the boy wanted to be touched, except by his mother.

This talk was different from others they'd had until then; his father's wisdom had run mostly to three themes.

'You can step off the footpath here, on to the road and into eternity,' was one often repeated lesson. Another was: 'You can be the best in the world at whatever you do, then round the next corner can come someone who'll beat you easily. You never know.'

The third was, 'Good times and success bring many friends, and everyone wants to know you. Bad times and no money send them all away.'

The boy liked the present talk. The three older themes needed only one airing: but this one, of uncertainty and limitations and misfitting words, opened up a subject that might well be endless.

It was good, being alive, and good too having a father and mother, sisters and brothers, and a house to live in, with a fine aunt. And Aunt Mira, too.

Each day was good, for each day was a window on the world. It was good, going to sleep at night and waking each morning in time for breakfast, but sleep took a lot of your time.

Each day, each little happening, each new thing he saw and therefore learned, was a chink of light shining on part of the world. Yes, shining out of the central life of the universe onto the darkness of his existence, so that little by little he would learn as much as he was capable of learning. Then he would die and others would do it all over again for themselves, in whatever ways they could manage. What they learned would be different from what he learned, because no one was the same as anyone else: no one would have exactly the picture of the world that he had, or any other person had, though at a distance they would look the same.

He didn't know why, but he loved this idea of difference.

Each member of the Blood family was different, yet they were a family, and that was good.

Aunt Ursula had a little poem about family that she recited to him several times.

> 'Lord, make the nations see
> That men can brothers be
> And form one family —
> All the wide world.'

He noticed that her mouth, each time she said the word Lord, had a faint shyness, as if it was a word she was borrowing. In his mother's mouth, Lord was like a happy and wholehearted 'Yes!' between best friends.

Good Dog, Dino

He felt good when Ivan Krenek and Stuart Kable, who lived up the other end of Country Road, asked him to come after school for a swim in the creek. He put his cossie on under his shorts and walked down the middle of Country Road with them. Judd Undermeier and Ally Bullo, from Federation Crescent, were on their way and Warwick Archer and Glen Merrilees, from the other side of the railway line, were going to wait at the corner of Creek Street.

Recent rain had left Spectacle Creek flooded, and it was a fine thing to stand on the bank and watch the water swirl by, to throw boat-shaped leaves, dry twigs or curled bark in and watch them caught in the eddies and whirled along to the water-race in the narrow neck that separated one round pool from the next.

A shelving bank of sand formed one side of the first pool. They threw their shirts and shorts off and made for the water. Galahs made a sudden hullabaloo and flew up into the air. In the distance a few currawongs clashed loudly with each other. Christmas bells grew higher up the slope.

Davis Blood thought he'd try to dive like Judd Undermeier, and got up on Toilet Rock — which had that pedestal shape in profile — and taking a deep breath, plunged in, his legs bending at the knees and entering the water with a second splash. The heavy rain had moved some of the submerged trees and dead logs into places that made the boys' local knowledge insufficient: he glanced his head on a tree, grazing his chest, stomach, and knees. He came to the surface dazed and began to float face down, caught in the current. The other boys watched in some alarm, with great interest and wide eyes, as his body floated towards the nose-bridge of Spectacle Creek. They stood there, but Dino, Ivan Krenek's dog, jumped in, grabbed the boy's hair in his teeth and made for one side of the nose-bridge of the creek, where the water raced through. The boy was beginning to come round as Dino pulled him in towards the bank. His knees hit bottom and he put his arms down, kneeling in half a metre of water, coughing and choking and trying to get the water up. Blood began to ooze from his forehead, his chest and one knee.

'Hey! Davis! You all right?' Glen Merrilees called out. The others were spellbound at the drama that had come so close to them.

'No one dive off that rock,' commanded Warwick Archer, as if that fixed everything. They watched the choking boy closely to see how a life and death situation affected someone. It was turning into an interesting day. Dino shook himself thoroughly and watched the half-drowned boy for a bit, then trotted round to the nose-bridge place, jumped the water, walked back to Ivan, reported in by looking up briefly, and sat by him.

'Good dog, Dino,' said Ivan mechanically. Dino acknowledged this with another brief look up, had a big yawn, and closed his mouth with a snap.

The boy Davis gradually stood upright, unhindered by his friends, still coughing, still choking, still trying to get up the water inside him. His friends stood back; if no one touched him, no one could be blamed for what had happened or what might happen. They had experience of hasty parents. One day they would make perfect employees, perfect public servants, and eventually they did. They would keep their slates clean, and their noses; their butts always covered; no colleague would ever be able to shoot them down in flames.

The boy Davis made his way home.

His father had told him many times about friends.

'While you're with them, you have friends. Turn your back, or go away, and they forget you.' But the boy's friends forgot him while they were there, watching him drown. No one likes me much, he thought. Then grimaced wryly and shrugged, for it was no use whingeing.

If All the Seas

At school Miss Thompson roped all her kids in to a common task. She outlined a sentence on a long paper strip, and had each boy and girl colour part of it. Next the class copied the sentence into their work books.

IF ALL THE SEAS WERE ONE SEA,
WHAT A GREAT SEA THAT WOULD BE

On the way out of the classroom, Davis Blood looked at the map of the world hanging on the wall. There was no time to stand around, it was time to go home, but something stuck in his mind; he couldn't say quite what it was.

Going Away

After school next day, when he'd got his school clothes off and had something to eat and drink — he was always thirsty — he and Lillian had a game in the front yard with a tennis ball. In the course of the game he suddenly grabbed the ball when it was Lillian's turn to have it. He did it in such a cheeky way that, as a reflex, she lunged for him, and when he ran away, she chased. 'Come back here! Come back to Mummy, little Davy wavy woo!' she called with smiles in her voice.

He was off like a shot, well away before she could get up a decent pace. He laughed, in surprise as much as triumph. But when her smile receded her face was left with sadness, as if he had gone away from her in another sense.

She accepted that all children grew up, but each time it was painful, and this was the last child she would have.

His sister and three brothers called his mother by her first name, Lillian. The boy began to think of her as Lillian from around the time he first outran her, but couldn't bring himself to be so familiar with her as to say it.

The House of Words

No sooner had he outrun his mother than several thousand years of formal moral teaching reached out and took a grip on him. Jackson Blood chose that afternoon to bring out one of his books, and to read to the boy. Perhaps from a desire to show himself, to himself, as not bigoted, the father didn't use the books of the Dissenting Brethren but something of a more general kind.

'Honour your father and mother, for your father who causes you is an image of God the Father; and your mother is an image of God the Mother who rules the earth, which produces us and all we live by.

'Have no hate for your brother, but love your neighbour and even strangers, as yourself, for whose heart is on goodness will dislike no one.

'Learn to love well, and gladden hearts all your life.

'Slander no one, give no false witness, for in hell are perjurers with mouths full of Yes and hearts full of No. Keep your promises; let your word be your bond, for the foundation of peace is good faith.

'When you come to die, be able to say: I have not killed God's children, for in hell are murderers. Not only that but avoid cruelty: don't wound others, for that is the character of the cat.

'Don't terrify others. When you come to die, be able to say: I brought no misery to others; I haven't been grasping; I caused no hunger, no weeping; nor did I help oppress others through my way of earning a living.

'Treat all possessions and property with respect, as if they were yours. Draw no false boundaries. Do not cause others to be robbed.

'Respect the old, and when you are old you will respect and revere the young, for they follow everyone, they live in the buildings we make and breathe the air we breathed before them.

'Respect the dead, for this shows humanity.

'Preserve humans, and their society. Be kind, show good will, for all misfortune is the concern of the good person.'

Jackson Blood took a break here to tell of a crippled Aboriginal woman carried by her family everywhere they went for sixty-seven years, then finished with some shorter sentences. The boy of six watched the book and his father's face; he hadn't moved. The smell of tobacco came from his father's clothes, his hands, and was in his breath. As far as he knew, his father was different from every other man.

> *'Fight for the good way of life.*
> *Treat the poor the same as the important.*
> *To ignore violence is to strengthen the violent.*
> *Loss is preferable to shameful gain,*
> *and death to slavery.*
> *Love learning all your life.*
> *When you are old your courage will need to be harder, your heart stronger, and your spirit more determined as your strength weakens.*
> *Don't be afraid of death, for while life is pleasant, death is natural.'*

He closed the book with the reverence he always accorded books, smiled at the boy, and got up. When he'd put his book away, he went out to see to his lettuce plants. They needed a drink every day, and their father made sure they got one.

The ethics he'd read to the boy wouldn't do him any harm; might even be good for him to see that other times had their own approaches. But a prickle of conscience remained. He could have illustrated with a story — this lad loved his stories of the war, of horses, of boxing, the circus — the Christian truth of freedom through obedience, denial of self, surrender to God.

He sighed, and went to get the hoe. Life was full of things not completed, or not done well. He'd attend to it later.

The boy didn't move for a long time.

There was a great difference here between these words and the words spoken at the meeting.

These were more like Aunt Ursula's. Why had his father said them? Had he departed from the words of the Meeting? There was a lot more to Jackson Blood than he knew.

In a continuation of this receptive state he moved gradually, a few steps at a time, around the verandah, down the front steps, among the flower beds, around the side of the house, the steep side, until he sidled, wandered, drifted near to where Jackson Blood tended his lettuce. Almost as if he expected, or hoped, some of this father's knowledge, some wisdom — to pass into him by virtue of his nearness.

He didn't know how to start talking to his father.

Seeing him there and since he loved talking almost as much as he revered the written word, Jackson Blood told him how the Aborigines made boomerangs from bent elbows of mangrove trees like those on the shore of Spectacle Lake; of nullah nullahs; of the woomera that helped throw a spear further; of how they hardened the points of their spears in the fire.

He had no plan of interesting the boy in primitive ways; he was trying to be a father.

The boy was grateful. It made him feel warmer that his father spent that time talking to him. He would remember the strange names and warlike functions his father mentioned, and he was attracted by primitive things. However, while his father was talking, though he'd been listening and taking it all in, he'd been occupied on another matter.

He had discovered what bothered him about:

> *If all the seas were one sea*
> *What a great sea that would be.*

In his mind's eye was the Mercator projection of the world map in Randal and Orville's room. All the seas of the world, with the exception of the Caspian, which was tiny by comparison, were one sea. There were no boundaries, no walls: all the seas flowed into each other, they were a common watermass.

The teacher was wrong. He would have to tell Miss Thompson the classroom strip had to be altered.

His father was talking still. The boy listened, but again he couldn't stop his thoughts, that went on in tandem with what he heard. If, to his father, God was master, and when he died he would see God's face, then when each of the family dogs died, would they see their master's face?

The family didn't know that in the classroom, a day or two later, as a result of his protest, a certain strip on the wall now read:

> *All the seas are one sea.*
> *What a great sea that is.*

Miss Thompson, too, ignored the Caspian.

God's in Your Head

When Lillian got home from work at the tent-making factory and had sat down to her first cup of tea, the boy came to the kitchen with questions. Into his mind now and then had come his parents' words about the omnipresence of God; he was ready for further information.

'Mum, God's everywhere, isn't he?'

She was dog-tired, but God and the family came first. 'Yes.'

'Then he's here, and here —' pointing to different places in the kitchen. 'And out there, and up the street?'

'Yes.'

'You can talk anywhere and God's there? In the dark too?'

'Yes.'

'Up in an aeroplane? In the Space Shuttle? On the moon?'

'Yes.'

'Under water?'

'Yes.'

'And God's a spirit?'

'Yes,' and entering into the little boy's eagerness and persistence, she quoted:

> 'Where could I go to escape your Spirit?
> If I go up to heaven, you are there.
> If I make my bed in hell, you are there.
> If I take the wings of the morning
> And sail to the uttermost sea
> Your hand is there to guide and hold me.'

He nodded, and went on excitedly.

'And you can't see a spirit or feel it and it passes through things and things pass through it?' He put it as he'd remembered his father saying.

'Yes. I think so.' She hadn't thought about the presence of God in such wide-ranging and specifically physical terms, merely knew God was constantly there, wherever she went, and she was constantly in touch with him.

'Then,' he said, with an excitement that was discovery and triumph combined, 'then God's in your stomach, cause that's part of everywhere! God's in your head! In your mouth! In your hands! In your bones!'

'I suppose so, yes.' And again she quoted:

> 'You knew my substance before I was made
> in secret, and strangely formed in the
> lowest parts of the earth.'

'So God's inside animals and birds and cats and dogs and germs and horses and lions!'

'Well, yes, that follows. All living things are children of God.'

'So you can hear God and he can hear you because God's in your head!'

'God is everywhere, yes.'

He was silent, hugging the knowedge to him.

God was in your blood and in trees and rocks and rain and air; in the sun and stars. He went out of the kitchen, his mother watching him go.

It was obvious: in your bones, in your blood, and everywhere. Right inside where no one could see or know, or hear what went on; most of all in your head. He would let the knowledge sink into him, and go about the business of being six.

The mysterious workings inside him would chew on this, and later prompt him to ask more questions, or come up with new thoughts. For new thoughts would come: he was sure of that. This was important. Where it would lead he didn't know, but that it would lead to something even more important he was in no doubt.

God was all through you, in the very things you were made of. What was that other thing Lillian had quoted, but that he hadn't paid much attention to? 'Made in secret, and strangely formed in the lowest parts of the earth.'

The earth? Were we made from the earth? That was a new thought. No one had mentioned that before, except for references to clay and dust in some of the things said by preachers at the meeting.

Yes, he remembered: 'In the sweat of your face you'll eat, till you die and go back to the ground, for you were taken from the ground. You are dust and you'll end as dust.'

Dust. God was in the dust, too.

It was that time of the precipice, when afternoon has been growing steadily near its end and suddenly is about to fall into night.

From the depths of the valley a baleful cry went up.

'Caprigel! Caprigel!' It was the strange bird again.

'Caprigel!' The bird called, then was silent, as night closed down on Kookaburra Valley.

Extremely Duck

None of the chooks had names. They didn't seem to have enough personality to stand out; this, though, may have been because there were so many of them and no one bothered to keep track of their natures and actions. There was a flurry of interest when chicks appeared, but it didn't survive their growing up.

All the ducks had names. Again, they were few, and easily picked out; but apart from that there's something about ducks that draws your eyes.

Winston Duck was fatter than ducks usually are, and waddled slowly around the fowl-yard with an air of importance. He was actually a drake, but he was called a duck because duck is a more satisfying sound to say. Valentine Duck was amorous and made a pest of herself to the two drakes in season and out. Kingsford Duck was always trying to fly and had to be weighted down with a short cord tied to something heavy enough to stop her getting airborne but not so heavy that she couldn't get about. Her anchor at that time was an old brass tap that used to be in the laundry before it wore out.

Extremely Duck was everything a duck can be; she was the epitome of duck. She had a wonderful waddle, a resounding quack, a gossipy nature, an alert stupidity and endless energy. It was a treat to watch her. She wore the other ducks and drakes out with her busyness; often you would see them looking over her head, or away somewhere, unseeing her, so her energy wouldn't suck theirs out.

Mister Flanagan

When Mister Flanagan the new cat came and was shown round the house and had his paws ritually smeared with butter for him to lick off, to make him faithful for life, and wandered into the kitchen, Aunt Mira got stuck into him.

'Hey you! Down there on the ground! Sockfoot! I'm here to lay down the law to new chums!'

Mister Flanagan looked up and miaowed long and loud. Just the one note.

'Keep that up, and they'll hunt you out. Or I will. I'm the talker in this house,' Aunt Mira advised him.

'Miaoooow!' said Mister Flanagan again.

'Hey!' called Aunt Ursula, wheeling in. 'Hold your tongue, new chum. Now beat it. Don't come back till dinnertime. Excede! Evade! Erump!'

'Cats are to be seen and not heard,' Aunt Ursula manoeuvred the book in her lap and began to read over by the window.

Mister Flanagan didn't move. He wasn't easily browbeaten.

'Go and wait for a dead bird to fall out of the sky,' advised Aunt Mira, enjoying the chance of a talk. 'You adjectival cat, you. There's big brutal men in this house, and a running-type child. Out in the yard and down the bush are highly skilled rats. If you stay I must warn you: Do not sit on the sheets! If you discover in this house a healthy tendency to hysteria, do not despair: in this stratum of society heroes sprout like spring flowers. You can be one! If you wander down to the creek, remember it's not rain water. It's a run-off of tears, shed for cats who lost their way.'

Without another word, or look, Mister Flanagan got to his feet and slouched out.

'Okay, that's it!' said Mira. 'Put all the lights out! I'm off!'

It was her own brand of sarcasm.

She sang loudly:

> *'Old woman, old woman, shall we both go shearing?*
> *Speak a little louder, sir, I'm very hard of hearing.*
> *Old Woman, old woman shall I kiss you dearly?*
> *Thank you very kindly sir, I hear you now quite clearly.'*

Aunt Ursula smiled in spite of herself as she read her book. Footsteps were heard on the verandah. Ursula lifted her head, ready to greet the returning school-boy. Mira waited, ready to burst into song, but both were beaten to the punch by Davis Blood.

> *'In fourteen hundred and ninety-two*
> *Columbus sailed the ocean blue*
> *Lost his boat the clumsy goat*
> *Teacher made him take a note.'*

'What is it,' said Aunt Ursula, 'that the more you take, the more you leave behind?'

The boy thought, his face relaxing with the effort going on in his head. . .

'Steps.'

'Footsteps, yes,' Aunt Ursula agreed.

'Where was Moses when the lights went out?' demanded the boy in return.

'In the dark,' said Mira sulkily. Everyone was stealing her thunder.

> *'Matthew Mark Luke and John*
> *Went to bed with their trousers on*
> *All yelled out in the middle of the night*
> *Lord, my trousers are too tight,'* she sang.

The boy answered her with:

> *'Stan, Stan, the lavatory man*
> *Washed his face in a dunny can,*
> *Combed his hair with a hunk of tin*
> *Scratched himself — with a safety pin.'*

'Davis! Where do you learn such things?' said Ursula.
'School. Why did the cow look over the wall?'
'Because she couldn't see through it,' said Ursula.
'Why did the bear wear a fur coat?' said Aunt Mira.
'Cause it looked ridiculous in a rain coat,' said Ursula.
'Because it didn't have a white tie and tails,' the boy said, then began to forage for some bread and peanut butter.

Aunt Ursula went back to her book, Aunt Mira went on raucously singing. As the boy cut the bread and spread it with butter, then dug out peanut butter from the jar, he looked at his aunts.

'I wish we were really here,' he whispered to himself, then wondered where the words came from. He was almost sure the kitchen, and he, and his aunts, were there. If you stopped still, and let your eyes calm down and withdraw, it was strange how like a picture everything was, out there in front of you — a quiet, still picture.

Moments of Unreality

Sometimes he had to tell himself to hold back from putting his hand on the stove or on the fuzzy red coils of the electric toaster. (Why couldn't he touch anything that existed?) He had to lecture himself when he was near the edge of a sudden drop. Things around him seemed sometimes not to be real.

Unreal things had no weight; his hand could stop a car, a bus, a tiger.

He had to teach himself over again that some things were too dangerous to touch, or to get in the way of. He found this at times difficult, for the car approaching in the street was sometimes a car and sometimes merely a steadily enlarging picture. As a picture it was weightless, and danger from it inconceivable.

It wasn't quite the same, though something like, when Lillian was standing at the ironing board, the songs inside her pushing to get out; ironing shirts, trousers, dresses. It seemed, as he tried to force himself to see things the way others saw them, that ironing shirts flat was ridiculous: why didn't she have a body-shaped mould, and iron the clothes in position as they hung or clung? The same with dresses, or jackets. Better still, if the mould could be slipped into a dress or shirt, and inflated, and heat itself up like the iron, even to having little steam holes, there'd be no need for the iron, and she could sit down to work.

You had to remind yourself that grown-ups did things for reasons you didn't know about.

It was a different unreality with Orville's tree. Wintry August had begun, full of blue skies and still days. The young willow was two years old and higher than Davis Blood; its second set of leaves was gone, its grey-green colour much the same as when it was a stick pushed into the soft dark soil. He could remember how it looked then, though his memory was patchy about the time between. He sat on Brown Rock and looked at it.

The eastern branch, that was once a mysterious lump, was as long as his forearm. A tree now, yet once a stick; alive and growing, yet once torn from its family tree and used to slash at trees and scare dogs with its fierce whistle as it cut the air.

The reality was both states. That whippy stick was a number of things. Unreality seemed to prevail only when you thought a tree had to be just a tree, a stick only a stick.

A different unreality pervaded him when at school his first pastel drawing — of a red apple — had been received with loud praises, and shown round the school.

He loved the fact that everyone was being so nice to him, and was praising him as much as Lillian did. But just underneath that enjoyment was a blankness, a numbness, as if he was away somewhere. The drawing was in the hands of smiling teachers, but not in his hands. It wasn't finished.

They thought, since the class was given the apple to draw and he'd drawn it, that the job was finished. It wasn't. He hadn't foreseen that they'd take it away. He wanted it there, where he could touch it and work on it more, and was under a kind of spell since it had been ripped away from him, as he felt; a spell which would remain until he finished the work he wanted to do.

Mass Baptism

It was Sunday evening. They'd had an early tea, and the boy, now seven, had done the washing-up, a chore which began traditionally at that age in the Blood family. He was off to Gospel Meeting with his father. It had been a day of sun and cloud, the August winds were late that year, and despite being Meeting night the late August sky was still not entirely solemn; there were smiles behind the clouds in the west where the sun hadn't quite slipped out of sight. As they passed the little park in Verdun Street at the top of Big Hill, he decided that birds, when they pull their heads down into their chests, as gulls do, and pigeons, have the appearance of deep thought, even of great learning. He wondered what they might think of later in the darkness: and all the other birds, too, who slept in branches of trees, on their feet all night.

The boy was reminded by the approaching darkness of how Grandma always put the flowers, that by day decorated tables and shelves, out of the house at night. They weren't dead yet, he thought, and still able to perceive the other plants in the garden that were alive and giving life. They must feel like ghosts already.

The sparrows were all in bed, also the starlings, the mynahs, the peewits. The clouds of rosellas had just begun to pass noisily overhead on their way to settle down noisily in the pines on Guringai Beach, as they did each day at sunset.

Jackson Blood held his youngest son's hand as they walked towards Alamein Street Gospel Meeting Hall of the 'Inclusives'. The boy was taking in everything around him, from the stationary houses, fences, trees, flowers, light poles, shrubs, meterboxes, to the nature of the two people walking — as far as he could know his father's nature and his own — and their peculiar situation on the surface of a peculiar world shaped like a soccer ball.

In the hall that night there was to be a mass baptism.

The boy noticed, as they walked, that the street looked different when he was with his father. He'd been along here alone, and the trees, the hills, the electric poles, the occasional houses, the sky — all had seemed personal. Somehow his walking with his father changed everything: the world looked official, the things belonged to no one and now he looked at them seriously with hard eyes. Alone, he looked at them with a sort of affection. They were closer then. They were almost his.

He had another feeling, a strange feeling, which made him slow his pace and drag on his father's hand; a feeling that what was happening here, round them in streets and backyards, was happening because of other things happening elsewhere. What at first sight seemed loose and separate was, he felt, woven together with other things and lives and happenings he couldn't see, and might never know.

It wasn't something he could talk to his father about; it would sound silly, because he couldn't express it clearly.

They walked steadily up the slope of Somme Street towards Alamein Street. From similar walks the boy remembered his father's previous words, in his own way. If he had been asked some time later to repeat all his father said, he would have been at a loss, and given back a sketchy outline not in the order it was given, but taking its own time his head reviewed all the things he had been told and arranged themselves into their order of importance to him.

Nothing is smooth, his father said, many times. With a microscope even the smoothest billiard ball, the most shiny ball-bearing, is rough and pitted; the closer you looked, the rougher it would turn out to be.

The boy queried 'closer'.

'I mean with a higher-powered microscope you can see more of the unevenness, until at the highest power we have now, with an electron microscope the idea of smoothness is absurd. Then, the smoothest surface is all rough. Even a razor blade is like a mountain range.

'Nothing is round; nothing flat; nothing straight; nothing ever finished; nothing is now; everything has some sort of weight. Everything is made of something, something smaller, nothing is separate.' It was like a sacred chant to the boy.

They had turned the corner of Alamein Street. Sixty or so people were standing outside the Meeting Hall.

'Plenty there tonight,' observed Jackson Blood. He wasn't the sort of man who would have minded if there had been three, or one. He was going, he didn't need others. As long as Mister Liston, the preacher, was there.

The boy found that his father's teachings sat with him well. To the father, they were the fruits of reading magazines and books, and hearing about those results of scientific research considered suitable for lay ears. He heard them and remembered: they weren't part of his soul. For the boy things were different.

He heard his father. He checked, as his father spoke, all the things he heard, with the things he had seen, and noticed without knowing that he noticed. They entered his head and became part of his mind, that inner part that is the mystery which is guarded and fed by mechanisms he had no access to, whose workings and composition were not known to him; where his self lived, where the record of his actions and intentions was kept, where the motive power that would drive him all his life was housed. It never occurred to him to talk about these things, they were treasure, he cherished them in secret. He added hints, clues and vague directions as he came across them, always ready to expunge one that was shown to be wrong.

They came up with the group of Meeting people standing near the sign that said the great sin was separation from God, and the modest notice board that told the times of meetings.

His father got a few greetings. Although he was a gregarious man, he gave the impression to those people of the Meeting, well-intentioned, good people, soft, not pushy, that he was sufficient to himself.

The boy noticed another thing about men who met his father. It seemed to him they looked at him as if trying to estimate whether it would be easier to be friends or perhaps less trouble, in the long run, to be enemies. Or were they saying: will I have to fight you sometime?

When they got inside the Hall, the boy saw that another of the things his father had said was shown to be true: there is always something under everything, there is no bottom. And so it was. What had been the floor of the platform at the preacher's end of the Hall, was shown to be only moveable boards. They'd been taken up, and a white-painted concrete pool was discovered. On tiptoe he could see the water level in the pool. He'd never seen a baptism in a concrete pool indoors. It was half the size of a backyard swimming pool.

So the floor had been lifted that had always seemed so strong.

It was to be expected. It fell into place beside the things he had noticed about the old houses in Alamein Street. The front bricks were different from those at the sides of the houses. At home, the big wardrobe made by grandfather Nelson Blood had a shiny, polished front and sides, but when you looked behind it, in the space between it and the wall, there was no polish, no shine. It was raw wood unfinished, a cheat, but to be expected.

Hymns began after a brief introduction. He'd noticed before that each Sunday the Assembly, as they called themselves, were made to sing as having certain feelings, then were preached at because they hadn't. The first song was 'I hear your welcome voice, that calls me, Lord, to you'. The singing was unaccompanied by musical instruments; which were worldly, and not tolerated. The strongest singers led, the rest followed, with greater or lesser intervals at the beginning and ending of lines, according to the singers' knowledge of the song. The boy noticed that if there was some memory of the tune, even though the start of a verse was ragged, the congregation had pretty well got into step by the end of it.

With the next verse the whole confusion began again. No one seemed put out by this, but it embarrassed the boy. He wanted the singing to be well done. There was a prayer from Roman-nosed Mister Liston, then a song:

> 'Just as I am, without one plea
> But that your blood was shed for me
> And that you bid me come to you
> O Lamb of God, I come.'

The big pool set in concrete on the platform was approached by four people who'd been waiting in a room off the preacher's end of the Hall. They were in nightshirts, but one woman wore full pyjamas, pink and white.

They waited humbly while more prayers and exhortations were said and another song:

> 'Take my life and let it be,
> Consecrated, Lord, to you.'

Then, with due reverence, the four were each in turn dipped into the waters of the concrete pool. They fell backward. The preacher, chest deep in water, holding them in his arms, the water taking most of the weight.

How cold it looked, the boy thought. After immersion they were set upright on their feet by sturdy Mister Liston.

They stood in a line, shivering and dripping as Mister

Liston began to pray, facing the congregation, with head up and eyes tightly shut, talking to the Lord.

The newly baptised ones shut their eyes, too. The boy saw it all. He even heard the man come quietly in the entrance to the Hall as the loud praying continued. He saw the shotgun.

He looked away towards the line of newly baptised, and was looking at them when the horrifying blasts began. He was still looking at the baptised when their nightshirts and striped pyjamas erupted with red splotches as they fell.

The man with the shotgun was very dark, with a hook nose, just like Uncle Hector; but Uncle Hector, though taller, moved quickly and softly, where the man with the gun trod heavily. He turned for the front door.

The boy saw his father spring to his feet and rush along between the Meeting Hall seats. He took off, and feet-first hit the shotgun man about waist high, smashing him into the side of the timber baffle that prevented people in the street from seeing straight into the Hall. The shotgun clattered into two piles of hymn books and bibles, scattering them, before it dropped with a crash to the wooden floor. The Hall was old, and the floor timbers tallow-wood, beautifully laid.

Jackson Blood knelt on the man's back, holding his right arm up near his shoulder blade. Each time the man moved, Jackson Blood moved his knee a little to the left of the man's spine and leaned forward. The man eventually stayed still, and was quiet until the police came, called by one of the preacher's three sons.

The boy looked at the carnage. Some people screamed, but most fell to their knees in prayer. Mister Liston looked after the dying and the wounded.

Davis Blood watched everything. What he saw he would possess for a lifetime. The holes in the baptised would trouble him until he died. Awful choking sounds came from the woman in the striped pyjamas. One man made a sound deep in his throat, like breathing with his nose and mouth blocked. He had twisted as he fell to the platform so that his face was upside down, in the boy's line of sight. Blood came out of his mouth.

The boards piled up at the side of the platform looked like firewood. They should never have been disturbed, thought the boy. The other two people sat up, covered in blood. Their wounds weren't so bad.

It was even more interesting when the police came. People tried to shield him, to stop him seeing, to prevent him entering into the events of the evening, but always he managed to get a glimpse round or between the obstacles pushed in his way.

'Like an execution,' a big person said. His father was the hero.

In one bound, one decisive act he had stopped a state of chaos and evil in its tracks, and allowed order to flow back, good steady, kindly, natural order, among good kindly, steady, ordinary people.

On the way home, much later when he'd been soaked so much in these events that they seemed nothing unusual, an unrelated thought came into his mind. There was God the Father and the Son as well as the Holy Spirit. But if the Godhead was a kind of family, why wasn't it a whole one? Where was God the Mother, as his father had read to him from the book?

He was tired, and yawning deeply, before he and his father were at the front gate.

In bed after he'd said his prayers, something from school mixed in his head with the baptism he'd seen. He was sleepy, and the words said themselves slowly in his head.

> *If all the executions were one execution,*
> *What a big execution that would be.*

Drawing Words

His father drew an umbrella for him, teaching him the look of words, by showing the shape of the objects. His father's hand moved quickly. Sure strokes formed the curves of the umbrella's stretched ribs, quick short arcs showed the boundary of the fabric. A strong straight line, with the handle on the end of it — and there was the umbrella. 'Uh for umbrella.'

The knuckles of his father's hand were brown and tight, the fingers massive and strong, the green veins stood up fiercely. They had been with him in other countries, and when he worked for a circus; they had held horses' reins, and the riding whip in the wardrobe, and an M16 for his country; they had fought, taped and gloved, in the boxing ring; they contained stories there would never be time to hear.

The pencil lead made a channel in the paper, with sides curved down to where the pencil's track flowed.

He watched as his father drew common objects — books, shoes, houses, animals, birds, boats, aeroplanes, tanks, cars. He wanted to be able to draw like that. With sureness.

Casually, in a few sentences, his father showed his youngest son perspective. He didn't know that there was a kind of folk-knowledge, passed on from higher to lower classes at school, that introduced this subject. It was in the form of drawings of the huge bows of an ocean liner, receding in size to the stern, bearing down on a rowing boat fifty metres from it, in which sat the person drawing it.

As the boy watched the drawings appear on the paper — the umbrella, bus, racing car, the yacht with sails full of air — he could feel the magic of the little representations conjuring up in his mind the action — pictures of things he'd seen either out there in the world or on television, or as other pictures in books. The drawings were short-cuts to the real-life objects, and therefore convenient, but they, and the words — umbrella, bus, car, yacht — were a great deal different from the umbrella you held in the rain, the bus you could pat with your hand outside school of an afternoon, or the yacht packed with busy crew coming about on harbour or lake.

He sensed also that Jackson Blood's purpose was the look of the words he illustrated, hoping to teach spelling; unaware that the boy knew the words already.

What Davis Blood was learning was to draw. Seeing her brother's interest, Danielle made sure he never went short of pencils and paper.

His first drawing to come to the attention of the whole family was of her. He'd been looking with Lillian in the family album and came across a shot of Danielle when she was thin and thirteen, and another when she played in a school musical at fifteen, showing her in a brief dancer's costume with her little bottom turned cheekily to the audience. The boy listened to his mother's story of how his sister danced and wiggled and swished up her little skirt in provocative innocence. He drew his sister.

He showed her angular as a girder, with a round head, stick arms, half-moon mouth and dots for eyes. She was surrounded by little forms shaped like two *U*s joined.

He called it 'Skinny Girl with Seventy Bums'. The family thought it a scream, and praised him without restraint. Even as they praised it he wondered where sheets of paper came from. Did they cut sheets, like slices, from a block of paper?

Aunt Mira demanded to see the drawing, and when they put it on the table near her, she looked at it a long time, then uttered a squawk.

'Who would have thought it! The Muse is among us, milked by a boy. When he was bubbling away in the amniotic darkness, who would have thought? What feats of Klee will we live to see? Oh distant beloved bums, what else will he find when he opens Pandora's pillbox? That a little collage is a dangerous thing? Where will this boy hang at last? Oh genital lad, we bow before you —'

But the boy was gone out of Aunt Mira's domain into the big room — where he sat with paper and pencil.

'Is he a native of Australia? Or is it just a phallacy? To test for phallacy: take down his decretals and waive his options, but never hit him in the genials!' came from the kitchen, then silence. Quite likely Aunt Mira had fallen asleep mid-sentence. Or it could have been that his father, or Lillian, knowing there was a Mozart program, had put the radio earphones where she could reach them. Mad on Mozart, she would listen, eyes shut, head moving slightly in time to the mysteries of the long-dead Mozart's melodies, those bewitching inventions which, when you come to look closely at them, seem to be spun from nothing.

'Davie!' It was Aunt Mira again. She rarely used his name. She sounded so miserable and alone. He got up and came to the kitchen door.

'Yes, Auntie?' He didn't usually give her a name, either.
'Say goodbye.'
'Goodbye?'
'Say goodbye to me. Please. Nicely.'
'All right,' he said brightly. 'Goodbye, Auntie dear!'
'Ah. That's better. I like goodbyes. People are so nice to me then.'

He knew he'd been had, but not quite how.

'I thought you were asleep.'

'Do you know, there were people I knew out west, had a caged bird and they loved their bird so much they painted the walls of every room to look like a forest, so she'd feel at home. Ah good old bad old days, when I was poorer than I am now and so happy, so miserable.'

'Are you all right, Auntie?'

'Duck! There's a loose boomerang in the room!' He ducked. She screeched and howled with ascending — if you can picture it — cascades of laughter.

Done again. He got back to his drawing table.

He began a series of drawings of the family, one by one, of the family eating at the table, of the animals, of Aunt Mira, of the outside of the house itself.

'The family eating meat,' he said, when Orville asked him what his latest drawing was.

Danielle was excited to find one day that the boy had drawn a vast bird covering the sky, from left to right across the paper, and the undersides of its wings formed the shape of a panorama of city buildings. She tried to find if he had drawn the silhouette of the city first, then over-arched the rest of the bird, but apparently not: it seemed he saw the bird as the 'power of the sky', as he explained.

'But there's nothing up there,' she said reasonably, trying to draw him out.

He wouldn't contradict her directly, that wasn't his way: he would feel as if he'd thrown something at her. He merely said, 'The sky is the top of us. What's above that is power.'

'Does the sky protect us from what's out there?'

'The power is there. Maybe the sky protects, I don't know.'

'And the power is a big bird?'

'No. It could be a bird.'

'Where did you get the shape of the city?'

He looked at her as if she'd asked a silly question. He'd been to the city. I see; I take what I see; I have what I take: they followed one another naturally.

I see, next thing I know. I see, therefore I can do. It was all so clear.

He was relieved when she went out of the room. He sat there. Words were a nuisance sometimes — most of all when people threw them at you as if they didn't matter, as if they were any old scrap.

He was happy. Outside, he could feel the sun showered its many rays gently on the earth, and the earth smiled. Flowers, paths, fallen leaves, waving grasses, trees, smiled. Bush rocks, friendly and grey, warm in the sun, smiled. The world was in a time of deep harmony, and he was in tune with it all.

He picked up the pencil and drew a fresh sheet of paper to him. Without thinking he drew a ball, then put strokes on it that stood up vertically. It had come into his head just as Orville first told him, that when the Meeting people put their hands up, as sometimes they did, pointing to Jesus — up there in heaven — then if people all over the world did that, all would point up in a different direction out into space like the seeds on a dandelion core. Heaven, then, would be like a bag surrounding the spherical earth.

It was only a thought drawing. He crumpled the paper, and began a drawing of the valley seen from his bed on the verandah, with the tall stringybarks, the young Sydney red gums, and the mass of turpentines, blue gums and all the varieties of eucalypts whose names he would never know.

Different

He noticed about himself that often, in the middle of a game with other children, he wanted to be away by himself, thinking of the things he went over in his mind by day, or walking, eating, going to sleep, or when he gazed off into the distance as the teacher was explaining something to one of the slower children.

Sometimes he wanted to be with other kids, but not often. He lived inside himself, his existence was contained by what he was and what he thought, and in the images that passed into his head and among which he wandered later, at his leisure.

He knew he was different, and that that knowledge was a thing to treasure.

He felt very much with all things round him: people, animals, birds, the backstairs, clouds, sky, bush tracks, Brown Rock, insects, grass, earth, his bed on the verandah, stars, trees, and the air of the valley. His eyes reached out, held what he saw, and, as if on the end of a long tongue, touched and tasted it; finally drew it back into himself so that what he thoroughly saw he made his own.

Once, sitting on the verandah and looking down into the grass and through the nearby fringe of trees to the valley, he thought within himself, in that language that was just beyond the reach of the words he knew, and which he called feeling:

> *I'm a container or even a kind of trap*
> *shaped like Davis Blood.*
> *Full of things that I've seized and pulled*
> *into my self-bag*
> *and which I now contain as part of me.*
> *This bag is growing, minute by minute.*

We are Bits of God

He was walking in the backyard, head down, with a piece of paspalum grass in his mouth: it was the white juicy shaft that had come with a squeak out of the shielding green socket joint. He was thinking of nothing. In this state his thoughts usually came to him. He liked the taste of paspalum.

Orville's tree. The bark at the base had grown into its comfortable fawn coloured roughness, the bark on the upper branches was still smooth and green. God was everywhere, therefore in Orville's tree. He stood under the curved branches, feeling the stillness the tree inhabited. How different it would be, to have to stay in one spot, like a tree. Still, God was in the tree, just as God was in us, and would teach the tree to defend itself.

God made us. He knew that. But if God made us and is in us, and God made all things including the world, as we are made from the world, and God is in all things and contains all things, then all things are made out of God; we are made out of God.

He hugged the thought. It was his. Nothing was as

warming as a good thought, especially when it was your own. Made out of God. God is therefore in us all; all are part of God.

He sat on Brown Rock. The stillness at the bottom of the yard was disturbed by a large brown and turquoise butterfly. God was in that butterfly, its geometrical flight was in God.

Again he rehearsed his new thoughts, to treasure them in memory. God in us, we in God. God in all things, all things in God.

It was good to have such thoughts. He was glad that the way things worked inside him, in the workings his parents had given him, allowed him to tuck such things away in his memory. They would emerge in their own time, changed slightly, as if some other thing inside had worked on them quietly with an insight that would surprise him.

Another thought fizzed up. What if he did bad things? What happened to the bit of God in him? Was it angry, or upset? Did it weep when he was naughty? Or hide away in shame? Or just shrug and hope for better days?

All that had grown was in the image of God — water, fire, stars, rocks, people, trees. His own life was new, but represented age-old life, perhaps life anywhere.

My Cat Ripley

After tea, the boy wrote a composition. It was one he'd often wished the teacher would ask him to write:

I will tell you about my cat Ripley.
He prays to God a lot on his knees, but opens his eyes when I get near, or perhaps one eye. It depends on how he feels. When he meets other cats they have a kiss or a fight, depends who it is. When he catches a mouse he has a game with it, but the mouse gets tired first and stops playing. My cat bites its head off then and leaves it where we can all see it.

At night after tea he goes out into the dark to keep watch over the house, in case baddies come. In the morning he lies out flat in the sun. The hotter the sun the flatter he lies. He loves the sun and his sides and head get very warm and good to stroke. Your hand feels warm when you touch him. My father says he is the same family as tigers and leopards and lions but not so big, that's all. Also he's not the same pattern as they are, he has lots of blacky-brown, with ginger and white round the face and chest, and one white paw. He stands up tall on his back legs and scratches the back of the turpentine trees. He's a good cat, but you wouldn't believe some of the things he brings back home.

He kept it with his drawings.

The Vow

*H*e had been bullied, belted and scarred by Papworths and Downies many times; the last was the day before. Always after those encounters he had taken the long way home for a week or two, until the memory of his defeat had gone.

This time, however, he decided to go through their territory the very next day, but with a difference. He kept the blood-stained handkerchief he had used the day before to wipe the blood from his nose, and coming down the hill towards them he tied it round his neck like a kerchief, with the knot at the back and the bloody spots fluffed out in front. He rolled his sleeves up so the grazes would show and pushed his school socks down so the skinned knee and the marks where two stones had got him on the front of the shin would be fresh and obvious. The sock had stuck to one of the stone marks, and pulled the scab away when he pushed his sock down, so it bled again, running down in a little stream.

Looking as if he was fresh from the fray, he met them as they came out of their gates and started to swarm towards him.

'Hey, lollylegs!' one of the Downies called.

'Let's get him,' said a Papworth.

'Looks like someone else got him first,' said the biggest boy.

'Have a nosebleed, did ya?'

'Who kicked ya?'

'Did your Ma belt the hell out of you?' Their mothers did, out of them.

One of the smaller Downies hit him in the back with a testing punch, and a small Papworth kicked him on the knee — a favourite Papworth trick. But somehow it wasn't the same as spoiling the skin and clothes of a spotless kid. The oldest boy called it off.

'Let him go. We got him yesterday. We don't want people saying we pick on little kids.'

They made way for him and he got through the ruck of enemies with only one more kick and an exploratory poke in the lower ribs — to see if he yelled. He didn't make a sound, apart from the noise of his school shoes on the unmade road scattering odd bits of ironstone and quartz gravel.

'Come back when the blood's dried and we'll give it to you again.' someone called. He kept his head straight to the front. One of the Downie dogs, called Cruncher because of his way with bones, ran at him, but the big boy called him back.

As Davis Blood walked home he smiled a little smile. I'm only one kid and it's not very brave to go getting Randal and Orville to bash them up, but one day I'll be back. I'll grow big and then we'll see. They think I'll always be a little kid like I am now, but I'll come back and get that lot, starting with the biggest, even though he did call them off me today.

He felt better after that. But fifty metres further along the street and he'd forgotten all about it. At the front gate he remembered his vowed revenge, and smiled. He'd never be able to reproduce enough anger later to get even. God must be in them, too, but what, he wondered, went on in their heads where all was hidden? Was it anything like inside his head? It couldn't be. It must be different. But how different? How could he get inside their heads, to find out?

The Timberyard

The boy's mother was ill in bed. Her kidneys, Aunt said. Each time a baby arrived her kidneys suffered a near-collapse, and now her child-bearing days were past, the kidneys remembered, and from time to time felt sorry for themselves, as Ursula put it, and let her know.

There was little supervision round the house for the boy to cope with at any time, but less now. His father was out in the world somewhere at work or looking for work; the boy was not clear which, a lot of the time. He sold things. He was a good salesman, having a humorous manner and plenty of talk when he was away from the family. The boy got up to all sorts of things. Possibilities for action seemed to open out wider every day. He had never felt the bonds before, of responsibility and obedience: he had adjusted immediately to whatever demands and restrictions the family put on him, and lived comfortably inside them. Each new rule laid down altered slightly the effect of every other rule.

He saw the adjustment that would have to be made, and made it. That was how life was: you learned what was what, and remembered. You changed with the changes. He could see the reasons his family had for each rule, even though he didn't accord them all perfect justice. He knew rules were mostly for the comfort of the rule-makers, not for his safety and bringing-up.

But out there in the world the rules didn't always need to be observed. He entered places where strangers and the 'public' were not to go; even boys of eight.

He wandered down along the shores of the bay at Applegreen Water, then the next bay, and the next. He discovered a vast yard where great bundles and stacks of timber were, where the smell in the air was like the smell of a deep forest. He pressed his nose to the stacks of pine, the huge rough-sawn balks of oregon. He let his eyes close a bit, savouring the perfume of the inner parts of trees —

with the bark ripped away. He put his hands on the roughness, he touched in awe the timbers nearly a metre deep and half a metre thick. Especially he loved the massive ones. Something in him was moved by their size and solidity; there was a sensual opulence, a luxuriance, a dignity in these timbers that had once been tall trees, thick at the base, living and breathing among the thousands of their relatives in a forest the world might never see. He hoped the most magnificent ones wouldn't be sawn into lesser planks, but remain heavy and whole, scented and proud, and eventually do a job that matched their strength.

Around him in the yard he saw thin timbers, wide and flat boards, bundles of laths; some lots planed smooth, some still rough. The whole method of sawing larger things into smaller, thicker into thinner, stood before him in the timberyard like a diagram.

The man responsible for keeping out thieves was not about to encourage tours of his territory. He saw the boy going from stack to stack, and the only thought in his head was that interlopers were thieves. In all his experience he had never known a stranger who would walk through and leave with nothing. Given the chance, he would thieve, too, if he could get away with it.

He crept up on the boy, and at a corner of a stack of tallow-wood flooring, lunged forward and grabbed at him. The eight-year-old's ears and nerves heard and reacted to the scrunch of boots just before his shirt was grabbed, and he was off before the man could settle himself.

When the man got into his stride on a straight stretch he gained on the boy. Seeing this, or, rather hearing it, the boy made fewer long runs down the lanes of timber, and cut round corners, dodging left and right. The man was slow on corners.

The boy was filled with fear, but a sense in him told him that if he allowed the fear to grip him, he would stop and grow rigid. He used the fear to drive his legs faster and think more quickly.

Five times the boy's shirt was nearly in the man's right

hand; each time the boy made a sudden turn and dodged away.

The boy had never been in the timberyard before and didn't know its plan. The man did. Suddenly the boy's run took him headlong on to a large platform of rough grey timbers. A wharf. There was the water, the bay. Another wharf seemed to be next to or just beyond this one. There was a gap, he'd have to jump.

He saw the distance while he was in the air, and fell like a stone into the green waters of the bay. The other wharf was many metres away. He narrowly missed a flight of steps down to the water, used by launch passengers. The water splashed up, the boy disappeared.

When he came up and took a breath, the man was looking down, grinning. He'd cornered the little bastard.

The boy swam towards the next wharf and pulled himself out of the water on to the wharf timbers, and stopped there, puffing. Only for a few seconds, then his breath was back. He embraced the upright pile nearest him and got a foot round it to the next horizontal timber. He could see, under the wharf, a way to get to the sunlight at the far end.

The man had no intention of getting wet. He stayed on the wharf until he remembered the steps. He descended, sat on a dry step and watched the boy, silently. The boy's fear had mostly gone; he was enjoying his adventure now. The black timbers, wet from years of daily tides, were friendly and broad underfoot. It was dark under there, he liked it: a hideaway, you could see out.

In the darkest part, he sat and dangled his legs in the water. He picked at the mussels, peered into the green depths, watched the sway of the sea weeds, saw small gangs of tiddlers swimming near the piles. What a good place to be. Once, he sang softly his school house cry:

> *Coolibah, Coolibah, brave and bold*
> *Coolibah, wearing green and gold*
> *Coolibah!-Coolibah!- full of zest*
> *Coolibah!-Coolibah!- is the best*
> *C double O.L.I.B.A.H. Coolibah!*

The man got up and walked back to his gatekeeper's hut. The boy sat, let his thoughts roam. He thought of his father, and how the life of the family went on, whether he was at home or not. It must be lonely, to be a father, he thought: sort of living on the edge of the family. Out on the margin.

When he looked up next, the man was gone. It was delicious being alone. The lights on the water were fascinating and compelled his eyes. The dancing reflections, the larger waves, lesser waves and waves on the slopes of other waves made him shake his head in wonder at the variousness of ruffled water. He drew the salt smell deep into him.

Round on the mangrove side of the bay the tide was out, the smell of black mud in the air. When it was just on dark, he climbed back towards the shore and pulled himself up on to the wharf, using some rocks in the bank for footholds. The man was still gone, the timberyard shut. His feet in their sandshoes fitted neatly into the square diamond shapes of the cyclone wire fence. He'd never climbed one before, and took an interest in each facet of the climb. Once on the top bar, and under the lowest of the three strands of barbed wire, he climbed down the outside of the wire, and walked home.

When he got there his shirt was dry and his pants nearly. His mother was up and in the kitchen singing,

> *'Father, I know that all my life*
> *Is portioned out for me.'*

His father wanted to give him a message from the past:

> *'When a chance comes, grab it.*
> *A chance lost is life lost.'*

And he, Davis Blood, had toothache. He reflected, as he put his hand to his face, that his father had probably missed many chances.

Speed, the Cat

Speed had come to the house on Sunday when everyone was at home. It was a sunny day in early November, the fire was lit in the backyard and the smell of grilling meat and burning gum branches was in a haze everywhere. A large scrawny tabby cat had come across the valley and now poked its head round the middle one of the clump of three turpentine trees and looked up the backyard of number twenty. A quick movement of the head was noticed by the boy, who said nothing, but took a piece of meat in his hand and slowly got near the cat.

'Here, puss,' he said, and held out the meat. The cat sniffed the air, hungry. The boy squatted down and held out the meat near the ground. The cat allowed herself to be drawn forward, closer, until she took the meat from the boy's fingers. He watched till she finished, then said, 'You wait here. Wait here now, I'll get you some more.'

The cat ate seven pieces of meat, and seeing it seemed a pleasant place, decided to stay. In a month it was fat as mud and never went back to being scrawny. It was slow and sleepy and never moved unless it had overwhelming reasons, so everyone called it Speed.

About cats, one thing stood out. No yelling would make a cat do anything, except get its back up, or just run. They wouldn't obey, not one of them. You couldn't command a cat to come, you could only persuade it, and to do that you had to plead a little. You had to lower yourself, or else offer something the cat valued above peace and immobility. You couldn't even get a cat to help you with anything, not even by coaxing. They would not work.

It's not that they were stupid. None was ever late for meals — which is the great test for stupidity — all changed their positions about the yard according to how hot or cold they were, finding always the perfect place to be.

They would all look you full in the face, and keep it up till it got silly; then they'd look away, having found nothing they desired. Their green eyes seemed like clear sea water over sandy bottoms: clear, but mysterious, telling you nothing.

Papworths and Downies

The boy went to school, though he felt awful. The cold that had taken up residence in him was a heavy weight in his forehead, his nose ran green, he began to cough. All day at school he coughed, and when time came to go home he went the quickest way, past the Papworths and Downies, even if he got killed.

When they came out grinning and looking for blood he was too weak to run or fight.

'I'm sick. If you fight me I'll fold up and probably faint on the ground here.' He looked at the rough stones of the street, and they did too. 'I'll be better on Monday. Wait here for me and I won't faint no matter how hard you bash me.'

He was a little uneasy at having made this speech. It was a sort of pleading, and that was weak, but they let him pass and he felt better. At least he would make it home.

On Monday, he had just got level with the Papworths' house, and they, together with the Downies, were in their front yard, milling about, restless and frustrated. They wanted to come and get him, but something was stopping them. An incoherent squodge of language arose from the more foul-mouthed. It seemed to form one large greasy, bad-smelling word. He hesitated a bit, offering himself true to his word, then walked on.

The boy didn't know what saved him until he came up with Randal and Orville leaning against electric light poles on opposite sides of the street, just where they could be seen by the bandit families. He hadn't complained, ever, but his brothers seemed to know what went on.

'How do you feel?' Orville asked.

'Pretty terrible,' he said.

'Did you think they'd get you?' Orville said.

'I thought they'd bash me up. They won't now.'

Randal said, 'Dogs don't fight tigers.'

At school he learned more worldly wisdom: that cheats never prosper; a copy-cat is a dirty rat; small things amuse small minds, but smaller minds look on; a cowardly custard is yellow as mustard; it was a virtue to mind your own business. He learned to say 'I'm bar!' when he wanted a rest from chasings, and 'Bags that one!' when he put in first claim to something found; or 'Sacks on the mill!' when he wanted an excuse to jump on a pile of bodies.

It felt good to know the right words to say among the other kids.

Down in the bush behind the house he learned to take young gum-tips, crack them across and draw them apart to show the little sheet of transparent gum. Putting it between the two out-facing sides of his thumbs he could make a musical sound when he blew edgewise to the gum. From there he graduated to tunes.

Drawing in Chalk

At home, safe from bandit families, the boy drew chalk figures on the side of the laundry which was below the fourteen steps and had always had a dirt floor until Preston and his brothers one day got the wind in their tails and concreted it. The side of the laundry was a fibrous plaster sheet, and the boy of eight found it a fine surface for his dramas of animals and birds.

He showed sporting scenes of birds playing cricket; dogs, with cats on their backs for riders, racing like horses do; a kookaburra policeman arresting a starling, which was perhaps intending to bribe the policeman with a baby lizard held behind its back in one claw; there was a bird of no particular type, a sort of utility bird, with a shopping basket full of things for her family. She was followed by miniature birds of different shapes. One was a wagtail.

The older members of the family didn't notice his mural until the weekend. He was relieved at that, since he thought he might get into trouble for drawing on the house.

If all the drawings were one drawing
What a great drawing that would be.

On the swing he loved letting his mind go limp — that's the way he thought of it — for then all sorts of things: spaces, scenes, dramas, words, bits of conversations, and unusual pictures, came into his head. A faint smile took up residence on his face. The world in his head was interesting, very pleasant, and stretched a long way from the old house at Bellbird Corner.

Various remedies, plenty of fuss, lessened the ache in his lower right jaw, which seemed to come from the big sharp tooth that Randal called a 'fang'. Randal was the first one to see him clutch his face.

Aunt Mira said threateningly, 'There's one sure cure for every disease,' but that information was considered inappropriate for a boy of eight.

His toothache was family property at teatime, when more remedies were advocated — cloves, hot mouthwashes, self-control — but the attention turned away from the boy when Aunt Mira pronounced, 'Sharper than a servant's child is an ungrateful tooth,' after which Ursula argued that 'servant's' should be 'serpent's', and everyone joined in.

It was a new experience for him, to have the family's attention slide off him so easily. He was relieved, also amused, and began to go over again, while he ate, the events of the timberyard. I love the smell of timber, he told himself. The man there thought I was going to steal some.

He came back to the general talk in time to hear Preston say dismissively, 'Fools are necessary. The wise follow them like shepherds follow sheep, or fishermen follow shoals of fish.'

'Sharks, you mean,' Randal said.

'Businessmen, he means,' said Orville.

Preston was pleased. He loved being seen to be on the side of the strong.

Orville was pleased too. He expanded his idea.

'He means fools provide a living for the smart ones.'

'Right again,' approved Preston.

Davis Blood had a question.

'Mum, a Christian wouldn't steal, would he?'

'Never.'

'Would you ever steal?'

'Absolutely never!' Though it was her temperament, not to covet others' things.

'Are you a Christian?'

'Of course Mum is!' exclaimed Orville.

'No, I'm not,' said Lillian.

'You're not?' said Orville.

'You're what?' said Randal.

'To be a Christian is impossible; being a Christian is an aim, an ideal you strive towards.'

'Oh,' said several voices. But it was the 'Oh' of disengagement. This was one of those subjects where interest quickly invited obligation.

The boy felt justified in pursuing the question. In that moment he apprehended that perhaps all things could be questioned, though whether they ought to be was another matter.

'You see,' Lillian said, 'Christianity is so difficult as to be impossible in practice. I try and I'll keep on trying till I die, but I don't expect I'll succeed where everyone else has failed, except one. Religion is all practice, and travel, and goal.'

What Will I Be?

Under the house, on the swing, Davis Blood thought: What will I be, when I'm older? What am I now? My mother says things like greatness, the best in the world, but what does that mean? People with lots of power, like kings and prime ministers and dictators, they have to be clever. It must be a minimum requirement. It must be good to be the best in the world at something, and have everyone know it.

And have everyone know you.

Power means telling people what to do and having them afraid of you, doesn't it? Perhaps telling them what to think, too. Being the best is sort of Up There, he thought. That, too, was pleasant. Lots of kids liked power, they were always telling you what to do and they wanted you to be scared of them. Others thought you were peculiar if you weren't madly active all the time; they had to be doing things, and never sat and stared. Still others would never admit to being scared, but insisted they weren't when they were.

As for me, he thought, I don't want to do what people tell me to because I don't trust them to have good sense, and when I'm grown up I won't have to, I hope. But on the other hand I don't want to be telling people what they ought to do as if they were children. So I won't order, and won't obey. The same with fear. I won't fear others, and they needn't fear me. That seemed fair.

I want to be free to do the things I want to do, knowing they won't hurt others. He remembered Aunt Ursula on freedom, 'We have a little, not enough; yet not so little that it can't be reduced if we don't defend it.' But he thought she was talking of a different freedom.

As he swung, his mind cleared of pictures. A song came into his head.

'The Lord's my shepherd, I'll not want.' As it sang in his head, he felt he was an audience, listening to it.

That must be how it was for Lillian, except that songs were singing themselves inside her all the time. What a marvellous thing a person's head was! Whole worlds are in there; lots of people; plenty of talking; and you can explain, argue, check over things, chuckle over your own jokes, and even listen to voices that say things in there. Memories were there, landscapes, faces, music, the sounds of people's voice. It was hard to think of things — apart from solid objects — that weren't there. Everything seemed to be represented in there.

Down along the valley a cuckoo screamed its intermittent call, as it had for three days.

The Big Storm

It had been unseasonably hot for days and the family felt suffocated. He had no trouble with the heat. The air was warm, that was all, and felt dry going down your gullet, into your chest where you could feel it still dry. His mother had wet cloths soaked in vinegar on her forehead, and people in houses up the street sounded frightened when they came out into their yards.

The sun was so bright, the day seemed to hang suspended high in the air, having little to do with the earth. At night everyone was glad of a little wind whispering round the corners of the house, and didn't mind the trees repeating what they heard.

In the afternoon, blue-black clouds approached, with a dirty light-brown cloud leading the way. The hills to the west limited the sky's extent; sometimes you didn't see the weather coming till it was right there.

Sheet lightning washed the sky, top to bottom, in a sick yellow. It was three weeks since the cuckoo first screamed. Jackson Blood referred to it as the rain bird.

At first the sound of thunder was thin, then closer, then overhead, accompanied by a clap of thunder like someone smashing down an iron lid near your ear.

Wind accelerated and the note the trees sang rose higher. In the distance grey clouds were smudged at the bottoms, as if a grubby hand had smudged a pencil drawing downwards. That was rain.

Wind made a whistle of the chimney top, as when Orville blew across the top of an empty soft-drink bottle. The storm on Gunsight Hill lashed the trees with zest. After a while, so impressed was he with the storm's fury that he felt the storm was in him, too.

Rain came slashing so fiercely down on the valley, it seemed like a raid. He watched it stabbing into soft dirt, drops like bullets hitting leaves and knocking them sideways. It cut channels in grass and footpaths. The gutters weren't deep enough to take the water away. Bread and Butter Creek down the back of their place was high and wide and odd things floated towards the lake. Sheets of water made the landscape lower down wonderful, bare, unfamiliar; he could hardly pick out where streets ran except for the electric light poles like grey splinters stuck in the world.

There was a certain fun about emergencies, with even the adults delighted as children, like when there was an electricity strike and everyone went round with candles, laughing.

He saw through the wet window-pane the trees, grass and garden flicker. A little waterdrop sliding down had power to make the whole earth move.

Once, he couldn't resist running out into the rain in bare feet to feel the hard drops hammer his head. He loved it. The confusion, the scariness, the thunder so loud that when it sounded nothing else existed on earth; the sheets of rain falling, not in columns but solid flat blankets of water. The wind pushed the rain, then stopped; pushed again and eased off. There was, to his sharp senses, no time of any length when wind or rain kept constant speed. All was change. No sooner this, than that.

There was so much water rushing in the flooded valley that the creek managed to look like a small river.

He still had to go to school.

The rain and wind, pressing at his back, drove him along towards school like a curse.

The rain continued for days. The black earth began to have a sullen smell. It was always wet. It needed water well enough, but being full of water all the time turned it sour. Perhaps hell was where all the world was stagnant, yet nothing died. Birds came out still, their little legs looked cold, thin as splinters. Sparrows have busy eyes, he noticed: uneasy, worried necks.

When Dany came home from the office, she said she'd probably write some music, 'A Suite, I think, for unaccompanied earthquake and solo cyclone.'

It rained for more days. You'd have thought there was no such word as dry.

The last day of the rains he was allowed to sit up late at night and the fire in the grate burned so low he found it hard to tell which was the more drowsy, he or the fire. Storms had become showers.

Morning was clear and sun-filled, the storms gone, but the light shook, as if the whole scene was unreliable, a paper facade over something meant to be hidden.

He walked up Big Hill in light rain, where he found, on the ridge that was Anzac Street, some well-made gutters. There, the flow of water formed patterns like half a fishbone, with slanting rib-like ripples coming out away from the concrete kerb. He looked closely and found the little ribs came from roughnesses in the cement side of the gutter. Further up Anzac Street the flow was less, but still the rib-like patterns persisted. They reminded him, though they were much tamer, of the fierce currents and deflections in the steep clay and stone gutters of Big Hill, where the water rushed in torrents past jutting rocks, and cut deep pools in the earth and exposed the white clay with thin black roots running through it.

When he went to school after the sun had come out again he saw places on the footpaths near the shops, where the rain had stood in pools. The sun had evaporated them slowly, leaving concentric irregular rings that showed each successive evaporation on the bitumen. Yes, he thought, that shows up all the little pools, so the path can't be flat.

He noticed the clouds a lot that spring, and the thought jumped into his head that perhaps never, in all history, had the same pattern of clouds repeated itself.

He'd taken pieces of white clay from the gutters at the side of the road and moulded them with his fingers into little shapes — a head, a dog. Now, on the way home after the rain, there was more clay exposed. He'd seen the pink clay in the big hole on brickyard hill and heard how it was baked to make bricks, and he thought he knew why it was good for bricks: when it was wet it was fine-grained and sticky, and when it was dry it got very hard. But why, he thought, remembering the black mud in the bay and how much of it there was, why couldn't mud be used for bricks? They could dry it and coat it with something to keep it firm, or mix something with it to make it set and not wash away when it got wet.

Why don't they do that? he said to himself, but he was home by then, and hungry, and forgot all about it.

What he didn't forget, but which remained poised somewhere in his consciousness, was that after he'd had an idea, or a moment of insight, something was different. As if he had grown suddenly bigger or had taken a step up, and now stood higher.

Newton's Sums Spread Right Across the Page

The boy sat in the kitchen after tea, thinking of nothing in particular, looking steadily from one familiar thing to another: table, crockery, dresser, wood stove, the box of cut wood waiting to be put on the fire, the mantelpiece and its objects, the blackened kettle, tea caddy, teacosy, matches, candlestick for power blackouts.

He knew them all so well that, in a sense, they were in him. Perhaps in me, he thought, are all the things in the world. Certainly all the things he'd seen in his three thousand days on earth he drew into himself like someone eating, or storing things.

'Aunt,' he said to Ursula, 'can people, ordinary people, make discoveries?'

She looked at him.

'Yes. Most of them, though, have been made before.'

She looked down, her eyes fell off his face, where they'd been resting.

'Take Newton. Early man knew all about the way gravitation worked. Sisyphus cursed it and pushed his rock back up the hill. People made arrows, they knew they'd fall to earth. A footballer, a cricketer, they know gravitation intimately, but who'd listen if they talked about it? A scientist is one who provides a mathematical equation for something even cave-men knew.

'See, Davie? Newton worked it all out in figures and published the right words to the right people and they took him seriously. And ever after we think of Newton when we think of gravity — until Einstein came along — not of besieged folk pouring boiling oil on invaders, or beavers chewing trees till they fall into position, or a man sitting on a rock at the doorway to his cave watching rain falling and earth crumbling and rock slides.' She wheeled in to the bookshelves and came back with a magazine in which she showed a picture of one of Newton's sums, rows and rows of figures, stretching right across the page and from top to bottom of the paper. There was no room to show the lot.

'The way you know whether you've made a discovery is to educate yourself, learn all you can, all your life: then you have background knowledge, know if it's a discovery, or just a repetition of a previous discovery.'

The boy went out of the kitchen and sat at the table in the big room, thinking of Newton and how, if he was lucky, he'd be learning all his life. Until the sun went down on him forever. But, he thought, harking back to his own special thoughts that God is in all things and all is part of God, even when he died he'd still be in God, so he wouldn't be entirely gone.

Only a Corner

In the afternoon the other kids had finished their drawings. Some were quick, and looked around for something else to do. Some were slow, and were laboriously guiding their chalks into the lines they thought might look acceptable when they'd finished.

The boy, though, was not in sight of finishing. The new teacher, from the front of the classroom, saw that he had worked only in one corner of the sheet of drawing paper. Miss Graves sighed slightly and let her arms hang. Try to relax, she counselled herself. Don't let anything get you down. Certainly not wall-to-wall school children.

She walked round the room, doing a circuit that would bring her at last to that boy with so little work done in the time. Who was that? Oh yes, Davis something. The other children called him Boysie. Blood, that was it. To reach him, she passed the desks covered with ordinary work, the crude thick strokes, feathery undecided attempts at lines, bright primary colours. The subject was Boats on the Bay.

'Well, you haven't done much, have you?' she said to the slow one.

'No, Miss Graves,' he said, head down, hardly disturbing his work on that corner.

Hopeless, she thought, about to turn away. Something caught her eye, something clear and — and what? She turned to him, bent down to look more closely at that bottom left corner. It was only one corner, but what a corner! Previous classes she'd had, where one or two children were much more accomplished than average at representing what they saw, had made her gradually familiar with types of talent she'd not met, but never had she encountered a child who hadn't spread out in outline some idea of what he was going to do on the rest of the paper. This boy was working meticulously on a corner, drawing details of trees, and people picnicking on the grass, presumably watching boats that would be drawn later, sailing on the bay. What could she do? The lesson time was just about up, there was no provision for long-term work on any of the projects she was to take the children through. She couldn't have him still working on this drawing while the others were moving forward to other work. But moving forward? What did that mean? This child was ahead of the others.

She tested him.

'Where is the rest of the picture?'

'Here, Miss Graves. The ferry is here and the two big yachts are here and here. The Customs launch is there and the two big tug boats there and there.'

She was doubtful. Seeing things before they were there on the paper was not an ability she possessed. Was he telling the truth? She turned to go away, then turned back and asked the questions again.

He replied exactly as before, his forefinger sketching in quickly the shapes of the yachts. Apart from the corner there were no marks on the paper, no outlines: he could see it all.

She decided to accept the boy's work as finished. She put it up on the wall that ran round the room, with two drawing pins.

Next day the boy came to school with a note. His mother asked could he be allowed to take the drawing home, to work on there since he seemed attached to it and loved drawing.

She let him take it home, on condition that it came back for her and the class to see.

At home, it seemed when he looked west that Blue Ridge had moved closer, and had folded Bread and Butter Creek more deeply, bringing it nearer to the backyard. It had always seemed further away; he must be growing up.

God in a Severed Head

One of the cocks in the fowl-yard was making a lot of fuss lately. It picked on the other birds, specially the young males, and made the hens' lives a constant flight. Lillian had noticed, and there was a sound of something like vengeance in her voice when she went among the fowls, took the malefactor by his throat and said, 'You'll do for dinner.'

He struggled and beat his wings, but she seemed to get a good feeling from holding his throat. When she had come up the various levels and terraces the bigger boys had made and was near the back of the house where the woodheap was, she changed her grip to one around its ankles, held it upside down, and the bird stopped struggling and fell silent. The boy, watching, saw her lips move in the endless song she sang.

Mother marched over to the woodheap, grasped the axe in her right hand and in one movement laid the bird's neck across the block and brought the axe down. She walked away holding out the dripping corpse, leaving the axe buried in the block, hard up against the dead bird's head. Its eyes were wide open, mouth too. God was in that severed head.

The boy watched it all. His gentle mother was a killer. He tried to reconcile this new picture of her with the previous one, in which she was reluctant to kill kitchen flies. As she got to the foot of the fourteen backsteps, her song broke out of its silence into sound:

> 'Oh Jesus, I have promised,
> To serve you to the end.'

And went into the kitchen with the dead fowl to pluck, clean, and cook for her family.

Davis Blood walked over to Orville's tree and stood

against it, putting his arms round its friendly trunk. Against his face it was cool, but not cold.

Orville had often spoken of it as if it was his young brother's tree, since he'd meant it as a present, but now that it had grown so tall and with so many spreading branches, he was rather proud of it, and didn't mind when young Boysie spoke of it as Orville's Tree.

When the boy sat down on Brown Rock, the bottom corner of the yard had a cool stillness that he liked. He wondered if Jesus ever planted a tree.

He remembered the moment during the Meeting on the previous Sunday night when the preacher's opening prayer began with what sounded like 'Oh, Internal God!', and he smiled as he bent his head and tried to keep his eyes shut and not watch the man fervently praying. He must have said 'Eternal'.

And remembered the mass baptism. Had some of God come out of the holes in the baptised? Had all of God come out of the dead? But no, he was in bones and blood, in what they were made of, so God was in the dead bodies.

And as well, if God is in the bits and what we're made of is part of him, then after death we'd still be in God.

And if God is in all things, he's in what we eat. But he didn't want to follow his thoughts that far, just yet. It was enough to remember words he'd heard at the Meeting, that the body was temple to the Holy Spirit, and acknowledge how close they were to his own intuitions, arrived at alone.

To make up for his wandering thoughts in the Meeting, he had made himself think of Mister Liston's words.

> *'Those who curse God, curse part of themselves*
> *Those who hate God, hate part of themselves*
> *Those who ignore God, ignore part of themselves.'*

His conscience felt a little better after this discipline. Mister Liston had gone on to talk of becoming friends with God. Davis Blood took that to mean being friends with the God in you, and in that form it had meaning for him.

He was in contact with the stars, the hills, clouds, the air of the valley, the thunder that came tumbling over Gunsight Hill, the soil that smelled so like life itself, the sun that powered the life around him. He felt it; it was his; he belonged to it.

He looked around. Everything he saw was alive.

In the Land of Noth

Aunt Ursula taught him one of her favourite wry rhymes:

> *'The trees are all covered with galls*
> *The kittens have gone to St Pauls*
> *The babies are dead*
> *The moon's made of lead*
> *And the houses are built without walls.'*

The boy had great success with it at school. An inspector was in the classroom the week after he'd learned it, and the class was asked for free recitations. The inspector laughed at The Land of Noth, and the teacher was pleased and told him so later.

He had the sense to tell Aunt Ursula of its popularity, and she smiled one of her energetic smiles.

'Just a little flotsam from the whirlpool of my mind,' she said. 'And I'm proud to say I'm modest about it.'

'I bet,' croaked Aunt Mira, 'that their little wooden faces lit up with apathy. All those poor souls from Moburbia, enemas of promise, proles apart.'

'You watch your tongue, Mira,' said Ursula mildy, 'or you'll get murdered for your puns.'

'I'll bury you all, bury you all!' screeched Aunt Mira. 'Lay out their decretals, fish out their genials, let it all hang out!'

'Your Aunt Mira is no gentleman,' said Ursula to the boy.

'Don't go brandying my name about!' Mira yelled. 'It's the twilight of the dogs! We'll all be up shortly before the great Computer-Dog in the sky. Worse than being grilled by a roomful of defectives. What will we say then to our cursors? That we were parallaxed by errors? That a little college is a dangerous thing? That too many of our enemies took a Samuel Pepys at our dairy notes? That we were seduced by a spirituous elite? That all too often we accepted invitations to a guilty party? That our political masters sprayed verbicide over us? No, the soft underbelly of our time is not to blame for us. Put the kettle on, Lily! Put the kettle on! Oh, her blood's worth bottling, that Lillian — the working mother of God, she is.'

She stopped. Her breath came in carefully calculated pants, her cunning little eyes shone as she looked about for nourishment. Tea-time was some way off.

The boy had been only half-listening. He looked at Aunt Ursula, ready to speak. Aunt Ursula was so tuned in to him that she felt the look, and her face was turned towards him before he got a word out.

'Auntie.'
'Yes.'
'You can see all of me, can't you?'
'Yes.'
'And my face?'
'Yes.'
'You can see when I smile?'
'Of course.'
'But I can't. Yet I know I'm smiling.'
'Oh.'
He went on, suddenly full of it. 'What I do is: I see my

arms, my legs, chest, bits of my cheeks' — he looked down at them to check — 'each side of my nose, and my tongue.' He put it out, and checked that he could see the tip.

'I see.'

'Or, in the mirror I can see me, but each bit in the mirror is opposite each bit of me, so what I see is not what you see.'

'Fine. I've got all that. What's bothering you?'

'Really, Auntie, all I feel I am is a sort of mask of looking, this shape —' with a finger he outlined a mask shape across his eyebrows, down to one cheek, round the base of his nose, across the other cheek, and up beside the other eye to the eyebrow he'd started from — 'like Randal's face mask for scuba diving, a sort of shape like this, all lit up, that moves round on legs, and grabs things with hands.'

'Oh? It's the same for everyone.'

'But you see me! They see me! I never see me!'

'Don't be upset. Eyes see other things, not themselves. It's the same for everyone. We must infer that we are ourselves. Nothing's as direct as we want; the world's not made to fit our words; everything is just as it is. That's our starting point. We made the words later.'

'But Auntie! How do I know I'm here? How do I know who I am? Who is this?' Holding out his arms, then pointing back at himself.

'Ah, that's a different matter. That takes time.'

'Will I find out?'

'You may. Lots don't, just go through life without thinking, unconscious as flowers, and die that way.' And remained looking at him, the smile still on her wrenched face.

'Does anyone else know?'

'Not a soul.'

'Not even Mum?'

'Not even Mum.'

'Does God know?'

'Yes.'

'But you don't believe in God.'

'Yes I do. My point is: I think he's responsible, distantly, for the effects of what he started, but isn't interested in leading nations, or humanity, this way or that.'

'But that he's there?'
'Oh yes. Since God exists, it's not necessary to invent him.'
'Pardon?'
'It can't be proved. Nothing that actually matters can be, but the most likely thing is that God is there,' she said comfortingly.
'The most likely?'
'The most likely.'

Floating Away

February was harsh with wet heat. All round the valley, the gums were wilting and weak, only the big old trees, with deep roots clutching far underground, were not affected.

Summer liked the coast that year and lingered into Autumn, into the May holidays. The Tasman Sea was warm still, and the days fierce. The wind, hot from the north, felt blue as the warm sea. You couldn't look at the sun; it was boiling, it might have splashed in your eyes.

Randal and Orville had gone shooting, over towards Fox Hill. Plenty of well-fed foxes had been seen walking boldly out of the bush and along suburban streets.

Davis Blood decided he'd walk through the bush to Pippi Beach and swim in the surf. From Kangaroo Point he went down into the valley, and Nerida Pass, among the tall grey gums, blue gums and black boy spears and crossed the Stepping Stones short of Maidenhair Falls. On the dark moist banks of the creek green delicate maidenhair ferns quivered as he passed and from those brown banks scented satinwood trees grew. On the flat he was surrounded by snake ferns, and the world was enclosed and cool. The call of the whip-bird, as it grew to a crescendo then whip-cracked suddenly, cut the silence like a blade. He noticed the green tinge of tall flooded gums, and that the sky was a long way off.

He headed north-east climbing the opposite side of the valley, where the chain of stepped pools was the home of crayfish. It was an hour before the coast lay stretched out north and south, on his left and right.

Pippi Beach was crowded as he looked down from the cliffs. All of us, he reflected, are living as fish live, under the surface of a sea, except we're bottom dwellers, and ours is a sea of air. Our roof is a murderous nothingness of no air; the fishes' roof is a murderous nothingness of air, which keeps them in very well.

He stepped back into the heath on top of the cliffs, and disturbed a firetail, which flew quickly over a large bush, and disappeared. The track was nearby, leading down to Pippi. For a second, he had been that firetail.

As he neared the beach he wondered: with the waves so regular, is it the same water washing against the shore all the time?

People lay on the sand, at all angles. He was reminded of moments on the shores of Spectacle Lake when the tide, running out, removed its support from small boats and they sagged sideways heavily on the wet flat sand. Far out, the horizon was lumpy with big waves. Near him, footprints and people disappeared into the water; the footprints forever.

What must fish think when a face bursts in on their world, where it doesn't belong?

As he took his first steps on the sand, he thought of the year before, when he was eight, and it was May, and how surprised and glad he felt when he'd run out of the surf at Driftwood Beach and found the sand colder than the waves. Glad, because it was a new thing he'd found.

On the sand a gull swept in. It shadow sat on the sand

before it landed. The gull folded its wings fussily and looked round to take stock of its situation.

It seemed to Davis Blood, standing in soft dry sand a metre or so above the water's level and about a hundred metres back from the edge, that the people swimming in the surf were tiny bobbing, capering things, distantly related to the human race. In the frames of his eyes, he could not, without an effort, summon up the realisation that they were more than manikins.

With a lofty nine-year-old smile he recognised that an observer, way overhead in the sky, would see them all, sunbathers and surfers, as tiny figures on a strip of sand, and little dots in the water confined to a few metres of the Tasman Sea. No more. Wandering a few metres out to sea, catching a wave, and getting a few metres' ride in to the shore. God must laugh. For some reason it reminded him of moments in front of the television when some special effect happened that looked so unusual that hands involuntarily reached for the control buttons, only to be faced with a notice —

Do not adjust the set.

It meant you were to adjust your expectations, adjust yourself. Get used to the unusual.

Davis Blood was the equal of anyone. In his head it seemed that the strokes needed to swim out past the farthest surfers were few. In his mind he felt the water flying beneath his powerful arms; so powerful that their stroking raised his head and chest above the water he churned, just like the hydrofoil in Sydney Harbour.

He ran towards the sea. Out of the soft dry sand, white in the sun, on to the hard packed wet sand, biscuit-coloured. Into the shallows, jumping the first broken wave, met by the next one at waist height, diving under the next breaking wave, surfacing in the smooth aftermath of the wave, swimming out towards the next, diving under, swimming on. Waist deep in the surf, the sea was a vista of small green hills.

Oddly, the surfers round him were full-sized humans,

not at all as small as he saw them from his earlier distance. He stopped swimming. Three times he tried to catch a wave back to shore as he saw others doing. He had never tried this before. Three times he was carried a metre and the wave rolled on without him. The fourth time he caught a wave much bigger than the rest, that stood over him like a cliff, its seductive cresting body inclined towards him. It lifted him, but where it should have conducted him smoothly to the shore, it broke over him and speared him head first into the sand. He knew what a dumper was.

He got up, rubbed his forehead and chest where he'd hit the sand, and immediately wanted to be back out where the outermost surfers were.

He swam again, dived under the waves as they came, swam when they'd gone. He put his feet down once, the water was chest high. He went out until he was level with the few surfers furthest out, waiting for the best waves.

He kept afloat with his arms, kicked his legs regularly, treading water. He could no longer touch bottom. When were these good waves coming? He kept afloat, waiting with the experts. Once or twice they looked at him, seeing he was nine years of age — how could people tell so quickly? — but nothing showed in their faces.

Perhaps he used too much energy treading water, more than was needed, but the waves began to come too fast at him, he was unready for each successive wall of water. Sometimes he seemed to lose the knack of treading water, and his body wanted to sink. He would try harder, kick faster. Then, without him knowing why, his arms seemed to lose the rhythm, his legs kicked awkwardly and he sank again. When he sank he felt powerless. His arms had no strength. The clear water was a net that held him softly, but with power.

The good wave hadn't appeared that would carry him capably towards the shore.

He didn't feel tired, just puzzled. He couldn't account for the occasional ineptitude and loss of flotation. He took a gulp of water. He didn't mean to. That, too, was a sign of failure. What was happening to him? Another mouthful of water found its way. The taste was wretched.

Next thing he was right under. The pale watery green of the sea filled his eyes. He fought to the surface, as if it had all been a mistake.

There was a deadness in his ears. The world was a long way off.

He went under again. It seemed he had lost all idea of how to stay afloat. Yet he didn't feel tired. Feel? He didn't feel anything. The water was sunny and light, slanting rays pointed down to the sand below.

His head was light. Nothing troubled him, the world was gentle, the water was the softest down, like when he was a baby, on the breasts of his mother.

The world seemed to be floating away, or he was. It didn't matter which. The world, and he, were slow, deadened. Floating, floating, away, away.

He smiled. Under the water he opened his mouth and smiled. Nothing was important. He floated.

Something had him round the chest, he struggled gently. His head was lifted out of the water, it lolled.

The rest of him wriggled, or struggled. It didn't matter which, the movements were feeble. Something pressed his chest, something else waggled his face from side to side, he began to choke and cough, weakly at first, but with increasing urgency.

He heard himself coughing and spluttering, a little before he recognised that it was he.

The big surfer in the red shorts caught a wave, with the boy held in one arm, and deposited him in shallow water. The boy stood, turned towards the sea, the young man turned him firmly towards the shore and said, 'That way, kid,' and gave him a push, waiting to be sure the kid got out of the water.

The boy was desperately giddy, but lots of people were there and watching. He kept an even keel going through the shallowest part; and with his head down left the water and dizzily made his way up the beach, between the bodies, to find his little pile of clothes.

On the towel he lay face down and from time to time water came up and dribbled away through the towel, back into the sand, and eventually back to the sea. For the first time in his life he doubted his omnipotence. He didn't feel much like a lord of anyone's universe; until he felt better, when all his old powers returned.

He felt shaken, though, by this first doubt. What if he'd drowned? When, at home, the last dog had just died, he'd lifted him up and found him floppy and heavier than usual. If he'd drowned he'd be floppy like that. When his cossie had dried he put his clothes on over it.

As he got up to go something occurred to him. When he was first in the water, and when he'd come out, he felt wet; when he was submerged, he hadn't felt wet at all. When he'd looked at his hand, under water, there it was, surfaces dull and ordinary, not wet and glistening; and quite at home surrounded by water. So fish probably didn't feel wet, either, and he'd thought sympathetically of them being wet all their lives, and wet sleeping at night in the dark, hoping they were still alive in the morning.

The Tramp

The young man slowly treading Country Road, coming in from the bush, was medium tall, nut-brown, and dressed in cast-offs.

The boy stopped bouncing a tennis ball and said, 'What's your name?'

The man stopped. 'What's your favourite name?' he asked.

'It's Jonathon.'

'That's my name,' said the man.

'Do you live down the bush?' said the boy.

'In a house with a roof, a floor and one wall.'
The boy thought a bit.
'A cave!' he guessed.
'Right on the head,' said the young man, yawning.
'Do you have a job?'
'No. Only living.'
'Did you ever have one?'
'Never.'
'Are you a swaggie?'
'I carry a swag, yes.'
'What do you do all day?'
'Sit.'
'And think?'
'Sometimes.'
Then the swagman added as an after-thought, 'When I can't help it.' And walked on.
The boy watched Jonathon slouch to the corner and go up Big Hill. He wondered if he'd come from Kangaroo Point, and past Black Snake Corner. But something told him Jonathon wouldn't have noticed, or cared.

What would he do up at Bellbird Corner? Get his dole money, buy cigarettes, some food, go to the pub for beer? Uncle Hector's words came into his head. 'If the drink gets you, you can skip manhood and go straight to middle-age, or skip both and slide into senility.'
He tried to imagine Jonathon ambling round the shopping centre, but couldn't quite. He'd be out of place in Pachelbel's Pizza, or Chaykovsky's Take-away Chicken. He wouldn't be allowed in the Beethoven Bistro or even Mozart's Salami Shop, the way he was dressed. Bach's Beefburgers weren't so choosy, or Vivaldi's Vegetables, but he'd probably head for the public bar at the Bullant Hotel, called the Liplock Bar because it was easy to get into trouble there, and often dangerous. Sometimes to him, Davis Blood, the people up there and the shopfronts looked touching, trivial and human as small babies.
He went inside. Danielle was home. For a while he stood at her door, fascinated by the sight of her record player, as

the sound flowed round him, watching where the stylus touched, unwinding music from the grooved disc.

Now and then he heard the new breed of young swagmen referred to, usually round the table, and usually to wonder what they ate, but the men of the family didn't seem to think there was much in the subject — he knew they were ashamed that Australia couldn't find everyone a job that wanted one — and it was soon dropped. Swaggies didn't get much to eat, apparently.

Next time the boy saw Jonathon the young man was just leaving the bush at the end of the street. He ran into the house and told his mother, 'Jonathon's coming! Can I go and feed him, Mum?'

He was so fired up with anticipation and pleasure that his mother cut and spread two slices of bread and butter without a word.

'What would you like on them?'

'He'd like apricot jam. The thick bits,' he said. Apricot was his current favourite. Lillian bottled a batch of apricots every season since a brilliant and entrepreneurial take-over baron had gobbled up her favourite jam manufacturer and in the name of efficiency abolished the thick bits.

He ran out just in time to intercept the young man, and offered the food.

Jonathon accepted it and sat on the earth bank on the high side of the road to eat. The bread and jam disappeared in four mouthfuls.

'A tap round here?' he said, wiping his lips with a big tongue that had a yellowy-brown stain in the middle. The boy had seen other tongues like that; they belonged to people who smoked. His father had one, and Mrs Vacchini in the fish shop at Bellbird Corner.

'Over there.' The garden tap just inside the fence was turned on and its flow directed into a thirsty mouth.

'Thanks, kid.'

'That's all right, Jonathon.'

'Who?'

'Jonathon. Your name —'

'Oh, that.' He had his drink. 'Sure. See you later.' He went off up the street.

Apricot jam will put strength into him, the boy said to himself, but noted that even this man, someone he'd helped, was trying to trick him. He would continue to think of him as Jonathon, but why hadn't he given his real name? Couldn't he bear the truth? Didn't he know God was in him? Apparently not.

Mister Williams

In fourth grade he began to get into trouble. He began to talk. Mister Williams, an enthusiastic user of the cane, repaid him, every time he was caught, with a stroke of the cane. At the same time he was first in the class in school work.

Perhaps the knowledge that he compared very well with the other kids in schoolwork, in music, singing and drawing, and now in sport in the playground, had an expanding effect on him. He was nailed every day for talking, but not in the least inclined by the brief pain of caning to stop. He enjoyed the notoriety.

His friend in the class, Lawrence Farmer, in answer to the boy's casual question why he was always getting into trouble, said, 'You get into more trouble than the rest of us because you're the cleverest and he's always looking at you.'

Lawrence was going to university when he was old enough. His father was an engineer, and he would be an engineer too. 'If I make the quota,' he said. The boy Davis Blood knew he wouldn't be going to university; his family would need him to be a wage-earner as soon as he could get a job. Nevertheless, he thought it unjust that someone passing the exams as Lawrence would, might not be able to get in, and thought the injustice was obvious.

Mister Williams increased the daily dose of cane to two cuts. He was fair in apportioning praise and punishment, but there was something about giving punishment that satisfied him more than giving praise. What a pity the use of the cane was to be abolished next year in state schools.

The boy's action drawing, in pastel, was outstanding; it was a cricketing moment showing a batsman completing a full blooded on-drive. Mister Williams managed to call him out to the front of the class, to praise him for his work and give him two cuts of the cane for talking, all in the space of a minute.

In the playground at lunchtime, Trent McGarrity held his hand out and said, 'Shake!'

Davis Blood shook hands.

Trent immediately came back: 'Spear!' Digging him in the ribs. And: 'Clip on the ear!' suiting the actions to the words.

It was a new ritual, to be tried out on anyone who didn't know what was coming. Davis Blood grinned, and went looking for Lawrence Farmer, who didn't know it. If he had, he'd have done it to Davis Blood, for sure.

His fingers still felt puffy and thick from the cane, and at one joint a purple mark told of a small blood vessel breached. It hurt to the touch, so he stopped touching it.

Licking Out the Cake Bowl

At home, in the kitchen, this newfound liveliness expressed itself in a bigger appetite. Around come-home time and again around tea-time he was buzzing about the kitchen raiding whatever he could find. If Lillian had a cake mixture in the bowl, he would be there to ask could he scrape out the mixture with his fingers when she'd turned out the rest of it into a baking tin.

Biscuits were never safe, apple peelings were sure to go down him as quickly as he could stuff them in his mouth. His mother watched him with smiling eyes, while her inner song unfolded endlessly.

Then out again he ran for another burst of play before the absolutely final call for tea.

Aunt Ursula did her bit, as she considered it, by giving him the odd reproof when she saw him at it.

'God'll turn you into an ant if you keep on stealing bits here and bits there.'

But he took this no more seriously than he did the other sayings about how, if he crossed his eyes when the wind changed, he would be struck like that with crossed eyes forever. He smiled at her, never knowing how she treasured the smile.

Aunt was left, looking at the spot where that smile had been. She stayed like that for some minutes, still warm from it. She loved him.

'You look at him,' shrilled Aunt Mira, 'as if he's canonisation fodder.' No one knew if Mira loved anyone or not, 'I hope he doesn't turn out to be one of God's hit men, or join the gaberdine swine.'

Ursula wasn't listening. She wheeled herself out of the kitchen, leaving Mira still talking.

'She could at least answer me back with an explanation mark. But I suppose that's asking too much. I always ask too much. Oh, chickens of my childhood, the fanatics of English have come home to roost. They're no help to me. Oh Mira, Mira! Sometimes you're as vast as the earth's orbit round the sun — other times you've shrunk to a corner of this kitchen, grateful for Mozart and a little cocky's joy.' She gave the sort of tremulous sigh that would have made even a stranger suspicious, and went on. 'Still, this turd plant from the sun in the Solace System is not yet a cowering inferno. I'm safe for a few million years yet. If I had a long enough tongue I'd lick out the cake bowl, too.'

Lillian looked across at Aunt Mira, but said nothing. As if she were alone, she sang softly.

'Blessed assurance, Jesus is mine.'

Aunt Mira craned her head forward to listen, but couldn't make out the words. She began to look cross. She didn't understand Lillian. She thought that unless you were abrasive, you weren't alive.

The boy found a line from last Sunday's Meeting running through his head, 'My food is to do the will of Him that sent me.'

It must be good to be sent, to know why you're on the earth and what's expected of you, he thought as he drifted out of the kitchen and into the yard.

He carried the old mattock down the backyard, took off his shirt and put it on Brown Rock in the sun. A minute later, he could be seen bent over, slogging away with the mattock in the soft soil, shifting his feet continually to the right so he made a row of dug earth as he moved sideways. He hadn't checked the mattock head, since he'd had no reason to do it before. When the head flew suddenly off, the light handle sped towards the ground and he had a moment of surprise before the iron head landed on his bent back and slid off to the ground.

It was old, the handle worn. Now it was in pieces. He couldn't leave it like that. No one else could use it, and neither could he. What would it take to fix? Would it be best to cut a sapling and make a handle? But if the head came off, the handle head was too thin, it needed to be made wider — something to pack the business end of the handle so the head would fit tightly.

He scouted round under the house. All he could find was an empty Ardmona peaches tin. He tore off the paper label, found the tin-snips and tried to cut through the top seam of the opened tin. Easier said than done. He used both hands to force the handles of the snips together. Nothing doing. He put his right knee on his upper hand, to force it down. His hands hurt.

Preston came past, stopped to watch. The boy looked up, Preston grinned. The boy repeated his efforts, pressing his weight down on the hands that held the tin-snip handles, to force them together and cut that top seam. He stopped, hands hurting again.

'Keep at it,' Preston said. 'You can do it!' And walked off, making no attempt to help, or even to offer advice. The boy knew what it meant: he was to find his own way there.

It took minutes of solid effort to work that top seam apart, but he did it. He went ahead and cut a rectangular piece of tin. He avoided the seam by making a right angle turn just before he came to it, and cutting back to the first part of the easier cutting.

He rolled a centimetre of the long side back on itself to form a seam, folded the tin round the head of the mattock handle, seam inwards, and laboriously drove a nail through two thicknesses of tin into the wood. The head slid down the handle and jammed itself on the tin collar. He lifted and dropped it, head down, on a rock a few times to make sure it was tight on, then carried it back down the yard to finish the row.

When he got into bed on the verandah that night, the westerlies were beginning. They hit Gunsight Hill, then dipped down to scour the valley. He thought once or twice how he'd like that wind to be full of people, new people, so the valley would be alive with voices and faces.

As evening closed tighter over the world he reflected that the evening air makes some things clearer: points of light, for instance, and the sounds people make. With a valley full of people he'd have plenty of both.

Going to sleep he saw grasses waving in endless paddocks, as when the family passed through wheat country to visit Uncle Hector's property, and Orville walking unsteadily and alone, far away. Orville was more than two years old with dead white skin and black hair before he walked, the family said. A bleeder, too. He watched Orville till he was out of sight. By then he was asleep.

Wit and Wisdom of an Oldest Son

Each day Preston left early for the office and worked late. Poverty had made a deep impression on him: he worked to succeed, to rise up out of and away from his beginnings. He wasn't a warm person, and Davis Blood had little to do with him, beyond hearing the odd argument or piece of talk with his brothers or the older people of the family.

Preston, now twenty-five and still at home, aligned himself with management and employer, where his father and Randal, now eighteen, thought of themselves as workers; his opinions reflected his orientation.

'People in employment,' he said, 'merely hidden social problems.'

He hated taxes. 'The most miserable corner shop, or dilapidated petrol pump, every grotty pub, every greeting-card-selling newsagent is a tax collector for the government.'

'In previous ages, the people wouldn't have stood for it! In our society the freedom to do what you want with your money is too limited. There's some freedom, but not so much that it can't be cut.'

When a new recession lurched like a mudslide down the slope of the economy and swallowed thousands, he would observe that floods make the river seem to be the whole world. When more banks failed or the stock market was scandalised by insider trading or more government controls or takeovers, he assured the family that for everyone burned in the flames there were many delighted by the spectacle of fires.

He joked with Dany about 'this bleak household'. When he was off to a conference on the Sunshine Coast he'd remark that 'Conferences are the opiate of the thinking classes.'

When Randal forgot twenty dollars he'd borrowed, Preston orated smugly, 'He who borrows and forgets, makes an enemy who doesn't.' Randal, though, was a difficult person to scare or impress. Being the family favourite once and now a local hero for his football prowess had given him strengths Preston would never understand.

His brothers hated Preston's wise sayings, but somehow his aura of success, being a company secretary, shielded him from their comments.

Looking over Orville's shoulder when he had his history book out for a project on Captain Cook's voyages, he said cleverly, 'History says that no one cares.'

Talking to Aunt Ursula he once said, 'Democratic socialism? How? If the process is democratic, how do you get socialism? If it's socialism, how does such a system tolerate opposition?' And Aunt Ursula had no answer, but that was because she agreed. Preston thought because her opinions often dug down to the roots of a question, that she was one of the ineffable Left.

But the passage that Davis Blood best remembered

occurred when Randal had a new sort of girlfriend; not one he boasted about, but about whom he was strangely silent, whose name brought on a diffidence and seriousness he'd never shown before. Randal was popular with girls, he seemed to move in a cluster of them.

'When you're young,' advised Preston, 'you're likely to take falling in love seriously — it's probably the first time you've thought much of anyone else.'

Randal took it; didn't take the bait or get angry.

Danielle came to the rescue by saying, 'And how's your string of girlfriends, Preston?'

There was no answer for a while, then, 'It's cheaper to hate than to love,' he said, and considered he'd got out of that trap well, and went back to his management studies in statistics.

Danielle knew her parsimonious brother well: he thought up sayings about the world and people instead of having to spend time — and money — engaging with them.

The Lady Vivian

Going home from school along Station Street, he passed a woman who brought her cats on to the front lawn at just that time. She began to talk to him each day. The cats were both large and beautiful animals, and so was she.

He began to stop there every day. She introduced him to the cats, Burke and Wills, which he genuinely admired. A pause followed in which he didn't know what to say, so he asked her if she'd like a cup of tea, as if they were at his place and Mum would get the tea.

She was happy with this idea, and insisted he come in.

He put his schoolbag on a chair and he thought she'd put the kettle on straight away. What she did was suddenly to grab him to her and hug him. He wasn't ready for it, and had to lever himself loose a bit, to breathe, for she was strong.

'The tea,' he said, struggling. She let him go and said, 'Yes, the tea,' and went to the kettle but she seemed to be looking back as if she thought he'd slip out. She put the kettle on.

'Call me Vivian,' she said.

She looked at him in an interested way, asking him to sit down and pulling her chair close to his.

They had their cups of tea.

Next day was a Friday. She asked him in straight away and the tea was ready. She seemed glad he liked his cup of tea, and gave him sweet biscuits. He loved sweet things. The cats watched from a distance, up on a bureau, their tails hanging down the sides of the polished timber, until Vivian decided that the cats were too important to be absent. She got them and sat close to the boy. She smelled sweet and glamorous, not like his mother, who smelled good without perfume. She held the cats so he could pat them and had them partly on her knees and partly on his, so their knees touched.

The skin of her knees seemed to have a kind of padding; he could feel there was bone underneath, but there was padding over the bone, and it felt delicious in a funny way. He hoped she didn't worry that his boy's knees weren't like that: his didn't hide the bone at all.

They found the sofa was more comfortable than two separate chairs. The cats were still on both their laps, and with the weight of both of them on the sofa, they seemed to gravitate towards the middle. Their legs were side by side, and hers were warm, much warmer than his mother's when he felt her against him. Their arms too, though hers were much bigger than his. She admired the light tan on his arms and legs and would persist in rubbing her hands over them as she said these things. His mother liked them too, and often rubbed her hands over them, but Vivian made him feel differently about it, in some way. Her hands were warm — as warm as Randal's or Orville's.

Her face reminded him, as he walked home, of a picture he'd seen of Adam and Eve in the Garden of Eden. They ate of the tree of knowledge of good and evil, but what did that mean? Why was it called the fall? To know seemed like a step up.

He remembered when he was tiny, and there were no crimes when he was alone in the bush. Perhaps good and evil came with there being more than one person.

Something bothered him about her face, but he didn't know what it was. He felt good that he knew another person, outside his family, who was warm, interested and nice to him.

Aunt Mira

At home in the kitchen scouting for something to eat, he asked Aunt Ursula: 'How is it Aunt Mira knows so much? She looks as if she's listening to a voice the rest of us can't hear.'

'Clever, isn't she?' answered Ursula. The other aunt was asleep, apparently.

'Where was she educated? I mean, who would have educated her?'

'She educates us, I think, but I admit she's uncanny, some of the things she knows. To listen to her, you'd think she always had her beak in a book.'

'Beak!' shouted Aunt Mira. 'O Pioneers! Analogy is the brother of assumption. Beak, indeed! Stop playing football with my associations!'

'Nose, then,' the boy said.

'Your king and country needs you!' Mira shouted. 'Needs you dead! Why is this house always in a beggar's muddle?'

Aunt Ursula's mouth stretched sideways across her face in the shape of a fallen-down triangle. She was smiling.

'Relax,' she said to Aunt Mira. 'Calm down.'

'No! Buck up! That's what's needed,' said Mira. 'Rome wasn't burned in a day! Who built the leaning tower of pizza? Who burned the book of love? Who fiddled with Nero while Rome burned?'

'I'll put a match to your tail,' said Aunt Ursula. 'That'll bring you back to the field. You old troll.'

'While I'm trawling the memory banks for verbal fish, you can go and shovel smoke!' advised Aunt Mira. 'Put a match to my tail, will you? The proper match for my tail is your face!'

'That's naughty, Aunt Mira,' the boy said, reprovingly.

'I want a bill of rights and wrongs!' shouted Mira. 'And so should you, guaranteeing life, liberty and the pursuit of girls. I believe in women's libido, the threat of liberation, that prose is prose is prose; in the vacillation of children, the de-snarling of society, that a man's best friend is his dogma, and that we are dreams of God.'

'I didn't know you believed in God, Aunt,' the boy said. 'That God exists, I mean.'

'Of course I do. I wouldn't want to believe in a God that didn't exist, would I? I admire all things and people that have gone beyond the limits of flesh. I believe in marriage, too,' she added with a cunning look.

'You!' said Aunt Ursula.

'The treaty of marriage is a fine thing, as long as it's supplemented by the protocol of love, and there's not too much emphasis on the genital singular.'

'What's that, aunt?' the boy said.

'What are the thirteen stages of man?' Aunt Mira Mitchell demanded by way of answer. 'I'll tell you. It's the story of the eternal misfortune of males, like Sisyphus, pushing their stones to supreme effort on the high peaks of love and having the whole enterprise collapse to square one. The stages are: agile, ductile, flexile, volatile, protrusile, labile, erectile, tensile, fissile, fragile, contractile, docile; thirteen is retractile, the last stage of all, and a preparation for the return of the first stage.'

'I think that's over the fence, Mira,' said Aunt Ursula.

'I think it's over his head, that's what I think. It'll be sometime yet before he encounters a warm statue and enters the lists of lust, and years before he sinks into the monologue of marriage. Just as well, too, with the Great Gynaecologist in the sky making sex so possible, the Great Joker in the sky making men and women so impossible, and the Great Epidemiologist in the sky making things so dicey.'

'Do you believe in Heaven, Aunt?' said the boy.

'Ah,' Mira said. 'To live forever, in light clothes. How charming. But among a million multitudes of amateur musicians? No! The orchestra's too limited and praise is boring.'

'But you believe in God!'

'I believe what I believe. You just see that you develop a feeling for women, a feeling for their geography, for their arts and sciences, ready for that first Gropius in the dark at the architecture of love. Just ignore their history, that's all. Oh, love! When assault has lost its savour, shall thy blunders be known in the dark?'

'He's only a boy, Mira,' Aunt Ursula said.

'Only! Lucky sod. Look at all the miseries he won't have, won't even know of, all his life long. Blithe spirits all! Hale and male and hearty! Everything simple and single! The universe measured by it, life and people sensed through its sensitive head, everything mediated by the male member and its moods! A fishing rod for floundering! Non-metal meat hook! Divining rod for underground streams!'

The boy was listening. Aunt Ursula was about to interject, when Mira took a lateral verbal leap.

'The Lost Verses of Cock Robin!' she announced.

'Who killed Cock Robin?' she demanded of the boy.

'I, said the sparrow, with my bow and arrow, I killed Cock Robin,' answered Davis Blood.

'Ah,' she said, 'but: who took his gear?'

'I, said the mole, to furnish my hole, I took his gear.'

'Who plucked Cock Robin?'

'I, said the crow, to teach myself how, I plucked Cock Robin.'

'Who took his feathers?'

'I, said the cat, to make a new hat I took his feathers.'

'Who's got his wife?'

'I, said the mouse, now she lives in my house I've got his wife.'

'Who ate his chicks?'

'I, said the mynah, for Sunday dinner I ate his chicks.'

'Who told the fuzz?'

'I, said the magpie, 'Cos I didn't get any, I told the fuzz.'

'Now, come on, join in! All the birds of the air were a-sighing and a-sobbing!' sang Aunt Mira, but the boy was silent.

Something in him whispered that though the differences between him and girls were shaping up to be altogether more complicated and dangerous than he thought, they ought to be plain and simple. But perhaps that was his 'simple and single' maleness, as Aunt Mira put it.

She was still talking, in that headlong way of hers. 'Forgive us our Christmases, as we forgive those that Christmas against us.' As if the words might fail and drop and die if she didn't give each one a vigorous push.

Not Often Enough

If some nasty kid raced round the corner of a school building and put out an arm towards the head of the first kid in reach and laid that kid flat on the asphalt, there would be blood and yells and the vicious kid hidden safely in the multitude milling round the basketball game.

Davis Blood was often asked to take the still-weeping kid home after first-aid.

Their mothers were sometimes home and gave him things to eat by way of reward. Once he got a plate of the previous night's beef stroganoff, and when he said, 'No, thank you,' the mother said, 'That's funny, he wouldn't eat it last night.' He was the injured kid.

At home, Lillian would tell him how nice it was of him to do good deeds like that, as if it were a sacrifice. She also told him how pretty he was, how good, how clever, how nice it was that he was never the one to be brought home sick. It was all part of being a good boy, and loved by his mother.

Anyone looking at him might have said, 'There's a kid that's sometimes scared, sometimes full of courage; sometimes greedy, sometimes generous; a mixture of good and bad; a normal boy of nine who may grow up to be a normal man, even a good one.'

But his mother said he was wonderful, beautiful, and strong, and sang like an angel and was the cleverest boy in the class, any class, and he believed her.

After she'd let herself go in this way she often burst into one particular song, as he had a drink of milk or something to eat, or waited to lick out the cake bowl.

> 'Come let us join our cheerful songs
> With angels round the Throne.
> Ten thousand thousand are their tongues
> But all their joys are one.'

Ten thousand thousand. That's ten million, he thought. That's not many. And looked in the fridge for something more to eat.

Some time before, he'd sat for a test, having only a hazy idea what its purpose was. Now, his father had word in the post that Davis Blood had gained entry to a class for 'gifted children', for the last two years of primary, and was to report to 1 Wycliff Street, Archerfield, in the new year, twenty-five kilometres away.

As he ate a sandwich he wondered what it would be like

to travel so far every day. It didn't bother him any more than that, and in fact he didn't think of it again. For as he looked up, and out of the kitchen window, he saw the daytime moon almost transparent, like a sliver of something cool that was dissolving and soon would be gone.

Without knowing why, he wondered if anyone knew whether now, here on earth, was now everywhere else in the universe.

The news that he was officially a gifted child did nothing to dim his mother's praises. She spoke about greatness, a future full of radiance, glory, fame. Sometimes he got sick of hearing it, but not often enough.

Constellations in his Head

As he grew older, his talkative phases became fewer. There were so many things to see and hear and draw into himself, so many new ideas thrown up by each new word, that these processes would be blocked, he felt, or at least hindered, by periods of giving out — for then he took nothing in.

'He's no talker,' the family began to say.

'He used to be,' his mother said. After a while even she didn't say it aloud, but continued to say it to herself. She hugged to herself every remembered scrap of his early days, for this was the bright one, the beautiful lively one she'd hoped for. The liveliness of the others was pale alongside the life in him. Yet how short a time it was: already she was beginning to live on memories.

Each day it seemed there were so many more things in the world than his father hinted, his teachers showed, or his books described, for behind the things he saw round him, he caught glimpses of other, related things stretching away into the distance. Behind a smile he saw all sorts of other smiles with different purposes and meanings; behind a bulldozed field he saw destruction and calamity extending to many countries, also the preparations for new fields, new towns, revised ways of life. Behind a sudden anger he saw the approach of silent revenge, passionate competition, murders, wars. Behind his own request for a second helping of his mother's bread pudding he could see, clustered like stars, pictures of starving children, splendid banquets, fields of grain, orchards, animals grazing, Oliver Twist, snackbars, slaughter lines in an abattoir, produce displays at the Easter Show, lines of kids at school getting spooned booster shots on their tongues, retarded children locked away in attics for thirty years chained to beds and fed on the floor, his brother Randal having steak for breakfast before playing football on Sunday afternoon for the district team in first grade.

There were so many things in his head. Each sight or sound or feeling, each person, each word, was surrounded by constellations of others.

He only had to think the word to make others visible. Then they teemed round him, coruscating, tumbling pellmell like water released from a dam; teemed and multiplied for a great way into the distance, until they seemed infinite. So much, and all spun from a word.

He didn't have this feeling all day. Perhaps a little at a time was all he could cope with.

Everything, he reflected, must have a sort of infinity in it, and each thing linked up with each other thing.

So their infinities intermeshed. He could just begin to get a picture of it in his head.

Like Dust

'Men?' Lillian said sharply, and was silent. Didn't even move her lips in song. The room waited, and Aunt Ursula.

Aunt Mira had fallen asleep in her corner after saying, 'The tax man can spell every name.'

'Males,' Lillian began again. Then, vaguely, 'They are here, sometimes here among us. We have no real contact.'

And stopped, as if talking in a dream. Or making a poem. She remained in the same position for minutes, then turned and started to sift flour, ready to begin making scones.

'Can we have dates in them today?' asked the boy, as if deaf to what had been said. But he heard.

His existence, and that of all males, had never been so problematical as in those minutes. They could all have blown away like dust. But they hadn't blown away. He was here, and he would like dates in his scones.

His mother turned her head and smiled full at him and said, 'Certainly,' though not with her eyes. He knew from her calm, withdrawn eyes, that she went on thinking within herself. Then her song began again.

It was good to have a mother who thought; even better to have a mother possessed by song.

Now and then Mira made a little snore. Aunt Ursula watched the boy and his mother, looking from one to the other.

Suddenly his mother had her arms round him, kissing his face. He twisted and turned, fending her off hard with one hand, then relented and gave her a tidy and judicious peck on the cheek.

'Don't do that!' Lillian said, frustrated and pained.

'I've got to have some power over you!' he said and stepped back. She looked at him sadly, but her song continued. He heard it in her. Then she smiled, and sang aloud:

'O love divine, how sweet you are.'

He felt relieved. She was over it, that thing inside her, whatever it was. He escaped to the backyard.

Foxes have holes, birds have nests, but I have the yard to play in, and it's the August holidays.

Behind her inner song, she continued to think. Men were little children that never grew up, never became sensible creatures. Well, except one or two, who help us in our destiny. They spend their lives sitting on their bottoms, counterweights to good order and regularity, hatching ways and means to gain what isn't theirs, hatching conspiracies against order and stability, hatching treasons of the spirit, wars and destruction.

We keep life going, keep the world family washed, clothed, fed.

We provide continuance, new life to replenish the old.

All things pass away; mothers and females continue.

Underneath it all, she was deeply sorry for men. All they had, to soothe them, was objects: things. Often they would invent objects, which complicated life, but nothing could fill the void in them.

Making

He made two things that afternoon. First, the woomera; the Aboriginal stick for throwing other sticks. He split a length of sapling about a metre long, using the axe and its weight to separate the halves. In the centre of one half, he cut — with the steel penknife Uncle Hector had given him on his last visit — a groove that ran nearly the length of the wood, then stopped three fingers' width from the end. The spear would lie in the groove, its end hard against the end, so that when he threw the spear by using the length of the thrower as an extension of his arm, the spear would travel faster and further.

His father had told him what a sophisticated idea this was. Not quite on a par with the boomerang, but nearly. It occurred to him that two pieces of cord, with a patch of soft leather in the middle just like the Biblical picture of King David's sling, would very likely do the same job, so when he had tested the woomera with two lengths of bamboo as spears, he found some thick string in the toolbox and a piece of leather cut from the tongue of an old shoe. He cut two slits, one each side of the leather — the steel penknife was very sharp — put one end each of the strings through the slit and bound a holding loop in the string with thin twine. With a loop in one string, for his wrist, and a stone in the leather, he had a sling. He threw a stone, for practice, and marvelled at the distance it travelled. He put a bamboo spear in the leather and holding it as he held the woomera, threw the spear. Yes, it worked in much the same way, but it was more satisfying with the stone. He tried ever larger stones till he found the best size, and sent that whistling down into the bush where it tore through the leaves of tree after tree, and, crashing into something he couldn't see, dropped to the ground, and was silent.

The big eastern branch of Orville's tree was heavy enough now to support a swing. He copied his father's method with the swing under the house, by digging out an old leather schoolbag and wrapping two pieces of it round the branch to stop the rope digging into the tree-flesh. There was rope under the house, and someone always left a bald tyre or two around. He rigged up two lengths of sashcord and tied each to an old tyre.

He had his first swing on Orville's willow tree at the start of its sixth year of life.

Holidays were good for making things. You had the time to yourself.

Dennis Yarwood

The sixth grade boy, playing cricket in the fifth and sixth area, sent the ball down to the batsman with all his speed. It was good, Davis Blood thought, seeing how quickly it reached the spot a metre and a half in front of the bat, after it left Yarwood's hand. All the batsmen were scared of him.

The boy watched until it was time to go in to school. He wanted to bowl like that.

He put the thought away, till next year, when he'd be allowed into the fifth and sixth play area. Meantime, he got hold of some old tennis balls that Randal and Orville used to play with and began to bowl at home after school.

He used an uphill run-up — all he had — and bowled against a small brick wall behind the laundry. He found he could get the ball down to the chalk-drawn wicket fairly quickly, and soon was able to get it to hit within the borders of the stumps about four times out of eight.

In the playground he waited on the edges of the bigger

boys' game — each day after school practising — until one lunchtime, five minutes before the boys were due to go back into their classrooms, he found he was near the ball, which was rolling loose after a hit, with no one running up to claim it and have a bowl.

Before anyone could stop him he ran to the bowlers' run-up, and, taking the same distance as Dennis Yarwood, ran full pelt up the bowling crease and let one go as hard and fast as he could. It wasn't straight, passing outside the wicket, but the batsman hadn't seen it bounce. Someone grabbed the ball, but a teacher on playground duty saw the fourth grade boy have his bowl, and made the boy who picked it up give it to the 'new bowler', as he called Davis Blood.

'This time don't try to bowl so fast,' he advised.

This was interesting. The rules about the fourth trespassing on the area belonging to the fifth and sixth were set in stone, as far as he'd heard, but here was a teacher, breaking them. Apparently, if there was a good enough reason, the rules could be waived.

The boy went back to the mark and did another run-up, trying to bowl faster than before. This time the batsman saw it but was too late getting his bat down to it. The ball yorked him and hit the wicket, which consisted of three stumps fixed into a block of wood.

The bell went. The kids poured back into school. The teacher asked the new bowler his name, and he went into class feeling a strange elation; more than when he was praised for other things he did well; far more than for his drawings, or singing, or for getting no mistakes in spelling.

The Birth Mark

The Lady Vivian was waiting for him, with her cats. When they were sitting in the darkened lounge with a cup of tea, she asked if he had any birth marks. He did. There was one right up the back of his left leg. She was interested in everything about him and often in the same things his mother found interesting. His body, for instance, and what he was like, inside. No one else was so interested, not even Aunt Ursula. Aunt was more inspiration than affection, he supposed. She pointed him outwards to the world.

The Lady Vivian was like Lillian, and then again she wasn't. The thing that really warmed him that day about being with her had to do with the fight he'd just had. At least it was one on one, and no kicking. Not that he'd told her, but having come from the excitement of combat and having felt for five or ten minutes that it was Keith Pooley or him, then to come into this quiet comfortable place where the only people were interested in him in a completely personal and wrap-around way, was a feeling of luxury such as he had never felt since he was a baby, when it was natural as breathing.

He was absorbed in these thoughts, and, being absorbed, even helped the Lady Vivian ease down his school pants, the better to see his birth mark.

'Oh, here it is!' she exclaimed with what he could only interpret as delight. Her delight warmed him.

His underpants were still on. His mother liked him to wear underpants. To keep him together there, she said.

Her fingers wandered over the place, and it was good.

'We are good friends, aren't we?' she said.

'Yes, sure,' he said. He felt they were good friends.

'You don't mind me looking at your birth mark, do you?'

'No.'

'What I mean is, if people are good friends, then the

things about them, the personal things, the things they cover up usually, well, they're not rude or anything to friends, are they?'

'No, I don't think so.'

'Neither do I,' she said warmly. 'I think everything about friends is part of being friends, whether it's your teeth or having a headache, or a birth mark, or what you did in the holidays or whether you like cats, or if you don't like tapioca pudding.'

'Urk,' he said. 'I hate tapioca. I've never liked that.'

'Neither have I,' she responded in a husky warm voice, her hands feeling good and friendly down the sides of his legs. Those soft parts on the insides of her fingers were certainly wonderful to feel on your skin. Sort of dry, so they slid over you. It was funny how you have delicious feelings in the most unexpected places, like the outside of your thigh, and several places on your knee. She was particularly gentle with the two halves of his bottom. She seemed to know where to find the good places.

He felt happy that he didn't feel wary about her, perhaps because she was so keen on everything about him.

'If you came one day and I happened to be just out of the bath when I came to the door, you wouldn't feel embarrassed, would you?'

He imagined she meant if she had her bathrobe on or a towel round her like his mother, or Danielle.

'I don't think so,' he said.

'Well, you sound confident about that,' she replied.

'I am confident.'

'Because we're friends.'

'Sure, yes.'

The Lady Vivian, in that deepish voice, also encouraged him to talk. She opened a large atlas, and with the boy close, showed him details of countries he'd never seen before except in the coarse outlines of the maps in school books. Gradually, she nudged him towards making up little 'imaginos' as she called them, about the deserts, promontaries, clusters of islands they encountered on the page. They sat close.

When he got home he felt strange, at first, that she wasn't there. Several times he wanted to say things that he would only have said to her.

If only a person could go everywhere and see every place on earth; if only the recording machines had been invented long ago, and you could see the interesting bits of history all over and over until you felt familiar with them. If only a person could get to know everyone on earth.

Sharing

The two boys were walking home from school past the windows of a place where big men played pool, and drank and hung about all day. A thing, a piece of something — it was paper — flew and wavered out of the window and settled like a big red leaf to the ground. It was a twenty dollar note.

Howard Spillane, the boy with Davis Blood, sprang forward as if he were the quickest boy in the world, and picked it up. Davis stood there. He was just as quick in springing forward as Howard, but the prohibition against taking what belonged to others was fixed in his mind and had not yet been overcome by experience and opportunity.

'That was bit of luck,' he said as Howard looked at the money. 'I've never found money in the street before!'

'You haven't found any now,' Howard said, pocketing the note and making things clear.

The boy Blood was puzzled. Howard had been friendly for a week or two, as if a bond was beginning. It seemed finding money put a stop to that. A small thing to get in the way of being friends.

Two men came pounding up behind them. Howard ran, legs going at a great rate, not bothering to look behind him.

'Look out!' he called. 'They've got us!'

Davis sensibly stood still. 'No,' he called back. 'They've got you!'

So that was another friend he didn't have.

Caddying

A pity, too, because he was one of the kids to announce his intention of going, in the holidays, to the Golf Course at Applegreen Water to caddy. It was a private course, with high fees, and wealthy golfers played there. He'd thought it would be good to have kids there that he knew.

In the event, of all the boys who'd said they would, only Davis Blood turned up. He made it a regular thing for Saturdays, and got good pocket money at Applegreen Golf Course for two years until just after he was twelve and began work delivering groceries for the Cooks.

After three weeks he became regular caddy for Mr Priestley, who had his round of golf with Mr Small, who had a close connection with chocolate manufacturing.

In the caddies' hut were boys from the district who sat, played cards, smoked and joked. He stood apart from them. He didn't know their jokes and could see no point in their constant testing abuse of each other. They swore so much that he imagined he could feel the words in the air, and sticking to him. He walked away. It was his fourth Saturday as a caddy. It was hot and sunny. On the way to the course at Applegreen Water he found himself pedalling automatically, his eyes full of the landscape ahead, which seemed to be stretched out like a banner, then a painting in which most things were still, though one or two moved without disturbing the painting's stillness. He was looking fixedly at this painting; he couldn't tear his eyes from it. It was as if he had no other existence, but was a pair of eyes only.

Cars were passing and crowding him towards the side of the road. One touched his elbow. He must wake up!

He was awake, wasn't he? No, his face and eyes felt locked hard in the static vision ahead. He shook himself, gripped the handlebars more tightly, struggling and fighting against the landscape painting and its unreality. He was in danger. He forced his eyes wide, worked his face muscles, and at last banished the feeling that he was living in a dream. But he had to guard against it, for it kept wanting him to slide back into his dream-state.

Once on the course, he indulged it. It was easy to slip in and out of it; all he had to do was remember to follow the flight of the golf balls. But the grip it had on him wasn't the same tight lock that had frozen him when he was on his bike.

Slipping into that state, he smiled inwardly at the thought of how like that funny boy up in Station Street he must seem, the one who would stop in the middle of the street, traffic and all, and begin to stare into himself.

Near the fifth tee, in an adjoining paddock, were cows, Friesians with high straight backs. As he waited for the men to hit off he saw three cows munching in a group, as if conferring. As he watched, one stopped chewing and looked round. The other two turned their heads, and for a while all three stared at him, mouths still. Then one by one they began to chew again, and looked away.

Caddying was a time for letting all sorts of things pass through his mind, the old man up the street at Bellbird, for instance, who never lifted his head but always watched the ground and walked so slowly it seemed his shadow was dragging him back.

The boy thought of the ground the old man looked at.

Was he fascinated by his future home in the earth, or afraid?

His beloved steel penknife, that he always carried in his right-hand trouser pocket, reminded him of how he'd cut his finger with it when he was trimming a piece of wood. Yet, even during and after the cut, he still loved his penknife, where if it had been something else, he'd have hurled it away from him in a rage

      As they walked in from the ninth green, he saw golf bags and buggies stacked outside the golf professional's shop. It reminded him of coming home from school one Friday afternoon and seeing a heap of something dull stacked over by the far corner of the verandah. It was only Grandma, indulging in sunlight. He didn't like her and she didn't like him, but her dislike came first.

The Judas Dream

      That same night the boy had a nightmare about Judas Iscariot. It had been four years since he heard the story of the betrayal of Jesus; now it had surfaced in a dream. This time he didn't lie awake wet and uncomfortable, but had the nightmare last thing before he woke in the morning. The story played itself over and over in his head after he'd dressed, had breakfast, and was on his way to school.

Judas was receiving the thirty pieces of silver, he was knotting the rope, he was hanging from the branch of a tree, ceaselessly, over and over. Even going in the school gate they were still counting the silver into Judas' hand. They got to thirty and started over again. The dream-play began to stop in the one spot and rehearse only one episode: counting the silver, getting to thirty and starting all over again. And again and again. It wouldn't stop, no matter what else he tried to think of.

When will Judas go and kiss Jesus? When will he get to the end of the story, so maybe it would stop? Then he could replace it with something else, like: I am the resurrection and the life. How could a person be the resurrection? Resurrected, yes. He could understand that, but to be the resurrection itself.

Will I ever understand things? he asked. All the people at the Meeting seemed to understand. They wouldn't just sit there if they didn't, would they? Surely they'd put their hands up and ask.

The Seated Potato

At home, alone on the verandah, he took out his pencil and the loose sheets of paper Preston had given him to draw on. It was a natural thing for him to do, he always felt good alone with his thoughts. The continual conversation inside his head, between him and himself, himself and others, or even taking the ways and words of others and rehearsing them to others again; this conversation, with its constant words, was impossible when he had to go and play with other kids. He could not have been himself without this regular internal dramatisation.

He drew a portrait of a potato sitting in style in a kitchen chair; a wall-mirror reclining on a sofa; a hoe sitting at table; a lion pleasantly taking a ride on a carousel among young children; a book lying in a bed; an elaborate polished chair lecturing an audience of spindly scuffed chairs; an engraved foundation stone — or coronation stone? — under the baby's high chair he used a few years before; a girl making up her face, which consisted of rocks and trees.

As he did the last one he was humming a tune. He sang some of the words, then hummed a bit. The words he sang sounded like: 'At the cross, at the cross, where I first saw the light, and the burden of my sins rolled away.' His absent-minded humming and singing as he worked seemed to him rather like a dream where things seem to happen independently of the dreamer.

Other things impinged on this dream-state. The music his brothers played in their room, for instance; kept down to a volume of sound considerably less than they felt happy with, at Jackson Blood's command, who referred to all their favourite groups and bands by the one name: 'Tawdry and Grot'.

The boy was accustomed to their music, though he'd never felt drawn to it. Perhaps he'd feel more affinity with it when he got older, though he doubted that he ever would.

For a minute he stopped, looking at his pencil. Were the drawings somehow in that lead? He smiled at the idea, reminding himself of the first time he saw a violin played, looking intently at the strings and the many-stringed and wondering the same thing: was the music in the strings? He was very young, then. Which promoted another question: was that small child somehow in his head?

Dream Day in the Holidays

There had been so many stories of nuclear accidents in different parts of the globe that each time the clouds grew hot and heavy, massed and grey, he wondered if perhaps they were tainted and carried death in the raindrops. But you couldn't stay inside all the time — that wasn't living. It was the last Friday of the holidays. He sat on the side of his bed on the verandah.

The valley below was full, he thought with wonder, full of air; some of it, the heaviest, settling under rocks he knew by touch and by sight, round trees and among plants dwarfed by other living things, yet never intimidated.

He went down the back steps, into the yard, down the three terraces to the bottom one, patted Orville's tree and sat on Brown Rock.

Brown Rock seemed placid at first, but its knowledge went deeper, he could see. It knew about nuclear things and wasn't shaken. The grains of sand that formed it contained God; each grain knew what it was. If one fell off, no matter, it could only fall into the everlasting. There was nowhere unsafe.

Around him rose silently the breath of the deep soil, and the smell of recent rain on the pine needles a little way down in the bush. Two bulbuls flew into a tree, then into another, then further away towards the neighbours' fruit trees.

He sat, arms round one raised knee, and looked directly overhead into the blue holes between clouds. He saw a hawk, stationary, high in the air over the valley, the feathers at the tips of its wings spread like hands. He waited for the descent that would signal an attack, but it didn't come. He nursed the thought that God was in the hawk and the bird knew. And didn't mind not being human, or a fish; but rather, proud to be as it was.

As he dreamed, it became that special morning when, like arrows from the north, dipping down out of the sky, the swallows are suddenly there, making the air look easy with their lilting flight up high and, swift as darts, dangerous with their low jet plane attack and aristocratic climbing turns. He was delighted by their artistry, and watched a while, then got up and walked through the bush to Kangaroo Point, where he stood on wide flat Point Rock, and looked down. Below Kangaroo Point, North Fork from his left joined West Fork from the right, and flowed south-east to the sea together; their combined shape reminiscent of a water diviner's rod.

He scrambled down the rocks, headed for North Fork, passed Wineglass Rock and Indian Head, crossed North Fork and walked all the way due east to Driftwood Beach. He stepped, clambered and jumped over the tumbled rocks at the north end of the beach.

The high cliff tops were undercut by wind, waiting to unbalance; upside-down rock pools were fretted out of the undersides of the precarious shelves of rock. He went looking for rock pools lined with pink, home to oysters, sea-eggs, snails. He put his finger into open anemones to feel them suck, and to check if they were warm. They weren't. As they closed over in response to his touch the pattern of white shell bits on the deep dark of their outer tendrils was like a miniature rockery.

Round the cliffs, layers of hard stone alternated with soft. Some soft layers were only the width of a hand, and in some of them, many metres below the cliff top, small rounded pieces of quartz were embedded. A number were being extruded by the erosion of the sandy rock holding them.

He picked one out. It was the same size as many he'd seen and touched in Bread and Butter Creek, and as smooth. That layer of soft stone was once a creek-bed, under all that rock. How many ages had passed since then?

He was thinking of it still, as he wandered slowly back down the beach. The sand, when the sea retreated, was flat as concrete. Where the waters of the lagoon slipped down to the ocean within their channel, the sand was ribbed, as if carved.

He trudged up the sand, onto the grass, and made for the edge of the bush. A swarm of gnats brought out by the warm day surrounded his head. The hills never go on holiday, he reflected, or the bush, or the sea. Nor do they have to go to school. They just are.

Coming back to the house as the day was being watered down to evening, the gardens front and back with their flowers and vegetables were not full of plants so much as reasons growing, reasons for his parents to work, reasons to care. By contrast, the plantain that he twisted over and fired like a gun, the soft dandelion, the different grasses in their seasons, summer grass and winter grass, grew with no assistance. They were his, they meant neither care nor work.

At the kitchen table, tranced still by the day, he looked at his food. The chop was a part of one of those lambs he'd seen pictured in his early kids' books, and in cutouts pasted round the rooms of kindergarten. The pictures gave no hint of the taste of lamb.

He was in bed but all the fish in the oceans of the world were in water all night and if they slept, slept suspended. They had no beds to lie on, and no backs or sides on their bodies that were comfortable for lying down. They had no roofs, walls or doors to keep out the monsters hunting them in the blackness.

It was lovely between the sheets as the westerly blew over the verandah railing, just above his head. Such comfort! Dinner had been awash with thick gravy. Just as he closed his eyes ready for sleep to take him, the thought elbowed its way into his head: who paid? What did it cost that I'm well fed? Who died that I might be full? Was the animal terrified in those last minutes when it knew that what it feared, what it had heard rumoured, was horribly true, and there was no way out? Did it wish it had long sharp teeth, and claws, so it could die fighting and inflict injuries before the knife came into its warm and secret parts?

Despite his sympathy for the lamb that died to feed him, he fell asleep immediately.

Reality Time

Coming home from the shops at Bellbird Corner carrying a plastic shopping bag of meat and butter, he pulled up short at the front gate to find Lillian belting into Jackson Blood on the front verandah.

After one moment of intense dismay, he realized it was a game. Lillian was punching Jackson Blood on the back, the side, and whichever shoulder presented itself. The boy noticed her fists: the thumb was forward, not wrapped round the knuckles. He winced, knowing how easily her thumb could be hurt against his father's tough bones, in that position.

He came up to them. His father's face was frowning with mock pain and terror. His mother saw the boy.

'Now I'll turn him round,' she said, and did so.

'Why?' said Davis Blood.

'To do the other side,' she explained, between punches. Her man's arms were crossed over his chest.

'You see,' said Lillian, 'it's his reality time. A few dozen more and he'll be done.'

How was it, he thought, that he didn't know his parents played games like this? Did he really know nothing about them?

'Mona Lisa'

Among his sister's art books he found a reproduction of the 'Mona Lisa'. He had heard references to the 'Mona Lisa' since he'd been a small boy, picking the strange words out of the air and putting them in the part of his head where unattached references were biding their time, waiting for another phrase to make them clearer. He felt no anxiety about their unfinished state. They wouldn't go away.

Aunt Ursula came wheeling up.

'Mona Lisa!' she said loudly. 'Too fat! The background: absurd! That sarcastic grin! To think they call it an ineffable smile!'

'What's ineffable?'

Then regretted it immediately. He knew ineffable from the Meeting: why did he have to pretend ignorance? Aunt didn't need propping up. He should try being himself, rather than trying to appear ten years of age.

'Something you can't get your tongue around. You can't find words to describe it,' she said in her usual voice, then went back to her loud-voiced comments, 'it's just sarcastic, I tell you. Derision and sarcasm about to break out like measles.'

The boy looked at his aunt.

'Never heard me like this before, I suppose?'

He said nothing, waiting for her to tell him.

'Well. Well, I suppose,' she said in a lesser voice, 'I suppose I was just trying to find something wrong with it. People keep saying how perfect it is. You can't take that sort of thing for ever, you know.'

The boy was more interested in the background of the painting, the queer green hills and the trees. Why were they there? Why were they like that? What world did they come from? It wasn't this one.

They didn't form a background that receded gradually from the plump woman's figure: they were miles away, looking unnatural. He thought the artist might as well have drawn some other design to put round the plump figure, for she certainly didn't look as if she was out in the open air. Were they — it was a new thought — not the background of the figure, but the background needed for the colours of the painting?

'I don't think it's a smile,' he said. 'I think it's a feeling. That's how I feel a lot of the time. Pleasant inside.'

His aunt watched him. He usually didn't open up. As for him, he was imagining some sort of geometrical design behind the figure. Diamond shapes? Irregular shapes? He realised he was turning it into a religious object, like a stained glass window. Then he thought: Yes! What a wonderful painting of a saint.

He wasn't allowed to follow his thoughts; Aunt Mira woke suddenly.

'Great Amazonian racing rats!' she screeched. 'What dreams I have! Freud's a fraud! It's rubbish, I tell you! Rubbish! Flotsam and jetsam rising from the uncharted depths of incoherence to float on the sea of stupidity and boredom that is my poor old mind! Noise, just noise, that's what it is! Ragtag and bobtail, odds and ends, off cuts and loose ends! The dust and detritus of years! Interpretation of dreams! Bahhh! Interpretation of fistulas, that's more likely!'

'Poor Mira,' said Ursula. 'Her thoughts bump around in her head, like bulls in a china shop with loose wooden flooring.'

'You're out of your trio,' grumbled Mira, calmer than before, but not inclined to be silent. 'Too many years at the mercy of coarse tutors.

'You can see what syphilisation has done to me. Now I'm a malcontent like everyone else. The private citizen rejecting authority. Let's all sing "Failure in F Minor", then get out the video of "Wild Raspberries". The deferential Australian turns like a worm. The submissive Aussie in revolt with a mild complaint and a threat to go on strike and hurt himself to punish others. By Saint Moronica, what it is to be a full-time female!'

'Can you make any sense of all this?' Ursula asked the boy.

'I think I can,' he said, with care.

'You have to have faith, and hope for clarity, when you're listening to Aunt Mira,' she said.

Lillian came in just then, singing:

> *'Strong son of God, immortal will*
> *Whom we by faith embrace*
> *Believing what we cannot prove —'*

'Lillian!' interrupted Aunt Ursula. 'What do you think of the "Mona Lisa"?'

'With the moustache or without?' asked Lillian, her song proceeding in a humming sound, its rhythm visible in the movements of her head.

Aunt Ursula gave up, and wheeled her chair round, grumbling, so quickly that the rubber wheels squeaked.

'Look at that,' accused Mira. 'You'd think rubber grew on trees!'

The boy followed Ursula.

'Aunt,' he said, 'what does she mean by go on strike to hurt themselves and punish others?'

Faced with a question, Aunt Ursula stopped immediately and gave her full attention.

'Well now. In some ways, strikes can be considered ritual self-punishment, intended to bring similar punishment on others. It can be looked at as having its origins in sacrifice to the gods, with the additional symbolic weight of the strikers sacrificing their own selves — that is, their money. Mira meant, I think, as far as she can mean anything, a sort of hysteria in which the striker holds a knife at his own throat and says: "Stop that, or I'll hurt myself!" like a child says: "Stop it or I'll hold my breath!" There's got to be better ways of drawing attention, or rectifying some situation, than going on strike; but those who strike are very conservative, traditional, unimaginative people. We're out of the trees one minute, into a bark canoe the next, then aboard a spacecraft the next; but all the time only a step away from our beginnings.'

'Do you know everything, Aunt?' he asked.

'Cheeky boy!'

'Do you? Yes or No?'

'Certainly not. And where'd you get this Yes or No business?'

'School.'

'Why are you being cheeky?'

'I feel like it. Besides, you don't go mad on me.'

'Mmf,' said Aunt. 'About Yes or No to questions. You've probably found that some questions, like: "Do you tell the truth?" are put in a way that limits the answer, for instance by demanding Yes or No. The right answer might be: I try to; or, sometimes; or, mostly; or, every second day; but Yes or No is too coarse an answer, not accurate enough.'

'Do you tell the truth, Aunt?'

'As far as I know. Except for mistakes in matters of fact, things no one can be sure of.'

'What things?'

'Well, I'm convinced the sun will rise tomorrow, but I can't prove it, so what I say about it might be a lie. But no, I haven't lied for many years. I guess I'm lucky.'

'Why isn't there something about telling the truth in the Ten Commandments?'

'Nothing's perfect.'

'But it's important!'

'Indeed it is. For me, it's the thing. Let me recite a little something I made up once.' Aunt Ursula settled her arms into a different, therefore more comfortable position. 'Here goes:

> *'Behind the lies, evasions, camouflage,*
> *There's a secret place your true self lives*
> *That knows the truth of what you think*
> *And say and do, and the intentions*
> *Hiding behind stated intentions.*
> *Lock that place; silence that inmost self;*
> *Ignore it your whole life long:*
> *It cannot be hoodwinked or destroyed,*
> *It knows and cannot forget.'*

He was silent for a while, absorbing it.

'Who did you make it for, Aunt?' he said at last.

She nodded her head a number of times, but it meant she wasn't saying. She'd written the lines for Davis Blood's older brothers and Danielle, but none of them was the kind of soil for planting such a sentiment.

This one was. Whatever she had to give, had had to wait all these years for him.

Ritual at Honeycomb Cave

The boy went with Orville and his father down into the bush. They left the wide clay track near Thunder Rock and went steeply down an old track through thick undergrowth with pink heath, conesticks, cigarette plants, the odd woody pear with its black flaking bark, tea-trees, a tree fern or two, pink spider-flowers, bacon and eggs bush, a tall needle-bush covered in white flowers, black-eyed susan, apple gums with their soft brown bark still blackened at the base from the last bush fire; bush pea plants, red-honeyflower, and Christmas bush torn off at the tops by visitors to the district during the previous season of goodwill; until they were at the cave mouth under Honeycomb Rock, which got its name from its wind-fretted ceiling. The ashes of many fires lay deep on its floor; its honeycombed roof and walls were black. Generations of kids and their fathers had come to roast potatoes in that cave, and Aborigines before them, for shelter.

Orville collected gum leaves, the boy helping. They strewed them, dead leaves brown and crackly on the bottom, and heaped green leaves on top. His father struck a match. The fire caught and billowed upwards. They stepped smartly back. The smoke was amazing. Orville took the potatoes out of their bag and put them in the fire.

They stood back out of the fizzing smoke motionless: three hand-carved bodies. Jackson Blood absently picked up a leaf from a cabbage gum, crumpled it in his fingers, and pressed it to his nose, inhaling its heady eucalypt scent.

The boys, big and small, sixteen and ten, waited for their father to say when the potatoes were done. When he decided they were, he stepped forward with a rough stick and prodded for them in the ashes, rolling them towards himself, out of the fire. He scattered the burning branches apart so each had nothing nearby to burn, and picked up the potatoes, juggling them from hand to hand — they were crusted with black soot, and hot — until the air had cooled them enough to hold. The boy got one with not quite so much black crust on it, removed what he could, and bit in. His teeth sank through the black into the white sparkling flesh of the potato. It smelled delicious, even more so than when they came out of the steamer at home. He peeled the black off, as he saw Orville and his father do. They sat around on rocks, eating. The gum tree smoke smelled like incense.

It was like a ritual, though it happened rarely. At home, his mother made every meal seem not so much ritual, as communion. There was a loving seriousness about the way she sat them down and then dished up the dinner. He thought of it as he ate his potato and looked round at his father and Orville. The bush plants and trees, in all their colour, came in a semicircle up to the cave mouth.

God is love. His father had often spoken of the God of the Old Testament, and the revelation of the God of the New. The boy remembered the words, but didn't understand. Why was God different after Jesus came?

Then he remembered a prayer talk on a Sunday morning at the Meeting, by one of the men who rarely spoke. These were delivered standing, sometimes with eyes shut, and were half prayer, half personal testimony; come apart into a lonely place, Jesus said to his followers. It was just before the feeding of the crowd. His father was a follower, but

Orville wasn't. Why was it none of the Blood children had become Christians?

I and my father are one, Jesus said. That was a different kind of family. There were no close resemblances, even of face, in the Blood family. Poor Dad, he thought. He must wish the whole family was with him in his concern for things spiritual, but they're not.

'Aboriginal people,' said Jackson Blood in a musing sort of tone, 'used to be at home here. Animals and birds, fish and crayfish in the creeks; lizards, snakes, wallabies, echidnas, goannas. They had their religion,' he mused. 'They seem to have been good people — vigorous, clean, manly, religious, law abiding, in good heart — until we came. What a curse we were to them! And what can we say of ourselves? We've been here two hundred years and still there's no Australian individuality formed, by which we can be recognised, or recognise ourselves. It may be another century before that happens.

'Poor blacks. Loyalty to their own ways wasn't enough. Decency, kindness, gentleness, respect, strict justice: not enough. It might have been a different story if they were tougher, coarser, more vigorous, hardnosed, determined, less welcoming, not so ready to step back to give strangers room.' He shook his head, the boy watched him, Orville looked out over the valley, where a dozen or so knobby redgums twisted their arms crazily, and stringybarks from their height looked tolerantly around them. Here and there a silver-leaf ironbark showed its tough black stem through the green and grey brush. Farther down the valley the stems of tall blue gums shone in the sun; they rose straight and tall not far up from the creek, and majestic turpentines stood close in their family clumps.

The Place of She-oaks lay across a fold in the land to the east. Nests of the black bull-jo hid among the shrubs, and the odd red bull-ant nest, with its quickfooted guards, cousins of the bull-jo, could be found on the sandy soil among rocks and plants.

'Is there no hope for black people, with us here?' the boy said. Orville had opinions, but he, and the other older boys, clashed too often with JB, as they called him; he said nothing. Orville and his brother looked up as currawongs cried out in their larrikin way; deep in the valley a whipbird's note drew out fine, then cracked at the end of a slow crescendo.

'The personal force in the individual will burst through, no matter what obstacles, what disadvantages are in the way,' the father said.

'There's hope for some of them?' the boy persisted.

'Yes. And for us, too. We are the pioneers, you know,' the father said, looking sharply at the boy. 'We. Now. What we are doing with the country is still pioneer work, though it mightn't seem so. We are arranging the future by what we do and what we leave undone.

'The sort of people we are is important. I'd like to see Australians that bow to no one but God; proud, noble, vigorous, clean Australians, who only take a backward step if they're about to counter-punch.'

He was smiling when the boy looked up to check. Davis Blood glanced away at a movement. A bold wattlebird with yellow on its front hung upside-down on a thin branch that bent under its weight, but didn't break.

'The only arrogance I'd like to see,' the father went on, 'is arrogance in the presence of meanness, ill will, bad humour: disdain for pettiness. Plain men and women: strong, open, cheerful, no tricks, no lies, candid; that's what I'd like to see. People who love the world of nature, look down on riches and indulgence, who work to have enough, with some over to give to those in need.'

While his father spoke Davis Blood noticed among the rocks the white petals of a flannel-flower between a brown boronia and a prickly bush whose name he didn't know. All these things had their lives to live, and contained God.

'This land craves a theory, a dream. Australia is a puzzle, there are mighty rewards for solving it. These seven states, yes these seven very different states, are seven stanzas to a great poem of the future, a poem being written now.

'But there has to be a largeness about the people,' he said in a quieter voice. 'A generosity with their thought and effort that they haven't yet got. Australians are shy of going all-out, of thinking big, committing themselves.'

While they'd been standing still at the cave's mouth more birds than the wattle bird had landed in nearby bushes, lizards had shown themselves, ants went about ant business.

The talk was over, the ashes spread. The three Bloods left in a flurry of movement. Birds and lizards went for their lives. The ants went about their business as they had before humans existed.

The Bush Book

The train journey to Archerfield, with one change of trains at Happy Valley, took forty-five minutes twice a day. At his new school for gifted children the kids all wore uniforms. Twenty or so schools were represented here. The classes were different, more interesting.

The first day he had to do a composition on sounds he liked and disliked. It wasn't something that really touched him, and he thought it came out rather wooden. He wished the teacher would set them something on the bush.

His chance came when the class were asked to compile a botany book of bush life, plants and trees. He spent a weekend on it and filled the book, using stamp hinges and sticky paper to fasten flowers, leaves, seed-pods, insects, to the blank white pages.

Jackson Blood's help was invaluable: he seemed to know each leaf, each flower, each beetle, teaching his son the differences between the various boronias, acacias, hakeas, melaleucas, bottle brush, grevilleas, banksias, eucalypts, and so on. The specimens too big to fix to the pages, he drew: the cup moth, a number of gulls, crusader bugs, sawfly larvae, yellow beetle, elephant beetle, auger beetles, a white curl grub, and an emperor gum caterpillar.

There was one specimen to which he couldn't do justice. He'd gone along Nerida Pass on the low track, till he came to the T-junction with Wallaby Track about a hundred metres short of Maidenhair Falls. He was crossing the small gully that contained the creek bed on a huge fallen log suspended about ten metres above the carpet of leaves. It was a place of fallen tree trunks, but there was a space below, clear of obstructions. Below, in the dim clearing, a lyre-bird stood and moved, its beautifully coloured tail erect in full display. He stood still on the dead, fungus-covered tree. The lyre-bird stopped, too, as if listening, then ran across the leaves under a rock and out of sight.

All he could do was draw it, just as he'd seen it, from above.

Nor could he do justice to the atmosphere of the bush, that feeling of wonder and delight at the delicately beautiful things that thrived in a tough environment, that enveloped him each time he set foot in it. The native fuchsias; heavy heads of blossom on white tea-trees; pink boronia amid green undergrowth; the almost translucent leaf of the wild pear seen against afternoon sun; blackened stumps from past bush fires; big peppermint trees whose leaves he crushed, whose perfume he breathed deeply; the blackboy spears, razor sharp sword-grass; the fierce acid of wild currants on the tongue; sudden sight of a golden wattle; a blue berry tree growing near the top of a cliff; the native pittosporums that Lillian called 'Sweet September' for their sweet pervasive spring perfume; the sarsaparilla leaves picked from the vine and bittersweet in his mouth: these were the bush he loved. Pressed flowers and single leaves stuck in a book conveyed nothing of that.

The other kids, however, didn't live near bush; they didn't have a back fence that wasn't there, whose absence allowed the bush to come right in the backyard. He knew his Bush Book would be considered excellent work.

He handed in the book on the Monday morning fidgety with anticipation as he waited for the teacher to get through the pile of books and come to his. First he had to negotiate a mathematics problem: a car travelling from A to B. It irritated him. Why not time the journey? Where was the allowance for starting speeds, time stopped in traffic or slowing for lights, hills, speeds through the gears, accidents, variations in the general traffic speed, variations in the car's road speed?

He asked those questions and was smartly sat on by the teacher. Let's keep it simple, it's just an exercise in arithmetic, and so on.

But why do it if no notice is to be taken of what would really happen?

The teacher absently lifted some of the books and chanced on a page of Davis Blood's book which had a pencil drawing of a codlin moth and caterpillar and branch, together with some acacia leaf specimens. Ignoring the class, he pulled the book out, and leafed through it.

He looked directly at the boy who was being a pest.

'Excellent work,' he said drily. 'I'll excuse your past attempts at evading the exercise; now do it!' and went back to the botany book.

The boy Blood got on with it, feeling very satisfied. Just the same, a problem that quoted a certain speed between A and B and wanted an exact answer wasn't something that could be encountered in real life: it was like an imagino that the Lady Vivian might make up.

The Good Life

Randal brought home for the boy a pile of thick white paper from the printing company he worked for, and among the different sizes was one that, although folded, opened out into a sheet more than a metre square. This sheet he took out to his favourite spot on the verandah, where he settled down to draw. But on what?

He hunted under the house for a sheet of wooden chipboard and found one big enough to put the paper on and keep it flat. He went to work.

He started with two hang gliders. One had a blue and white barred wing, the other was crimson with a white stripe. Lower down he drew a tall crane with a rigger — a dogman was the word his father used — high up in the air with his foot in the wire rope sling, hanging on with one hand, looking around him as the crane driver swung him up and around to where his next piece of work was.

On the edge of the picture, where the rolling country and the bush began, a party of shooters in a truck were careering into the open country.

Farms started around the western edge of the picture. The farms had patchwork quilt layouts of vegetables, fruit trees, grapes, passionfruit, watermelon vines.

In the little shopping centre he drew a crowd of people in the streets, bright shop windows, offices where people could be seen working at desks, men by the roadside digging holes for drainage repairs, building new shops, and traffic of all descriptions in the streets and parking lots.

A school near the shopping centre had all the kids out in the playground, at lunchtime.

Over on the river three fishing boats were coming back into port circled by gulls looking for scraps as the decks were cleaned down.

He drew suburban back gardens, with neat plots where vegetables and flowers grew. He put in, last of all, many-coloured washing on backyard clotheslines, blowing and flapping.

He hadn't noticed any of the family coming by, or heard anything that went on anywhere except in his head and on the paper, apart from his mother carrying ironed clothes into the bedroom and singing the words 'I heard the voice of Jesus say, come here to me and rest.' When he finished he gave a great sigh. While he was working his breathing was shallow, his mouth open, an arc of tongue in the corner of his mouth. He looked at his work, held it up, looking at every detail.

He put the drawing on the big table. As the family were gathering ready for dinner, Randal asked him what he called it.

'A good life,' he answered.

His older brother said, 'It looks like an ordinary sort of life to me.'

The boy said nothing, just looked pleasantly up at the older one of nineteen. Yes, that's what's good about it. Why were older people so often unhappy and dissatisfied with their life? They knew no other life. Why didn't they fit in better than they did? Not all discontent is divine discontent. Perhaps it was just talk. He had noticed people often like to say strong things rather than weak: criticism sounded stronger than agreement, wilfulness than contentedness.

The Log

In the afternoon he went down the bush short of Kangaroo Point, to where his father and he had been the week before. It was a place of rocks and scribbly gums and blue peppermints; bush flowers were thin on the ground here, and once he startled a ground-bird, probably a quail. There was the log they had left, its cut end dry and still a bright colour, with the pink-red at the centre, the heartwood.

He stood near the middle point of the log, and pushed it with his right foot to roll it and expose any centipedes or spiders that might have camped there. It rolled over. Exposed insects, and some visiting slaters, ran from the light.

He had a go at lifting the log from the lighter end. It wouldn't come up much more than ankle height. He stood, and looked round to see what tools the bush had given him. There were rocks and stones. He got a flat stone, ankle-height, lifted the log again and slipped the stone under with his foot. The log was off the ground at one end.

He rolled rocks across nearby so they'd be easier to slip under, and before long had the log's light end waist-high off the ground, though only precariously on the pile of rocks.

When it was high as his breastbone, he thought now's the time to see what I can do. He took a rest for a few seconds, but couldn't bear to keep his hands off it any longer.

He got in under the higher end of the log, and cautiously put his shoulder up under it. In that moment he remembered the pad his father used — a folded sugar bag or cornsack to protect the point of his shoulder. He had no pad. He would have to try without one.

He tried again, putting his shoulder up against the under side of the log's bark. He straightened his legs, but his waist was still bent. He remembered something he'd heard from his father, and bent his legs, straightened his body, and came up under the log, with only his knees to straighten.

Fortified by a couple of good deep breaths, he straightened his legs; his shoulder took the weight. It hurt a bit. He pushed up harder, until for one satisfying moment his legs were straight and the top end of the log was off its supports. Carefully he pushed the log upright, where it took no lifting, only balancing. For some thirty seconds he held it upright, balancing it.

Once more he put his shoulder against it, letting it lean on him, but he misjudged something — the timing, perhaps — because suddenly the weight was too much, he couldn't oppose it, it was going to come down taking a path through him. He skipped aside just in time for it to go crashing Bomp! on the ground.

He went home happy. He had lifted it. One day he would put it on his shoulder and walk with it.

Poetry

Restlessly he went over to the bookshelves and picked up Lillian's poetry anthology. In the next hour he discovered English poetry, and in particular some sonnets of Shelley, Keats and Shakespeare that compelled his attention, and, having made him captive so that he read them again, enraptured him.

> *'When I have fears that I may cease to be*
> *Before my pen has gleaned my teeming brain.'*

He read it again, half aloud. The sound and length and

rhythm of those vowels! The desperation of the young poet in the face of relentless time!

> 'My name is Ozymandias, king of kings,
> Look on my works, ye mighty, and despair!'

and,

> 'Nothing beside remains. Round the decay
> Of that colossal wreck, boundless and bare
> The lone and level sands stretch far away.'

His skin prickled with the emotions called up by the words and rhythms. It was a form of music.

As for Shakespeare, he couldn't get enough of

> 'Shall I compare thee to a summer's day.'

and,

> 'When in disgrace with fortune and men's eyes.'

and,

> 'O never say that I was false of heart.'

and,

> 'When to the sessions of sweet silent thought.'

He read them over and over.

Under the spell of the music in the words he leafed further through Lillian's poetry anthology, discovering Christina Rossetti.

> 'Remember me when I am gone away.'

and Elizabeth Barrett Browning's *Sonnets from the Portuguese*:

> 'If thou must love me, let it be for naught—.'

Matthew Arnold's 'Sonnet to Shakespeare' finished off that afternoon's discoveries. Something in him was sated. He had to put the book down; he felt physically averse to looking at the words a moment longer.

He went out into the yard to chop wood. When he breathed the fresh air of the valley it seemed so delicious that it struck him that while he'd been reading he'd hardly breathed at all. He'd been so still. He picked up the axe.

If all the axes in the world were one axe
What a great axe that would be.

The words he'd tasted were, in their way, as delicious as the air of Kookaburra Valley. He was glad all the poems in the world weren't one poem: he wanted lots more. A magpie's liquid, elastic notes arched, extended, descended and curved in the valley air.

He attacked the wood with full, vigorous strokes. Jackson Blood had told him, disapprovingly, of the energy wasted in such a method, and advised a shorter, efficient chopping action, but his father's method omitted the wholeheartedness and the joy. He loved the sheer effort of pitting himself against the wood and the axe.

He kept on chopping till he felt like a pause, then sank the axe-blade into the soft earth and stood up straight, puffing a little, raising his face to the sky. A sliver of silver moon rode high in the blue. It seemed as insubstantial as a smear of cloud. It was too early to see the first stars.

In a recent school library book he'd read of Messier 31, the Andromeda galaxy — 1,600,000 light years distant. He'd tried to imagine one light year, even worked out the figures on paper. Eleven digits. Then tried to imagine that multiplied by 1,600,000. It was impossible, yet that distance was only a tiny fraction of the universe — which God contained.

Then he tried to take in the other thought: that what an astronomer now saw as Andromeda was by courtesy of light that left that galaxy 1,600,000 years before.

How did they know it was there still? How could they possibly know?

He shook his head and picked up the axe again, aimed at the wood and thought of poetry.

Travelling so far to school each day didn't worry him, it was good really: he had time for lots of reading. There might be books in the school library with more good poems.

Those poems he'd read a short while before seemed to have in them a substance, a sort of nourishment. What was it?

He put the axe down and stood by the chopping block, thinking. Almost like things you could live by; pointers to better ways of thinking, new ways of feeling; better things you could aim for and keep in mind, and some day even reach.

He ran up the back steps and helped himself to a biscuit, a Monte Carlo. In the middle of crunching it, when his mouth was nearly filled with the dry bits, he wanted a drink of water. He felt very clever that he could make a channel in the crunched bits with his tongue and get the water through that, hardly melting the biscuit.

Fight to the Death

It is an axiom of life in school, and universally accepted, that boys in lower classes are inferior. This is what simplifies each boy's relationship with all other boys.

This fair, thick boy, being in a lower class, was inferior. When he insulted the boys in the special class as a bunch of sissies, it was up to any boy in a higher class to make an example of him, and fight.

In addition to being inferior, the fair thick boy picked his nose in company and ate the pickings. This was a damning trait, but the primary transgression was to give cheek to your superiors, as if you were an equal.

'You're on,' declared Davis. 'After school. To the death.'

The fair boy had no option but to accept the challenge.

All through arithmetic and as the school day unrolled, Davis thought of how he would fight that boy. Everyday English passed in a dream of blood and dust. Geography made him think of flat places, free of impediments, in which to fight, space to punch and roll, to grapple and throw.

Just after three, when the grounds cleared of teachers and kids, there were a dozen or so waiting to watch the fight to the death.

Davis Blood saw the fair boy, and went over at a half run.

The school bags were put in a heap, and the boys strung themselves out to make a rough enclosure for the two to fight in.

Davis went for him, punching at this Semeon Metachek head. The other boy gave way under the onslaught but didn't cave in. He returned punches of his own at the Davis Blood face.

Davis, impatient, went to grapple with the boy's body. He seemed to go in with his head, then put his arms round Semeon as if to lift him off the ground and throw. But Semeon, even though inferior, was not as light and insignificant as the wrath of Davis wanted to think. Semeon put a headlock on him immediately, and hung on. No matter what Davis tried to do that headlock remained in force. Semeon had his right arm round Davis' neck, and his left hand held his right hand in position.

Davis made a grab for Semeon's privates, and encountered a short fat penis, not noticeably different from his own Sylvester, whom he'd christened in the winter months because the little chap seemed so small and lonely down there. A proper Christian name might cheer him up. They don't hurt, except on the tip, so he released it and went for the testicles. His hand closed over the tight little bag and squeezed sharply. Semeon let out a yowl. His arms relaxed their hold for a second while Semeon took in some breath to aid him to fight the immediate pain. Davis slipped out of the headlock and began to punch wildly at every part of Semeon that presented itself. Semeon recovered from the pain of his crunched testicles, and began to take an interest in the new direction the fight had taken. He too punched wildly.

Semeon, though, with his wish to be equal, couldn't match the fury of the boy from the higher class who wanted to observe the traditions. Semeon wasn't angry enough, and his skill wasn't remarkably greater than his opponent's. He began to lose the fight.

The fists of both boys were red and scratched. They stood and slugged at each other, sometimes hitting, often not. Both puffed, and their energy seemed to come in bursts. Sometimes it seemed to decline at the same time, and both noticeably slowed. Davis had bursts of greater energy at more frequent intervals, and he was first to begin faster punching each time.

He noticed that after a period of steady fighting, his anger, that had its headquarters somewhere inside him, boiled over, and he made sustained bursts of punching until the strength seemed to drain from his arms, and they became heavy planks belonging to someone else. Then a moment's rest, a dodging away was needed, and the speed returned to them and they were his again.

Their faces were red and puffy in places, both had split lips, both kept on punching.

The fight took a break when Semeon's front foot didn't obey him, and slid forward until stopped by a stone, when he lurched forward well within range.

Davis caught him with a barrage to the side of his face and head, jarring and overbalancing him. He went down. Davis stepped back.

The crowd of boys yelled, 'To the death! To the death!' Meaning he should go in for the kill. Semeon was getting up, shaking his head.

The boy Davis felt he had won, and it had been a good fight. He didn't feel like going in for any kill. He confined himself to waiting until Semeon was newly upright, then flooring him again with a smothering barrage of punches.

'To the death! Death! Death!' chanted the onlookers, but Davis didn't move while Semeon was down. This boy, with a bruised and smeared face like his own, was closer to him in that moment than the boys he rubbed shoulders with every day in class and playground. Yet he was inferior, in an inferior class.

'Death! Death!' yelled the onlookers.

But the boy Davis waited until his enemy got up. Semeon shook his head, no more, and turned away.

Davis went over to his school bag, picked it up, wiped his face with his handkerchief, and walked off towards home.

Semeon went the other way.

Neither spoke to his supporters who, Davis thought, would probably have liked a death, rather like the onlookers at suicide scenes on television, who shout: 'Jump! Jump!'

Davis had gone a fair way when he discovered he was uncomfortable and sweating-hot. He didn't like the feeling. He would take everything off as soon as he got home, and have a shower. Before he got something to eat.

On the way home in the train he thought of nothing, just watched the parallel lines of blurred objects as they passed him. He sat at a window seat, head still, eyes unblinking.

Fighting was silly. But that wasn't the whole story, it was more complicated than that. He saw again the ring of kids and the furious fight they enclosed. Enclosed. He'd seen on television a collapsible stock fence that could be taken out into a paddock and erected from the back of a truck. Someone could do the same for a ring to fight in. The idea could be used, a portable collapsible pen, to enclose kids at play. There was an invention waiting to be made, he thought, and his usual smile reappeared on his battered face, after being absent for some time.

If all fights were one fight
What a great fight that would be.

It occurred to him that it was a while since the Papworths and Downies had harassed him.

His thoughts switched to one of the lessons they'd had that day. One of the kids said that birds dream, while still in their eggs. And they'd been told of swifts migrating, and mutton birds, and the cranes of Africa. Those birds spent all night in the air. Did they sleep on the wing? Did they dream too?

Walking along Anzac Street he listened for birds' cries. The fight was gone from his mind. Yesterday the birds' voices were merry, but now he was sad to find they were full of sharp threats and fears of predators and wary of sudden death. He'd learned of the food chain, and how the killing never stops, night and day, down to the smallest bundle of fear, and how we humans sit at the top, preying on all else; but the circle is completed by the very smallest things, bacteria and viruses, which have the power to bring us back to earth.

Crossing the vacant block the track went through the reeds of the wet patch. In other lands, at night, the moon's rays would stripe through the tall reeds and the trees, making a pattern of tigers. Perhaps boys in those places wouldn't make bush trips alone.

He didn't remember the fight until he got to the front path. It set his teeth on edge to see the cat on the verandah licking its fur. He'd seen a hairball in the museum retrieved from some animal's stomach, and the slight irritations awoke something like a quiet business-like anger, and he was right back there, battling with Semeon Metachek in his head.

God was in Semeon, whether he knew it or not; even if it didn't show. But if he didn't know, then the part of God in him must be hidden, or obstructed, confined within something. Perhaps even chained up.

Country Road Galapagos

At home he set up a straight stick in the ground about a metre high, marked off twenty-two paces, and bowled at it.

After a while he found the way to hit it most often was to look at it, and only it, for five or so seconds, and never to take his eyes off it as he ran up to bowl. He began to hit it twice out of four times. In one spell of five balls he hit it four times; but missed the next ten. He swore at himself.

He understood well enough. There were plenty of kids who couldn't hit the one stump no matter how many balls they bowled at it. He was accurate, to a point: but there was a lot of arm, a lot of things to go wrong between the head's intentions and the hand's release of the ball.

It was like in drawing. His hand tried to draw what his head saw, but never quite made it. Sometimes it nearly got there, and he was glad then; but mostly it was off the mark, and always the thing his head wanted was in advance of what his hand could do.

Not long after, when Orville came home, and kids from other parts of Bellbird Corner came down to the flat of Country Road outside the Bloods' house looking for a game of cricket, Lillian joined in. The boy was anxious at first for his mother's dignity — he'd never seen her as relaxed as this about play in public. Because she was his mother, he'd thought she was a possession of his. It began to dawn on him that this wasn't so.

Other things dawned on him. His mother, so gentle and smiling, so cheerful and kindly, was a physically strong woman. In the house she was loving and energetic, but due to her endless song-cycle, rarely spoke. When she did it was always delightful, just as when she suddenly sang aloud as she worked. But standing at the wicket, with cricket bat raised, then bringing the bat down in a wide arc to meet the ball, he saw that there was great power in her stroke. For one thing, the tennis ball thumped into Gordon Sawyer's stomach before he got his hands up.

For another, she dished out a casual, playful backhander to solid seventeen-year-old Orville during the game, for some unimportant piece of cheek, that sent him back about four paces.

Perhaps he was off-balance. But the boy, watching, didn't think so. Mum was really strong. There was a lot about her he didn't know. It made him feel a slight sadness.

When she ran up to the mark to bowl and a sneeze came over her, he was at first embarrassed by the thunderclap of it, until he noticed that the other kids looked at her in awe. When she bowled, her long arm didn't seem to come over fast, but the ball flew like an arrow, with no curve in its trajectory. She specialised in the yorker. He complimented her on it, then without thinking, began to explain what a yorker was, until he saw the shadow of a smile under her brows and realised she knew perfectly well what it was.

'Sorry, Mum,' he said.

'That's all right, young Davy wavy woo,' she said cheerfully, then resumed her hummed song, and walked back with the ball for her run-up. He knew the tune, it was one of Mister Lichfield's favourites at the Meeting: 'Hail, thou once despiséd Jesus'. He took particular notice. She hummed the tune all the way up to the crease as she bowled the ball. There was a slight break in the time as her arms came over and she released the cricket ball; the break had in it a piece of the grunt that a hum becomes when subjected to the physical effort of bowling. Then the song resumed.

For no apparent reason the words of Jesus came into his head: 'Remember, I am with you always'. Always was a word he liked, it was smooth and heavy; you could lean on it.

Just then, he had a great wish for everything to stay the same; for his mother always to be that age, to be singing under her breath, to be strong and admired; for himself to be eleven and able to play cricket in the street; and for

Country Road never to be covered with bitumen, for then traffic would fill it, as traffic did to other streets at Bellbird Corner that had been surfaced.

His imagination travelled further. To have things stay the same here at home would be a little like the conditions on the Galapagos that the class had studied at school, rather like a laboratory where a population was allowed to grow undisturbed. But of course the Galapagos wasn't undisturbed any more; all sorts of domestic animals were introduced and had become predators. Neither would things stay the same in Country Road.

A Tenor

*I*t was a regular radio programme that Danielle listened to: 'Great Singers of the World'. Many times the boy had vaguely noticed it, but until that evening he'd never really heard it. Something about the notes, and the way they were produced, pierced him. The presenter had taken one of the Verdi set-piece tenor arias and invited the unseen audience to hear four differing treatments of it: first by Caruso, then Gigli, Björling and Pavarotti.

The words mattered nothing: the lyric beauty of the song transfixed Davis Blood. More than that, the sound of the four voices vibrated in time with something inside him that was just ripe to be reached: the heavy manliness of Caruso, the tender caressing Gigli, the clear northern heady tones of Björling, and the noble ringing grace of Pavarotti.

Several times he shivered, feeling a wave of cold come over his wrists and arms, climbing up his back, his neck and face, and over his scalp.

How it must be to produce such sound! To stand on a

stage and have every eye in the packed theatre focussed on you. Just to be at that focal point must be to step up into another existence. To carry round your profession, your career, within yourself: no paraphernalia, no props. To open your mouth, let free the sound only you could produce, and to loosen the flood of feelings in others — thousands of others at a time — that were flowing in him now.

His voice would break in a few years time, his father said. If he could become a tenor, would he want to? He had tasted some of the possible sweets of such a career in advance; the attention and praise of two primary schools; but what if he did become a tenor?

He put the question away inside him, conscious of the shadow of another feeling: that his inner receptacle was a great excuse for putting off decisions and actions.

When he saw Danielle next, to talk to — you didn't interrupt her during a programme — he arranged to listen to some of her operatic records.

Danielle's face first said she was pleased. After a few seconds, though, the difficulties of arranging to be home at certain times clouded her face. Besides, she was twenty-four, and the family expected her to leave at any time. He would have to be careful, and make it easy for her to oblige him, or she'd cancel the whole thing. He didn't want that: she had lots of records and tapes. He could learn from them.

The Cave of Life

At school on Monday he had to write a composition about a girl, from a girl's point of view. He sat and tried to think. What did he know about girls? Desperately he began to write:

'Pollyanna Whitmansfield looked at the rather sunny beach and the sky, across which darkening clouds were racing eagerly; too eagerly, she thought. On her face was a troubled expression. She remembered her home, dimly, and the ancestors she'd come from, but the clouds and threatening weather were driving her mind towards the Cave of Life, and presently her legs would follow.

'The Cave of Life was a refuge, but she preferred to think of it as a place to be explored. It was known to be dangerous, as many had gone in and never come out again. To add to her worries the cave was extremely dangerous at high-tide-in-the-stars, and that tide was quickly coming in.

'Swiftly she ran across the beach, her elbows at a funny angle and hair streaming in the wind. She stopped just before she came to the cave. PW's heart — they all called her PW for short — began to thump with caution. She went in about five metres and when she looked back to the entrance of the cave saw only a dim light. After another ten metres, all was black. To her horror, something felt wet round her ankles. She screeched. It was the tide.

'She felt her way along the slimy walls and with mounting horror heard pounding waves outside the thin walls of the Cave of Life. She made her way along branching passages until she was thoroughly lost, then heard a noise of knocking in the walls. Round another corner and she was saved. There in the sunlight was her father and a huge crowd of excited spectators, who looked at her constantly and plied her with attention, hot drinks, hugs and smiles.

' "You've learned not to be too curious, I suppose," said

her father. But she couldn't answer without a lie, for the answer had to be Yes to your father, so she said nothing.

'Being too curious had made her popular and famous and everyone knew her face and pointed her out in the street. That's what she learned, and that's what she liked above all. But she still hadn't explored the Cave of Life. That would come later.'

He knew nothing about girls. The teacher made no comment. At least he'd handed it in, even if it was no good.

Next day it came back with 7 out of 10 and the comments:

> *More imagination required*
> *Why the 'Cave' of Life? What is intended*
> *by this image? In what way is life a*
> *refuge?*

But it was obvious. Life was a refuge from being nothing, from never existing, from being a bodiless possibility.

As Long as He's Good to His Mother

Aunt was reading a book that raised questions she couldn't wait to put to him. It was about prisoners and enforced servitude.

'Okay, then,' she said. Which meant Pay Attention. 'What is mankind?'

He'd have to guess. 'Mankind is every sort of person there is, past and future.'

'Hmmff. Another one: what should mankind do?'

'Everything.'

'Smartypants kid. What d'you mean everything?'

'Everything other humans have done.'

'Everything?'

'Yes, why not? If they don't, they can't be humans like previous humans were, and that's where we get the idea of humans from, isn't it?' It was as much a guess as before.

Aunt stopped a while, and thought. Now and then she'd raise her face to look at him, all screwed up round the mouth and eyes. She had to work hard just to say anything.

'Everything, you say. My God. And what would this smart human kind try to be?'

'Human.'

'My God! What about ideals? What about trying to make human kind into something better than this?' She gestured around, but all that was there was the clothesline full of shirts, underwear, towels and sheets, trees in the backyard, a valley full of bush down the back, three sides of a grey post and wire fence, assorted shrubs, bushes and his father's vegetable garden. 'No more than human, and no less?'

'Yes, Aunt.'

'What's life for? And don't give me any smart answers.'

He thought about that a bit, 'Just to be here. Just to keep on doing what people did before we were born.'

'Hmmff.' It was louder than last time. 'You could at least have said, the purpose of life is its function: to borrow elements from inorganic element cycles and use them to turn energy into children. Something I'll never do.' She subsided a little. 'You've done pretty well there, although I'm surprised to hear you come out with that position. Let's look at some of the things that go with it. I take it you believe mankind will always have war, factions, classes, national interests, opposing religions and the rest?'

'Yes,' he said slowly. 'Different people think differently, they need different religions, different ways of life.'

'And you don't think we ought to try to become a higher form of life? No, don't answer that, I know what you think. So, assuming you don't want humankind to tear itself to pieces, you take the position that humans ought always try to reduce the wars, the frictions, reduce the harms and antagonisms?'

'I suppose so.'

'What else? Don't you wish people good?'

'I don't wish them anything. Let them go.'

'Heaven and earth! Do you know you've got a philosopher out here?' she called to the kitchen from which had been floating the sounds of *'Himself he could not save'*.

'As long as he's a nice boy and good to his mother, and doesn't try to be too this or too that!'

And this from one who praised his cleverness and once spoke of greatness! What had happened since he was little?

Aunt looked at the kitchen door as if she wanted to kick it in. She hadn't moved her legs in thirty years, since the fifth column in her nerves and muscles struck her helpless.

'Hmmff!' she said louder than ever. 'What about humans having courage to go on in the face of a bleak, empty universe?'

'Human *is* to have courage, Aunt. The universe isn't empty, or bleak, it's interesting. If it wasn't just like it is, we wouldn't be here.' He was guessing, taking a risk under pressure of her questions, but thought he had a fair chance of being near the mark.

This time she said 'Hmmff!' more softly. It sounded like a satisfied grunt.

When I write things for school, he thought, I don't give good comments. I do much better when I answer questions. Perhaps Aunt knows how to ask questions.

Time

It was a day like other days, but before breakfast something had changed forever. There, at 20 Country Road, at the table, his father was reading the morning paper. The paper truck had tossed it over the fence onto the verandah, waking the dogs briefly, but not Davis Blood.

It was pleasure the boy saw on his father's face as he turned the broadsheet pages. There was defeat, too. Jackson Blood knew now he could never expect to be admitted to the inner circle, the Fellowship of the Dissenters, but neither could he part from his beloved tobacco. He'd given up one hope, and gained the daily paper, symbol of worldly affiliations, and pleasure.

When the boy got home from school, there was the paper still on his father's chair, crinkled and thoroughly read. His mother saw him looking, and smiled.

Did his father have a battle with himself before he finally ordered that paper? He'd often wondered, usually as he said the 'gentle Jesus' prayer at bedtime, if Jackson Blood, as far as he knew a hard and stubborn man, had struggled violently with himself, and perhaps wept large and heavy tears, before he surrendered to his gentle God, the God of his fathers.

Going to sleep that night — or was he already asleep? — he heard a deep, serious voice: 'Why are you here?'

Was someone on the verandah? He looked round. No strange shapes disturbed the familiar nightly outlines of the verandah.

'Who are you?' But the voice was in him.

Why was he here? He tried to think of reasons why, of things he might do in the future which would supply the answer, but all he could think of was his answer to Aunt:

to go on living as others lived before him. It wasn't enough. There had to be something he must do, different from what others did.

He fell asleep, puzzling over it, and woke after a bit, feeling he'd been involved in nonsense adventures, which he thought he could remember, but which faded faster than he could reach out after them, except for one in which he laughed himself to death.

Nonsense is only sense re-arranged, he told himself, and slept again.

This time he dreamed of the Bloodfather, strong and stern, whose blood runs in human veins, who demands that we act by the best rule we know, who keeps a list in our hearts of what we do, adds all the things we've done right and all the things we've done wrong. Every time we act, a note goes into the list kept within us. He writes it down, and constantly reminds us of the total.

It was the idea contained in Jackson Blood's reply to Preston's amused question one day — Preston thought the details of life trivial, and couldn't understand serious attention being paid them — when he asked: 'Why live to such an austere standard?'

'Because one day you'll be judged by it!'

It was Saturday morning. After he'd chopped some wood, he went up to his favourite place at the big table and got some paper.

He would write a sort of poem. He looked down at the paper and let his eyes go limp, unfocussed. Something in the district. A lake, the seashore, a hill, maybe. A hill. Brokenback Hill, where some of the kids used to go for stone fights, just up from the little old house at Platypus Creek where the Pogsons lived. It would deal with time, for once his father rejected the world's news, but now he was changed. Once he, Davis Blood, was a baby and now a boy of eleven; and now he didn't know what he would become, but one day he would know.

On Brokenback Hill

In the beginning there was nothing there but rocks,
till a man made a wall out of the rocks.
The wall was there many years.
A woman planted a vine by the wall.
The vine grew on the wall many years.
In the end the vine withered and died.
It hung on dead to the wall for as many years
As it hung on to the wall alive.
At last the vine crumbled to powder.
The wind blew it away.
After a long time the wall fell down.
There was nothing there but rocks,
As it was in the beginning.
Slowly the rocks crumbled to sand.

The Seven States

Years ago, Jackson Blood told his youngest, the Pogsons had sent four sons to war; their cousins who went numbered seven. Of the lot, five came back. Their little house, perched on a small rise that led up on one side to Brokenback Hill and on the other side fell away to Platypus Creek in the valley that in turn rose up and became one of the ridges covered in bush that ran from north to south. The house was part timber, part fibro-cement sheets; painted green mostly and having a small concrete apron at the back step; cannas on the wet side where the garden tap leaked against the house; corrugated iron on the roof, bleached grey with one rust patch to each sheet; a heap of weeds up the backyard growing round an iron-bound wheel off their old sulky; a plum tree not far from the back door; three azaleas and an old hydrangea round the south side near the front step they never used; rows of beans and potatoes on the path that sloped down towards the street and the wide entrance with no gate, that they always used; paspalum and stumps round at the front of the house leading to the unused front gate; leaning spotted-gum fence posts for a front fence with three holes in each post for the eight-gauge wire that didn't rust in forty years; a side window that was never shut in the bedroom of two of the lost boys, where now Glen slept.

Glen Pogson was one of the noisy ones at Bellbird Primary. He was no good at anything, but a pleasant enough kid. He had long eyelashes; girls envied him. In the house of cowards there is no weeping, but their little house was a house of heroes.

The spirit of a country is in the people, Jackson Blood said. The Pogsons were and had been modest, quiet, enduring, good-tempered. 'One day, Australia will be a nation of nations, a race of all races. The quiet virtues of old Australia will be needed, to diffuse among our welcome visitors, and act as a balance for diversity.

'I believe in democracy, but not in a dead level for all. I believe in having millions of strong individuals in my democracy, people pushing against their limitations, trying always to rise and do better, no matter how far they fall. It's fine to have help and give help in adversity, but when it lapses into a habit of leaning on others, waiting for others and not getting out and stuck into life, then it rots everything else. I'm guilty of it; maybe that's why I see it so clearly.

'I believe each person must be given a chance, but must give themselves a chance too. Each is capable of some understanding and appreciation of the best there is, and the best is available.

'The individual is important. Once the individual is able to have self-respect and wants all others to have self-respect, the nation can look after itself.

'New Australia is coming, son. The Seven States. It's on the way. A land where the average person is conscious of containing extraordinary things, where the democrat has the old aristocratic virtues, where the maker, the worker, has the traits of the philosopher.

'I won't see it. But I lived my life without thinking much about it, until I was older. The Seven States will need ordinary people who think. It's the people themselves taken all together that are great potentially: they make the nation.'

A Second Birth

*H*e'd been sitting on the edge of the verandah, legs over the side, warm in the sun, his mind playing with thoughts that ran lightly this way, and that. Or were those thoughts playing with him? he asked, in a mental aside. Some were thoughts that arose as he sat on Sunday in the Meeting, and one phrase came back to him:

Except you are born from above.

It was addressed to living people, so it meant another sort of birth. A rebirth? An entirely different birth? Since it was Jesus speaking, it must be a birth of the inner person, a spiritual new birth. What would that be like?

On the face of it, there would be a lot of interesting things happening to you if you were born one person, then later, reborn differently, for there was no doubt about it, the whole spirit of the thing implied great inner difference. Such difference might well be detectable in outward actions, but its most powerful evidence would be in those inner spaces of the head, those plains, mountains and cities invisible to others, where music and people and talk went on, and lives were lived, none of which could be seen or heard by others, only their outward traces and shadows detected.

Being Himself

'What are you going to be when you grow up?' asked a lady at the Meeting on Sunday. Her hair was tied in a bun; she was a round face and a smell of lavender. She kept standing too near him.

He didn't know. Obviously you had to be something. In his family, people were themselves, weren't they? Why couldn't he just be himself? He smiled, to put up a protection against being thought cheeky, before saying he didn't know.

'I expect you're shy, or something,' and she moved to someone else. He was relieved, but not shy. She had wanted an answer, where he would rather have talked about it. He would be big, but would he become something?

He walked away, head down: people butted in less if they couldn't catch your eye.

No. He would become more himself, though how he knew this he didn't know. Perhaps his singing voice had something to do with it, or whatever his mother meant when she said, as she often did, that he was 'artistic'.

If, of course, God was to intervene and tell him what to do as with the Apostle Paul, then that was different. The problem would be solved.

It was difficult to pin down the person he was. Sometimes he seemed to be one boy in one place, another elsewhere. Which was the true one? Was there no one person? Was it natural to be a number of different persons, different ones for different places?

At the Meeting he wasn't the same boy as he was at school; down the bush he was different from what he was at home.

Differentials at the Dance

At the school dance he watched the girls. Why did most of them wait for boys to come to them? Was it because the evidence of the boys' actions in approaching was the only way they had of judging whether that boy wanted that girl? What happened to their own desires, their own inclinations, their own choices? Was it better for a girl to go with someone who wanted her than to wait for someone she liked who may not want her? If so, that was just a calculation of convenience. Were their egos so frail that a refusal was a tragedy? If so, why were the boys willing to risk it? Why did one have more to lose than the other from a little risk?

Or was the hanging back a signal, an encouragement to the boys to take a risk and be seen to be assertive? Was it only when the boys felt they were active and aggressive males, dealing with less active and less forward beings, that their confidence remained? Perhaps theirs were the frail egos. Perhaps it was they who needed this differential most, and the girls knew it and gave it to them, since it cost nothing to give, and returned the girls what they wanted: the approval or envy of other girls and a new source of attention to themselves.

Even so, the girls' chances of satisfactory encounters seemed like a lottery. It must be a peculiar feeling, he thought, to have such important matters reduced to the level of a lucky dip.

Jonathon

The boy saw Jonathon again coming up Country Road from the bush. His walk was slower, his body slightly bowed. It was a year since the last time and Jonathon seemed ten years older.

The boy went inside, got Jonathon's money that he'd saved up, and walked after him. Jonathon took it without acknowledgement or gratitude. He didn't care if he got nothing.

On the way back it dawned on Davis Blood that he hadn't needed to run to catch Jonathon. The outdoor life and having nothing to do, couldn't be all that good.

The Shoe

Lester Batty was a thoughtful boy with a prominent lower lip, many freckles and a complexion without a trace of pink. He even had freckles on his lips.

Davis Blood hadn't known Lester could draw well until the teacher gave the class a commission to draw a shoe. It wasn't due to be handed in until the following month. He went home, put his shoes, which were new, on a table, and decided to draw the left one. He drew the smoothness, the shine, the neat laces, the unworn heel, the general look of affluence that the shoe exuded. It shone. It was brand new. He rarely got new things, and when he did he cherished them.

Lester Batty went home, took off his battered, bent, lined and creased, scuffed and worn shoes, and made a similar decision. He drew the craziness, the worn and defeated leather, the scuff-marks, the curve of the worn heel, the uneven sole, the laces that had lost their metal ends and were splayed out in fluffed threads, the frowns and creases in the instep and toe of the shoe. He drew a shoe that had lost its shine. Every day for the month he added another touch. Every day the shoe advanced in age and weariness; every day the drawing followed. He ended with a grandmother of a shoe, full of experience and character, exhausted by life.

The teacher gave him the prize.

The boy Blood thought about it in his disappointment. The plodder had won. He, with his natural gift, was a loser. He had lost because his shoes were new and lacked character.

The Growing Pile of Drawings

When his father and uncle and aunts talked of important things there was so much talk of the Universe it was as if everyone knew exactly what it was. He sat at the big table and let his head wander over the images he had of what some parts of the Universe were: the wide canopy of stars at night, the pictures he'd seen in books and his father's magazines, of radio stars, distant galaxies, of vast numbers representing in terms of time these vast distances; and the apparently never-ending nature of the whole thing.

Perhaps to a force or being who made all this possible the thing was small and manageable, maybe no bigger than a fishtank.

He drew such a fishtank and set a hand by it, holding a magnifying glass, trying to see the Universe of galaxies this hand had made possible. He set a table nearby, with tablecloth, plates and eating tools; the contents of the tank were to be plundered for the meal.

He didn't like the indefinite nature of his thoughts and the drawn images. He screwed up the drawing paper and looked round with an annoyed expression.

Randal's continuing contribution of drawing paper was something to be grateful for. Still life, that's what. He drew the Sydney Tower and other tall thin buildings as dried flowers in a vase. He put that aside, too. Nothing went right today.

He drew next the outlines of Utzon's Opera House. He reached for his pastels, coloured the sky orange, the Opera House blue, used bluish-white water for the harbour, with a red nearer shore. Impatiently he put it on the growing pile of drawings.

He let the pencil wander gently across the next clean sheet of paper. The line became the upper silhouette of a recumbent body, yet it outlined hills and valleys. He wrote 'Body Hills' on the sheet as a title, and put it, too, aside. He could fill it in anytime, since the idea was there.

A portrait, he thought. He looked across at the mirror set in the sideboard, catching sight of his own face. He lifted his hands as he looked in the mirror, and made a small square with his fingers and within the square he framed part of his own face. He would draw part of a face, that's all, and give it a black border. Two eyes, nose and mouth, the portrait consisted of. He blacked-in the border and held it at arm's length. It was good. Funny how it didn't seem to matter how faithful the drawn shape was to the seen shape: all sorts of different shades and types of character came out of misdrawn, inaccurate or clumsy lines. And if he had something of the seen face, just something recognisable, then almost any sort of addition created facets of character the face might conceivably have in the eyes of various viewers. It was more than freedom: it was licence to do as you liked.

He put this on the finished pile. He was attached to them; they were things he'd made.

Face up in the morning paper was a black and white photograph of a section of terrace houses. To the left and right of the photo the terrace extended into the borders formed by the newspaper's black lines, cut off at both ends. There was an idea.

He took one of Randal's sheets of paper and drew the terrace, but not cut off with a black border; instead, he broke it roughly off at both ends, leaving jagged brickwork. He draw a sea round it, a surf bearing it up, and a sandy shore which it approached. 'Surfing Terraces' would be the title. He drew some black people with spears standing on the sand, looking with amazement as the terraces surfed in towards them.

As a last touch he put a face or two at some curtains and a cat sitting on the front door mat on one of the terrace houses and pot plants on the verandahs of others.

He put that drawing aside with satisfaction. He listened. The house was quiet. He put another sheet in front of him and sharpened his pencil on the emery board Orville had shown him how to make.

He drew the same terraces as before, this time plonked down in the wastes of Central Australia, desert all round. A lizard peeped round a terrace corner where shade fell.

As a last application of his terrace idea, he drew a sailing ship of the eighteenth century towing out to Australia the same broken block of terraces. Migrating families looked from every window.

The Swan Song

Once, Aunt Mira asked to be taken to see swans. The nearest were in the big lagoon park at the old settlement on Blue Ridge river. The family set off in the car, Jackson Blood and Lillian in the front seat; Danielle, the boy, and Aunt Mira in the back.

Lagoon Park was mainly a water park. You can drive through on roads that wind between groves of trees and flower beds, and you come upon water all the time, since the water is confined in a man-made shape like nothing so much as a piece of a jigsaw puzzle, with one or two inlets and five or six rounded shapes, or nobbles, if you look at it from the air.

They lifted Aunt Mira out of the car and set her down near the edge of the lake. When picnic things were spread out five swans appeared. Aunt Mira talked to them a long time. The family fell on the picnic.

At home, Aunt Mira was asked what she talked about. She replied that she asked why swans only sang when they were dying. She said it was because they lived a life without thought. Only when they were dying did they realize they were alive and what a marvellous thing that was. They died, singing their sorrow that they hadn't been glad all their lives at the wonderful gift of life.

'It was a cry for empathy,' she said, 'from the flip side of life. No laughter by request. Heart-rending songs swans sing, music to strike at your hamstrings. All hearts and hounds, every symbol clashing. Ought to be recorded for radio, played over the muesli-lovers' stations. Not the only birds, either, that can be plaintive at the tops of their voices.'

'Did you find they were your mental equals?' Ursula wickedly asked.

'Hrrk!' shouted Mira. 'Equals! Their conversation had all the cut and thrust of an obituary column. A case of a mucklewit talked to ficklewits, a brilliant individualist at the bar of a parliament of fowls. We were proles apart.'

'Was there anything at all you found to admire?' said Ursula.

'Well, the males were firm, but the females were divided,' said Mira dismissively. And began to hum a tune, then to sing in a cracked sort of voice, 'Oh large and saline sea, like a blanket cover me . . .'

With hardly a pause, she launched into another sea of words.

'Why do so many young women get about in such a haunted manner? Because the world's full of bachelors gay, that's why! All those young things dying to perform labias of love. Oh, would some beast the giftie give us, to see ourselves as beasties see us!

'Did I tell you about the time I was in the tropics? In the monsoon season it was so wet the paling fences put down roots and the surf was fresh water; so windy it blew the dog off the chain. In the dry season it got so hot the keeping time for a corpse was down to a minute and a half, and so dry all the brothels had to close.'

'Mira!' Aunt Ursula said sharply.

'Present,' said Aunt Mira, giving a sort of salute.

'He's only a boy.'

'And life's only a comedy of Eros,' answered the redoubtable Mira. 'Remember what the women in the prison camp said: As flies to wanton boys are we to the guards: they unzip us for their sport.'

'This one's not a wanton boy,' said Ursula seriously. The boy hoped Aunt Mira wouldn't allow herself to be silenced.

'Well, you can lead a hearse to water, but you can't make it tell the truth.' She yawned loudly. 'Jessica Christ I'm sleepy,' and shut her eyes, then opened them.

Seeing the boy watching her with big eyes, she said sadly, 'Unhappiness. Everywhere. Can't be avoided. But I'll tell you —' she leaned forward to claim his attention. 'By altering your outlook, your behaviour or your location, preferably frequently, you can attain different varieties of unhappiness.' As if it were an important secret.

She went on.

'There are five billion, you know. Five billion breaths taken in any ten seconds. So tell me this,' and stopped.

'What?'

'Where will the oxygen come from for tomorrow?' The swans were long forgotten.

Then she shut her eyes. Her head wavered slightly, then wobbled crazily, then fell forward on her chest so abruptly and with such force that her eyes jerked open. She was fast asleep, eyes wide open, seeing nothing but what was inside her head.

Sex Change

It was holiday time again; primary school was over for him. After the six weeks holiday he would go to school by train, all the way into Sydney.

The very first Monday of the holiday he called round at the Lady Vivian's. As he rounded the corner into Tobruk Street a girl was coming from the opposite direction. She was about fourteen, one of the Larter girls from Mafeking Road. She stopped at the Lady Vivian's gate just as he did.

'Where do you think you're going?' she demanded in a rough voice.

'In here. To visit.'

'No, you're not. I am. When were you last here?' she asked suspiciously.

'Three or four weeks ago,' he said.

'Well, beat it. I'm visiting today. It's arranged. He's expecting me.'

'He? Who's he?' he asked.

'Mister Vivian, that's who. Anyway, none of your business. Piss off.'

But the Lady Vivian —' he began. Her coarse laughter interrupted him.

'Lady! Ha! You stupid kid. Lady! What did he do, wear a dress and put make-up on?' And she went towards the front door, hooting with ugly laughter.

The girl turned at the door.

'Go home, little boy. Give other people a go.' She knocked in a confident manner on the panelled timber door.

He hurried away, not wanting the Lady Vivian to catch sight of him — or whoever she really was. He certainly wouldn't come back where he wasn't wanted. His best friends were in his own family, after all. Perhaps he would never have a friend, a real one, that he could be friends with for years.

> *If all the friends in the world were one friend*
> *That would be lovely.*

That would be a dream, he thought dismissively. He was too young to be sad about it.

Instead, as he walked back along Tobruk Street he thought of names, and how names sounded when people were talking of those who were absent.

He made a little plain-verse, as he called it, out of his feelings on the subject, and said it over to himself on the way to the brow of Big Hill.

> *When the person is not there*
> *but the name is said*
> *the name is like a living shirt*
> *hanging by the collar*
> *in the hands of someone who doesn't know*
> *the person as a person.*

He ran all the way down Big Hill to the bottom, where Country Road was, and home. He felt free. He remembered the faces of Adam and Eve, that the Lady Vivian had reminded him of. The face of Adam, it was.

The person who was once the Lady Vivian had indicated a belief in God, but if he did believe surely he wouldn't have lied — dressing up to look like a woman when he was a man. Unless he believed God was just a word, with nothing behind the word; deaf, and powerless to remember.

The Wanders

At the age of twelve Davis Blood suddenly, impulsively, lit out because he felt convinced his father had no time for him, perhaps even disliked him. Weren't all the others strong, and blonde? Weren't they all by nature craggy, angular, difficult to get on with, fond of taking strong attitudes, quick to quarrel, hard to appease, impossible to satisfy for long? Except for Danielle, whose nature seemed, with some differences of breadth, tolerance and spiritual energy, a pale copy of her mother's.

Only he was happy, smiling, brown-eyed, even-tempered; except for his angers, the sudden accesses of hate that came from some-mysterious-where; except for the strength of hostility that shot up, like a geyser, from inside him and forced him to perform actions that accorded with it.

He always expected those. They weren't the self he felt himself to be. They hurt no other person.

His father, he felt, admired the unthinking, rough, male ways of his older brothers; he was still doubtful of a smiling boy with red cheeks and a mind attentive to others. He couldn't see that the boy's attentiveness to things around him, the fact that he had lots of time for looking and listening, were possible because he had no internal irritations, no need to bluster, intimidate and prove himself. His mother had convinced him of his worth and something in him had needed little convincing.

His work at school seemed to bring signs of excellence. Still, the world held many schools.

His father's rages, like his, were short and sharp. The vicious thing in him would suddenly erupt, the voices inside threatening and promising immediate and wholesale destruction; there was no standing in the face of these outbursts. It would have been impossible, because foolish, to do anything to oppose the outpouring. And it was so loud.

He believed in God, but when he was furious and creating fear around him perhaps his respect and fear of God was temporarily gone. Otherwise, Davis Blood thought, how could he do it, knowing God was all around, listening and watching?

His father was a mixed man, perhaps a good man. Davis Blood knew that the estrangement between them, slight or even imaginary as it was, wasn't only on Jackson Blood's side: he fended off his father mentally, and perhaps JB felt it. Davis Blood wanted to be better than his father.

He was used to suburban trains, and had no uneasiness about getting out of the house and making his way to the station. To have bought a ticket would have been repugnant to his feeling for privacy: he hated the thought of having to decide on a destination and state it. Who knows if, in an hour's time, he would still want to go to the place he had a ticket for? Assuming he had enough money to go to a place far enough away.

He waited for twenty-five minutes down the end of the platform, discreetly hiding behind a large-leaved privet. The end carriage wasn't empty, passengers going to Happy Valley sat there since the overhead steps were at the back of the platform. He enjoyed the rocking of the train for the two stops before Happy Valley, the feel of the wind coming in his open window, the solidity of the other passengers, the smell of the train, the loud rushing sound as they went under a bridge, and the lesser roar of cuttings they passed through.

At Happy Valley he got out with the rest, and made his way up near the indicator board to look for a destination. Only fifty minutes wait for a train north, into the country to the lakes of the central coast. He sat down with other travellers, who settled quickly into that quiet moroseness that humans are so good at, particularly when they travel by train. He couldn't keep still for more than a few minutes, though, and had to explore the far end of the platform. There was another set of overhead steps at the north end, a good view from the top over the surrounding houses and flats of Happy Valley. The people there had tennis courts, buses, plenty of shops, banks, squash courts, supermarkets, television aerials, a few parks. Many lights were on in houses and flats, for it was dark now.

It was boring to wait. Perhaps he ought to get out of this station and walk. No, it was better to get a long way away. Would things look clearer to him then?

The long train going north, drawn by two diesel-electrics, had a peculiar rhythm to it. Was it the different railway lines in the country, was it the different type of carriage, that made this difference to the ride? It was smoother, as if the distance between the sets of wheels was greater; the carriage seemed to sway less.

Mia Mia drew slowly towards the train, and it had only taken a little over an hour from Happy Valley. Would he get out here? He looked at the place. A small shopping centre, a few lights, and there was the water, at the north of the station, sparkling under the moon.

This would do.

He jumped off — he was at the back of the train and went back to the end of the platform where the sign said NO WAY PENALTY $50. He ducked round an oleander bush and scrambled up the embankment to the traffic bridge over the railway lines.

On the roadway he looked along the platform. No one had noticed him. There was a railway person collecting tickets and checking the passes and periodical tickets of the Mia Mia people coming home from work. He didn't look up.

The boy crossed the bridge and walked down the slope towards the bus stop and the taxi rank.

The main street opened off Railway Parade. He could see takeaway food shops, and neon signs of chemists' shops and a newsagent's. Some shop windows were lighted, there were Chinese, Vietnamese and Indian restaurants, and an old dim cheap place with a narrow frontage and men in shabby clothes hunched inside over mixed grills.

Walking along past the baby health clinic and the Mia Mia Medical Centre the boy could see a place to go. There was a piece of land jutting out into the distance, and past that the rhythm of lights on water. There might be a wharf there. He went faster.

The cold planks of the wharf gleamed in the light of the moon.

He found a set of steps down to the water.

He sat on the third step. His head came above the top of the wharf, he'd be able to see anyone coming.

After he had taken in all the things around him that could be seen, he felt pretty much at ease with his position. In a short time he felt a wave of sleep pass over him, and his eyes thought about closing. He lay down on the second step so he could see over the top. His body settled down on the hardwood step, he relaxed. He experimented with the idea of sleep, closing his eyes, breathing steadily.

A few minutes of this and he felt refreshed, and the thought of sleep went away. He lay still, having been told that if the body gets its rest, sleeplessness matters less.

He lay there a long time, with only a few looks over the top step to see if anyone was coming. He began to feel cold. He stayed still, hoping his body would warm the air around him if he didn't disturb it. Perhaps it did, but not enough. He froze.

Overhead, the sky was clear and the stars shone brilliantly. They were distant, unimaginably so, yet seemed so near. Just overhead, in fact. But for all that, he felt that he, as a person, was almost nothing; no more than an eddy of air that hardly stirred the leaves of the nearby mangroves.

He decided to endure the cold no longer. He got to his feet, took a walk round the wharf, looked down into the water, out across the bay along the railway line that led north, then turned away from it all and made back to the road. He crossed the rail line again and headed for the road where he could hear the heavy traffic north and south. He found the highway, and made north until he came to a side road that went inland, and out of which he had seen coming some semi-trailers, big rigs that, he reasoned, couldn't have come from the bush and farming country in there, but must have been taking a short cut to avoid the toll gates.

He went west, into the dark. The occasional truck spotlighted him from the distance and roared up and past. After a while the street lights stopped and the darkness seemed, if anything, softer with the lights gone.

He walked until approaching morning began to lighten the sky, in that peculiar light before dawn. Cocks in the distance woke and the heavy-eyed but remorseless boy, plodding steadily on, heard them without expression. The exercise of walking had formed a protection round him from the cold, which he felt on his surfaces, but which, he also felt, could not penetrate while he kept going, and created from within himself the continual shield against the world's cold. He was hungry, pincered by crab claws inside where he couldn't reach to soften the pangs.

Before the sun came up he was in orchard country. He climbed over the rabbit wire. Gratefully he pulled some carrots, knocked the soil off and ate them. Walking through the paddocks, he came on a hectare of rockmelons. He sat on the bare hilled earth and cut one open with his faithful penknife, and scooped it out. It was good.

Early season oranges shone in a neighbouring paddock on the other side of a rabbit wire fence. He took a shirtful and sat just inside the fence, near the road. Several trucks passed, loaded with cabbages and cauliflowers, Valencias and potatoes.

His burps, he noted, were satisfyingly of rockmelon, even after four oranges.

After sun-up, he felt tired. The light was crowding in on him, trying to get into his eyes and the adjacent parts of his head. Through the bone, if need be. Home. Get home. No matter what home is, or who likes you, get home.

He was a stranger wherever he went, it seemed; to people, and here to trees, to the way the streets were laid out, the shape of the land, the way the hills were disposed.

It wasn't his land. He was a stranger here and would always be. It was a stranger, and didn't want him.

Apple gums he passed were weeping dark red, their tears solidified on the powdery blackened bark.

'Watch out for your friends!' they called out. 'Watch out they don't drag you down!'

Friends, he said. What friends?

What kept trees straight up? When he had a log on its balance point, only a touch was needed to keep it up straight, but let it lean a bit and the rest of its weight began to tell. It got very heavy. The easiest thing for trees, to survive in a wind, was to be straight up and that's what they did. It was clever of them to do the thing that was the smartest thing to do.

Walking, almost blindly putting one foot after the other, he withdrew into his head, allowing the rest of his clockwork body to carry him on.

Down the bush one day, under a rock which he lifted, crouched an anteater, its spines showing and pointing towards him like a crown of thorns.

Would he savagely hack at the animal with his axe? Of course not. The calm beauty of the afternoon forbade it. Instead he went further east until he came out of the bush on a cliff in sight of the ocean. He could see the earth's curve on the wide horizon. The sea was harvested, as he'd heard in class, but not farmed, not sown. He had stepped back from the edge of the cliff just in time. A crack appeared under his feet, and the very edge of the eroded rock hung there for seconds before it slowly broke, and fell to the scattered rocks soundlessly far below.

He got a lift in a truck loaded with cabbages back to Mia

Mia station, scaled the train to Happy Valley, changed trains and got to the front of the suburban train for the few stations home. He was falling asleep every minute or so. He didn't notice the driver of the electric train look at him and see he was nearly asleep. He got out at Bellbird Corner, right at the front of the station. He went round the brown painted fence past the No Thoroughfare sign and clambered quickly up the steep clay and shale embankment to the post and rail fence, climbed through it and went, glare-struck, home. The driver smiled. He'd been twelve once.

He went round the back of the house when he got home, and didn't see his big brothers spot him as he came up the back steps.

'Get on that, will you.' said Randal.

'Just about out on its feet,' said Orville.

'Does Mum know?' said Preston.

'Who knows what Mum knows,' said Randal.

The boy quietly opened the back verandah door and came in.

'Davis, is that you?' called Mum, interrupting 'What will it be to dwell above'.

'Yes, Mum.'

'Where have you been?'

'I just came up from down the back, Mum.'

The brothers laughed. It was literally true, but not the truth.

'Yes, Mum. I saw him,' Randal said.

'Are you sure, Randal?'

'Yes, Mum.'

'Very well then. Come and have your breakfast, Davis.' Her song resumed, half in words, half hummed:

> 'And with the lord of glory reign.'

No more was said.

The brothers knew, his mother knew, and Davis knew they knew. But the code was that if he didn't want to talk about it then, he might want to later. And if not later, then maybe not at all. Either way, he wouldn't be pushed.

He was home safe, that's what mattered.

Nothing was solved, though. His father, next time he clapped eyes on him, treated him to another dissertation on his beloved Seven States: about the future life to be lived by Australians; how it wasn't easy to see what will be, though the most confident will see furthest; how timidity and tiredness must be done away with, and vigorous pride, human force and making things new will take their place; how love is necessary to understand people, the universe, the Seven States; and above all, that strangers must be welcomed along with the strange, the diverse, the new, the independent.

Under it all, the boy thought he detected that his father was still looking somewhere over his head: talking to, but not seeing him.

There was something else, too.

For the second time in his life he had serious doubts about his place in the universe. It seemed, now, that he may have been childishly mistaken to think of Preston, Danielle, Randal and Orville as merely older strangers who happened to live in the house, rather like unofficial uncles and a youthful and informal aunt. Instead, it was beginning to look as if they were, and always had been, rivals he had never guessed at. Hadn't Lillian treated them, spoken to them more roughly than she spoke to him? With less adoration, less reverence? Hadn't she praised him daily for years for his beauty, his cleverness, his understanding? But what if she'd done the same for each of them, years before? What if her present roughness with them was just familiarity that had grown with the years? What if she loved them as much as she loved him? And what if there were just as much reason, in them, for that love?

Where did he stand now? And why did it matter?
And what sort of boy was he, if his own father didn't like him?

The Punching Bag

One afternoon he rooted round under the house until he found a sugar-bag in good condition. He filled it with a piece of hessian that he folded up tight, tied the bag at the top and plaited a length of sash-cord long enough to tie one end to a verandah floor-joist and the other round the mouth of the bag.

It became his punching bag. He jabbed with his leading hand, then let the other fist go with a big punch. He'd never seen a boxing match, just a few highlights on television news, and punched as he thought it ought to be done. Jackson Blood had told him about thumbs when he was small.

Whenever he had steam to let off and the swings under the house, or under Orville's tree, weren't enough, he used the punching bag. He learned quickly not to give it a glancing blow, which took skin off his knuckles.

Punching the bag was satisfying. He could belt into it as fast as he liked, and as hard.

He began work for the Cooks around that time, delivering groceries on their shop bicycle with the carrier basket, on Fridays after school and sometimes Saturday mornings. If there weren't enough deliveries for all day Saturday, he would set off at noon to caddy at Applegreen Water. He was never without pocket money.

Pleasure

It was a Saturday when he did the groceries for two hours, played cricket in the street on the level patch for an hour, went on a message up the street for Lillian, had lunch, then because he felt full of energy went to caddy at Applegreen Water golf course, riding Orville's old pushbike. He had a milkshake on the way back, smelled his sunburned arms — he liked the smell — and pedalled home up Hat Hill and along through the next two suburbs to Bellbird Corner.

He was pleasantly tired, glad to sit at the big table with the two french windows open, facing the sun, able to see the valley spreading away down to the west, then rising in grassy slopes to Gunsight Hill with its tall grey gums inserted into the steep, shadowed slopes.

He had a pile of paper, his pencils and pastels, and the box of watercolours Preston bought him for his birthday.

'You ought to take some of those up the street and see if the shops will put them in the windows. I think people would pay money for them.' This was high praise, for everything had a money value to Preston. He had moved out, and now had a bachelor's flat near the city, visiting the old house at weekends.

The boy smiled for the thought, but if he gave them to shops to display, he wouldn't have them.

Often he got new ideas from what he'd done before. Preston had been scared by being poor, and had worked night and day to get on in the world. At twenty he had been company secretary for a venetian blind manufacturer and now, at twenty-eight, finance director. He would never be poor again.

The boy was made of different stuff. Being poor didn't matter. He wasn't scared. For him, it was what he did that mattered. To be was more important than to have.

He smiled again as he drew a big sheet of paper to him. And the pleased expression stayed on his face as, with tongue at the corner of his mouth and curling, he began to draw. This would be a series of drawings of people viewing things. His mother's pleasant voice came intermittently from the kitchen. Saturday evening dinner was a big meal. 'It's finished, our blest Saviour cried,' she sang.

Number one was of a painter in the country painting a brown hawk, wings extended, motionless in the air, looking down, waiting for the slightest movement, eyes open and unblinking. Behind the painter, sitting on a stool at his easel, was a fence. Three hawks on the fence looked over the painter's shoulder.

Number two was of an artist in a beret, wearing a small tufty beard, painting a bank robbery going on across the street from where he had set up his work. A group of police stood behind him, looking at the painting and up at the bank across the way, waiting for the robbery to happen on the canvas.

Number three was a drawing class, showing easels, students and model. All except one of the students drew the body of the model, her head and arms. The odd one out started from her fingers.

His mother's endless song had different words:

> 'Now thank we all our God, with hearts and
> minds and voices.'

then became a musical hum.

The boy got up and went outside, took a few dozen swipes with the axe at the big log with all his strength, ran down the back of the yard where the bush began, picked up a rock and hurled it towards the creek, waiting to hear it crash and tear through leaves and fall heavily.

He walked over to Orville's willow tree, put his arms round it to see if they met — they didn't — felt how warm the trunk of the tree was, pulled some grass, chewed the soft ends of the stalks, and ambled slowly back up the stone-bordered terraces to the back steps.

Back to pencil and paper. He breathed deeply with pleasure. The house was quiet. Aunt Mira talked to herself occasionally, Aunt Ursula was out for the day, his mother in the kitchen. He would make a water-colour.

The Opera House took shape in cream-white sails, sailing down the Harbour towards the Heads, followed by a retinue of small craft. No, he washed out the small craft and drew city buildings following the Opera House out to sea. 'Sneaking Out', he called it.

In another, a room of a house admitted the sea, in which fish swam, seaweed grew and strange plants waved. This he did in pastels.

Also in pastels he drew a Buddha with a bronze shine on his skin. Naked students, boys and girls, threw darts at him. Darts stuck in his flesh, blood ran down from the punctures. The students went forward to retrieve their darts and have more shots.

In pencil he drew mountains and vineyards in the shape of a sleeping Greek god. His chest and head, hair and beard, his legs and feet were all parts of the landscape. There was no border to the earth side of the god, he merged with trees, grass and soil.

Also in pencil — everything happened much quicker in pencil — he drew ancient soldiers fighting hand to hand with short Roman swords. Their shields were of metal but each was in the shape of a baby: chubby body and legs, with arms spread above the head, and bandy legs.

He laughed out loud at this one, and for a moment Aunt Mira, who had begun mumbling to herself, was silent. When she resumed he called out, cheerfully, 'What are you grumbling about, Aunt Mira?'

'Wanton buoys, tossing restlessly in Spoon Harbour.'
'What?'
'I'm not grumbling, I'm mumbling,' she said. 'So there. I share the machismo of the stiff upper lip.'

He smiled, and went on drawing. Aunt Mira's top lip was stiff indeed. As he drew, some things from school played over in his head. We — humans, other mammals, birds, insects, fish — are made of the earth's common elements: carbon, nitrogen, oxygen, sodium, potassium, iron, zinc, copper, calcium, phosphorous, hydrogen and so forth. But how? How did flesh come from carbon and water and the rest? How did the flesh of trees arise? Were we cousins of plants? They used carbon, oxygen, carbon dioxide, water, and the same trace elements we used. Where was the difference? More importantly, what was the similarity? After all, they breathed, they had circulation, they had immune systems and chemical defences, just as we did. If he could only look at it from a new angle, see that similarity in a new light, he might understand.

His patient fingers drew, undisturbed by his thoughts and his youthful feeling of overpowering ignorance.

Axioms

He had qualified for entrance to a prominent secondary school, and now travelled by train to the city. With his school bag full of text books he sat in Room 26 among his new schoolfellows.

It was his first Geometry class; the book lay open before his puzzled eyes.

It was a statement on axioms. He knew later he should have read it as 'things we will assume to be true for the purposes of this exercise', but he didn't. He simply read the words of the axioms and didn't like them. Surely it was beyond commonsense to think that a whole high school career in geometry could be founded on 'things we will assume to be true'. Who would tolerate that?

The book said on page two: 'A point has position, but is said to have no magnitude.' If only he had given due weight to that 'is said to have'. He didn't. The glaring error of the proposition was all he could see.

His father, from his earliest days, had impressed on him that anything that exists, right down to protons, neutrons, electrons, down to the quarks that compose particles, has some magnitude and some mass. His father maintained this latter point about mass, as a personal thing that suited his own temperament. He knew the 'authorities' said there were massless particles: he just didn't believe it. In justice to him, he made it clear to the boy that in this he went against the prevailing opinion, all the time deriving a great pleasure from the fact that these particles were not visible to human eyes and had to be taken as a reasonable hypothesis, on trust. Faith was his word for it; the same faith which, spurred by his spiritual need, made God real to him.

The boy, in his own times of thought — while sitting in the bath or on the lavatory, going up to the shop for his mother or waiting downhill from the tees on the par five and long par four holes at Applegreen Water for Mr Priestly to drive — went even further. He felt that words have weight and size.

The way he put it to himself was that each thing that requires a word to denote it, has mass and magnitude, as does the word itself. And not only magnitude but reality: a word was an object, a thought was a thing. So that while being was something that is, so also was non-being. Reality included all that could be thought about.

Later, when he read well ahead in his school science text, he would decide privately that if a word was all that was necessary for existence, then space itself was an object. But that was eighteen months ahead.

If he'd been older, and known more, he'd have said matter and thought have a common factor, which is information, but that, too, was in the future.

Within himself, and in his own time, he was not accountable to anyone for his thoughts, was free to follow whichever way they took him. But this was different, he was in class. Here he was accountable. Here it was the beginning of the school year. Here there was a teacher eager to get on top of a new class.

Mr Cummings must have been drawn by some intuition

to ask the boy to stand and explain the definition of a point.

Davis Blood had to stand: that was an order; but he couldn't say something he knew was wrong. His father, the Meeting, all the people he respected, knew that was the same thing as a lie.

'Come on. Out with it. Don't stand there like a stump,' said the mathematics teacher. 'We haven't got all day.'

'I can't. It's wrong,' the boy said helplessly.

His face was hot. The class grinned at his discomfiture.

'The geometry book's wrong, is it? Is that your problem?' The class laughed. The boy felt the red creeping past his cheeks up into his hair. He tried to loosen his collar, but he'd tied the knot in his school tie too tightly.

'A point has position, but no magnitude. What's wrong with that?' said Mr Cummings.

'It's wrong.'

'Wrong? Are you going to correct the book? You're here on your first day in geometry and the book's wrong? We can't stop and waste time with this sort of nonsense. Sit down and bring me tomorrow the axiom written out a hundred times.'

If only he'd bent a little, realising it was a game of pretend, he wouldn't have been embarrassed in front of everyone: but he hadn't learned to bend. He sat down, the lesson flowed on. He heard nothing for a while, he was in such turmoil.

Nevertheless he knew they were wrong, all of them. They'd found a simplicity, a regularity, that wasn't in the world. They'd found order and certainty at the expense of what was so. They'd tried to abstract from reality something that wasn't there till they created it, and they created it because they needed it. He, and his father, had no need of such comforts.

All these people, boys and teachers, thought there really was such a thing as a straight line and a circle, but he, and Jackson Blood, knew such things could never be: there was only the idea of a regular and perfect circle, the idea of a straight line, the idea of a flat plane surface. No matter how painstakingly or small they were drawn any apparent smoothness or straightness could be shown to be of the order of a mountain range, and at the bottom end were particles and whirling electrons composing the bits of pencil lead, the ink, the paper surface.

A few minutes after his red-faced shame, he found the class parroting words to the effect that when equals are added to equals the results were equal. Nonsense founded on illusion. Nothing material, no object, was, or could be, equal to anything else. His father had told him, but more than that he knew it was true, he could feel it, deep inside him. Such a proposition as the boys recited was true of numbers, but numbers were abstract, they were an invention. Were the people who wrote the geometry book trying to do things with physical objects that properly belonged only to the abstract? He didn't know. His alp of ignorance again, pressing him down.

'There can be only one straight line joining two given points.' Two points drawn where? On a flat piece of paper? Then he could see how at least two lines could be drawn joining those points. On a crinkled piece? On a roadway? The question then became: what is straight? All this aside from the fact that nothing could be straight; there was no such thing as a point without magnitude; and a flat or plane surface was impossible to achieve in practice. And if impossible, why was it necessary to use those words, which reality turned into lies, or dreams at best?

If those words, and this system of geometry, didn't describe the world, what were they?

Games. Why not say so? And were other disciplines more games?

Then what, he asked himself, is the world? I don't know, he had to answer, but they don't know either. I do know that the order they think is there, isn't there. It must be their thinking about the world, with classifications and divisions, that gives the appearance of order to it. Yes, he told himself, the order is in their sentences not in the world. Of course they find order: order is what they're looking for.

Why were they so concerned that this equalled that?

If two countries were powerful, were they equal? If two

people were rich was that equality? If two women were beautiful, were they the same?

Why did they crave equality, congruence? The natural world outside got along without them.

He was aware he was side-stepping the point made in the book, that it was all a fiction, a thought experiment, and he should treat it with 'as if' and 'is said to have no magnitude, length, etc.' But deeper than that was the objection that such a fiction had no firm link with reality. It was founded not on what was, but on 'is said to'.

It was not grounded in reality, not anchored: it was floating.

Perhaps there were other geometries, starting from more acceptable first principles. But there again, did they all start from a set of axioms manufactured by humans? If they did, if they needed axioms, instead of arising straight out of how the world was made, then they too were ungrounded in reality.

As he got ready to close his book at the end of the period and move with the class to the Science block, he thought rebelliously: I have magnitude and mass, therefore I am. Then his eye caught the first sentence, headed axioms; 'All mathematical reasoning is founded on certain simple principles, the truth of which is so evident that they are accepted without proof.'

Without proof! How dare they! He slapped the book shut angrily and looked up — right into the eyes of Mister Cummings, who gave him another hundred lines on the spot for petulance and lack of self-control.

Accepted without proof! Then it was floating! They admitted it! His thoughts were not just obtuseness, pigheadedness. If there were other geometries, this place of doubt, of discontinuity, of ungroundedness, this break, was the place they might begin; from their own 'as ifs'; from other made-up, unprovable axioms! Was geometry of any kind simply a fabrication, and not something arising out of the way the world was, as it had certainly been represented to him? That was shocking! If this was true, then geometry, any number of geometries, were just guesses as to how this world might be constructed. It wasn't information, it was supposition. Geometry told nothing about the world, only about geometry. And yet they'd said education was to prepare you for the world. Which world?

An ungrounded world of supposition, he said bitterly. Two hundred lines wasn't supposition though: it was fact enough.

Other thoughts, stretching beyond what he had grasped, seemed to be taking shape in his head, but the whole class surged out of Room 26 and onto the timber verandah, heading for the Science block. The thoughts became cloudy, dissolved, receded, then vanished. Helplessly, he went with the other boys, wishing he could stay in his seat and try to recover those lost thoughts.

School didn't give you long enough to think, he reflected unhappily; only time for a first reaction.

He walked up the asphalt slope of the playground towards the next lesson.

He had to learn geometry. Rebellion at this point was futile. Their control was absolute. He had to learn what they gave him, or be failed.

The feeling of ignorance and incompleteness was all through him, as if he'd been soaking in it. The shame that went with it, the self-consciousness that made him feel everyone could see into him, pushed him further away from others, further into himself. It seemed that in the geometry class he was destined not to be in the top bracket but, in one of Jackson Blood's phrases, stone motherless last.

Perhaps He was Stupid

In Science, when the teacher, in running over their primary school work on measurement, got to the old metre, once indicated by two marks engraved on a platinum-iridium bar at Sèvres, he had the same problem. Where on that fine line was the measurement started, and where on the second line did the length of the metre show? How can you make a mark in metal without taking some of the metal away? In which case the line was a trench, no matter how slim. Similarly with the method that succeeded it in 1960. Where was the exact point where 1,650,763.73 wave lengths of radiation corresponding to the transition between the levels $^2p_{10}$ and $^5d_5$ of the isotype $^{86}_{36}$ Krypton, were exactly one metre? He did not concede the teacher's point that if it was near enough for ordinary purposes, it was good enough: it was wrong.

The other kids had no trouble; they acted as if the axioms were true and possible and thought no more about it, accepting the convention.

Perhaps he really was stupid.

At any rate, he learned what he was being taught: that now, in high school, work and joy, education and truth, theory and reality, were separate. There was no question here of science working, working, trying to glimpse the face of God. You had to assent to things you disagreed with, for the teacher giving the lesson was the one who marked your tests.

And the tests were wrong, based on misinformation. Yes, he agreed with the practical value of measurements: lines, angles, squares. Houses, cars, bridges, tall buildings, were built by them, and they were accurate enough for such work. But why hadn't anyone admitted it was rule-of-thumb? Why try to make theories out of it and have it sound grander than it was, as if this was how the world was?

No Axioms

On the way home in the train he looked at the buildings — attempts at certainty and simple dimensions — then away from them at the trees, fruit, flowers, rocks, grass, leaves, clouds.

Mr Cummings' geometry had nothing to say of them, and could have nothing to say. They weren't spheres, or circles, triangles or squares, cubes or straight lines; they had no plane surfaces, no flatness, no consistent depth or height or length. The world of nature had no fairytale axioms; it needed no 'things we will assume to be true'. They just were. They laughed at measurement, at geometry, and at humans, too, whose words weren't up to the tasks they were given.

When he left the train and began the walk home he got talking to a boy in Anzac Street. Bruce lived further up Country Road in a house whose backyard butted on to the big vacant block that went right through to Anzac Street. He was idly hurling bricks and half-bricks into a clearing on the vacant block. Then going to where they landed and hurling them back.

Davis Blood joined in, and found he had the ability to hurl a half-brick quite a long way. Holding a full brick lying along his arm, with fingers acting as a stop, he could hurl it, straight-armed, never less than the length of a cricket pitch.

Bruce was fresh home from school at Marist Brothers in Narrowneck. This was a good game. The pleasant savagery of effort went a long way to helping him forget the ridiculous figure he cut in geometry, and his irritation in science. Bruce looked a good prospect for a game now and then.

The Brilliant Kulakovsky

In Room 26 next day he looked across in admiration at one of the boys, a fattish, curly-haired boy who had come only a year or two before from Europe. Kulakovsky had no difficulty accepting the fictions on which geometry was founded; he had no embarrassments, no trouble with teachers. He was good at everything except practical subjects, sport and music.

The boy didn't envy Gene Kulakovsky: that was useless. He was glad others were smooth enough not to stick at the little points he was finicky about. Kulakovsky got full marks in his first lessons. The teacher's face showed a quiet satisfaction: they weren't all thick-headed dum-dums. It was a pleasure to teach the smart ones; and there were quite a few in this class: Verbruggen the technical one, and Peters, with his feeling for heroic poetry and intuitive love of science; Pye, Lucy, King, Chambers, Scott, Whitfield, Blanks, Yeo.

Buildings

He felt the shame of his geometry confrontation settle over him like something stifling, yet growing onto him. Without having experienced anything like that before, he knew it was something he would remember for the rest of his life.

He consoled himself when he got home by drawing a skyline of big-city buildings, each one in colour. He liked the idea of a coloured city.

He drew on one of Randal's wider sheets of thick paper a series of buildings constructed with no straight lines. He liked the city of colour, but was proud of this one.

He went out into the yard and attacked the wood pile for a while, then back to the big table and went on drawing. Homework could go hang; perhaps he'd do it on the train in the morning. His mother's voice came to him in a snatch of song: 'Praise my soul the King of heaven'.

Buildings submerged in quicksand; a carpet of buildings from mountains to the coast; another of roads twining into and out of tall city buildings, some with roller-coaster slopes, and one road coming straight up against a blank wall, right in the foreground, with a blockage of congealed traffic.

He liked altering the world.

> 'Sun and moon bow down before Him,
> dwellers all in time and space.'

Lillian sang.

Next he had an idea for a Big Dipper, on which buildings were having rides. Then a carousel, with buildings on the backs of the horses, in the chairs and on a ride shaped like a shark. The next in this series showed a landscape in which everything was a building: mountains, boats, cars, people, houses, animals, trees, rivers — all were either single buildings or composed of buildings crowded together.

Another, in its way a repeat of the Big Dipper theme, showed single buildings coming down a hill on a slide, which was a sort of mat. One variation had them falling in a heap at the bottom, the second showed them walking away round to climb the steps and have another slide.

Another drawing showed all the buildings in a cityscape as skeletal; another showed a city rising, or sinking, in the middle of a lake; another pictured unwanted buildings dumped over cliffs just like wrecked cars sometimes are.

The last drawing he had time for before tea was of a stretch of coastline with all sorts and shapes of buildings being built in one area, crowding against and elbowing others, which fell into the sea further along.

'Okay buildings,' he addressed the assembled sheets of paper, 'that's all for today.' He had his wash before tea to forestall the question from his mother.

He would much rather have gone on drawing.

One or two boys at school, particularly Thompson, were keen on drawing, and their background knowledge was greater than his. They took trips into the abstract, producing clever shapes, intricate designs.

He wasn't comfortable with something that referred mainly to the mind and cleverness of the artist: he wanted more shared ground between maker and viewer.

After tea, when he took out paper and a soft black pencil, he had the urge to draw a cartoon. A group of identical faces was framed on a wall, and a person, with a face unlike any of those, was pointing and saying, 'That's me, third from the left.' He was about to crumple it, but relented, and added it to the pile of drawings. He felt rich, to have so much paper. Good old Randal; he was moving out shortly, to live with his girlfriend Krista.

On another sheet he drew a forest, with no trees, only television aerials. Animals peered out of the metal undergrowth, impassive, wide-eyed like Rousseau animals he had seen in Danielle's art books.

Last thing before going to bed he drew, in pastels, a mountain with a large hole in the middle, through which could be seen a city in the distance, with spires, tall buildings, houses, roads, traffic and a lake. He kept it for the idea, though it was on the weak side.

He went to bed with not one lingering thought of his humiliation at school. It would rear up often enough to have him squirm as long as he lived. Instead he repeated to himself a passage he'd read in a school library book, 'Don't be a chameleon. Stop pleasing others. Find your own soul. Listen to no one.' Advice to the young Mozart from an older man. He hugged the words to him as he got comfortable in his bed on the verandah, breathing the air that came straight up from the valley over the wooden railing.

As if in opposition — or was it in addition? — other, more familiar words surfaced in his head.

'If any one thirst let him come to me and drink. For the hungry I am the bread of life. For the lost I am the door, the way, the truth, the light of the world. For the dying, I am life.'

Faith, he heard himself recite in the fortress of his head, using the familiar King James version his father quoted, is the substance of things hoped for, the evidence of things not seen. He began to paraphrase it, just for fun, while he waited for sleep to come:

> *Faith is the assurance of things hoped for,*
> *the conviction of things not seen,*
> *the substantiating of things hoped for,*
> *the evidence for things unseen,*
> *the guarantee of what we hope for, proof*
> *of the existence of unseen realities.*

And again:

> *faith gives substance to our hopes, and makes*
> *us certain of realities we do not see.*

He enjoyed ringing the changes on the familiar words, and quickly went to sleep. When Lillian checked later, there was a faint smile on his face. She bent and kissed the smile. As she tiptoed away on the verandah boards, she could be heard softly singing:

> *'I need you every hour*
> *Teach me your will*
> *And your rich promises*
> *In me fulfil.'*

A Corner They Turned

On the verandah outside Room 26, Turner, one of the boys, read a poem about sex. The talk was all of girls and physical equipment and the logistics of sexual adventure for a day or two, then it passed as if forgotten; as if it was a corner they turned, and having turned it, it was behind them.

Behind them collectively, that is. Individually, it was a different matter. Each, no doubt, followed his own path.

Davis Blood felt the tide of physical longing at all sorts of odd times of day, and the temptation to do something about it.

Once, at home when the house was quiet, he gave in to it joyfully in the toilet. When the interesting thing began to happen a fierce penetrating joy filled him: down to fingers and feet, all through legs and body: it was everywhere in him. At one time, for only a few seconds, he thought he was leaving himself.

Then it was over. All the rapture drained away. He felt the desolation of fulfilment and its sharp loneliness, which in turn, he felt briefly, could sprout impatience, anger, hatred, even violence. When he flushed the evidence down the toilet, he wondered, with some amusement, what it would do to the fish when it got through the sewers into the Tasman Sea.

He went with a new soberness into the daylight, to bounce a tennis ball. As he passed Lillian's front garden, he could feel the flowers turning to face him. They knew. He could see it in their eyes.

Something he noticed, then and later, was that he could never recreate afterwards, in his memory, the feelings he'd had, and their deliciousness. Unless he did the whole thing again, of course.

When Does One Equal One?

His geometry disgrace was with him still, though he thought of it less as time passed.

He liked algebra, where you could denote any number by a or x or anything you pleased. It was rather like attaching descriptive labels to large objects, then detaching the labels, and playing with them instead of the objects. He enjoyed that detachment. Numbers were good: they didn't try to mean anything.

It was when he thought of sheep or people or things he knew, like chairs or houses, and tried to apply numbers to them, that he felt uncomfortable.

What was it that bothered him?

In the train on the way home, he stood in the corridor, the afternoon sun hot on his face and his grey serge school uniform. When he got a seat, he sat slumped, head forward. Gradually his thoughts began to swirl, then form shapes in his head.

He knew what felt wrong about numbers applied to things. If you had one house and added another house to it, you had two houses. It was the word 'one', the number, that falsified the position, with its spurious air of being equal to any other 'one'. One equalled one when you were talking of numbers, and only then. Even 'one' written or printed could never be the same as 'one' written or printed elsewhere. Try as you might, you could never get the writing, or even the printing, to be the same. As well, the position was different, and the paper beneath it, even if on the same sheet. Only the idea of 'one' was the same: the sticker you detached from the object or from the word on the paper. The names of numbers were themselves a kind of algebra. The idea of one equals the idea of one.

Lots of things humans invented, including words, seemed to be brave but vain attempts to bring order to a real world full of roughness and indeterminacy, and empty of straightness, flatness and consistency, and equality.

The Tidal Wave of Blood

The boy was twelve years and eight months when he had the family dream of the tidal wave of red. He told his dream at breakfast. He had watched the wave approaching from a long way, seen it when it was near, crashing over coastal beaches, cliffs and everything in its path. He told how he looked down and saw the countryside blood-red, and watched the wave-front as it surged inland over the mountains, out of sight, leaving the land, its lakes and rivers, all red.

Aunt Ursula and Danielle reacted immediately to the way he'd seen it.

'Down!' they chimed in together. 'He was above it!'

It was the first time in the family's story that a dreamer wasn't engulfed in the flood, with descriptions of the warmth and stickiness of the blood, initial feelings of friendly compatibility, gradual sensations of suffocating, and on to final transformation. He'd watched it go inland, past and beneath him.

Bloods of the past: Viscount Blood, Lord Brougham Blood, Alexander Blood the dwarf, Captain Cunningham Blood, Nelson Blood, James Blood, father of Jackson; all had the dream, and none was forewarned — warning the young wasn't the family custom.

It took strange shapes when interpreted by past Bloods: the sea will turn to blood; the mountains will liquefy; earth will blaze and be roasted like a beast; planet earth will become the next red planet; a liquid planet, red as a billiard ball; a ball of solid blood for God to play snooker with forever; the blood would vaporise and girdle the planet with red clouds, from which red rain will fall.

The Bloods of the past died various deaths, all to do with blood. One was caught and eaten in Africa by jackals; one was carved up and eaten by fellow castaways on a boat; one was killed sniping at the enemy in wartime; one was taken by a crocodile; one shot by gun-happy larrikins in the bush; one had his blood pressed out of him when a building fell on him; and one drowned in his own blood in a knife-fight.

Present-day Bloods didn't try to guess its meaning.

'The boy's had it, has he?' said Aunt Mira. 'Ah well, tempus fujiyama. The West sinks slowly into the sun. Not one of them ever able to work out what it means. Funny cattle, Bloods. No instinct for tidiness. Myself, I couldn't resist trying to get its meaning.'

'It doesn't mean a thing, Mira,' Ursula said. 'A dream doesn't mean: it just is. You know that, it's like a shower of rain. When it's over, it's gone. There'll be another, but the drops won't all fall in the same place.'

'No need to preach.' She sounded cross. 'You're not Pope Jones, and I'm not Moby Duck.'

Lillian's voice came from the bedroom, where she was folding clothes:

'When peace like a river attends my way.'

Ursula smiled at the sound, Mira ignored it.
But Lillian had other thoughts, of her dear and only brother Eddie. He'd emigrated some years after her and tried to establish himself in a country town, west of the continent-long divide, the north–south blue ridge of mountains marking the closely-settled eastern coast off from the rest of the land.

She'd often wondered if the tidal wave of blood was a metaphor of a flood of humans conquering the country and being eventually assimilated by it; or was it a symbol of a world haemorrhage of weakness and death? For dear Eddie it was the latter, dying in a pool of blood on a verandah in Orange.

'When sorrows like sea-billows roll.'

as she finished folding Danielle's pink and patterned sheets.

Davis Blood had packed his schoolbag, swallowed his second piece of toast and marmalade, kissed Lillian goodbye, and was on the front steps about to leave for school when the strange bird that came through every few years let out its strident cry.

'Caprigel! Caprigel!' resounded angrily in the valley. And once more the cry: 'Caprigel!' Like a warning.

Woman Reclining

Sunday morning before ten, when he would have to get ready to go to the Meeting, Davis Blood got out paper and pencils and drew a woman reclining. She was as big as the landscape; small villages and parts of two towns were crushed where her body rested. The villages that remained were tiny; ant-like people walked the streets.

He did another on the same subject, with the female reclining among farms and trees, surrounded by tiny herds.

Happy at the thoughts that crowded into his head he quickly worked the huge reclining body into the mass of pipework, compressors, turbines, scaffolding, tanks and retort vessels of a chemical company, such as he had seen on a class excursion to Botany Bay.

He extended the idea to the crowd watching and listening to Hitler at a Nuremburg rally in the thirties, as he had seen on television. The woman's form lay crushing a section of the regimented crowd, but where her body wasn't, the audience were standing unharmed, stiff and obedient.

The next one showed the recliner in a scene from Eden; some animals were crushed under her, others meandered over the gentler slopes of her body.

He had ideas for doing the next of the series in space with satellites for company; on the moon watching the earth rising; and in a vast picnic area with the uncrushed people still drinking and eating their barbecue food, but he was called to get ready for the Meeting, and that was that.

Metaphysics

Treating it in the terms he'd been taught, he began to do well in mathematics, particularly in algebra, but also in geometry, though of course geometry had no real foundation since nothing could, within the real world, be equal to anything else.

He did acknowledge that the angles, lines and areas that in class were 'proved' equal, were, roughly speaking, of much the same size, but that was surely to do with his psychology: he perceived those likenesses; for practical purposes he was prepared to turn a blind eye to a discrepancy here or there. But to pronounce the word 'equal' was to set foot in metaphysics and begin to construct a new, and ideal, world.

Nevertheless, even though he couldn't let go his first conviction that geometry wasn't standing on firm foundations in the world of objects, but was somehow floating, unattached in a world of abstractions, he could see that it was a beautiful idea, and that working with perfect forms, in the ideal conditions of 'as if', would continue to be interesting, perhaps even enchanting.

What shapes, what ideal contours there were to be drawn! What pleasure there would be in searching through them for equalities, harmonies, odd and interesting relations, as long as you accepted the convention, as long as you didn't try to apply it where it didn't belong.

There was, too, the pleasure of drawing, for the lines and angles, circles and curves, were capable of wonderful combinations. Geometry and straight lines, angles and regularity were not the natural world of the bush, the beach and Kookaburra Valley, but it applied to some of the world he lived in. It made possible the construction of houses, electricity poles, railway lines, cars, shops, tins of food, knives and forks, furniture, the pencils and paper he used. The straightness — even though it could never be perfect — together with the regular surfaces, were some of the things that could make life clean, neat, predictable. There was often comfort in a clean, shiny, regular world.

He felt a bit mean that he'd been so particular, so critical of something Mister Cummings was trying to teach in good faith. He thought it might be wrong to doubt everything. Well, perhaps not wrong, but a waste of time.

The metalwork class was a long way from metaphysics. He'd enjoyed the hand-tool work of the previous year, but now the boys were allowed into the world of machinery.

His first sight, at thirteen, of the metal turning lathe brought to mind the image of music unwinding from Danielle's records when she used to live with the family, as the machine tool moved closer to the metal rod, and bit in, unwinding a thin shaving of steel, which curled away, and broke, and fell with a clatter. The music of the lathe wasn't the same as his sister's music. Making a metal centre-punch, with a tapered point and knurled handle, was so absorbing that neither he, nor the other boys, noticed brushing the borders of hunger at lunchtime, and were reluctant to leave the workshop. Verbruggen, particularly, was in his element; he worked weekends in his father's workshop at home.

The Clay Thingoid

His latest thingoid was a flower vase, made in the form of a squat figure kneeling with arms round a deep clay jar. It was his word; 'sculpture' seemed pretentious.

He used the oven in the kitchen, after a little persuasion of Lillian. The work came out well enough, but the colour disappointed him; it was weak, and said nothing. He had a lot to learn about pottery.

Aunt Mira watched him examine it.

'Your proudest possession, is it?' she cackled.

'Of course not.' He didn't want her sort of talk just then.

'Can you take it with you?' She meant when he died.

'Of course not.'

'Why bother with something you can't take with you?'

'Because dying's not living. Everything stops eventually, but that's no reason to drop everything before it happens,' he said sharply, annoyed at the pretentiousness of this talk.

Aunt Ursula wheeled in, and he noticed she wore a tight black woollen sweater. Attention divided between his vase and Aunt's sweater, he noticed with surprise — yet he had seen them, been near them, all his life — that Aunt's breasts were big and heavy; they had a tilted cheerfulness, a jauntiness that reminded him of those cheeky black tugs on Sydney Harbour, painted with steam-engine green, and bows curved high in a grin.

The vase sat in his hand, and he was miles away. Aunt had been everywhere; she had never rested in her ceaseless embrace of life, her fight to keep the final stillness at bay. This clay, though, was as dead as she would some day be, though God would still be in the bits; while some things would live forever.

He could imagine himself dead — but not dying.

It must be embarrassing, being dead. People can do things to you and you can't stop them. Wash you and swear at you if you're dirty. And let you drop, even let your head drop; or let a fly stand on your eyeball.

And what would live forever? From some mysterious place there came into his head an intuition, that the wonder and the power was in life itself, whatever life was, and that life was stronger than death.

Life itself was the eternal thing.

He gave a little shiver. The two aunts were regarding him.

'You need a wood-fired kiln, Davis.' Ursula gently said. 'To get character into the surface.'

'It's no good. I'll throw it away.'

'Let me take it.'

'But it's no good,' he said, handing it to her.

She wanted it because he'd made it.

'Won't hold water!' mocked Mira.

'Just see that you hold yours,' said Ursula.

He saw the vase on her mantelpiece later along with several other things that had been his. He was too innocent to see how like a shrine it was.

Aunt Mira Sings

Aunt Mira, hearing carols all round the place at Christmas time, sang one of her own for the occasion. She was shushed in vain.

> *'While shepherds washed their socks by night*
> *All seated round the sheep,*
> *A bar of Sunlight soap came down*
> *And they began to weep.'*

'Why did they weep?' said the boy.

'Soap gets in your eyes,' sang Aunt Mira.

It had been a long time since she'd given them a song.

'Vacillating rhythm,' she began, then said in her usual voice, 'or is it vaccinating rhythm?'

'Has anyone been giving her wine?' asked Lillian. 'You know how she gets. She should only ever have a sip or two.'

No one confessed, but Orville had a sort of cockeyed grin, and Aunt Mira was too canny to point the finger at her benefactor. She loved red wine particularly, though at times suffered with a headache from it.

'The road to ruin is a ten-lane highway,' Lillian said, and blushed fiercely; firstly at the thought that she sounded like Preston, and secondly at the realisation that she didn't like sounding like her eldest son.

'Let me tell you the story of the sick stock-raider,' Mira said, lurching verbally. 'One of the derisive rich, grateful for each nude day, who exposed his genials while kissing in the park. Been out to lunch with a private member. Discussed the Sale of Gods Act, the Poor Food Act — looking at their curious meal — looking curiously at their food — were served a whiter shade of ale, complained about the performance of the Skin Quartet, threatened to report the management to the Ministry of Dirt, and begged to be treated for percussion.'

Lillian had things to do, and left the kitchen. After a bit, Orville did too. The boy was left alone with Aunt Mira's nonsense.

'Finishing his shot in the park, he observed children gambling on the grass. "They that live by the sward shall die by the sward!" he roared. He was spurious, and a quick walker when roused. "We must cut expenditure in the pubic sector," he muttered. Three crows bent solicitously over a dead pigeon. They looked up from the carcass and said they were having a ball. A male carcass. This was like a blow with a bar of irony. Should he take the ball by the horns? It was Gland's End, the Sport of Spivs. He was reduced to healthless laughter.'

Looking out the window, the boy's face had an arc of smile as he listened to Mira's senseless monologue.

'Was he having the thyme of his life? Not since he'd left his indentures in a glass. Not since Australia played the West Indies at Lourdes. Not since the action replay highlights of the French Cricket Test of '91.

'Still in the park, he came across a youth with a facile mouth, playing an urbane trumpet, accompanied by a female human, who advanced on the sick stock-raider determined to bring him to momentary justice.

' "How'd you like a weekend on the Cross?" she asked, her voice sweet as a razor. The noise of music deafened him.

' "What huge beasts you have," he said. A large bottom followed her. The strains of music showed on the young man's face.

'He stopped playing and said, "This is a concerto for strumpet and syndromes."

' "It's a strumpet solo," the woman said, linking upper limbs with the sick stock-raider. They walked on, but on what?

' "All I wanted was an in-desk look at life," he protested.

' "I'm cleft by grief and sorrow," wailed the woman. "But I'll give you the tongue of your life when we get to close quarters. It'll just be a symbol wedding. I may have to stop for a short period, even though it goes against the groin."

' "Are you one of the print-handicapped?" she said. "Or on the brink of munificence? In short, how are you off for fifty-dollar notes?"

' "Is this an arm holdup?" he queried.

' "Certainly not. I'm the pillow of rectitude. You can hold it up, can't you? Or is the law of graffiti too much for you?"

'The noise of music sounded well behind them now. "Ah, the Pubic Symphony," the woman murmured. "Just look at the children," she said, pointing to specimens of the young gathered in groups, drinking and playing.

' "Boys retching towards manhood," she said. And of others, "Trying to pull off the impossible. Went to one of the new non-educational schools, I bet."

'Their faeces tell the story.

'He patted her beasts, realising her possibilities. "The breathing hills," he said. She smiled tenderly.

' "Mammaries are made of this," she assured him. "I'm in the nude for love," she hummed. "Let's go and match our accessories, share some assumptions. We'll soon have you grinding to a halt."

' "I'll enjoy being in your vicinity!" he said.

' "You come in my house," she advised. "We'll soon take down your decretals." ' Aunt Mira laughed at her pet phrase.

The boy went to the sink for a glass of water. Some days he seemed to do nothing but drink.

Her croaky voice followed him: 'Hit him in the genials!' Then her crazy laughter. The carols were forgotten.

Magic Squares

Mr Cummings set the class a puzzle for the weekend. He wanted the boys to construct what he termed a 'magic' square with sides of four units; each of the sixteen small squares was to be numbered in such a way, using numbers one to sixteen, that across and down, diagonally, and in as many other symmetrical ways as possible, the sum of any four numbers was to be 34.

'The whole point of the exercise will be lost if you get the solution from your parents or other members of your families, or if you look it up elsewhere. I want you to do the dog-work yourselves,' he said.

In the train home Davis Blood closed his eyes, visualising the problem. Sixteen squares. Smaller than a draughts board. Shifting numbers about, manipulating them. Draughts. That was it!

On Saturday, after he'd finished his grocery deliveries, he looked through the old toy box under the house and found an aged set of draughts. He painted consecutive numbers on them to sixteen, and arranged them in a square. It was easy to find combinations of 34, not so easy to arrange them so the vertical rows matched, in sum, the horizontal rows, and so on, to symmetrical groups of four numbers throughout the square.

By three o'clock he had solved it.

His answer, which he wrote out for school, was:

9	6	15	4
16	3	10	5
2	13	8	11
7	12	1	14

He counted twenty different ways to make 34, then tried for more. He got to ten more then, for a rest, ran down to Kangaroo Point, his head empty of everything except the bush.

The brilliant Kulakovsky's solution looked different,

7	12	1	14
2	13	8	11
16	3	10	5
9	6	15	4

and for a second or two on Monday Davis Blood thought his own was wrong, until he saw each was the reverse of the other. Verbruggen, who wore a new Christian Endeavour badge, had a solution that gave far fewer combinations.

In spite of his beliefs, he was beginning to enjoy the abstract certainties of mathematics; chiefly algebra, but also the properties of numbers themselves. He spent hours propagating primes and trying to find a pattern in their distribution.

On the way up the hill from school he found himself overtaken by Mr Cummings. He turned slightly to see who it was, and the teacher turned his head at the same time. The boy was surprised to find himself spoken to.

'Well, Blood. What's your main complaint about geometry this week?'

'No complaints, sir.'

'Something must bother you.'

'Well, it does, sir. Proof.'

'Proof? Theorems, you mean?'

'Yes, sir.'

'I see. Do you mean you object to proof?'

'Not if it is proof, sir.'

'Listen, you don't have to call me sir outside school.'

'No, sir.' If he had to call someone sir at school, he was going to call that person sir anywhere. To change outside school was more humiliating than any sir at school.

'When isn't it proof?'

'Well, it starts off with axioms. That's the trouble.'

'Still axioms, eh?'

'Yes, sir.'

'You feel axioms somehow weight the demonstration in favour of the demonstrator?'

'Yes, sir,' he said excitedly. 'It gets a start. The rest is easier, because of axioms.'

'So instead of proof, it's just being consistent with what was laid down?'

'Yes.'

'Quite right. Year seven boys aren't supposed to be so picky, though.'

'No, sir.'

'You didn't take enough notice of the "is said to be", did you?'

'No, sir.'

'I remember hesitating at that, myself, at school. But what you should keep in mind is that school is about learning to fit in with the world others have made for you. You inherit their geometry, ready-made. And perhaps build on it, if you're lucky,' he added wistfully, as if that's what he'd like to have done, and didn't.

'Axioms are just rules. Mathematics is a game. We made it up out of language mostly, as a useless interest originally, then extended and applied it in answer to problems we had. There's no mathematics in the bush or on the beach.' He sighed, and looked round at the trees in the park, the derelicts on the grass, the few monuments, the aggressive wall of city buildings beginning only a few hundred metres ahead. 'And no morality, either,' he digressed.

This was a familiar sentiment to the boy. He said, 'Not until there were at least two people, sir.'

'Eh?' said the teacher. 'Yes, agreed. As long as you leave out the animals.'

'Oh. I didn't count them, sir.'

'Something to think of, eh, Blood?'

'Yes, sir.'

'So basically, as someone has already said — Russell it was — in mathematics we don't know what we're talking about, or care whether it's true. Free creations of the human mind. We base our lives and work on those free creations.'

The teacher stopped and stood on the grass near the statue of Cook, and gazed towards the same sliver of Harbour. The boy was so absorbed he still carried his heavy schoolbag.

'But I thought — '

'You thought education was about knowledge, and knowledge was based on experience of the real world.'

'But geometry is supposed to be knowledge, sir, and it's not based on experience,' he asserted firmly.

'No?' said the teacher, smiling at the boy's tone.

'Can't be, sir. Nothing can be equal to anything else.'

'No. But for practical purposes —'

'But equal, sir! Equal!' he insisted.

'No, fair enough,' Mr Cummings conceded.

How absolute the boy is, he thought, remembering half-forgotten Hamlet. He went on, 'Our knowledge comes from us, it's not based on experience. Geometry is a theory, as science is a collection of theories. Everything we say about the world is theory — observation is theory — and no theory can be relied on to be the final truth. But go on,' he said kindly.

'I've thought about it, sir, and only abstract things can be equal: concrete things can never be.'

'Oh, have you, indeed?' the teacher said, smiling. 'I agree. Equality is our concept, our need, our word. We've built equalities into the theory, and built the theory on axioms: properties and relations we can't prove because they don't correspond with any reality. Language itself doesn't correspond with the real world: we have no word that accurately describes the surface of a pond, the surface of the sea, or of a mirror. Language reaches out towards the object, sometimes touches, but never encompasses it.'

'Yes, sir. No flat planes. Nothing straight. No points with position but no magnitude.'

The teacher laughed. 'Euclid rides again. Back to that, eh, Blood? Well, point taken. They're all ideal concepts, no relation to reality. We made the system, we didn't find it; we made the branch of metaphysics we call science, and we made the logic which tells us these things — geometry, science — are floating, not based on logic or experience. We also made the language on which our logic depends, and from which it grew as a kind of grammar. Language doesn't correspond with the real world, can't cope with it; so can our logic be sufficient?

'Logic tries to be certain about the uncertain, precise about the imprecise — words — about the trivial, the changing, the unknown. Like science, it's a human construct; it has no rationally secure foundation.'

'Science?' the boy said, not sure he'd understood the earlier reference.

'Science is a construct, not grounded in experience or logic. I consider it a branch of metaphysics, and tease my friends by referring to it as one of the arts, like music. You see, the so-called laws of science can't be proved and therefore aren't certain. Science is a great help to us, but it's a collection of imaginative hypotheses that may be improved on or found lacking at any time. In fact, it's become wonderful and full of promise, a paradise for those artists and visionaries at present miscalled scientists who are restoring mystery and wonder to intellectual life.'

He stopped. The boy waited, hoping he would continue.

'Where were we, Blood?'

'What education is about, sir. People seemed to be saying, when I was younger' — the teacher laughed aloud at that — 'that it's about the world around us.'

'The natural world?'

'Yes.'

'It isn't. The natural world itself, without our contribution, is a dark mystery. All we know is our constructs. All we can eat is what we've found by trial and error to be safe. Our shelter is what we've made. We're funny little animals — scavengers, like the rest — made from this earth who one day woke and found ourselves here and have puzzled over it ever since. Who are we? What are we doing here?

'Apart from those practical things of food and shelter, the efforts of human reason to try to grasp the world that's actually there are like a swimmer in the sea trying to stay afloat. It's a struggle all the time, until the day when strength is gone and the swimmer sinks. And world and mystery remain. We have to make do with what we find here, and with what we are; and at the same time we're expected, each of us, to learn over again all that history has passed on to us. Keep swimming, Blood.'

For they had arrived at George Street. The teacher walked on, the boy ran down the steps into the railway station beneath the busy street. It was the last day of school before the holidays.

Mister Cummings wasn't so bad, after all.

Lillian's Chair

Lillian had a special wickerwork chair on the verandah. It had stood there for all of the boy's life. If she sat reading, her song was stilled. If she sat without a book, it was given free rein.

'Of all the gifts your love bestows,' she sang, and the boy listened. He had never been able to answer the childhood question about loving his mother. Your mother was your mother, a fact of life, like your mother's headaches, or meals every day, or going to school; but what was love? No one explained. If you didn't ask too closely what love was, of course he did.

Aunt Mira suddenly erupted, 'Your proudest possessions are what you take with you when you die!'

'All you can take,' Lillian said mildly, 'is what you are.'

When she lived at home, Danielle sat in Lillian's chair on several occasions, and Randal was the one to spot that those were times when she was deeply involved, as she put it, in a relationship. It annoyed her that Randal was so quick, but not half as much as when Preston came in, having heard Randal's diagnosis, and pontificated: 'Females about to marry ponder many things. Such as sudden riches, sudden heart attacks and how much superannuation there'll be.'

He was so thick, so self-important, that he expected laughter. Danielle was doubly annoyed, because that time she had been thinking of marrying the latest man in her life.

Aunt Ursula was no better than the boys. When she deduced that Danielle was thinking of bringing her lover's bachelorhood to an abrupt halt, and learned that he was nearly twenty years older than Dany, she too was guilty of speechifying.

'The reason women marry men older than themselves isn't respect or dependence or any other fine-sounding thing: it's that light on the hill, that reward of age, that beacon of comfort, order and peace: widowhood!'

A lot of it was Dany's fault. She was too quiet. It encouraged others to fill the silences.

Davis Blood, though, had thought Ursula looked magnificent as, with arms raised dramatically, she finished declaiming through the dreadful tangle of her disability.

Danielle got up out of the chair and swore. Ursula said, reasonably, 'Who ever saw a sad widow?' Dany ran out, nearly in tears, but more in fury. She hated others' opinions. When she was silent she wanted the rest of the world silent, too.

'Oh, well,' said Ursula. 'They say everyone gets their desserts. I've been lucky, so far.'

The chair sat empty, the others still grouped round it, as if its presence held them.

'She doesn't know what she wants,' Preston observed, not without a little sympathy. His own life was lopsided enough. He wanted the managing directorship, but had little else.

'Women don't want anything,' Randal said, out of his knowledge of the world. 'At least not anything in sight.'

'Women,' put in Aunt Ursula, 'are the world's philosophers.' She was enjoying the artificial conversation.

'Go on, Aunt,' Preston said. 'How can they be? Where are their books?'

'Books are unnecessary. Now you watch a woman shopping: choosing, deciding. Women know no decision is wholly right. They're most comfortable when circumstances force their hands and the thing's done. Before that happens, they're happiest picking at the problem, turning it endlessly this way and that. Lost in endless contemplation of its possibilities.'

'That's being a philosopher?' said Randal. 'A man just goes zap! And makes up his mind, like that!'

'And women have to fix the mess later,' said Aunt. 'No, my point is that women actually think. Anyone can decide like your zap! Anyone that doesn't want to take care.'

When they'd all gone their different ways, the chair sat there.

A detached observer might have seen, in each one departing, a slight hesitation. As if they were checking to see if the chair was filled with the presence of the one who, though she said little, was the soul of the household.

Now Davis Blood, some years later, had recreated the whole scene in his head, simply by glancing at the chair. In a year's time, he thought, or fifty, he'd be able to recall that scene though by then the actors in it were dispersed.

Would that mean the scene was still in existence; still, somehow, alive? Certainly it would exist, as images in his head, along with myriads more, until his own death liberated them.

Certainty

Some things had certainty. Words sometimes had it, mathematics had it, logic had it. Those were things humans had constructed. The law had it, religion had it, Marxism had it: the natural world didn't have it.

Mr Davenport, the science teacher, applied the theme of certainty to measurement, and gave the class a practical example that filled Davis Blood with pleasure.

'Suppose we're making machinery and we need a special batch of carbon steel — specifying the carbon, the other additives and so on — and we need this steel in strips of, say, 59 mm. Now, depending on the degree of accuracy required, we can get this steel made to the finest margin of which our best tools are capable — it may be we need an accuracy of within a hundredth of a millimetre. But if we wanted, and could pay for it, we could get it to within millionths of a millimetre. But where the exact point of 59 mm lies is something we don't know. With better instruments, more accuracy, the steel may be closer to 59 mm, and closer and closer; but exactly is not something we can experience. We may, by chance, have exactly 59 mm, but we could never know, for certainty here is illusion. Not only do we not know exactly the measurement of the steel, but we can't be certain of our measuring tools.'

In a way it reminded Davis Blood of the Social Studies lesson on the French Revolution, when the teacher said, 'Well, you know, freedom's a funny thing. It can't ever be claimed and held, because it won't stay still. The word moves about; there's no certainty on what it means. But it can be fought for, and that's the point.'

The Anger

It was days since he'd spoken to anyone in the house. Even when he went up the street at a quarter to six on Saturday morning to work on Kendall's bread cart, he'd snatched something to eat without a word.

His head seemed like a heavy lump equipped with eyes held in a frowning position, not moving far to left or right. His whole body seemed set in a forward position so that straight ahead was the only way to go, with no bothering about people or things to one side.

As he walked, his family noticed his head-forward, eyes-narrowed look, and kept out of his way. His habit of looking silently, deep into the object before him, trying to enter it with his mind, was around him, and went with him, all-encompassing as air. Only now the object was himself. Not even Orville chipped him about it. If he was feeling peculiar, he had a right to do it and be allowed to get over it in his own time.

He stood, aimlessly, in the dining room, not seeing himself in the mirror, only dimly aware of the yellow and silver sunlight outside on grass and trees and flowers. It was coming, he could feel it in him.

The anger grew. He could feel the swelling in his chest and down further as it gripped his stomach. On an urgent impulse he went to his Jonathon-tin and emptied the saved money into his own savings tin.

He couldn't blot Jonathon — or whatever his stupid name was — out of his mind, but he could remove his money and abolish his money tin. Screwing it sideways, lid against the rest, until the wire hinges gave way. He stuffed the two twisted pieces of metal in the rubbish tin and banged the lid down hard.

What was there to do? He couldn't draw, or read, feeling like this. He wanted to hit something. No, more than that, he wanted to destroy — to be so powerful that one blow would lay things flat: houses, people, obstructions, so that a savage spree of his violence would leave a typhoon's trail.

He forced himself to stand there, letting the feelings from within flood him, yet not stopping the scrutiny of them made by yet another, more considered part of him.

He was two people. He'd felt that for some time. At least two. Quiet and docile in house and classroom; all that his parents and teachers could ask in the way of discipline, attention, teachability.

He was a different person when he sat alone at the big table, either thinking while doing nothing with his hands, or using his pencils or pastels to think. Different, too, when he ran down into the bush, the axe in his right hand, his elbow bent as a shock absorber for the weight of the steel as he ran from rock to rock, up the hills, and down into the cool valleys.

Different again he was when some wrongs done to him built up inside until he blew up with sudden violence.

And still different when the slow explosion inside expanded into consciousness and he was filled with rage and hungry for destruction and the sounds of crashing and breakage. Which he held in, always.

Jackson Blood wasn't a man for endurance, he'd often said, but for speed over short duration. Was he like his father? He ran down the back steps to the toolplace and got out the four-pronged hoe. The prongs were long and wide; a tool that could carve out a large sod with every blow.

He went down to the lowest terrace that his brothers

had made, where the soil was deepest and darkest. He started to dig near the place where a back fence would have been, and completed one row. Then he turned with his back to the fenceline and worked on the far edge of the row he'd dug, hoeing into the unbroken surface that stretched in front of him, digging in, then pulling the sod towards him, into the ditch made by the digging of the first row. He worked up to a good speed, and from there gradually began to work in a fury. Just behind the fury of work a fury of mind followed, till it caught up, and he worked in a state of extreme anger, haste, and violence. He went on like that until his arms ached and his hands began to lose their grip, having clenched tight for so long.

He dropped the big hoe and let its shiny smooth handle lean against his shoulder. He wasn't angry any more, though he still felt the pleasant excitement of having been angry. Digging was good, violent action satisfying, the aftermath pleasant.

He reflected that while he'd been furiously working, it would have been impossible for him to drift off into one of those dream-states of unreality in which the world seemed frozen into a stationary landscape painting.

Perhaps there was freedom from feelings of unreality in constant movement, action, plans, noise — any sort of intensity. If so the equation was: To escape unreality — do!

But he had no wish to escape any of the feelings that rose from within; he wanted to experience all that were there.

When the anger subsided he felt a twinge of fear — mixed with shame. The shame! Ah, that was something. It was shame that he hadn't done something to match the feelings in him, to be worthy of the frightfulness within.

What sort of person was he? Why did he — so sunny, so equable — contain such violence?

What words did his parents' religion have for such as he?

>'Become as a little child?'
>'Born again from above?'

> *'God is love?'*
> *'Love your neighbour as you love yourself?'*

These didn't answer the springs of anger in him.

> *'Be perfect, just as your Heavenly Father is perfect?'*

Yes, that covered it, but what comfort was that? How could anyone be perfect? Or was there some future use for his angers, that would bend them into acceptable shapes?

He forced himself to sit at the big table. His eyes looked out of the french windows to the sunny afternoon, but his head saw nothing. He sat for a long time.

Suddenly, as if awakening from a sleep, he noticed the turpentine leaves, shining in the sun.

A breeze lifted them, their undersides fluttered and showed white. How beautiful the world was! The anger was gone. He smiled, glad it was over. He felt good.

Aftermath

In the sky to the west, white clouds in a queue idled across the sky. Leaning out over the verandah rail, he saw the valley trees fidget among themselves and share out sly noises, though some of their movements were, he perceived, silent.

It occurred to him that even the flight of a fallen leaf could be calculated if all the factors acting on it were known. But who could know that? He raised his eyes to Gunsight Hill and thought of the Old Paddocks over the western side of the railway line, down on the flat, site of

Waratah Mile, the first settlement in the district, wondering at the mysterious way that knowledge of things around trickled into him along a separate vein of time, while he was dreaming or occupied with other things. At the edge of the Old Paddocks he saw in his head treetops speaking quietly together of breezes they had known. Some from as far away as Madagascar were mentioned, that touched Perth, then collided briefly with the Indian Pacific on the Nullarbor, and bore to Bellbird Corner scents and dusts and exhalations that went to the head like wine.

He walked out into what before had been landscape, and became part of it, an element of the bush he loved. He loved the curves and rises, folds and dips, outcrops and grassy flats of this land and these hills so much, he felt it reasonable to imagine they might be made for him to love. All through the bush, all year, he reflected with joy, leaves hang down, rain falls when clouds get heavy enough, cliffs wear away, trees grow, branches fall, birds fly till they can fly no more. Everything does what it's suited for. It was obvious; it was also wonderful.

There was comfort in such stabilities. All things appear to end, but continue in another form; other things leave their previous forms, and grow together to replace what appeared to end. But of course there is no end, for God is in all things, whatever form they take, and God was both before, and is after, mere things.

Off the main clay track through trees of mountain devils, wild currant bushes, the low-growing whistle-plant, he came to the little quarry where men round about found slabs of white sandstone for paths and patios. The grain was regular, well-defined, no trouble to split. Jackson Blood had taken some for the front path, using his old brickie's bolster and three-pound hammer to cut it, and the wheelbarrow to trundle it home.

Rain had dissolved stains out of fallen gum leaves, leaving brown leaf-shaped prints on the white stone. He stood, feeling the chill of evening coming on, remembering a story of Jackson Blood's in the mountains, hungry, and after the kill warming his hands inside the body of a sheep.

Further down the slope towards Little Paperbark Forest, arriving at a place of saplings, he took it into his head to play a heartless game with them. In this game you run like mad, jump in the air and take the young tree high, and if it holds, you stop in the air and swing back and round: if the tree goes, you end up on the ground, holding the top end of a splintered trunk. He loved the young trees, and he loved butchering them sometimes, as if all were his to have or to destroy, like a wilful child.

He simmered down, went back up the slope, and headed for home.

A pale smear flickered across the track. He looked up in time to see a soldier bird pursuing its stiff muscular flight to a honeysuckle tree, which it approached at a height lower than the bottom branches, then with a sudden upward swoop — it was a climb but its speed was that of a swoop — landed abruptly on a branch near the top of the tree, hidden by leaves.

He felt like applauding the bird's clever way with the air, and its wings, and the apparent freedom in being able to get off the ground.

He smiled all the way home, friends with the world.

A Makeshift Existence

Monday was the first day at school after the holidays. In a playground game with a tennis ball, he chased the ball into year twelve territory, lost it to big Artie Mauther, and only just escaped being caught by the big boys. He'd been in danger brought on by a temporary feeling of invulnerability, and got back to year eight territory mercifully without being scragged.

On the way home from school he ran into grey-suited Mr Cummings again. The teacher glanced down, then looked ahead, and waited before he spoke.

'So, Blood. You seem self-contained, Blood.'

'Yes, sir.'

The man laughed a little, a sort of out-breath through his nose, not opening his mouth. Probably at the 'sir'.

'Good work on the magic square.'

'Thank you, sir.'

'Do you believe, Blood?'

'In what, sir?'

'In anything.'

'Yes, sir.'

The teacher wasn't listening to the boy. Words were in him, and must come out.

'Inside you, that's the important place. People make Utopias, where safety is king, but the only safety is inside you. People can't get at the you inside. That's your refuge. Do you have strong convictions?'

'Well,' he started.

'Get some quick,' Mr Cummings said. 'Strong beliefs support you in times of trouble, keep you going, keep you together. Lack of belief leads to falling apart. I know. I started off believing in nothing. A mistake. If science, rationally unsecured, can be respectable, belief can be. It's absurd for the individual to take the professional philosopher's aims for himself, to be a truth-seeker forever, holding off from commitment to belief until final truth is attained. Sometime, somewhere, he must leave this doomed expedition and settle down to live and work and grow children. Having no final truth, he must accept, trust, believe; or construct his own system.'

The boy said, after a bit, 'Yes, sir.'

They crossed the street to the park in silence.

'Sir,' said Davis Blood, when they set foot on the grass.

'Yes, Blood, what is it?'

'When you said: we have to make do; would you say more on that?'

The man looked down at the boy. He'd said those words weeks ago.

'Very well,' he said automatically. This boy was hungry; he wanted to be talked to. 'There's the world of nature and the world we've put together. We can't live in the world of nature; if we could, we would, but we need clothes, houses, cooked food, clean water, drugs and doctors, employment, and so on. We provide them, they're not put out ready. We eat whatever we can kill, or find, or work out how to grow. But these things we use as scavengers, they weren't put here for us. They're what we've found we can use. They're here on earth for themselves, not for us; we have to bend them to our will.'

The boy remembered Ursula saying something similar, and nodded.

'Many of the vegetables and fruits contain poisons, and all contain bacteria. Animals, particularly, have bacterial problems, so we cook them to kill the bacteria. Our own very accomplished immune systems tell of vast interior battles in the distant past, as the ancestors of our genes resisted invasion attempts by smaller bodies.

'In other words, we're here, and if we can find some way to go on living, we'll do it. Just as every other living thing does. What I'm trying to get across is that we at present have lost the idea that we're only one of many competing organisms, and nothing was put here specially for us. As for our bodies, we're made to walk upright, to eat, defecate, grow, reproduce: for action. We're not made for rest or sleep; our bodies have no recognised parts adapted for lying on, as feet are for walking or running. We have to keep turning at night, to keep the circulation going. It's all makeshift. Staying alive, survival: all makeshift.

'At any moment the ground may explode or open up beneath us, an asteroid too small to be detected may blot out a city, a tsunami may devastate islands and coastal towns — all with no regard for human dignity.'

He hesitated, as if about to stop walking, but went on.

'At any moment our own frail mechanism may stop because of a tiny blockage or two. Even food is an enemy.'

He said these words with something like despair — mixed with annoyance — and the boy glanced up at him. Mr Cummings went on in a stronger tone.

'We have to be aggressive enough to kill, so we can eat, but must tame our aggression so we can support large human populations without destroying each other. Balance is the word, Blood, and good sense. But the question remains: What are we?'

His voice sank on the phrase, as if he was hit by a heavy defeat.

The boy was silent. The teacher stopped, standing near one of the park's specimen trees. He put a hand against the tree trunk.

'Not exactly fighting fit, Blood. Just rest a bit.'

The boy stood.

'Are you okay, sir?'

'Be right in a moment, Blood. Small pain.' He looked into the distance, out over the Harbour. He put the other hand high on the middle of his chest.

'Now,' he continued, supporting himself still. 'Other things flow from our makeshift existence. We find ourselves here and there's nothing ready for us: no numbers, no poetry, no stories, no history, no philosophy, no morality, no geometry! Not even language, on which all the rest is based! So what do we do, Blood?'

'We make them, sir.'

'Right. We have to provide them. There's nothing here waiting for us, but we have needs. Huge, grinding needs. We've chanced on a way to talk, since our larynxes are in a suitable position, and we construct language. Our needs will not be denied! We need things to think about, we need problems to work on. We need conversation, we need words of caution or encouragement, we need stories, we need opinions — on our ancestors, on ourselves, on our futures — we need morality so we can live together without every disagreement or frustration leading to murder of others and revenge murder of ourselves. We need geometries, we need to feel we're on a journey towards better things. We need meaning; we must imagine it, create it, supply it. We need God, something higher than we are, to venerate and emulate, and more than that, to tie us in personally to the Maker of the Universe.'

He stopped talking. His arm was tired. He leaned against the tree, both arms by his side. The boy waited, trying not to look worried.

Mr Cummings drew two big breaths, and went on.

'Do you know, Blood, that at the seashore, in the mountains, the desert, there is no evidence of a God?' He looked down at the boy.

'No evidence, until we came along. We see things that we take to be evidence. But this is the point: Gods come from us, from our needs! Just as geometry, and houses, and statues' — Captain Cook stood nearby, gazing night and day over the harbour — 'Problems, books, languages, philosophies, poetry, numbers: they all come from us!

'We need geometry, Blood! Once we found it could help us to navigate and to build better, it became indispensable. We can't wait till its logical and philosophical foundations are underpinned and secure before we use it: they may never be. But it works for us, and we need it now! The foundations of science are floating too, Blood, but we need it. Daily we use the parts that work. At the frontiers of science the powerful and original imagination is king, for science is guesswork, hypotheses; but the journeymen, the tradesmen of science are indispensable — their science works!'

He paused for breath.

'Better now, Blood. Let's walk again.'

They started off.

'Truth is another matter. We may approach it, more nearly every year, but can never know it.' He quoted:

> *'If by chance mankind spoke final truth*
> *He could never know it, for mankind's truth*
> *Is bound in language, it is a rope*
> *Woven from a web of guesses.*

Apologies to Xenophanes. But we need houses and dams and bridges and roads and mines and machines now! We need geometry now, Blood!'

They crossed the wide street. On the other side the teacher stopped and, face to face with the student, said earnestly, as if trying to impress it on the boy, 'Active unbelief is a way out of commitment, towards the territory of complete freedom — aimless, ungrounded, anchored to nothing — a most dangerous and empty existence.'

Mr Cummings was silent the rest of the way to the station.

The boy said, 'Bye, sir,' and escaped down the underground steps.

'Yes,' the teacher said absently, and continued on.

The boy went over it several times on the journey home. It was a mark of confidence that a teacher had said something to him that came out of his life, rather than off a shelf in his mind marked 'for school'. But the makeshift nature of human life, coupled with the warning on lack of belief and the idea of inner refuge: these were important matters. And the notion of need, governing all.

As for the rhetorical question: 'What are we?' He could hear it still, repeating itself over and over in his head. Mr Cummings' voice had been heavy, as usual, but on that phrase it dropped, it seemed to be frayed slightly, with a despair Davis Blood had never before heard in the voice of an adult. As if he might soon die without ever knowing the answer.

The Child as Thinker

His thirteen years of life seemed to be packed with things to think about, to learn, to decide on. In the Meeting he had been faced with the problem of the place of mankind in the world, in the universe, in relation to his fellows, in relation to God. He was familiar with ideas of revenge, punishment, justice and the varieties of wrongdoing. Life and death were common words to him. He found his way easily among ideas of right and wrong in the family, in the street, at school.

At home he'd been made familiar with the political ideas of the past that were in current use. The popular exploits of science were part of the background of his mind. The geography of the country and its customs he learned about from the talk at the table of his father, brothers and uncle.

At school and in the street he was given practical demonstrations in the fields of revenge, punishment, justice, approval, the workings of hierarchies, the problems of authority and power, and given exercises in recalling things he had learned, as well as practice in the mechanical operations of arithmetic, singing, and now algebra and geometry, history and English.

As with geometry, he didn't always accept what he was told. In English, a relief teacher referred to one of the novels they'd be grappling with later as an example of a 'stream of consciousness' method, and likened this to a river. But Davis Blood's own consciousness wasn't continuous, rather a succession of bits of consciousness. There were moments when he was conscious of nothing, moments that later he had no memory of. His consciousness was intermittent.

What he had learned, since the day of the axiom, was not to make a big issue of it, as if he were Horatio holding the bridge single-handed against the enemy; but to work out what he thought, and develop that.

Orville's school science book, in its last sections for the advanced kids in year 12 at the end of secondary school, dealt with light, and quanta or packets of particles. It transported him to a world the rest of his studies didn't deal with: the world of air, sky, ground, the land itself; light, sound, gravity. The attempt to describe the nature of the world and the universe he found fascinating. He joyfully indulged his imagination with speculation.

Perhaps space, he thought, the intergalactic medium, isn't mere absence of matter. Perhaps it's not nothing, but a thing itself, a form of matter; something that, if you push it here, will push against something else over there.

What rot, he thought at first, smiling at his nonsense. But further on in the book, which he read when he ought to have been doing English homework, he came across things that made his fancies seem not altogether nonsense.

He encountered serious discussions of speculations that all things are forms of the same thing; that the separate parts of which the universe is composed are connected and communicate at a fundamental level, which means there is not the separateness in its parts that one would think, but a strange form of wholeness. This seemed reasonable to him from his science-class familiarity with the proton, electron, etc, basis of matter, though he knew more than that was implied. In addition, it accorded with his feelings about God being in all things and all things contained in God.

A further speculation was that the parts that go to make up the material universe are in some way conscious, though perhaps unthinking, participants in its workings. In other words, such parts may 'know' and act accordingly, and also deal with information they receive, seeming to be organic in some way we haven't yet imagined.

The speculation that satisfied him most, though, seemed to knit together parts of the others, as well as appealing to little favourite thoughts and hints of thoughts he'd had since he was small.

It was this: that nothing is independent of other things,

all things are — what was the word? — with everything else. What he did, then, affected all the rest, in however small a way. All affects all else. And, another element: the separate parts are aware of the whole. Being made of the basic bits, they recognise the basic 'bitness' of other bits. Which implied, or reinforced, the idea that they are in contact with each other, as if something tangible existed between them, needing only a push here to register a bump there.

Further, even communication between bits here and bits there might be unnecessary, because both are bits of the same entity, both are they! One bit knows what is the situation with the other bit, since each feels the presence of each as if they are inhabited by a common consciousness. In which case, again, there may very well be a 'now' which is now through the universe — to answer his question of childhood.

It was airy, heady stuff, made of words and imaginings and possibilities; and the fact that he couldn't follow any of the equations didn't bother him. He was glad to have found so congenial a particle physics supplement.

He mentioned some of these things to Aunt. She was happy for him, and seemed, because of her wide reading, to have heard most of the things he spoke of.

After some talk of what the universe was like, Aunt said, 'Realities are like spheres, and there are many. They interpenetrate so that any one thing may share a number of different realities. You know your Venn diagrams? Well, like that, only with spheres rather than circles.'

Which gave him more to think about, as he straightaway got busy trying to build a mental picture of interpenetrating spheres. The picture he came up with was similar to the linkage between the shells, the different energy levels, of electrons, as Orville's book explained.

Good Old Aunt

He was having one of his silences when Aunt next wheeled up. Her subject was morality.

'The things you do are important,' she said. 'They add up to more than half your life. The system of *do's* and *don'ts* is called morality — it fits us to live with others, without murder.

'People usually just feel their way into the system. Those who don't get the point — that you can't expect to do anything that comes into your head — have trouble. They come up against the system, that everybody, more or less, agrees with and supports. I say "more or less" to be accurate, but in practice so many people do support the system that it's impossible to beat it, and runs over those who oppose it. The thing you need to agree with, is that it's good and worthwhile to live with others, at peace, and you need to have that firmly inside you.

'Some day you may get a feeling for the whole system, the whole mass of ways people have of working together, living, trading, forming alliances together, competing, learning, holidaying, amusing themselves, rising in the world, ruling others — the lot — but most people don't. All they get is how to get on in their own little corner.'

She watched him, knowing he was defiantly inside himself, but knowing also that he was wired to register her words, even if he gave no sign.

'Getting back to the personal, to conduct. Some believe in judgement after death. They're right in so far as the final verdict comes only at the end of life, but the salient point is that continuing judgement is in you, and proceeds moment by moment. No one and nothing is going to put everything right at the end. There's no punishment, no reward. All there is, is a resultant person, moment by moment. You are what you do. What you are includes what you have done. You contain in yourself both punishment and reward. The government of human affairs is in human hands. If you wish to punish murder, you can do it. If you say tit for tat, then that's what you will do. You effectively decide what is improvement and what is bad. You can go either way, from moment to moment. If you fail to choose, then that is a form of choice.

'The nature of humans, with their greed and acquisitiveness, aggression and violence, appetite and laziness, together with the better things, is the nature, I believe, of any life that could arise.

'Anything that can choose its actions moment by moment; anything that can think "I"; anything that has the ability to act on others, will be selfish first, and get what will make it comfortable. When it's comfortable, it may then feel free to think of others.

'You see, God is love, and also hate, plus many other things. God is God of good and evil too; God of matter and spirit, of life and death, of light and darkness; God of all. Of ants, too. Ants are just as valuable.'

The boy was silent still when she finished. He went into the kitchen for something to eat.

As for Ursula, she gave in to a little theatrical despair, knowing it would be heard, and amuse the boy, but that no one else would take the slightest notice. She declaimed:

> *'The truth has killed me; this is the resurrection!*
> *Why do I waste my time on this planet with*
> *People who hear all, but say nothing?*
> *And roads that never run on time.*
> *They wonder why I sometimes refuse to move*
> *Or why I sing raucous songs in city banks*
> *Or eat a messy lunch in my wheelchair*
> *Parked on the pavement in Pitt Street.*
> *If only I could take off this wheelchair like a dress*
> *Give it to St Vinney de Paul for the poor*
> *And go buy a new body at a fashion shop!*
> *Still, the die is cast and can never change his spots.'*

Good old Aunt. But his thoughts weren't on her words. He was thinking of his sister's art books, full of coloured reproductions. He was back at what he perceived as the break, the apparent fracture, in what the art books seemed to show as a continuity in painting. There was a break there, he felt sure. Something in him made him feel that at that break, that unexplained discontinuity, there were discoveries to be made.

The Fracture

How did painting, or painters, get from Corot's and Constable's trees to Soutine's Big Tree? From Renoir's faces to Picasso's? From Van Eyck to Van Gogh? He couldn't understand that step. He could follow, fairly well, he thought, how a painter could travel from Canaletto to Seurat, Gauguin and Monet, to some of Cezanne, but what was it the later painters were seeing? It was as if their paintings had become almost independent of what the world looked like. Were they about seeing? Were they painting something inside themselves?

How much more there was to see in the world — to learn, to try to enter in sympathy and understanding! So much. It was all ahead of him.

The Fall-out Shelter

After school on Monday he ran home, threw his clothes and shoes off, put on shorts and sandshoes, grabbed a piece of bread and butter, scraped it with peanut butter as his mother ordered — she didn't like excess — and crammed it into his mouth as he raced down the fourteen back steps to the tool place.

He picked out the old worn mattock with the rounded and blunt blade, carried it over his shoulder down the back yard which was stepped into three level terraces bordered with bush rocks at the bottom level.

Brown Rock was the eastern boundary, the turpentine trees were the southern border where the bush began. The soil was deep. There was over a metre of soil before the clay started.

The fall-out shelter he was building would be deep, for the earth was sandy and soft. He would go down as deep as he could, digging out any floaters he found, until he was into the clay and down as far into that as possible.

He attacked the work with eagerness. There was homework to do for school, but he could do that after tea, or in the train tomorrow.

The mattock bit deep into the dark brown earth, dislodging the odd earth-covered stone, beginning to waken and expose long shiny green centipedes with golden legs. These hurried quickly out of sight under a lump of earth or, if they were cut in two, each bit wriggled furiously.

By five o'clock he had got down to a floor of pale grey, the glimmer of moisture showing in tiny spots. It looked so finely put together, a little like wet rock.

When he was called for tea, which usually happened five minutes before the dogs were called by a spoon on a plate, and which was enough to bring the cats, he had got down to his waist. He picked up the tools and ran with them to the tool place, then up the fourteen steps to have a quick shower.

The next day he carried on down into the clay and finished Tuesday with the hole at neck level.

Everyday he did some work on the shelter. In a week the floor was down to the end of the clay and on rock. He could stand in the pit and the sides were over his head.

He cut down eighteen young trees hardly more than saplings, stripped them, halved them, cut them to length, and put them across as roof supports. He boarded the sloping approach channel and put in a door. His last job was to lay the square sides of an old iron water tank over the roof supports, overlapping them to make a roof rain couldn't get in. There was a rise in the middle of the roof where he laid one of the trees lengthwise in the middle to raise the iron and slope it down towards the outside edges.

When the blast of the bomb came, the family would be inside, the devastation and heat outside. But how could he keep out the poisoned air? Oh well, it was a blast shelter, then.

Randal was so impressed with the boy's work that he bought a new mattock-head for the boy, square-bladed and sharp. Davis Blood took the old one off its handle, washed it, carried it up under the house, gave it a smear of oil and put it on a rack in a place of honour. Each male in the family had used that mattock-head. Even the vertical blade had been worn right down; it had been used for splitting rocks.

No one in the family said much about the shelter, or even looked as if they noticed.

Except Kellick

Except Kellick, the new dog. He watched the boy's efforts intently, often with head sagely on one side, giving an impression of deep thought.

Kellick had been offered round the district after the two Fox kids and their father had been killed in a late-night car accident, near Honeysuckle Bend. They had loved Kellick, and Mr Fox, a retired circus performer, had spent a lot of time with the dog. The sight of Kellick hanging around the house moping was too much for Mrs Fox after the three were buried. The Bloods were always good for a stray or two. He was a sort of anchor dog. However you wanted to go, he wanted to go slower.

He had an unhappy cast of mind, and since there had been those three deaths in the family he came from, the Bloods allowed him time to settle in. He was part bull terrier, part foxy, but that didn't explain much. His new family thought it might have been his early environment, but it was more likely just the way he was. He had a sad, despairing expression.

A part of his colouring was black, shading to brown at the edges. The tip of his tail was black, so were two round spots on his rump; he had a black saddle that had slipped to port. There was colour over his eyes, on parts of his head and ears, but apart from that he was white. On top of all that he had long ears.

When the time of mourning was past, the boy was able, now and then, to get him to run. His was an awkward, sideways, rolling run, as if he had too much muscle in all four legs, and none would yield priority to any other. He seemed happier after his runs and the boy was encouraged by that to take him up to the shops. At first he stood alongside the porcelain dog that collected for the crippled children appeal.

Then, when he saw people were looking at him benevolently, he licked the porcelain dog's face. When there was applause, he climbed up on the painted dog's head and balanced there. More applause and laughter.

When the boy went to the Uniting Church with some kids he played cricket with — as a sort of rest from the Meeting — the dog followed the boy inside and sat in a chair. He followed the service, apparently, for he nodded in time to the hymn. Attendants were going to remove him, but he directed a look at them of such mildness, almost sweetness, that they left him there.

At home later, the boy told what had happened, and suddenly said: 'Sit in the chair!' The dog jumped up like a trained performer and sat in the nearest kitchen chair, head up and eyes front, beaming. The difference from his usual morose expression was amazing.

'He can do tricks,' Aunt Ursula said. 'He's a trained dog.'

'He's a bit of a chuckleberry,' Jackson Blood said drily.

'Can I call him that, Dad?' the boy asked, glad for contact with his father in such a cheerful situation. His father's monologues on his researches into the Epistle of the Romans were not homely, nor were they exceptionally cheerful, being about grace, justification, and mercy. And his talk of the Seven States was largely over the boy's head.

'Sure. Huckleberry Chuckle, Chuckleberry Hound, whatever you like.'

'Why don't you give him some more commands?' said Lillian.

'Yes,' Ursula added. 'He's probably got more tricks.'

'Go to sleep!' said the boy sharply.

The dog's eyes brightened. He sprang down from the chair and lay flat out sideways on the floor, fast asleep instantly.

'Watch the telly!' said the boy.

The dog sprang up, sitting on his tail and back legs, front legs straight, staring straight ahead, and didn't move. Everyone clapped. The dog gave three bows: one to his right, one left, then a deep inclination of his head to the front.

'Read a book!' said the boy. The dog sat up, same as before except that he held his two front paws up near his chest, his little palms spread as if they supported an open book.

'He's good!' said Jackson Blood. 'Dig your grave!' he commanded, 'and lie in it!'

The dog dug frantically, clearing the invisible dirt backwards between his hind legs, then lay down dead in the hole, eyes shut.

At some commands he did nothing; they weren't in his repertoire. But he spun like a top, standing on two hind legs; he barked once at the appearance of one finger and so on up to ten barks for ten fingers; he sang; he mimed going up the ladder; he pretended to do a thimble and pea trick.

But at the end of his performance he waited patiently, then gave a little whine. He knew more, he wanted to show what he could do, but he couldn't tell them the right commands, and he couldn't do a trick without the right command as a trigger.

Many times the family got him up to his tricks in front of an admiring audience, but each time, after they'd exhausted their commands the dog was left disappointed, knowing he could do much more, but helpless because they didn't know the words to say; and resumed his hangdog air.

The boy was troubled by it. Sometimes at night when he was in bed waiting to go to sleep he remembered the dog's whine, his restlessness, his helpless impatience. What if people knew more than they knew they knew? And didn't know what to say to bring it forth? Was he, himself, capable of a great range of achievements, but helplessly handicapped by not knowing the commands that would liberate all he knew?

The dog began to get around with a little more pride in himself once his talents and training were known. As well, he started getting up early. He developed a few strategies to wake the boy at a fitting time to start the day, and the fitting time for the dog was around dawn, on the dark side rather than the light. Perhaps he wanted to give them more waking time to think.

When his methods involved making a noise, he irritated the other animals and they put a stop to it. None of the human side of the family knew exactly how it was done, but Uncle Hector suspected the other dogs threatened him with a going-over.

The boy blocked off the dog's attempts to get into his bedroom section of the verandah, but the dog got round that, too. He concentrated on the door of the boy's sleeping quarters.

He knew Davis Blood could feel him concentrating. Admittedly, the boy felt nothing until one morning, getting up to go down the backyard early, he opened his door to the verandah and there was the dog, concentrating on a part of the door level with his eyes. The dog knew that once having seen him, the boy wouldn't be able to get the fact out of his mind and it would visit him every morning like guilt. The moment he woke, he knew the dog was there, willing him to remember.

For weeks he was a mental captive to the dog, until he got angry, yelled at the dog, and was free. Next morning he had forgotten the dog's presence.

Kellick kept his vigil for a while longer, then he too abandoned it.

Orville, in his free time, took Kellick in hand, and trained him to jump on to his old skateboard after he, Orville, had got it rolling. Kellick soon was able to push it until it had a good pace, then jump on and be carried fifteen or twenty metres.

It was a fine sight on Saturday mornings, up in Bellbird, on the paved area of the new shopping mall.

Next, Orville took Kellick to Driftwood, or Pippi Beach, and stood him on his Hot Buttered Surfboard, walked him out into the surf, turned the board and let Kellick take a small wave ten or fifteen metres towards the shore.

Orville enjoyed the dog's cleverness, and Kellick seemed to enjoy the audience his teachability attracted. Under it all though, when the applause waned and the attention ceased, remained a sad-eyed look that reminded the family of all the unknown and perhaps wonderful exploits that could be called up if only they knew what commands to give to plumb the depths within him.

Fillings

He'd seen aquarium fish in the zoo, and spent a few minutes looking, then passing by, as the queue moved, but never had a chance to sit still and watch until he waited for an hour in the dentist's waiting room for a filling.

When he got home, his jaw and lip numb, he felt like having a crack at the woodheap. After a furious fifteen minutes he raced up the back steps to the big table which rested calm in the afternoon sun, to his pile of paper and pencils, pastels and the rest. He gathered them round him like a fortification. Now and then he touched fingers to his numb lip, but as he began to draw he forgot.

He drew aquarium people who swam in Tank City. As they swam, their insides showed, like toy fish. He coloured it, and put it away on the pile with the others.

My works, he thought. A smile started on his face, and after that spread right the way inside, and lit up his inner spaces. My works.

What if everyone drew pictures? He did a drawing of city streets lined with pictures at eye height.

For a moment he felt the brush of a large thought, then it was out of reach. What was it? He tried to push his brain to follow it. What had it been? He had felt suddenly larger, blown right up, big enough to contain populations, continents. He could recall that, but the thought? Gone. Where?

Where do thoughts go? Not out of one's head, certainly, for he'd known some that he'd recovered, after a time of forgetting. So they must be in there, somewhere, waiting to be remembered. The head was a marvellous and mysterious thing. So much of life went on in there.

He went to the kitchen for a drink of water.

'You have a pre-frontal dichotomy!' snapped Aunt Mira. 'Watch out for your soft options! Each life is at its capacity!'

'What?' he said catching on quickly. 'Each life? Even the lazy ones?'

'Each life is at its capacity.'

'Thanks, Aunt.'

'Chastity begins at home, remember!'

It was useless trying to converse with her, sometimes, but always interesting, even though baffling. Usually, it was better to keep her talking than try to make links between her outbursts.

'Would you like to go outside, in the sun?' he said, thinking how she spent her life indoors.

'Copy the hoi-polloi? Busy doing nothing but tan their hides? Not for me! That's fit only for croutons! The life of the zero hero! Those who wilt at windmills. I'd never contemplate it! I've had all the exposure to the effluents I'm going to have.'

'Would you like something to eat?' he said.

'No, by the jaws of the Madonna! With *my* teeth?' she shrilled. It was a joke in the family that Aunt Mira had no teeth to call her own.

'Where's my teeth? Who's got my teeth?' she yelled. 'Bring 'em back or I'll call in the armed forceps! Oh, where's a Ponce Charming to come and fit me for teeth?' she lamented. 'I'll take the tiniest, shiniest pair. Oh, the honey of age is sweet when the acid of youth no longer bites to the jawbone. Where's the mad Prince of Dentists? He's off courting Cinderella, that's mad keen on balls! Watch out, Cinders, or you'll be drilled right to the socket!

> 'Oh gums to the right of him
> Gums to the left of him
> Into the valley of teeth
> Rode the mad dentist!'

She stopped suddenly. 'Well, don't stand there gawping! Don't you appreciate uninhabited behaviour? What are you trying to be? A Nobel savage? Are you waiting for the vibes of Marx? Or are you just another member of the bland?' She turned her head away, then back, to fix him with her bright, beady eyes.

'Beware the God beneath the skin,' she grated, and was silent. He waited a bit, thinking she might have stumbled on his discovery, but she had fallen asleep. She slept most of the day, but you could never count on her being asleep when you said something about her.

The Vaulting Pole

Jackson Blood casually mentioned, in a story to the boy, how people in another time and place used vaulting poles to fly over obstacles and cross dangerous creeks. The boy, attracted by the idea of an advantage in jumping, but more by his father's obvious interest in vaulting, took the axe into the bush and scouted around for straight saplings from which he could cut a strong pole of about two metres.

The most suitable were young eucalypts. The sappy outer bark, often about a centimetre thick, added nothing to the pole's strength: it had to come off. He stripped it with the axe, holding the sapling upright and working downwards, then reversing it to bare the wood at the top of the pole.

Back home, he ran with it, held out in front, straight at the front fence, dug the thick end of the pole into the grassy ground, and lifted himself on the pole as he jumped, clearing the fence easily.

From the verandah, in a corner of the honeysuckle, the new dog Wildash looked out, startled. He looked this way and that for a direction to run, but was better off where he was, and stayed.

The boy set himself to vault the small cypress on the front lawn. It was as high as his head. Even as he ran up to it, he knew this was wrong. There ought to be a penalty for failure, and there wasn't with this. If he failed, his feet hit the top leaves, that was all. He ought to jump things where failure meant a bar knocked down, or a fall: that way the greater incentive would force him to try harder.

He cleared the little tree, then searched under the house for some old tyres to put on the front fence to make the going harder.

By the time he'd satisfied himself that he could vault fairly well, he had cleared the fence plus four car tyres.

He went up into the house for something to eat.

His new-found ability to use the vaulting pole was an asset when, next Sunday, Bruce's cousin Marie came to visit. She was a blonde girl with a narrow, graceful head and pretty face. She brought a girlfriend — Julie. Bruce's family were at church. Marie leaned out of the window and watched as the boy vaulted the two-metre side trellis that supported a grape vine and separated the front yard from the back.

She smiled sufficiently often for both boys to feel encouraged to go inside the house and while Davis kissed the blonde girl on the lounge, Bruce kissed her friend in another part of the room.

He enjoyed this business. Marie's mouth was soft and sweet. He left, reluctantly, when it was midday.

The smell of Sunday dinner came to meet him when he was nearly home. Lillian's roast had never smelled so good.

At the kitchen door, her song burst out:

> 'Guide me, O thou great Jehovah
> Pilgrim through this barren land.'

As he ate, his thoughts returned to the two girls. He'd like to have tried his hand at kissing both of them. Perhaps next week.

With Death There's No Knowing

Davis Blood's English class was given an assignment in advance: they could do it over the weekend and hand it in on Monday. A subject of your choice, said Mister Johnstone.

He thought vaguely about it in the train on the way home. At least he wouldn't have to write about someone else's crummy subject. What would he write of? The bush? Sport?

A woman in the seat ahead, across the aisle, had an afternoon paper open at page three. Beside a picture of an undressed blonde girl was a headline:

Leukaemia tragedy
Girl, 7
Mother's story.

That would do. He began it on Friday afternoon, did some work on it the next day, and finished it Sunday, making it as sorrowful as he could. Bruce's cousin had gone back to her home in the country. Kissing practice would have to wait. He called the subject of his story after the girl he hadn't kissed.

Julie

She was only seven and leukaemia crept up on her. No doubt to death she was a tasty morsel.

'Mother.' she said, when she was only a little sick and Mum was upset, 'when I grow up I'll look after you.' The doctor had said not to tell the child. Mother couldn't say much.

'Don't worry, mother.' the little girl said tenderly, 'I will. I'll look after you when I get big.'

Mum was crying, but not loud. Not loud enough to upset a child beyond the point where she felt helpless in the face of big people's sorrow. Just a little wet near the eyes, trying to smile.

The time came, and it was only a matter of months, when even the little girl could see that she wasn't ever going to grow up.

'I wanted to look after you, mother,' she said. 'But I'm really not going to grow up, am I? Not ever.'

Mum couldn't say anything. If she opened her mouth to speak — her lips and teeth were pressed together to make sure she didn't — the crying would start. It would be loud, too loud for a little girl to be allowed to hear, and how would it stop?

The little girl looked over Mum's shoulder at something. She spoke to the thing she saw, 'No, I don't want to go. Not that way.' Her voice was serious.

Only seven.

'Mother, I won't leave you.' And she turned her mother's face towards her, so they were looking into each other's eyes. 'I won't ever leave you. I'll always be with you. You'll know I'm with you. I'll always look after you.'

She looked a long time into her mother's eyes.

Then she settled slightly in the bed. She was dead, her eyes still open.

'Julie!' her mother called after her, 'Julie!' But Julie was too far.

It's years since then. Julie is in a wood coffin under the ground. They laid lots of flowers on the coffin and waited while the men shovelled the dirt in on top. Waited till the end.

Since then, there have been times when money was short, or the other kids needed this or that. Sometimes big things, sometimes small.

Always, when they really needed, they were able to manage. They might be short of money, but somehow, at the last moment, money was found. Ever since she died it's been like that. Every single time.

Her mother sometimes says, with a kind of wonder, 'Julie said it would be like that. She always said she'd look after us. She said always.'

She was only seven, and to death a tasty morsel. But you never know with death. Death doesn't always win.

He handed it in on Monday. On Wednesday the class got them back, with marks and comments.

Mister Johnstone had given him 6½, and the comment: 'Sentimental, pretentious, derivative'.

The boy grinned. He hadn't expected any different. What did Johnno want: originality?

Religious Drawings

Often things he saw gave him ideas for drawings in the instant he saw them. A television advertising campaign for a financial institution used Ayer's Rock in different coloured drawings and photographs; the boy saw it between segments of news. He had no great interest in the news; news happened reliably every day, you could leave it any time. He went gladly to the big room and sat with paper and pencils.

He pictured the Rock in the air over Sydney; then out at sea, floating and being gradually populated by sea plants and creatures and birds; and, thirdly, the rock covering all of Australia. He made a blue-bordered devotional picture of Christ in white robes, such as he'd seen in the lounge room of Bruce Kelly's house in Country Road, with the chest cavity opened and dark, displaying a brightly lit golden Ayer's Rock complete with jewelled sash across its middle.

As an extension of this last idea he drew people in the street — shoppers, children, policemen, couriers — with their chest cavities opened: in each chest was Ayer's Rock, plus sash and jewels.

He did a series in this showily religious way. He drew the figure of Christ in eight different poses. In successive chests of Jesus he showed: a football badge of a prominent club, a glass of beer, a woman, a new car, Christ himself, a coin, a landscape, an ordinary man, Lazarus.

He put them where no one would see them, not even Aunt, then, regretting this subterfuge, added them to the top of his pile of drawings. If it was good enough to draw them, it was good enough to acknowledge they were his.

Resurrection of the Joggers

Coming from school towards the railway station he was overtaken by four joggers in padded shoes, singlets and shorts. They puffed, their bodies were wet and shiny, as they thumped towards heavily trafficked George Street.

As he went into the throat of the railway, down the steps to the rank rock walls enclosing the platforms, he thought of things he could draw about joggers. He could see a burial service, an open grave, and joggers passing in the background a few metres away.

He hoped he would remember it. He often forgot ideas that, when he got them, seemed so big and bright that he could never forget. He should have made sure by noting it down in words, then later he would have seen again the picture his mind's eye first saw, and could have drawn it.

He didn't do that. Instead, he thought of the scene as it played itself out along the street outside the graveyard, with the funeral cortège approaching. Just as mourners and cars got near the gateway, a stream of joggers ran out in single file.

By the time he was in the train, his head had assembled pictures of joggers travelling through the wide expanse of Ravenswood Cemetery where at nightfall the wraiths of the dead rose up from their beds of clay and streamed after the living, in a mixed procession of earthbound and airborne.

He smiled as he thought of angels on plinths within the cemetery grounds; angels on high in jogging shoes; and joggers running between rows of graves, in the aisles of the dead.

Last of all, he imagined the day of resurrection, transformed into the resurrection of the joggers. He imagined that scene painted on the meeting-hall ceiling. But the Dissenting Brethren believed ornamentation was worldly, and therefore despised it: it would have to be removed, and go to a church. Churches were more compatible with worldly things.

When He was Older

In the train on the way to school, he thought perhaps when he was older he'd be able to go to classes and draw live models. He leaned back, his head against the window frame. He imagined a female model, world-weary, massive. His imagination ran with the image: she was being sawn in sections so the students could see what she was made of; she was prodded and discussed; faces and hands poked all round her and laughed at everything she was. She grew huge as a sea in another imagining. The students became sailors taking depth-soundings of this sea.

Next she was a building which the students, as workers clambering inside and all over her, were building. Last of all she was dismantled by wreckers, to make way for a new building.

He looked at one point on the rushing earth the train passed; it was a blur as his eyes registered only streaks parallel to each other. It was pleasant, seeing nothing but that blur of movement, thinking of nothing but that, and only limply of that; letting his imagination idle.

Grandma Died Suddenly

He left school at ten o'clock as his note from home requested and went along as he'd been told, to Ashwood Railway Station and found the funeral director's place with the rest of the family there, waiting. Grandma was to be buried at Ravenswood, and if he hurried afterwards, he would get back to school in time for the German lesson.

There were relatives round the grave that he'd never seen before.

'They're a dead loss, that lot,' he heard Randal say, 'except they fill out the numbers at a funeral or a wedding.'

Over the empty grave they sang 'Thy will be done, O Lord, whatever the cost', and 'Oh, what a debt we owe'. He looked round at the bowed heads and wondered what was going on inside them.

What happened to the silver handles? Were they left in the earth to tarnish and gradually oxidise? Or did someone retrieve them so they wouldn't go to waste?

The text of the speaker, Mister Halliday, was, *'I am the resurrection and the Life'*. After more prayers the shining casket with silver handles was lowered into the grave. In the train on the way back to school he thought about the resurrection of the body — no one had ever come back, no ordinary people, that is. But resurrection meant something that would happen later.

Did it mean Grandma would be resurrected — actually come to life — the blood flow again, the injuries to the blood vessels in her brain heal up, her memory return? Would she be as she was? And if so, as she was at what age? Just before her death at eighty-three? Middle age? As a young girl? Would she be resurrected as a child, a baby, with eternal life to live over again from the beginning in nappies?

He made it back to school with only ten minutes of the

German lesson gone. He was red and sweating, but it was worth it: German was his favourite subject.

Would Grandma qualify for eternal life, as was preached in the Meeting? He remembered Aunt Ursula's remark about it.

'Humans who can't wait for the weekend to come, or Christmas, or their holidays, dare to think they can handle eternal life, with nothing to look forward to, and nothing whatever to do.' But that didn't describe Grandma, who didn't seem to enjoy anything.

And there was resurrection.

But now he was at his school-desk, and his books out.

As he settled down to strong verbs, something else from the funeral came into his head. As they'd been waiting at the graveside some of his cousins had been having a friendly argument about God: should it be He, or was there a case for She? They divided strictly along gender lines. But his thought had been that God was neither He nor She, but They, in terms of the trinity, as preached at the Meeting.

Finished with it for now, he gladly went back to *sterben, starb, gestorben; graben, grub, gegraben*. He like the strong verbs table; it was an epic poem composed of three-word lines.

As he went lovingly over the table, pronouncing each three-word line, there were thoughts in the background of his mind that went back to a time when he was small.

He'd checked with Lillian that God was everywhere. Once that was established, many things flowed from it. God was everywhere therefore in everything: through the universe, throughout the planet; within the individual fish, bird, animal, bacterium; in human bone and brain and blood. In effect, all is made from God, therefore all is part of God, since God includes all that is. If we are constituted of hydrogen, oxygen, nitrogen, phosphorus, iron, carbon, potassium, arsenic, sodium, chlorine, manganese, magnesium, copper, zinc and the rest, then God contains them, and they carry part of God.

If God contains all that is, then Grandma, as she broke down in the grave, into her constituents of metals, gases and other elements, would be dispersed but not destroyed.

Her chemical elements would go back into the common inventory of the planet.

Finally, her elements would separate out into protons, electrons and any other particles of which the elements were composed, and they, too, would be conserved, not destroyed. They were the immortal bits: Their lifetime as protons, for example, was scientifically guessed at ten years to the power of 31. So Grandma's constituent parts would still be around. Her components, at least, had eternal life.

It was almost what the Meeting people had said when he was young: 'And the spirit returns to God, who gave it.' Except that now it seemed that not only the spirit — her life? — returned to the common stock of all life, but the components of the body returned too, though in a more basic form.

> *Sehen, sah, gesehen.*
> *Sprechen, sprach, gesprochen.*
> *Denken, dachte, gedacht.*

Mr Allen, the German teacher, 'Froggy' to the boys, called the class to order and gave a test that occupied the last ten minutes of the period. The brilliant Kulakovsky, a native German speaker, always came first. Davis Blood was never able to head him.

Grandma's Resurrection

Later in bed, he thought of the burial service and 83-year-old Grandma in that polished maple coffin, lowered into the hole after one of the Brethren spoke of the Resurrection. Would she really, one day, be alive again?

He couldn't believe. It was too indefinite. How was it

done? What happened to the scattered dust and gases to bring them together? The protons and electrons which by then would be parts of other things? Or was it a metaphor? Did it mean: live in memory? On the face of it, it seemed impossible, even absurd. If it happened as they said, there was no purpose in death: death provided room for a next generation. The important thing was life continuing, not the individual. Everlasting life for the individual human personality was wrong. He couldn't believe it. Decay, yes; dispersal, yes; immortality of the particles, yes: but eventual re-assembly, no.

How could he ever say any of this to his father, Jackson Blood? He would be saying his father was wrong. He would be denying the worth of the beliefs his father spent his whole time studying. Yet if he didn't believe this, he had to reject it all, for you accepted the body of beliefs, the whole package, or rejected it.

If only they didn't have that bit to believe in. Did they really mean resurrection of the body? And did body mean body?

How much simpler it would be if all they meant was the same message as was contained in Aunt Ursula's saying, that she had used in conversation at the table:

> *To speak of the absent is to make them present;*
> *To speak of the dead is to make them live again.*

And how much less greedy it would be if they agreed to say, with him:

> *We're made out of God;*
> *God contains all that is;*
> *We go back to God.*

And so much more humble, more suitable, to consider ourselves part of all other life; our fate the common fate.

The Operation

For two months, he'd had pains, then one Saturday, his fourteenth birthday, the doctor rang Happy Valley hospital. Emergency operation. He was dozy with morphine on the operating table well before Doctor Geeveston got there.

Lillian and Jackson Blood came to visit at 4.30 as he was coming out of the anaesthetic minus his appendix. Jackson Blood had a present of a red tie for him. It had small red squares for a pattern, woven in such a way that the silken material shone differently depending on which angle you looked at it. He was hazy from the anaesthetic, and kept slipping back into a dream of wide paddocks in which the grass was white. More of the family came for the night visits; he was in better shape then. The five metal clips over the wound pained a little, and he was hungry. He wished later he could have kept the appendix they'd taken out of him, but he'd been too casual to ask for it.

In the morning he read a newspaper. It was interesting to see the things that were always in newspapers, no matter when you picked them up.

He liked the tie, dreaded the food, and didn't know what to say when the men in the other beds told jokes they thought funny. He endured the visiting hours. He was glad when he got to his feet and made his way to the bathroom alone. Hospital was awful. The worst thing was its smell. On the way home in the bus he could smell himself. Hospital had soaked into him in a week. He smelled of sick people, dressed wounds, mysterious diseases, and dying. To take his mind off it, he tried to imagine what it would be like to be one of the basic elements. He tried water first. Endlessly slippery. Then he tried to imagine how the gas hydrogen, that they'd ignited in the science class, could, by joining with oxygen, became water. He tried to be hydrogen, and be oxygen, and to picture them joining. He couldn't get the picture. As for hydrogen being hydrogen because it had one electron orbiting one proton, and oxygen being oxygen because eight electrons on two different levels orbited eight protons plus eight neutrons — still less could he understand that. How could the elements be so different just because they contained differing numbers of the same basic particles? The mystery of it was beyond him.

He imagined the smell of hospital was stinking out the bus.

In the train back to Bellbird Corner, he opened the windows wide, to blow it away.

Strangers Holding Knives

Back at school the following Monday, he was nearly caught by big boys for a bootpolish job on what was beneath his underpants, but since they'd picked on him for sitting quietly, he got to his feet and cleared out from there, and looked for Verbruggen and Peters. He still had the bandages round his stomach, where some of the holes left by the clips were weeping, and the lower end of his scar was still open. Standing in the schoolyard, there came to his mind a picture he'd seen on television, of a jailyard with the men milling around, playing, talking, arguing. What if he were ever in prison? With all these kids? You couldn't change the people, you had to be with whoever was there.

He looked round at the other boys, eight hundred of them. No. He wouldn't like being cooped up with the same people all the time. Jail wasn't for him. Whatever his angers did, he would keep out of prison.

It reinforced the feeling of his being essentially alone. The way he put it to himself was that even if people jump off a cliff together, they drown alone, just as he, so recently on the steel table with the gutters for the blood, felt the needle alone and went to sleep alone at the mercy of strangers holding knives.

On the Friday afternoon he went along to Lawson's grocery store, the biggest in Bellbird outside the supermarkets. They wanted a boy to deliver groceries Friday afternoons and early Saturdays. He got the job. It paid much more than Cooks, who were mean, and more than Kendall's bakery, and they provided a brand new bicycle with twelve gears and a big basket for the goods.

On his weekly visits Preston made jokes that Bellbird Corner had no banners, marches or demonstrations, no fire-bombs or signs of revolution, only an addiction to open air, sport, entertainment and the beach. Preston was right.

He didn't say much about the managing directorship, but later Aunt said she thought he had it in the bag.

Randal visited once a week, too, usually on Saturdays, since he played with a district football team, usually on Sundays.

Danielle visited less often.

Two Loves

Without quite realising how much he enjoyed it, he had taken to running on bush tracks. He ran to Kangaroo Point now; the axe in his hands felt as if it was rearing to bite through thick red bark into the pale wet outer flesh of one of the turpentine trees on the eastern rim of the cliffs.

How he enjoyed those first strokes as the blade sank into the soft sapwood and left straight, sharp-edged gashes. And that first chip that flew was huge.

He was happy. Light danced from the shiny eucalypt leaves, the earth-smell rose round him. He walked in it, and in the softening air. The gold of the August wattle had become darker, heavier, now September had arrived; new leaf was beginning on the tips of the trees; new grasses peeped fresh green against the pockets of black ash that remained from the last summer bush fire.

He laughed, half-loud, at the bush spread out below him when he stood on Point Rock. He had no need to gather it all in his hands, to own a piece of paper describing it, to fence it off: it was his. He came down to it, walked in it, every weekend; sometimes after school during the week: he loved it. Its shapes and smells, its silences and spaces, its gullies and slopes, rocks, caves and valley sides: all were in him and round him, like the air he breathed.

It was pleasure to be there, to be alive within its life.

It was a different pleasure from that of cutting trees. He held both within him, neither one inhibiting the other.

As he stood there, white clouds caught his eye, high and heaped up. There was a hippo's face. Over to the south a map of Papua New Guinea; it gradually altered its shape to that of a giant eagle. The hippo's jaws widened in a laugh. If I had a pencil and paper, he thought, I'd copy that down.

The rock he stood on had two cracks that met in the shape of an elbow. There were drawings in the rocks, figures in the sky, traceries on the white bark of scribbly-gums, curling vines of sarsaparilla and its bitter tasting imitation, patterns of leaves growing and leaves fallen. He felt rich to be surrounded by the riches of the natural world and by ideas and promptings there for the taking.

Orissa

On the corner of the north-south highway as he was coming home from school on Friday, there was a dark-eyed schoolgirl in navy tunic and white blouse with a striped school tie. She glanced at him. He watched her. Her name was Orissa; she wore copper bangles. Other boys said she had shiny bronze breasts, and could fight.

For a moment he was back in the bush, on the high flat-topped ridge leading to the Point among the shoulder-high brush. Words sounded in his head:

> *'The landscape is speaking to me*
> *the form of the land is trying to reach my mind*
> *why that hill there?*
> *what is the meaning of that valley?*
> *why do I feel elated to see this hillside falling*
> *subtly, gracefully, to the creek; then rising*
> *in curved steps to that green ridge?'*

Orissa was joined, in his mind, with the landscape he knew that was so close to him; so much part of him that he didn't need to know he loved it. He followed, caught her up and spoke to her. Her voice was low and musical.

'Piss off,' the low and musical voice said. 'Small fry.' But her eyes! They looked at him, pupil to pupil; he felt her gaze entering him, locking on to what was inside him. The landscape was speaking to him.

He understood Orissa's language, but not that of the landform. Orissa was created harmoniously. Had anyone tackled the barrenness, the stony hills, the dry watercourses of the land that inhabited him? Her watercourses were moist and healthy; you could see wetness in the lower edge of her eye, the wetness covering the pink surfaces in her mouth.

'She won the squash today,' a kid said, passing on his left. He saw no one but Orissa.

The voice said, 'Wrists like iron. Watch out she doesn't deck you. Likely to, if she doesn't like you.' He watched her go.

Over by the Pacific Milk Bar stood the merciless girls that hung out there every afternoon after school. They called obscenities to him. He knew what they wanted. If, in answer to the gibes, he turned on them and swore, abused them, or turned their words back on them with a brutal joke, they would be happy. He'd be accepted. But doing that would mean using their methods, becoming like them, and that he would not do.

Boys were there, too; rough and reckless, the sort the girls admired. But it was all appearance, and language: their words were far more dangerous than they were, and singly they said nothing, and their recklessness was just stupidity.

He dreamed that night of Orissa in blazing day. Shadows fell on her wherever she stood. The shadows clung, and began to eat. She grew gaunt, bony, skeletal. Her eyes were derisive still; even as they dissolved, the sockets stared scornfully at him.

How could he find the language the landscape was speaking? If he could just read it. As they had seen in discussions at school, Australia was not only distinctive in its own right, but, leaving aside Antarctica and the continents under water, stranger and both older and newer than other continents. He thought of one of Ursula's sayings: 'Perhaps, in traditional societies, men kept women under, knowing that women don't care much for men — as men are forced, by their biology, to care for and be dependent on women — and once in power women will dispense with men . . .'

Orissa had two plaits of hair hanging down her back. Her back was straight. Seeing her legs, he had an ache for the wide warm flanks of the lady Vivian, the whole world's lady Vivian, the real lady Vivian, without the deception: expanses of warmth and acceptance and rest.

He loved Orissa. He wished, walking home alone along Anzac Street, that he could express his love to someone, as if it were a boast.

How her voice glittered! Yet he felt, in a blind intoxication of praise, that even her silences were music.

Behind it all was the conviction that she saw him. Her way of looking at him, full in the eyes, said that she understood what he said, and even when he didn't speak, she understood him. Perhaps that's why she was derisive.

Dinner that night was real, in a half-hearted sort of way, but it wasn't till he got to bed that he felt he was with Orissa. His first dream was one in which he could clearly see her voice. It was moonlight. His second was full of wild, exaggerated delights — full to overflowing.

Spears

At home on Saturday in an ecstasy of making, he formed an aboriginal figure with two spears. He built the body up from clay, using painted twigs for the spears. He sharpened the points, then, before putting them with the figure, on an impulse made the points blunt. Not just blunt, but rounded-blunt. It was on this aspect of the making that he lavished the most careful attention.

He didn't care what the family said when they saw them: they had to be like that, and like nothing else. What a feeling those spear tips gave him! He felt he had made something profound, but that was the wrong word, he knew: he had made something personal.

He wanted to make spear points like that and plant them all over the deep soil of the backyard, all over the bush behind the house and beside the track right on down to Kangaroo Point and along the banks of the creek to the sea.

When he'd finished and laid the tools aside, he put his new thingoid apart to set it off. He looked back at where he'd been working. The scraps and bits left on the place of work seemed timeless, as if a thousand years before an artist had heard a call and gone, taking his talent but leaving the tools.

Lying in bed that night, unable to go to sleep, and unwilling, he thought of what it must be like to await those spears. To an enemy, an opponent, a partner in fighting, what it must be like to fear, yet to long for, as inevitable, the hurt and initiation of that tip. It might tear the flesh. It must tear the flesh.

The soil of the continent is thin, he reflected, apart from a few favoured volcanic or coastal places. Thousands of years ago, were there men who looked up to the clouds and cursed them for passing by, as they do most of the time, with rain unshed? And cursed again, when flood carried the best soil away to the sea? Were there boys like him who looked round and wondered what would have to be altered in mankind or in the composition of nature, so that we could eat trees and leaves, or boil stone and sand for nourishing meals? Could we turn silicon to carbon, nitrogen to oxygen, or vice versa?

Remote from him at that moment, perhaps in bed, possibly dreaming, though not yet unconscious, Orissa lay. He was conscious of her presence on the planet, without knowing the house in which she breathed.

How old our land is, he reflected. Every stone, every hill, every ridge far more ancient than it looks, much more than we think. With a pang, he remembered Jackson Blood, the man who fathered him, rubbing his right knee where the cold got in and the ache was deep. Some of him was old, yet short of fifty.

He watched every afternoon for Orissa, particularly Fridays, when he was delivering groceries on the bike.

One Friday he heard that others had watched for her; they had seen her going home late after sport and dragged her into a van. Only the kids round about seemed to know, he didn't hear it mentioned at home, where Lillian or Aunt usually got to hear everything. Perhaps she told no one.

She put up a fight and was marked when they'd done with her. The next time he spoke to her she advised him to do the same as last time, but in a milder voice. He went home hoping she hadn't lost any of her fire. A girl with breasts of bronze, and copper bangles, ought to stay strong, if not invulnerable.

It was at one of the freshwater pools he swam in that he saw her next. She was diving off Sandwich Rock — it was shaped like that — as he came round the bend in the track down to the sloping earth that became sand at the water and was called Ned Kelly's Beach. He'd startled a goanna a little way back and its sudden alarm had startled him in turn, but everything else was forgotten when he saw her. She didn't tell him to piss off, just kept to herself. He tried not to look at her body when she came out of the water to dive again. But he was aware of her every time her shoulders left the water; her skin drew his eyes as if with cords.

Her neck, just below and behind the ears, and the back of her neck above the shoulders, where the whiteness disappeared under the dark hair, had a look about them that he would remember after many years. That fine skin, that whiteness. He was puzzled that he felt breathless. How strange it was that a smile, a toe, an elbow, could be such valuable things.

As for himself, he felt ordinary enough: just a face with mouth, nose, eyes and ears walking along on legs, with arms visible at times. How silly Orissa would think he was, if she knew how obsessively he pictured her, and how often!

Thoughts of her pervaded his hours, coloured many days. It was a kind of takeover, a feeling that the strong essence of her, her essential self, invaded him: she was an aggressive, conquering spirit. He couldn't stand against her.

Sometimes these preoccupations left him no time for better, more constructive thoughts, and he felt isolated, confined, trapped. Was her effect on him close to being evil? For, while he was obsessed by Orissa, nothing else mattered. She drove out everything.

Other times, it seemed her influence over him was the reverse of evil, for, instead of sexual contact, she seemed to stand for more intense life, an added richness, an intermittent freedom from aimlessness and unreality.

To him, she seemed perfect. Yet, in calmer moments, he knew that was the wrong word: she was incomparable.

The Male Imperative

Carrying round inside him images of Orissa seemed to spur thoughts of other, larger things. These thoughts would come into the light of his head where he could see them, at all sorts of odd times: having a shower, or tying his shoelaces before going to school, or with his spoon halfway between plate and mouth at breakfast.

They dealt with what he ought to do, what he ought to be, and they came often. Some he'd heard from his father and brothers, from books he'd read, or people he'd heard talking; though he felt he'd have thought them himself, without the aid of others. These thoughts typically addressed him as another person.

> *With what you've got, whatever disadvantages,*
> *With no equipment, no weapons, no learning,*
> *From any beginning*
> *You must go up against the best.*
> *Whatever you choose to do, you must have a go!*

You must try!
No standing back, no detachment,
No excuses accepted. At the end of life
You will judge yourself on whether
You gave it everything you've got.

John the Baptist

It was a Friday. In bed that night he didn't go to sleep right away. The pillow sank into a hollow, his face felt surrounded. He propped himself up, thumped the pillow to get the hollow out, and settled back on it.

'Who are you?'

Who was that? A deep, serious, almost sorrowful voice sounded in the room. It was the sort of voice you paid attention to. Who am I? he thought. Just me, of course. Davis Blood. Boysie.

'Who are you?' He sat up. It was the voice he'd heard when he was eleven at the special school at Archerfield, and it wasn't in the room, it was in him. It wasn't asking his name, but who he was, inside.

He waited, in case there were more questions, and while he was waiting, fell asleep.

He woke hot and frightened. He'd had a nightmare. Salomé had demanded the head of John the Baptist, and her demand had to be honoured by her father, Herod. A soldier went down to the cells to measure John the Baptist's head for the plate the princess would choose for its display. He came back and showed the diameter of the head and the neck. After some time spent thinking of the colour of John's hair and his complexion, Salomé sent the soldier away with a polished silver plate bordered with designs in blue enamel, since that would show off his hair to the best advantage. Also it would make a gorgeous contrast with the colour of his blood.

It was a year since he'd last heard the biblical story. Why had the machinery inside him that went on working while you were asleep, picked on this night to remember that story? At thirteen he had come home from the Meeting thinking about it, horrified at the thought of the girl's revenge on that good man, just because he wouldn't do what the state wanted.

In the Meeting, John was said to have died willingly, but how did they know? What happened to the rest of him after the head was gone? Did they put it all together in a grave after the princess had finished playing with the head?

No, he believed Salomé kept the head. She played with it, lifting it off the plate, putting its lips to her breasts in turn, then clasping it between her breasts, her arms round the curly locks, the blood still dripping occasionally down her dress past her stomach and on to her silk-covered thighs. She kissed the cooling lips, kissed the still-open eyes, then with a swear-word pulled the prophet's lower jaw down and kissed him inside his mouth.

She put the head back on the plate, sat on a chair and watched it. Then, looking round in case someone was looking, she unloosed her silken gown at the waist, and took the head in both hands, lifting it off the plate.

'I'll make you look at me!' she said fiercely, and crushed the bloodless face against her body.

He spent a long time trying to forget the pictures in his head. The sensations that accompanied these imaginings persisted until he was called at six for his cup of tea, before breakfast.

Alterations

One thing that relieved him of Salomé's presence was the taking of a few lumps of white clay dug from the water channel that served as a gutter for Big Hill. He watered and worked the clay in his hands, separating out the few rust-coloured roots that grew like veins in it, and filled an old IXL peaches tin with the half-prepared clay.

He pulled out a piece that fitted easily in his left hand, and kneaded it thoroughly, ridding it of tiny lumps of still-dry material, rounding it into a ball of well-worked sticky clay. He dried his hands, and flattened the ball out into a flat disc shape.

With a narrow-bladed putty knife that he found in his tool-box, he began to make two bow-shaped depressions, facing each other. The work was detailed, careful and exact. The clay allowed him to make and remake, to alter and restore. He made a replica of Orissa's lips. When he'd satisfied himself they were a copy, he altered the shape of the top lip, flattening a fullness that made them, to him, less desirable, less eloquent. Into the middle of the lower lip he put a deeper cleft. That done, he extended the middle of the top lip just a fraction down, so that it nestled in the cleft of the bottom lip. They were no longer Orissa's lips, but now were perfect, just as he wanted them to be.

On Cat Island

Davis Blood went with three other kids — Digger Smith, Aub Field, Sam Marsden — and hired a boat from Spindle Head, taking it north through the widening bays into the wider mouth of Blue Ridge River. They fished a bit, letting the boat drift; then started the motor again and went east, turning south into Mandrake Water, so called because of its resemblance on the map to that plant, with short pointed arms and legs. All went ashore at the northern tip of Admiral Rocks. It was a day of very light seas. They mucked around a little, dropped in a fishing line for an hour, then the other three wanted to climb the cliffs and explore.

Davis Blood, though, headed back to the boat.

He sat in it for a while before starting the motor. The others were out of sight; he was alone. He didn't look back. He headed for Cat Island, which looked, from a distance, like a cat curled asleep on the floor with its rump high one end, its head low at the other.

He kept to the sheltered side of the island and found a gap between rocks where a little shelf of sand looked promising as a beach. He got out, pulled the craft on to the sand, pulled the line from the bow as far as it would go. He wrestled a rock over against the biggest of two rocks on his little beach and wedged the rope between them. He knotted the end so it would be held between the rocks.

He had looked down on the others' keenness to explore the Admiral Rocks, but things were different now. He was by himself, as he liked to be. He clambered up the nearest rock to get a good look at the best way up to the top.

At the top, he stood and looked east into the distance, where sea met sky in an indistinct line of haze. He stood enthralled. More than the words meant — horizon, distance, sea, haze, colour — there was a blurring of something more than colours, something more than words. It ran through him, filling him, but he had no words for it.

He stood there for many minutes, then climbed down on the ocean side of the island, where the deep sea swell crashed slowly on the rocks of the island. He marvelled at the green body of water, so translucent, as each swell reared up against the island and showed its breadth and mass. He stood and watched the hushed bulk of each wave, fascinated by these glimpses of the roof of another world.

He made his way up to the top of the island again and looked with satisfaction all round. How wonderful it was to be the one human, alone and undisturbed. He sat on a pale pink rock warmed by the afternoon sun. Plants struggled to retain a hold on top of the hill; hardy, shiny plants that wouldn't give up their lives easily, that would take scars, drought, or mutilation for years before they weakened, and even when their life was reduced to a few stalks and bent roots, they would hang on. Whatever it was inside them that had such fierce persistence and passion for life, perhaps was in him too.

He hoped so. That was to live, surely: to be old and bent and still have the fire of life alight in heart, blood and eyes; still to hang on, still to breathe, still to set one foot after another.

Wedged into a crevice between two rocks he found a glossy women's magazine, open at a page showing fruits and desserts; on the facing page were colour pictures of roast meat and two steaming soups.

Apart from the appetising look of the food, there came into his head some words from school, when boys like Verbruggen, Kulakovsky and Thompson were talking of art.

The photograph had superseded representational painting, they said. Portraits, events, landscape: photography had pushed them back into a corner, limiting their scope forever.

He understood, he thought, some of these effects, but something bothered him about the boys' cheery and final dismissal of painting. Even his sister Danielle's camera seemed to take different photographs according to which film processor she went to; therefore the colours were unreliable, untrue: they couldn't be guaranteed. Could any photograph be believed? No, he answered: photography was as subject as painting to the accidental. It was fiction, too. Creative even.

And could a photograph show the life in a face, the character of a place, the mood and feeling of an event, without being of such limited scope that it was trivial? Could a photograph contain poetry? He concluded that it could, in the hands of a good photographer, or as an accident, but that it didn't necessarily supplant the work of a good painter, who might have happy accidents, too, as well as insight and ability.

An open boat drifted a hundred metres away, slowly making for the upstream shore, carried by the tide. Over there, what was that? He saw a group of people way over on Admiral Rocks, where he and the other boys had been.

He scampered down the slope towards the boat. Gone. That was it, drifting out there. Vaguely he hoped the breeze that always sprang up in the late afternoon wouldn't swamp it.

But if that was the boat, was that group over there the boys he'd left on the Rocks?

He sat in the sun. Perhaps they would see him. He stood and waved. It was too far away to see if they replied. He didn't realise that with a background of rocks he couldn't be seen.

He watched the boat. It rose and fell in the incoming waves that travelled up the throat of the estuary that became the Blue Ridge River.

He would be late for tea tonight. He didn't know that his friends hadn't seen him climb on to the island, but thought he'd gone overboard. Even then they were working out how to get home. They would have to get lifts from visitors to the place, the tourists that had comfortable cars and were adult, and responsible.

He explored the island again. This time, he looked all over it, just in case other visitors had left something he could eat. Maybe there were good places to hide from the rain, and the cold. He decided the west would be warm to start with.

It was a comfortable island. Walking about on the top of

the rocks was easy, and the feeling of being in charge of a piece of the earth was good. He loved owning things, and the things he owned he made his own by constant handling, and using; by looking and touching, turning them over in his hands until he knew every feature, every line, mark, crevice. On the island he had a wonderful thing to get to know intimately, but it would take so long. If only he could live there.

But his family wouldn't allow him to stay. He had an education to get; besides, the law compelled you to go to school.

He stood still on the topmost point. Into his head he gathered the idea of the island. He could feel its shape inside him, as if he was able to miniaturise the island and tuck it away in him.

He felt warm towards this mass of rock licked by the sea. He would treasure the feel of it in him, the stumpy trees twisted and bent, the rocks cracked across in straight lines, all in the one direction — the massive boulders at water's edge, the rocks fallen before them with only their heads above water between waves. There were small plants in flat patches of sand, mosses on the south side of some of the rocks, tiny flowered plants unknown to him. Did bees come all this way across the salt water to care for the plants on Cat Island?

When it was sundown, and he hadn't found water except for a small pool trapped in a wedge-shaped junction of rocks and shaded by a balancing rock, he went to look for a hidey-hole on the western side where the sun was warm. He found a shelter where he could look out at the faraway lights on land. He sat in the last of the sun, then lay down and, without intending to, fell asleep.

He was awakened hours later by the sound of a helicopter's hard rackety sound of blades slapping the air. He sat up, went outside his shelter, and saw the chopper tilted, coming over the water towards him. It rose and turned away, sweeping back towards Admiral Rocks.

He made out craft in the water, with lights and machinery. While he watched a diver surfaced. He heard the far-off sound of voices.

He yelled. His voice was swallowed by night and wind from the south-east. He waved, then felt foolish, for he was surrounded by darkness.

He whistled. Its piercing note would attract attention, he knew, if he kept it up long enough.

He saw one man in a launch look round, cautiously.

When would he have a chance to be on an island again? What if he lay low and kept his whistle to himself? But Lillian would think he was dead, she'd be upset. Why was it so hard to get away from people? They'd be OK without him, once they got over being sad. Then they'd remember all the good things, most likely.

He ought to go back. Mum, the family, school — they pulled him back.

He stepped forward, took a big breath and whistled. This time the diver, standing on the deck of the launch, and the first man, both turned their heads. He whistled again, getting a strong upward and urgent sound in the note, before he let it drop down at the end.

Both men pointed at the island.

Next minute a spurt of light shot from the boat and began to crawl over the island. As it came nearer to him, the boy began to wave excitedly. This was just like scenes he'd seen on television. He jumped up and down and waved his arms, as he'd seen rescued people do. Then the light hit him full on, and stopped him.

'That stopped my little gallop,' he thought. He covered his face with both hands, to shut out that smothering light. It came through his fingers. Could they see him? He thought he'd better give a wave, so he removed one hand, and waved.

He heard their voices. The light stayed on him. Then a loudhailer blared.

'Stay there, son! Stay right there! We're coming to get you off.'

What if he'd been able to stay there a few days? With water and shellfish, he wouldn't have starved. If only he'd come with matches to light a fire, a knife to get food, something warm to sleep in. A fishing line, of course. That was the way to live. He could go anywhere then. A nylon sleeping bag and the other things would fit in a very small pack. How old would he have to be before he could just go?

And the dream he'd had asleep in the shelter. He remembered bits of it. It was a morning, and he'd come round the side of the island, found a cave he hadn't seen before, and there was this woman, sitting on a rock, playing a guitar. A real lady Vivian, with worlds to teach him. He was convinced that women knew, far more than men, what really mattered.

Now it would never happen. At least not till he was bigger.

Home in bed he went to sleep. A confused dream took hold of him. He was alone in a boat, the sea was high, nothing to steer with. Then the woman with the guitar was with him, dark hair falling on both sides of her face and neck, coming together below her chin and spreading out flat on her chest. Her hair was fine and shiny. They weren't in the boat any longer, they were on the island. They woke together in the morning sun, smiled at each other and went to get water. They scraped shellfish off the rocks together, ate together, drank from the same dish.

He recognised the dish. It was the same one Mum had given him the hot soup in when they brought him home. The dream dissolved. He slept, and dreamed again. This time he was alone, on the island, on the flat rocks near water level. Small pools of water were all round him in sculptured holes in the rock. He was tall, he'd become a man. Suddenly he got an idea from the rock pools! By turning the situations round him on its head, he came up with an idea for protecting water in pools and dams in the dry, hot inland. He invented a shade in the form of inverted cones in one continuous piece of heavy plastic, supported by aluminium poles that fitted into each high point. The downward pointing cones had holes to let rain water in, to fill the dam. Evaporation rose inside the cover, condensed on the plastic and ran back down the sides of the inverted cones into the dam again.

He woke, sweating, the sun full on him.

Shakespeare

It was hot in Room 26, the air thick, not moving. Warm breath from twenty-six boys rose invisibly, circulating under its own dynamics, raising the temperature further.

The class was collectively bent over the books which lay open on each desk. Davis Blood had his finger placed in a later page — 73 — and was at the moment looking at page 61 of *The Merchant of Venice*. There was a choice: memorising one of two passages. The one on page 61 was Portia and Shylock.

> *Then must the Jew be merciful.*
> *On what compulsion must I? Tell me that.*
> *The quality of mercy is not strained;*
> *It droppeth as the gentle rain from heaven*
> *Upon the place beneath:*

He went over the words again. Marvellous words. He kept that place and turned to page 73. Speech of Lorenzo:

> *How sweet the moonlight sleeps upon this bank!*
> *Here will we sit and let the sounds of music*
> *Creep in our ears:*

Where did the author get these words? And why these? His eye went down the page to another of Lorenzo's speeches.

> *For do but note a wild and wanton herd,*
> *Or race of youthful and unhandled colts,*

The words must have come from within the one who wrote them; but from where inside him? What gave rise to them? To be able to dig such words out of your head must be a marvellous thing. And there were other, more marvellous words, in the tragedies.

Other authors studied in class were, in the main, like Shakespeare safe and dead, while their words, in the form in which they wrote them, were still there to be read. The boy thought often of the after-life these authors had achieved, and wondered at the power in their words that gave them such life. Some, even, grew in majesty and importance after death. This, too, was a wonder.

To a large extent these authors were teachers. The class teacher was merely a guide among these monoliths.

Such wonder-humans were beyond reach: that went without saying. What they did was the most important of all human activities because they left a recording of their minds, their imaginations, their sensibilities; their voices went on speaking down the ages, their influence continued while civilisation persisted. The life in their works was lived far above the heads of ordinary people, of whom he was one; and in his youthful opinion, above the painters whose works he studied, admired and wrestled with.

Uses for People

He had delivered the Friday groceries for Lawsons. His pay was in his pocket, his legs tired. Three of the deliveries were big and up the steepest hills in Bellbird.

At the big table, he worked off his feelings by drawing a shop with people on shelves for sale. A packet of breakfast food was behind the counter serving a customer in the shape of a soap packet, with two wrapped people being the sale item. The cash register read fifty-seven cents.

On another sheet of paper, he extended the idea to buildings. Mini-buildings were doing the work, manning the cranes, laying the bricks, forming the whole building. But the bricks were people.

The idea of a building, an unusual shape: he took more paper and drew an immense building in the shape of a landscape, that stretched far away into the distance. Windows, doors, balconies appeared, as if stuck into the landscape.

He went back to the idea of practical uses for people. He drew giants drinking from people-shaped glasses, cups and mugs; giants nibbling on a bag of people-lollies, people-sticks, and a giant baby sucking a people-dummy.

He felt tired. He went down to the woodheap to liven himself up with some fierce chopping. It didn't work. He ended up sitting on the biggest log in the yard, gazing at nothing down in among the trees of the bush, as they were gradually permeated by the increasing darkness, and finally saturated by it. He walked slowly back up to the house for his shower and to set the table for tea. He felt very strong, but slow.

Dedication

It was Saturday, near noon. He was in the kitchen, alone but for Aunt Mira, the radio on. He heard the first few notes of a Schumann piece he'd heard once, and dived for the radio. When he'd listened to it before, its seriousness and passion attracted him, but he hadn't really heard what it contained.

He listened this time, looking hard at the radio. He was hungry for what the music was saying to him. He bent and rested his head on his arms near the speaker, drinking in the notes. Closer he moved, until he felt compelled to cram the music into him. His ear was flat against the speaker, his hand went round the body of the little radio and pressed it against his ear, until it pained. He turned the volume up till it blared straight into his head. His eyes were wild; he felt high and hard and lifted up.

The music was eloquent. It was also, in his head, a stepping stone to violent action. He felt he could do anything, he was capable of anything with that explosion of feeling in his head.

It stopped. He almost dashed the radio down on the kitchen bench in anger. When the music was gone, what took its place was — nothing.

Widmung, the announcer said. Dedication. Aunt Mira said nothing, for once, as he left the kitchen.

Outside, a shower began. Huge drops, big as hail, rained on the iron roof. Lightning flashed its violet light over everything, thunder boomed in the distance, the sun was out overhead, between heavy clouds. Hail started, then tailed off. Steady pouring rain began. Light shone through the silvery globes of water as they fell heavily. The trees were wet and shining in the sun. Steam began to rise from the ground, and from the dirt of the road.

He loved it. The world around him was bursting with life and vigour. Raindrops flicked the wet gumleaves on nearby trees, so that they flashed in the sun like shining steel.

He watched, waiting for more thunder. None came. No more lightning?

With a sharp outbreath of impatience through his nose, he went inside to the big table, full of purpose.

Landscape

I'll do a landscape, he thought as he got out thick white paper. Could a landscape be done as an interior? If so, an interior of what? Of the body? If you walked into a human thorax, the arteries, covered bones, the hanging organs nestling together, could perhaps be treated as sunlit objects.

Could he do a landscape as inside a building? Open the door, look inside, and there are green pastures, trees, animals, and farm buildings. In the building next door a different scene; a fishing village, maybe. Or, displayed in a paper bag, a landscape of mountains?

Or, and this seemed more likely, a landscape set like a plant in a large earthenware pot; with roads, houses, plots of land, trees and fields, all contained and domesticated. This could be placed on a table along with other pots containing different landscapes, ready to be deployed on a verandah as Aunt's pots were; or a balcony. Yes, he liked this one, and began to draw.

Pictures of Pictures

Monday was a holiday. He divided his day between the woodheap and the big table.

With paper in front of him he began to dream on to the paper, using the point of the pencil as part of his head. As it wandered here and there, making lines longer and shorter, a peculiar comfort arose within him. He was in charge, here, working on this paper. No one else could do what he did in the way he would do it.

A forest of statues grew under the point of the pencil. He had seen an encyclopaedia picture of a petrified forest, and his forest looked rather like that. Everything perfectly still, rigid, dead.

He went from that to a drawing that he called 'No Real World'. This was in three parts: one an empty stage; one a desert; the third a room in a large house, of the sort he had seen at the houses of the rich Dissenting Brethren.

In each of these places — stage, desert and room — he drew the natural objects to be found there, as representations only. On the stage, the actors were pictures of actors. In the desert the saltbush, the gibbers strewn on the desert floor were pictures of saltbush, pictures of gibbers, pictures of spindly plants, pictures of the horizon. In the room, the piano was a picture, the curtains pictures, the tables and chairs — all pictures.

Finished, he got up quickly, dropped the pencil, and ran down the back steps.

'Wait for it,' said Aunt Ursula, in the kitchen, to Lillian. They both stopped still.

Seconds later, the sound of fiercely energetic wood-chopping came up to them. It travelled across the valley, also up the slope of the hill to neighbours in Anzac Street, who knew exactly what it meant.

Some of the neighbours felt sympathy for the family, such a big family and still with a wood fire in the kitchen. The neighbours hadn't been touched by fashionable ideas of going back from microwave to wood stove. Neither had the Bloods: they'd never left the era of wood.

His Particular Balance

The log he brought up from the bush this Saturday afternoon after he'd delivered the groceries was short, but nearly half a metre thick. His father, who had so often reproved him for attempting things beyond his strength, shook his head, but said nothing. The boy was sweating freely, his steps abrupt attempts to retain the balance of his load, the axe held in a tightly clenched fist, eyes fixed on each step as he took it.

If all the trees in the world were one tree, what a great tree that would be. The world-tree, in fact. The primary school saying came into his head, and he would have smiled, but he knew a smile could relax him and he might drop the log.

He came slowly off the road, over the grassy verge, through the front gate, concentration absolute and unbroken, down the side of the house to the woodheap, where he let the log roll off his shoulder, and stepped smartly away in case it bounced back on his foot.

His father watched him wipe his face with his forearm and saw the beginnings of the satisfied smile. Then, standing the axe carefully against his trophy, he went walking, not running, up the back steps to the bathroom.

When he came out fresh and showered, his face was still red with the heat of his body and the load he'd carried. He looked down once from the verandah to the log, then went in to sit at the big table. He picked up a pencil.

Lillian's voice came to his ears:

> *'Jesus, the very thought of you*
> *With sweetness fills my breast.'*

That voice was home to him.

His fingers on the pencil felt thick and distant, as if they were no longer so close to that inside, thinking part of the finger, the place where long use teaches the person on the other end of that finger that it is indeed a finger, his finger, and all is as usual. All was not as usual. The skin where it touched the pencil felt so cushioned that it seemed nothing would ever be able to hurt it in the ways it had been hurt before.

He marvelled now that so light a touch could hold the pencil firmly, where before he'd gripped it. His fingers felt invincible.

> *'To those who fall how kind you are;*
> *How good to those who seek.'*

He experimented to see how lightly he could touch the paper and still make a line. On the paper a fine network of lines appeared and grew into a spider web. The web was strung between the two edges of a chasm. He put a man in the web, in the place where a working spider would be; not in the centre, but immobile, off to one side, waiting for prey.

Later, elbow on the table, head resting on an open hand, eyes dreaming out over the afternoon valley, he thought of the components of his life.

The joy of growing strength. The growing exhilaration and joy he felt in running, together with the making, the drawing, the thinking in words, and those companions of his childhood, the dream-states without words, seemed to be in balance; a balance peculiarly his.

Dreaming, or halfway to dreaming, he drew two lines of hills from left and right, converging in the middle of the paper at a point slightly higher than the two sides. As he drew, letting the line wander a little, he was struck by the way one side resembled the outlines of a prone human leg, seen from the feet. He drew the other leg to correspond to it, as nearly as one human leg corresponds to its mate. A pair of giant legs converged at the giant crotch.

He drew a procession of tiny men — then added women and children — advancing towards the giant crotch, which now was equipped with a ladder; and already little people were climbing the ladder and disappearing into the doorway of the crotch halfway up. The doorway was framed with leaves and branches of bushes and trees, much as the entrances to old houses still are.

As an afterthought, he added some pets to the procession, making it Noah's Ark, with a difference.

He heard his mother's voice,

'Inscrutable Jesus, Spirit of Love',

and the thought came to him that he dimly remembered she had been singing aloud all the time he was dreaming, yet for most of that time he hadn't heard her.

Somehow he had screened out everything but his work.

Adam and Eve seemed a good thing to dream about, for no better reason than that they happened to step, illuminated, into his head at that moment.

He drew Adam beneath and touching, a huge leaf that curled at the sides, and from round the edges of which the Eve-spider peeped. A hole eaten in the leaf showed the snake poking out its head. A mass of turns of spider's thread round Adam, holding him fast to the curled leaf, and the drawing was done.

On the same subject, and bearing in mind what he'd learned about spiders from books in the house, he drew a large vigorous Eve-spider in the centre of her web, and on the edge of the web, advancing warily, a tiny Adam.

He put these drawings on the bottom of the pile. The family might think he had sex on his mind. Though why shouldn't he?

But they were his work, why hide them?

He restored the drawings to the top of the pile, threw the pencil across the table and went out into the afternoon for a run.

He loped easily down to where Country Road had its beginnings in the bush, and from there on into its solitude.

As he ran it occurred to him that if he could make his legs go faster with the same stride length, he could run faster. In a clearing he tried running on the spot, lifting and pushing down his legs as fast as he could, then making them go faster still. What he found at first was that the faster he tried to go, the lower he lifted his legs, one improvement balanced by one shortcoming.

He ran deeper into the bush, along tracks his feet didn't know well. Several times he stopped to run on the spot, each time pushing the speed of his legs to their limit. He ran easily all the way home, had a shower and settled down again at the big table, eyes bright, eager to get to work.

Return Match

At football on Wednesday he was for a few seconds at the bottom of a ruck. The opposing forwards, hunting in a pack, had dived on him, like a rockfall. The words in his head at the time — there was no tune to it — were, 'the peace of God that passes all understanding'. How they got there he didn't know — they were familiar Meeting words. He was lying face up. A boy with red hair and ginger hairs on his top lip grinned down at him and stamped his foot quickly and efficiently on his face.

After the game he found a mirror in the dressing room. What would he tell Mum? The straight nose she was proud of was no longer straight. There was a lump one quarter the way down from the top.

On the way home in the train he remembered the grin and the red hair, and the ginger hairs on the top lip. He would have to wait for the return match in the second round. To stand over Ginger Lip on the bottom of a ruck would be a pleasure.

He sat back, thinking up ways to get his legs to run faster. Perhaps on his back, cycling his legs in the air? Maybe suspended on parallel bars, working his legs against no other pressure than the air?

He grinned at his thoughts. The picture of Ginger Lip floated into his mental vision. He knew he wouldn't stamp on Ginger Lip's face. The peace of God.

Why not? There was something in him, perhaps connected to his angers, that would savagely enjoy the feel of that face, or maybe any other face, under his foot. He didn't know exactly, but he guessed that the reason he wouldn't bother to take revenge was simply the bother of remembering, annoyance at the feeling that revenge bound him to Ginger Lip in a transaction that he, Davis Blood, had not originated. He'd rather take the knock, then wash his hands of the matter. That passes all understanding.

'You will keep him in perfect peace . . .'

Ah, there was a tune to that!

'Whose mind is stayed on you.'

He jumped from the train and ran up the steps of the overhead bridge. Into his head came the renounced revenge, and it was clear to him. Of course he wouldn't bother with some trifling knock, or insult: but let the cause be something his heart was bound up with, and then!

Yes, he reflected grimly, then we'd see how easy it is to forget or forgive.

When he crossed the highway he began his run home. He'd read ahead in the science book, and had come to particle physics. Were particles, at the very smallest level, like Ginger Lip and himself? Did they have likes and dislikes? Did they coalesce, as kids do in games, and sometimes fly apart, as in a sudden quarrel, or when they all went home? Did they have intentions? Did some conditions, and some other particles, suit them, while others didn't? The book said nothing of these matters.

Class Boundaries

That night after tea, he was getting ready to do some drawing when Aunt called him in a loud voice, from the kitchen. Preston was visiting, and sat with Randal and Orville in their room.

'Hey, Boysie!' her painfully produced voice called.

He recognised this tone. It meant: don't come, we'll talk in a shout from where we happen to be.

'Yes, Aunt,' he said. But whose voice had said: Yes, Aunt? How did his voice get down there? His voice had broken!

'This social class business!' She gave no sign that his voice had changed.

'Yes, Aunt.' This time it was the high boy's voice he was used to.

'Those old terms, middle class, working class, once meant something more precise than they mean today, but that was in another world. It might be easier for your own understanding — if you looked at it like this. Ready?'

'Yes, Auntie.' His voice went deep again. It was unpredictable.

'Right. The class boundary that means most is the one between the bottom class that doesn't bother to stir itself, and the next one up, that tries to rise in the world. Can you hear me?'

'Yes, Aunt.' And the whole house can, too.

'The boundary is between those who plan and save and train themselves and care what happens, and those who don't care, don't save, don't plan, don't try to learn new things — just won't stir themselves!'

She was talking to the rest of the house as well, but the ones she was trying to reach were Orville and Randal, who had recently talked of dropping out and going on the beach, up north.

There was no telling if the two brothers heard, or not, but there was one who did. Preston was usually impatient with interruptions, and more so when he was doing nothing at all, but in this situation he was glad to weigh in with his pronouncements.

'Never mind, Aunt, there's nothing to worry about. Mankind will always be such that no matter his condition, the desire for something better will never be extinguished.' He spent most of his daytime hours at work, and hadn't heard of his two younger brothers' heresy.

'Apologies to Gorky,' said Aunt drily. 'Yes, or to put it another way, no matter what utopia fathers erect, sons and daughters will want it different.'

Later that evening, his voice again did its ups and downs at the table, making everyone laugh except Lillian. She smiled, but he saw in her face the slight sadness that had been there years ago when he was six and had outrun her. For her, this was another going-away.

Aunt Ursula didn't appear to notice. Aunt Mira had her head down, eyes closed, and a Mozart programme on the radio coming through the earphones into her head. She looked contented, and comfortable in her pink outfit.

He'd heard his aunts talking of 'Little Wolfi', and Aunt Mira talking — softly: always in awe of this someone — of 'brilliant dreams and castles in the air', of 'sadness under the ecstasy', of 'miraculous adventures of feeling', and as always, of how when you looked at the music closer, and closer still, it seemed to be constructed of the simplest building blocks imaginable, almost arising from nothing: a few notes, part of a scale.

It reminded him of the science class, and the building blocks of matter, which, the teacher and the science book said, were simply unobservable particles and electric charges: in themselves nothing much at all.

Next time he was by himself he tried singing with his new deep voice. He started somewhere near middle C, went nearly an octave down, came up to the C above middle C, then found he could only sing a few tones above that, before his voice broke back into his boyish treble.

He would never be a tenor. Goodbye to singing, then. His beautiful boyhood voice was a gift from a clear sky; he'd done nothing to earn it. Anyway, it was too easy, being given your profession to carry round with you with not even a bag of tools, like a plumber has, or a doctor. A singer was a servant of music that others wrote. It wasn't enough.

He didn't grieve, but it was one door on the future shut.

Rages and Observations

After one of his sudden angers, the boy sat at the big table, not wanting to talk to anyone. He bent his head over his paper, making light pencil lines. The lines connected to show a woman reading in a park, one arm was affectionately round the shoulders of a small child who was boring into her side with a pneumatic drill. Chips of rock and rock dust flew out of the hole made, though she seemed flesh and blood enough from the look of the rest of her.

The boy he first coloured-in as a stone boy, then when he repeated the drawing on another sheet, he made the boy flesh and blood and the mother a reading statue. He like the second one better.

There was a peculiar mental gap set somewhere near the middle of his rages. Into this gap thoughts came, often quite calculating thoughts. Sometimes they were so different from what he was doing, so foreign to the spirit of anger that possessed his whole body, that he was tempted to think the anger was not real.

He had just smashed to pieces a large rock down the backyard where the bush began. He pounded it until it was a flat piece of yellow sand grains. Not even a small piece of rock remained, to hurl down to the creek.

In this most recent rage, he stopped and coolly listened to the words that sounded quietly in his head: 'A man of violence, a violence such as we have never seen.' then got on with the storm of furious anger that had taken him over.

Where did such calm observations come from? Where did the anger start? He would not follow up the question. It was in him, that was all. It made him uncomfortable to dwell on it.

When he went back into the house, calm and relaxed, Aunt Ursula, who had not long come home from a visit to some Sydney friends, wheeled up to him, and, apparently with no reference to anything, said, 'Some of us are given a sort of civilised discontent, you know. The more life has said "Yes" to us, the more we have the urge to say "No!" The more comfortable and loved we've been, the more we admire privation and austerity. The safer we've been the easier it is to yearn for danger and the sight of blood.'

He looked at her, puzzled. Had she seen him pound the rock to powder in his frenzy of murderous anger?

He smiled at her, trying to disarm her suspicions, but already she had a smile on her tilted face; she knew.

He found he could say nothing. He was acutely uncomfortable. He hated people seeing into him.

Hanging Out to Dry

After school on Monday, he chopped some wood for the fire and dumped it in the wood box beside the stove. Coming out of the kitchen he looked down from the back verandah.

The clothes hoist in the backyard was something he had never properly considered as a subject for drawings. He washed his hands, and went to the big table.

In an hour he had done six drawings on a clothes hoist series.

One showed cars pegged out, like the day's washing, to dry. The second showed ordinary people hanging out to dry; the next, animals; the fourth, guns; the fifth, houses; the sixth, world leaders of the day.

He wasn't satisfied with his treatment of the idea, but they would do to go on the pile. He could look at them later, when fresh ideas would occur to him, as they always did.

No Softness

At school he went to a few lunchtime meetings of the Christian fellowship. Some Christian Endeavour badges were in evidence, and some of the Student Christian Movement. Their way of talking about Christian things was different from that of his father's people at the Meeting. They talked about the Lord stepping off into the air to taste its colour and feel its songs: how he inhales the fantasies of children, the breath of tomorrow, the thoughts of yesterday.

They prayed that sometime soon people would send up balloons in church, turn tired cathedrals into cafeterias, paint gravestones like the rainbow, write their names in the sunset, play football in the park with cripples, sing in asylums, grow flowers in garbage cans, turn bombs into boomerangs.

He found the sentiments sickly, but there was no doubting their kindliness, their spirit, their keenness.

He felt more at home after all in the strenuous atmosphere of the Meeting, where nothing was exaggerated, where there was no softness, no pretty visions, where the individual faced his God, was emptied by repentance, healed and made whole by faith and filled with joy of the Holy Spirit.

Another thing he noticed was that, while in the room with these young Christians, he didn't think. That is, the usual flow of converse that went on in his head, stopped. He waited for the others, and when they spoke he thought about their thoughts. He felt uncomfortable doing this.

I'll keep out of groups, he said, in that conversation place within him. I want to be free to think, unaffected by group opinions, group fashions, or by the subjects others happen to be working on.

What had happened reminded him of a short sermon Aunt Ursula had preached to him not long before.

Nevertheless, it was due to them that he sat down in a

lunch hour and hammered out some verses loosely based on his reactions to their more sober notions and to one particular hymn they sang:

SPIRIT OF FAITH, COME DOWN.

Spirit of God plead now
With him that I most fear
That mingled with my secret vow
That strange sweet voice I hear.

Great love of God speak now
The words that I must hear
Toward your humbling throne I bow,
Your mercies' robes I wear.

Strange hosts within one heart
That wars upon itself.
Lord let me not from you depart
Until my soul has health.

Strong Arm of God reach down
And pour upon my soul
The grace that is to others shown
That makes the spirit whole.

No Explanation Supplied

Sitting at the drawing table, the winter rain pouring down from the west and the french windows closed, he sat doing nothing. He was in a dream, and didn't notice the rain stop, nor the sun come out through a break in the clouds, shining on the green wetness of the valley.

Through the curtain of his dreaming state, the sparkle of a falling raindrop caught his eye. He woke from the dream, and saw the window framing the dripping sunlit scene outside.
Windows.
His pencil felt as if it were part of his hand. He drew five windows. Through the first was a vision of the sea, with waves like juggernauts. The second opened on to a desert of level sand and scattered rocks.
The third was full of flowers, the fourth of faces, the fifth was a jungle thick with city buildings.
He drew the five windows set in a curved wall, and furniture in the space before the wall.
There was no explanation, within the pictured space on the paper, of the scenes shown. He smiled with satisfaction.

He put his drawing pencil on the table, and the latest drawings on his pile in the drawer. It was not a Sunday when he'd wanted to go to the Meeting with Jackson Blood. He'd stayed at the big table all day, working intently, in that state of concentration where he hardly needed to breathe.
For days the world was the same colour as the weather: grey as ashes. This morning, the clouds began to break up, the pouring rain stopped and became sun showers.
The sun was bright, the shadows hard-edged. It was afternoon. He got up, went out on the verandah and

watched his valley for a while, allowing it to flow into him. His eyes roved round, touching loved and familiar things.

Suddenly he felt so happy, so full of spirits, that he simply stood and yelled. No words, just the sound. When the yell wasn't loud enough, he screamed. One of the dogs began to mutter anxiously.

He ran to the front of the house, jumped the fence and off down into the bush. He would just give himself a short time there, then come back and get on with more drawings.

He slowed to a walk, and as he walked, he could feel all round him the day burning slowly on, the winter sun hot after overcast days. Sun-filled clearings steamed. Once, a brown quail hurried away through the low brush.

The sogged earth, the wet leaf-mould got in his nose. It was something he would never forget. For once, he went slowly, enclosed with earth and trees in the one dream.

This was called crown land, and in a country without crowns, he thought with amusement but no bitterness. It seemed irrelevant to the age-old rocks, and to the larger trees, which might have been saplings when his white forebears arrived.

The moon was beginning to show against the fierce bright sun, which had made it insubstantial as a jellyfish.

Just off the track he noticed a tree blasted by lightning during the storms. Long splinters of torn and ripped wood stuck up towards the sky; a thick fallen branch lay against the base of the tree. The exposed wood, once so private, seemed oddly dry. As if the fault for the rift lay more in the tree's weakness than the violence of electricity.

The sun was burning low in the west, the shadows soft, with blurred edges that moved as you watched.

It would be good to be here, to live and breathe in this patch of hilly bush a long time.

Perhaps, since everyone seemed to leave their place of birth, he could take his with him.

He turned for home, so full of the landscape, so heavy with it, that he could only walk. Running would have done violence to it.

Thoughts of Others

*H*e walked out onto the side verandah, thinking of a sentence that came up in Mr Davenport's science class.

'Perhaps, as Haldane said, "The world is not only stranger than we imagine, but stranger than we can imagine." '

But is it? We are formed from the minerals and gases of this one planet, this special mixture, and therefore it is exactly right for us.

Why may it not be that, since we are so much of it, so attuned to it because formed from it, that we can see it as it is? Couldn't it be that cosmic visitors would indeed see the planet differently but not as it is, because of their differences? And not see things we see, because they don't know what they're seeing?

He looked out over the valley, leaning on the square timber rail of the verandah, his feet touching the fibro sheet where it met the grey floorboards. His mother's voice came floating in from the front garden.

> *'Man of sorrows, what a name*
> *For the Son of God who came . . .'*

A movement on the left took his eye, down the backyard past Brown Rock, where the line of trees bordering the bush started. From between two of the turpentine trees, the Catamaran stepped lightly, picking their way through invisible barriers, up the terraced yard to the back steps. They went everywhere together, usually side by side, like a twin-hulled cat. They had been down the bush, probably discussing the pros and cons of going wild: whether to strike out on their own, grow to enormous size, terrify the homes, people, and pets that lived on the fringe of the bush; or stay here in comfort and honour. They inspected their food for the close of the day, set out on twin plates;

then wolfed it delicately and licked the plates clean. Opening their jaws wide — each of them at the same time — they looked languidly round for a drink.

That, too, was provided. They would stay at least tonight. It was a daily decision.

He loved watching things and people, particularly people. If he could be hidden, he would see what other people do when they were by themselves. A fly on the wall. Alone in a crowd, it was possible to see some things, but not enough. If he could know what others thought; what words they said to themselves in the cells, or cathedrals, of their own heads. Ah, that would be something!

He felt he knew nothing of other people.

Often when he had watched people who were alone, he saw they still had a shell of carefulness on; they seemed to act as if someone might be looking.

How could you ever get close to the truth about others?

But wasn't there something sneaky about wanting to be invisible? Like being a spy, not the sort of thing a decent person would do.

His mother sang,

> *'Guilty, vile and helpless me.'*

Did she mean that? When had Lillian ever been vile? Even guilty was unthinkable. It was exaggeration. It was like trying to imagine her with a sin. She wouldn't know what to do with it. But there, he didn't really know his mother, certainly not in that place where she was herself — in the privacy of her head.

Everything is Slightly Possible

As he ducked into the kitchen for a drink of water he heard Aunt Mira's voice from her corner.

'I'm dying.'

He got the glass of water and had a swallow, then went over to look at her.

'Dying.'

Her head was down. She was ruffled, defeated.

'Are you pulling my leg, Aunt?'

'I'm dying of lack of love.'

'You!'

'Others love me, I know. The lack is in me. If only I could love. Someone; anyone; the world; each day; just to love something!'

He was suspicious of her. She was a wily old bird, with a piece of cheek or crackling sarcasm as quick as a flash if you were unwary.

'You'll survive, Aunt. Just keep breathing in, then out.'

She'd used that sentiment on him several times. He went outside.

Confident in her command of language, Aunt Mira commanded herself to say nothing. She was unsuccessful. Words escaped, in spite of her.

'He's very single-minded, that boy: loves only himself. But he's too young to worry. Oh, I'm so unhappy. Nobody bothers to love me anymore.'

Ursula wheeled in.

'No one ever did, to me,' she said. 'Not since I was sixteen. But one has to keep doing, that's the thing.'

'In my case, it's keep being,' replied Mira.

'Being is soon done,' Ursula said.

The two aunts were always careful to show no intemperate benevolence towards each other.

'It's all right for you. You can get around.'

'Stop complaining. Lighten your load with hope!'

'Hope!' Mira cackled.
'Yes, hope. You can do it. Everything is slightly possible. Remember, time heals all wounds.'
'Time wounds all heels, more like it,' objected Mira.
'No. Time's wounds all heal,' insisted Ursula.
'Oh! Oh!' called Mira loudly. 'I'm being hit over the head with blunt concepts!'

The Seven States of the South

It was Friday afternoon and his father was home by five, having picked up a week's casual work with a plumber and drainer.

Five days of contact with the world had topped up his confidence, and also given him energy for a denunciation of the kinds of people he didn't want to see in his future Seven States of the South. He summoned his son, to tell him. Sitting in his kitchen chair near the window, he said,

'Yes-men, rogues on high salaries, parasites on the party system; criers, cringers, crawlers, whingers; the lice hiding in the undergrowth of big organisations; haters of truth, lovers of the false front; those who can shape their faces to please everyone they meet; the long-term planners of the sly transfer and the sneak promotion; slaves and rubber stamps; the servile, the shifty, the mean. And reserved for special horror I include the survivors — those who announce the word about themselves with pride — who glory in throwing overboard everything except their own interests, and everyone who might survive to deprive them; who die with ease, but no dignity.'

By this time Jackson Blood was dying for a cigarette and

began to roll one from his favourite tobacco. The boy was left wondering who would inhabit his father's Seven States!

The Joy of Making

*H*e was fifteen. He celebrated by making two trips to Kangaroo Point that Saturday after he'd done the groceries for Lawsons. Standing on Point Rock, looking down with satisfaction on the thickly wooded slopes and the valley — that led eventually to the sea — and round at the trees on both sides of the rim of cliffs above the slopes, he picked out two mature turpentine trees standing with smaller members of the grove. He attacked the larger one with joy. Under his breath he sang — the exertion giving the words a savage tone — 'Oh love that will not let me go, I rest my weary soul in thee-ee.' He was steeped in those words.

Under the warm bark the timber was creamy, soft and sappy; the axe was sharp; yet it took a full three minutes before the sigh, the soft snaps one after the other, the loud crack of the last uncut tendons of wood to break under the tension as the tree began to fall. The heart wood was red; it smelled lovely, yet strange, like an unfamiliar vegetable cut ready for the table.

He bent over the stump. A faint warm breath rose from the sharp spikes of wood that had snapped. He put his face right over it, feeling the warmth. There came still a faint sighing from the torn, jagged needles of wet living wood.

He cut into the log in such a way that he made two scarfs about a metre apart; then rolled it and cut two more as twins for the first two. He cut out the raised parts on either side and left a piece in the shape of a wide board of red heart wood. Carefully, he chopped this board from the tree at both ends of its length. It was a great waste, but he wanted only the red heart wood, and that section of it.

Before he left the Point he cut three slender apple gums, trimmed them and left them lying together hidden by their own leaves and some underbrush; he put the small billet of turpentine under his left arm, held the axe in his right hand and loped home.

At home he got to work with the plane and smoothed one side, then the other. He tried the adze at first, but the grain was wavy and the blade jagged the timber and lifted large splinters that would have ruined the surface. He managed to plane the surface flat; the bottom side was impossible to smooth properly with a hand tool. He had made a thick, heavy cutting board for Lillian to use in the kitchen.

He had a problem with his mother: she was always reluctant to change her habits, and though after a day or two of looking at it suspiciously she began to cut meat on it, she often looked across at the old pine board she was used to, which she couldn't bring herself to throw out. She thanked him, but her attitude was like when Jackson Blood did some painting: she would ask for the job to be done for months, then when the job was under way was fretful at the dislocation and mess. Did she think things could be done immediately, taking no more time than they took to say in words, like magic? Or did she feel the mess dirtied her, if it dirtied the house?

Next, he took rope and a shoulder pad, and walked back to the Point for the apple gums.

The valley was on his right as he left Country Road and entered the bush. He walked, enjoying himself. Up high, the moon sailed through brief clouds, like a bright dinner-plate. He'd awakened that morning before dawn, to the feeling of the heavy dark being raised off the earth, and the earth in response, breathing more freely. Yesterday the sunset had been simple and grand, looking as if it tasted of God.

He remembered the moon on other recent days. One day it was white, so high, and the sun so bright it seemed like a tablet in water, dissolving. One night, looking east from the kitchen window, it was big and buttery. It had slipped out of existence as it moved past the window frame, then gathered in a hunched image in the rippled window glass, then again slipped past quickly as he moved his head.

When he was much smaller, he'd imagined heaven up there, until he'd learned of the earth's shape, after which 'up there' had to signify a spherical envelope containing the planet.

What was heaven, wherever it was placed? Well, it couldn't be as the Christians said. Young as he was, he could see the emptiness, the slow weariness of eternity, the awfulness of happiness infinitely prolonged, and the pain, for gentle souls, of contemplating others no matter what they'd done, suffering agonies on a similar time scale; some of them friends and family. It was too horrible.

He looked down into Kookaburra Valley and caught that air it had of understanding what he was thinking.

'You know, don't you?' he said aloud.

The air was delighted. Delighted with the world that produced it, delighted with its duty of flowing among the objects it encountered, passing across land, then sea, then land again, forever.

At that moment there was no wind, all was still, yet the bush had a busyness, a hum, as of a myriad invisible activities. And the whole was so triumphantly another world: not nothingness, it was another state of being.

As he walked on, the feeling that the air was full of the scents of earth and leaves, sunned rock and bush plants, was gradually overwhelmed by something he'd never felt before, not even at night, waking in pitch black dark. It was a silence he could feel, above and below, in earth and sky, pressing round him, silence in which everything was submerged, lost, far away, deeply padded with atmosphere. It was vibrant, though soundless. He stood still, feeling it intensely for the first time.

This slope, this valley, was like a place from which

everything had gone, leaving the feeling that life had been there a moment before.

For him, in later years, it always had that feeling. Never once did he come upon it when that vanished life was there: always it had gone a moment before. A few birds' cries, rustles of snakes or animals, a flurry through bushes of a quail, the fall of a dead branch, these hardly echoed, they weren't enough to dispel the feeling that a lid was clamped over everything, forming a cocoon.

Later still, this silence acted on him like a drug. In addition, a hunger grew in him for its uncertainty, the feeling it contained that the world might shift, anything could happen. With such expectations hanging like a cliff overhead, a person, a race, might wait forever for something to open that cocoon, and end up doing nothing.

He resumed his walk towards the Point, dazed a little by the powerful feelings in him.

When he'd carried home the three apple gums, he barked them, then made saw cuts in such a way that when he stripped the rounded sides away he was left with flat planks from the middles of the trees, each with white edges and pink heartwood. He planed them smooth, cut each in two, and had six of equal length. He would use them for a table top, or bookshelves, later, but the interesting work was done. He put them under the house to dry out.

He'd seen a dead tree down there, short of the Point, blown over in a storm; it was spotted gum, tough hardwood with a tight, wavy grain. One day he could cut out its centre, too, and have a whole table top. It was an idea.

Beginning of a Death

It was now, at fifteen, that he discovered his father was dying. Jackson Blood had gone to the doctor a number of times, had x-rays, had come home with reassurances and the prospect of another fifteen years of life. The family had heard these things at the table at night and it didn't occur to them that they weren't being told all the truth. That sank in gradually, without words. His lungs' wartime exposure to chemicals had eventually claimed him. And, Davis Blood privately thought, his heavy smoking.

Since he'd been too proud and independent to continue collecting a tiny war pension, he now faced great difficulty in getting his war disability recognised. For months he made the long journey down to Sydney, waiting hours in a queue, sometimes all day, a sick man. The rest of the family heard these things later.

He began to spend much of his remaining time in a veterans' hospital with bush surroundings, and when he came home it was like a visit.

After an absence, the boy noticed his father's strong tobacco smell. It was in his clothes, his hands, in the familiar yellow finger-stains, even noticeable when he'd been to the lavatory. Davis Blood felt ashamed that he noticed it so much; it seemed like disloyalty. He sat in his chair in the kitchen endlessly gazing out of the window. The boy didn't know what he thought of, but wished later that he'd asked him.

Once the boy was in the kitchen, just home from school, and standing near the oven. He looked at his father, whose eyes were wide open and still as he looked out to, and beyond, the camphor laurel tree and the grass of the yard next door. He imagined he could see reflected in the gloss of his father's eyeball a green valley in which grew a castle from a small rise on the floor of the valley, and all round were steep mountain sides, enclosing the valley. Cows grazed and ruminated, horses cropped grass and swished lazy tails. If he should go into his father's room while he was asleep and lift one of his eyelids, would he still see that valley, or would there be no sign of life, or would it be night?

Nothing was said, but the beginning of his death was in the air between all the members of the family.

Several times the man wanted to talk to the boy, and when he did, spoke not of St Paul and grace and justification by faith, but of Australia.

'The first Australians had it right when they held sacred the land that nourished them, since it is, mostly, a fragile land. No wonder the Europeans found only Aborigines here — our neighbours didn't want it, it's full of problems, it's too hard. Look at the map — a huge belly and nothing in it. Deserts, erosion, dry plains, hills without water. This country can't be conquered or subdued, only understood. Its glories, as land, are in the past. All we can do is nurse it, delay its final demise.

'Unless someone comes along with ideas for it, either to change it, or do something other than cultivate.'

He also spoke some visionary words which made a great impression on the boy.

'We Australians, like the original inhabitants, are in a dreamtime of our own; the dreamtime of a remote future. What we do in the next thousand years will be the stuff of myths to those who come long after us.'

All round, it seemed because of the nuclear threat, voices proclaimed a version of the biblical Last Days, yet here was his father asserting a long future for mankind. He took the thought away with him, to think about.

Only You Have the Answer

Several times Aunt saw him looking at Jackson Blood and with nothing to say, as was the case with him most of the time, and after noticing this for a while, she said to him, 'You're the unusual one, the strange one. It will be your destiny to live forever.'

'How can I do that, Aunt? Everyone dies.' Was Aunt joking?

'Not everyone dies,' she said sturdily. 'Work it out.'

'But —' How old was Aunt? In her fifties, for sure.

'But me no buts. You work it out, alone. No one you ask will have the answer, only you.'

She watched him obsessively. Each day she was hungry for him to be back home, around the house when she was, where she could see him and catch the flavour of what he did, as if she knew he would leave them soon, though still physically there.

Suddenly he picked up a ball and had a game with it, bouncing it against the brick work of the front steps. She watched his enjoyment, his quickness, his easy balance, and the fact that his mind was obviously on something else.

Lately he did everything suddenly. He was sometimes lazy, dilatory, working in fits and starts, when he was forced to, or on a whim of the moment. Often he would rather do nothing but sit around thinking, yet when he picked up the axe and went for a log to carry, he behaved as if possessed, and if he worked at his drawings it would be all weekend.

He confided in no one, not his brothers, or even his mother. She realised with sadness that he trusted no one. He often said nothing for days.

He was profoundly alone.

Waterbury, the Dane cross, had gone greyer round the muzzle than a few months before. And that was a strange thing: Waterbury greying and not dying, while Jackson Blood was dying and not a grey hair in his head at forty-eight.

Finishing School

Spring, and the soft airs; new leaves unfurling and opening out with the shine of newness, the tenderness and translucence of flesh that hasn't set.

Seen from the kitchen window, the new camphor laurel leaves were the lightest green, nearly transparent, the succulent green of the breaking waves on Driftwood Beach, just below their white crests. There were caves of quiet air between the heads of leaves within the tree's inner space; silent caves whose texture and warmth he tried to imagine for himself. That air, enclosed by such bountiful green, that quivering quietness, seemed an ingredient of poetry, almost an emotion in itself.

The evergreen gum trees put out new leaves at the crown, the new translucent leaves growing dark amber first, their borders juicy with new sap and a polished metal sheen when the sun glanced from their surfaces. Orville's tree was a mass of light green leaves, its trunk massive, its branches strong. It was as wide as half the block of ground the house stood on.

In October the flowers on the outer borders of the pittosporum branches opened and exhaled their sweet heavy scent all round; the border flowers, despised freesias that grew anywhere, sweetened the air; a reminder of new growth and the fragrance of the earth.

He had not long turned fifteen. For him school would

soon be over. Any further schoolwork he did would have to be done in his spare time. With his father sick and two of the boys and Danielle gone, the family needed another earner.

Danielle was long gone, in the city sharing a house with friends. She started an exodus, for soon Preston had moved out to a flat in the city. He still worked for the venetian blind company where he was first company secretary, then financial director and now managing director. Leaving with words of wisdom to his youngest brother: 'There's money in everything: in love, in hate, in the aged, the young, the sick, the lonely, the unloved: the ingenuity of humans has no limits. Dollars everywhere, kid! It's all there, waiting.'

Randal had gone off to live with his girlfriend, and visited once or twice a week. Orville had done his degree part time and was due to go to Teachers College in the new year. The boy moved in to what had been Orville's and Randal's pale-blue room with Orville when Randal went.

He'd had the bed on the verandah all those years. It was strange to sleep in a room. He spent some time under the house cleaning up the old mattock head they'd all used and worn out: he filed off the oxide, shone it up with emery paper, wiped it with an oily rag, and put it in his new room. He picked it up often, his hands going all over it, as if trying to sense something of his brothers and his father, that might be clinging to it still; something of the years they'd lived, something of those selves of which he knew almost nothing.

The Third of October

Among a pile of books and papers Danielle had left, undecided about whether to keep them, he came across a folded pamphlet on meditation.

Find a quiet place. Sit on a straight-backed chair, feet flat on the floor, fold the hands in the lap. Fix the eyes on one spot, or close them. Relax. Empty the mind, thinking of nothing. Keep it up for 20 minutes.

There was no one around. He sat over in the western side of the big room. He would try it.

He fixed his eyes on one spot. The spot kept moving, and he kept thinking of how to hold it still, so he shut his eyes, let his body go limp. He stayed like that for a while, thinking of nothing, seeing nothing but the backs of his eyelids. Then something happened.

He was looking into a cloudy cave that dropped straight down into the ground. A pale mist swirled up and round, within and below the cave mouth, obscuring the depths. He was standing in a desolate region, high in the mountains of his mind.

Several voices seemed to twist together in the sound that rose from deep down there. Voices without words. He strained to hear. Then clear words came in a deep voice.

> *'We are the eternal! Eternal,'* added the echo.
> *'We are the eternal!'*

He felt the skin of his face creep, and his neck. Something tightened his throat. He swallowed, eyes shut, peering down into himself. The voices were still twined together into one voice, and echoed in that deep cavern. He waited. He could see nothing but depth and pale mist.

> *'You have been preserved, protected, given all you need!'*

And a long silence.

'When will we hear from you?'

Hear from me? Hear what, he thought. Or had he said that aloud?

'We are eternal! What would you expect?' was the deep reply.

His eyes prickled, as all the tears he'd ever had in him wanted to come out. He waited, listened. There was nothing more. As he looked down in that deep cavern in himself, the pale mist grew paler, the black depths lightened, and with a final swirl, all vanished.

What had happened? Something, someone, some Ones had spoken to him. Why? But what did that matter?

Hear from me? he repeated. What do they expect me to do?

My food is to do the will of Him that sent me, came into his mind, but what did that have to do with Davis Blood?

Perhaps he'd imagined it. But no, that was silly. One thing, though, struck him. These voices of his didn't come from some fanciful region of sky, but from the depths of the earth. Well, why not? God was in the earth, wasn't he?

'Davis!' called his mother. 'Come and lay the table!'

Was this what Aunt meant, and his mother: that he was a special person? Were there really things he was to do? Had to do? Things that were eternal in some way?

'Davis! Come and set the table for dinner this instant! My goodness, that boy's becoming inattentive. I always said he was a dreamer.'

'Yes, Mum,' he answered. 'Coming.'

A peculiar, happy calmness possessed him. For a few weeks he wore a slight contented smile; an outward sign of the altered state of things within. Some times he felt that objects in his path, or visible in the distance, had the power to stand up and out from things near them; and once or twice they were ringed by a glow of colour; outlined, rather. The colours reminded him of the part-spectrum that is seen when light glances off glass chamfered at the edge and has that glow within the edge, or casts it on what is near.

When will we hear from you? The phrase came often into his head, and the fact that it rose from out of the earth. Hear what? The antiphonal sounded within him.

Flexibility

He took Randal's 12 gauge shotgun, broke it, and, carrying the two pieces in a sugar bag, went walking up the hill between the railway line and the new white temple, where the bracken was never less than knee-high, and where dense bush began past the temple grounds. In his pocket he had four cartridges of BB shot. Two rabbits fell under the shot in the first hundred metres. The gun-blast echoed off the temple walls and the high railway embankment in quick order, back and forth, like a ball bouncing.

The corpses, as he held them by the legs on the way home, were horribly limp. They swung like soft chains from his hands, still warm, but a warmth foreign to his own warmth: pathetic, only recently alive, that warmth said. On the grass, where he skinned them, the full awfulness of shooting small animals with 12 bore BB shot stared him in the face. He went ahead, but nothing could disguise the purple-black holes in the light flesh, and in the kitchen the torn bodies were looked at with raised eyebrows.

He'd helped the household, though. The women watched his responsible air — they knew he knew he should be going further at school — they felt the strength in him, that prevented one complaining word coming from him. More than that, Ursula saw the pride and confidence that filled him to such an extent that he spent not one moment regretting what had to be, but changed direction instantly without apparent stress.

She felt great pity. Was it confidence that produced such quick obedience? Perhaps it was. But if not, what was it? How did he take so easily to hardship? Was it flexibility, or something else?

He Dreamed

That night he was in a groping jungle, cold and dark with many leaves; he had time only to try to dodge sideways as the descending tree-snake bit him six times about the face. There was nowhere to take cover: all round him the trunks of trees and great derisive leaves of wet succulent plants pushed against him.

The bites didn't hurt. The snake was gone, perhaps back high in its tree. There was no path, but a way forward seemed to be slightly open in front of his feet.

Instantly, the jungle was irrelevant, for he was no longer there. He didn't question the change. Movement down in a shallow pit took his eye: people without skin writhed, some singly, some together. Those together touched; they began to wrestle. His teeth were on edge as he watched the skinless surfaces scrape, each against each. Wasn't that sand and gritty stones in the pit? The wrestling forms grew savage with their opponents; they tore at the face, they scratched at the unprotected flesh; vines began to entangle them, mud to obscure them. They became movements in the surface of a pit of mud, and gradually submerged. All ripples ceased.

He woke, with the skinless forms still filling his head.

Men Worried Him

On a Saturday morning that was full of small children, bright colours and pets, the boy was standing with Waterbury near the supermarket, on the paved part where seats were fitted among the garden beds and ornamental pools and waterfalls. He noticed men sitting and standing around; outside the gambling office — the TAB — and along outside the pub. The seated men watched the crowds of shoppers stream by. Davis Blood walked Waterbury near them, and stood.

As he watched the men watching, he waited for signs in their words that they had seen the people as he had seen them, had noticed and been affected by their simple joy in sun and leaves, in water and sky, in other people.

As he waited longer, it began to seem that they hadn't even noticed. Why weren't they joyful at the joy around them, why weren't they glad at the life in the small children, the mixed joy and duty in the faces of the women? Why weren't they moved by the smile of the day itself?

Were men different? The women could feel the happiness of the day. Of life, of lively children: it was in their faces and voices. Not the men, apparently.

Did they see differently? Did they see different things? Did they see, not people, but objects; like stumps, blocks and impediments? When a child ran, laughing and shouting, were they immune to the infectious mood; did they see only an object moving and emitting noise?

He decided that men were essentially different, and he was different from them. If they spoke Estonian, they couldn't be more foreign to him. If he lived here in Bellbird Corner another sixty years, he'd still be a stranger, forever outside their world.

Men worried him. It would be awful to be like them when he grew up.

Transactions

Friday, after lunch, in Social Studies discussion — it extended over two periods, with the last one a free period — some of the boys were talking of a bright future they'd read of, a Utopia in which the state will have withered away and all people will be equal and free from exploitation, all will have jobs, all will be educated, all will share the ownership of the means of production, the banks, the market. There were other glowing things waiting for mankind in that future, but it wasn't all bright, Davis Blood thought, but dark; for all of it was as yet unseen.

The way the others spoke, those good things were inevitable, as if mankind had found the secret, and knew how history worked. That was the way the world was moving, they thought, as if it were a locomotive on rails, aiming for a known terminus.

He could see that their Utopia was an answer to the problem of the poor and the straggler in society, and appreciated the attraction of this generous future, though he wasn't clear about the benefits of having the state wither away, but his understanding baulked most at something much simpler.

'You seem to think times can be made good for everyone at once,' he said when it was his turn. 'But inequality, riches and poverty, lazy people and energetic, good times and bad, alternate, come and go, all the time, in wave formations. It's the way societies and people work. Some people climb, some slip down, some save, some don't; some care, some don't care. Your plan requires people to be altered. If they're not changed in their natures, not even coercion will work: the same old things will always happen. And why shouldn't they? What's bad about people being different? Your idea seems to be a society with no casualties and everyone on the same level. What's bad about being poor if everyone has a chance to change if they want to? Some don't want to, some do. People are all different, but you want to treat them as if they're not individuals.

'It seems to me you're trying to make sense out of a myriad random currents of action, the actions, interactions, aims, hopes, thoughts, of many individuals; but such things have no rhyme or reason in the mass, only a resultant. There can be no one solution to all emergencies, no one single destination that everyone will arrive at. Even if they did, who would be content to stay there? How would you make them stay? By force? If so, where's freedom?'

This provoked strong condemnation on all sides, and he didn't get a chance to say more. The sneers and jeers went on quite a while. Even Kulakovsky and Verbruggen joined in. Thompson and Pye looked at him as if he was a cretin. Even Petersen and Lucy looked superior. He wished he'd had a chance to say that he thought changing people's natures — in the mass — was impossible.

For it seemed to him that must be what they were aiming at. What lively-minded person would ever be content with a goal arrived at by others, by his forefathers? What state could ever exist that wouldn't change? What sort of world was it, where nothing was unforeseen? The sheer numbers of the world's people, the countless varying actions, desires, impulses, accidents, quarrels, jealousies, misunderstandings, rose in his mind in all their dizzying complexity, and made him wonder that the other boys couldn't see it.

They seemed to possess agreed meanings and words and know of necessities he could see no reason for. His own words were simple, theirs had a technical, almost scientific flavour. He felt inferior because he knew no theory-weighted words for his thoughts, but their solemn words irresistibly reminded him of the more obscure preachers at the Meeting, and their dogma was just as ironclad.

Behind their words, as they ignored him and continued, he saw they had in mind an ideal order, somewhere in the future, and in this ideal state, if he understood them, human folly would be abolished, or so contained that it wouldn't rock the boat.

How could that be? Why was it necessary to think of an ideal order? Surely, if there was such a thing, it would only be a stage on the road, to give place to another later, and with lots of upsets in between. And to express such a nebulous thing in words, surely would require loose, easy words, the widest possible terms, so they contained hints only, and almost no specific information.

He fell back on the example of geometry. If geometry was founded on nothing that existed in the natural world, but on man-made axioms and a practical need, and there were as many geometries as there were different patterns of axioms, and the different geometries all had their uses, and more could be constructed at any time given the imagination and the will to do it, then how could people imagine that one man-made theory of economic and political behaviour, however often revised, could be final truth, or give rise to an ideal order?

The more they talked, the more iron-bound their theory seemed to be. Perhaps they thought it was the embodiment of hope for mankind, but to Davis Blood it seemed their strict prescriptions left no room for hope. And no room to move, either: freedom was squeezed out.

To them, what he said was no argument: he hadn't used acceptable terms. But he knew it wasn't an argument, merely the outline of an approach; why couldn't they see what it implied? He felt it pointed to something substantial, though he wasn't altogether clear about it, himself. The trouble was, the points that he felt mattered, to do with who we are, what we are, and how we became ourselves, weren't covered by their theory, or even noticed, and the things he thought good and satisfying about present-day affairs, they thought trivial and not worth preserving.

Lying in bed that night, he returned to the Social Studies discussion. If there is a way some things have always been, including people, and always will be unless people change, then you'd expect that way to assert itself no matter what changes come about.

If, he thought, we call this way: some rich, some middling, some poor; then you'd expect to see this pattern assert itself anywhere even if everyone started off rich, or started off poor. If it was called: some energetic, some lazy; or some inventive, some dull; some quick to understand, some slow; or some quick to action, some slow — then where is the sort of government which can legislate and enforce laws against these differences to make people equal? And if you didn't enforce it where was equality?

He'd heard, from talk at home, of places in the world where equality was legislated for, yet, as Preston, at thirty-one, managing director, took delight in pointing out, the children of the party heads and top brass went to the best schools and scored the best accommodation and just happened to live where they could get the best doctors.

But that was only a narrow example. He thought of the people he knew, however slightly: boys and girls, friends, neighbours, relations, shopkeepers, idlers in the street. He lay thinking of them, their faces, words and familiar attitudes floating on a screen in his head.

Somehow he saw them a thousand years ago, then several thousand, then ten thousand, when people were leaving the hunting life to settle on the land and grow things. He saw them again when some people began to come off the land and live close to each other in market villages, where farm produce was exchanged, where trades began and flourished, where gold began to be valued as wealth and money was invented, where a house became property and some saved enough to buy more than one; where some drank or gambled their money; where some were too lazy to be worth employing; where some loved fighting and were employed as soldiers; where some loved planning, intrigue and power, and became rulers or politicians; where some loved quietness and thought and became poets, or loved argument and became philosophers or lawyers; where the torrent of personalities, abilities and levels of energy interacted to produce the wonderful variety of human activities. The sheer numbers and combinations fascinated him, and enlarged his vision.

Twice he woke from trivial dreams, with peculiar phrases in his mouth.

One was, 'All transactions tend to capitalism.' The other, 'Life itself tends to the middle class.' Perhaps he'd read them somewhere. But if so, he'd forgotten where. When he woke it was pitch dark; he had the impression he'd been grinding his teeth for hours. He checked, with his fingers, to see if they'd been worn down to stumps.

Transactions, he thought. Why that word? Transactions could be a name for all the things people do; they add up to what's called daily life. Why was he thinking of capitalism last night? Only because the Social Studies discussion had dredged it up, a haversack word to hold all sorts of things. But the kids at school used it to hold things like exploitation, greed, oppression, war, alienation, cruelty, poverty, unemployment, hunger and neglect. He thought such things could exist under any political system, depending on the circumstances at the time.

Perhaps his idea, that with a little latitude in the word's meaning, capitalism with its throng of transactions, was daily life, was not too far from reality. After all, transactions of any sort, personal or public, involved an exchange and a reckoning; one had to give something to get something, whether love, money, security, respect, employment, and there was a power balance and a power relation. Perhaps the kids at school needed a different word to account for the evils they worried about. Their solution to the world's problems seemed to dodge any idea of a reckoning, and certainly the idea of a legion reckonings for as many transactions. As well they hated the idea of casualties, of failures. They wanted to insure against pain, loss, failure, against all mistakes. That was as far as his thoughts took him. He wasn't sleepy, but reflected that whenever he talked, even to himself, he sooner or later reached a dead end. He slept because he could think no further.

At breakfast he said casually, 'What's capitalism, Aunt?'

Aunt Ursula's eyes gleamed. It was a while since he'd asked her a question.

'Capitalism starts with property. The common use of the word has to do with surplus money or credit. It involves using your own or other people's money to breed more money.'

Here was no broad definition that roped in the daily and petty transactions of friendship, agreements, alliances, arrangements, bargains, compromises, concessions, terms of obedience and good behaviour, contracts of marriage and fidelity, the giving of a job and the acceptance of it, the sharing of lives and time and property, associations for common interest and pursuits: the giving of something and the getting of a benefit.

'If you're having trouble with this at school, keep in mind that often the well-meaning, the caring, the progressive don't understand the profound and paramount importance of money and its transactions.'

'Thanks, Aunt.' There was not time at breakfast to tell her of his idea of transactions. He would leave it lie in his head, knowing that things he saw around him would add to it their increments of information, in support or rebuttal, correction or extension.

'Hey! By the way,' she said as he was about to go. 'The virtue of capitalism — as we know it — is that it has the unintended side-effect of a liberal political system.'

'Thanks, Aunt,' he called back. The teacher had covered that point, but as an aside. Miss Mumford was a socialist.

He ran down the fourteen back steps, down the backyard past Orville's tree, to where the edge of the encroaching bush was marked by the clump of turpentines.

Under the Skin of the World

Home after Wednesday sport he made straight for his drawing table.

As an exercise he drew the first thing that came into his head. It was the world of ordinary appearances. Under the skin of that world, was a lower world visible through a tear in the fabric of the earth. It was a repository of abstract paintings, surreal objects; vegetables with eyes, legs and clothes; people with peeled skins like bananas; cooked babies with apples in their mouths piping hot on a serving plate; weapons, such as guns, walking on legs in a fusion of the organic and inorganic.

Following this he did a similar two-part drawing of a beautiful day. Statues in a park were doing their own paintings. Underground were various burrowing animals painting banal events from their lives, and the banal objects that surrounded them: rocks, drips of water, buried bones, insects, worms, burrowing animals. The statues above, in the park, by contrast painted ordinary human figures, drawn from the life they saw round them as they stood on their marble or concrete bases within the limits of busy cities.

Mister McCarville

The boy was faced in English with a sentiment he'd often heard from his father, who loved stories on the 'dark horse', the unfavoured one that confounds informed opinion by winning. The usual teacher was off sick, a temporary filled in for the last two periods of the day.

This strange teacher, large and bearded, jovial and leathery, who continually looked out of the windows as he talked — unlike the other teachers, who stared avidly to see what evil the boys got up to — told them of life in a country town thousands of kilometres to the west. He told them of a boy his father went to high school with, a backward, awkward kid who lived a long way out in the bush, who'd had to get primary school lessons by radio, and mail, who knew little of the ways of a small town like Ajana. He told of how the kids grew up; some went here, some there, some became men, some women, and some other things. He told of years passing; fields ploughed or left to turn back into bush; families growing and passing away; ghost towns; gemstones, gold and mineral fields; mining ventures, death in the desert, massacres of the past.

The kids in Davis Blood's class listened. The teacher didn't look at them once, but no one did evil in that classroom that day, despite the certainty of not being detected, or if detected the certainty of being ignored. When the teacher occasionally stopped, there was a flat silence, and almost you could hear the kids saying: Go on!

Mister McCarville went on. Time passed, people got old. Sometimes people remembered young Stoop, short for Stupid, the awkward kid that wasn't smart in anything. Then they'd go on to speak of something that mattered in their daily lives at Ajana.

One day, when Stoop's classmates all had grey in their hair, Stoop came back.

He came back in a big car, dressed in expensive clothes. Someone remembered his surname and when they saw his face they remembered. Without knowing it was Stoop, they knew his face from newspapers, magazines and television. He was Sir Stuart Claxton, just as once he was Stoopy Stu; the same but not the same. Now he was a great man, famous for being Sir Stuart.

He stayed a fortnight, going out to his old home, looking up people he once knew, and their families. Everyone he met called him Stoopy still, no one could find the word Stuart, and certainly no one was going to call him Sir. One kid that had been in his class, always a lively cheeky kid, now the local butcher, called him Sir Stoop in the little pub, but only because he had an audience of shoppers.

Then he left, and apart from a mention now and then, he was forgotten. Except for some families he'd helped with money.

He resumed his life in the cities of the world. The little town resumed its life near the western coast of the biggest island continent on the face of the earth.

When they talked of him later, he was Stoop still, just as he was all those years ago.

The boys in room 26 stayed silent. They asked for no message or explanation from this strange teacher. The message was in the story.

It was Friday afternoon. Mister McCarville left the room. The boys went home for the weekend. Everyone went quietly. They had more to think about from that one lesson, than from all the others laid end to end. Not so much from what he said, but from the pictures he drew and the way his delivery, or manner, or personality seemed to create vistas between and behind his words, vistas that stretched away into the distance in their heads.

The Dawn of Poetry

Outside his pale-blue bedroom was the dark-leaved pittosporum tree. Many times he stopped near the open window, and looked out into the cool silence within its canopy of leaves. A branch would end with perhaps six or seven branchlets, and, on each of those, three or four twigs with a handful of leaves on each. Behind each group of leaves, and before the thicker grey and spotted branches, there was a space, and under the shelter of the outermost part of the leaf canopy, there were many of these spaces. Watching them, feeling their coolness, he felt for the first time the same sort of feelings he had when he read the English poets from his mother's old anthology of poems. What a marvellous thing it must be to write words like these, that produced such effects! With her brother's inscription and quotation from Tennyson inside the cover, written as she was leaving England to migrate to Australia, it was Davis Blood's first poetry book. He'd read a good deal of it, but now at fifteen, the words and feelings joined together and bathed him in emotions he hadn't known before. When he felt them those first times, they seemed to penetrate his body, down his legs to his feet, to the tips of his fingers and inside him. He felt he was breathing richer stuff than air; his body filled, it seemed, with a strength that felt miraculous: he didn't know where it came from. The world was wider, yet he felt he could do things that once would have been beyond him.

When he went out in the yard and put his hand on the eucalypt's flank, he imagined he could feel the silent, indrawn life of the breathing tree, the quiet conversations it had with its neighbour trees.

How could these feelings and intuitions be put into words? Sometimes it seemed a shabby thing to try to squeeze fine and beautiful bits of the world into old, familiar, and makeshift words. They deserved better. Yet those poets he'd read, whose phrases and lives filled him with feeling, somehow had surmounted the problem.

Though they started with old and ordinary words, they had joined them together in such a way that powerful emotions and memorable images rose from them, and the whole composition took on a life of its own.

What a marvellous thing to be able to do! He shook his head slightly. How could I ever do such things? he thought.

Aunt Mira seemed to read his mind. No sooner had his feet hit the verandah after he'd run back upstairs than she screamed out: 'All becomes prose! Poetry rusts to prose!'

He looked into the kitchen at her.

'I'm not going to tell you to shut up, Auntie. You'll only keep on and on.'

'That's the way,' said Ursula. 'Don't encourage her. She's just trying to get attention.'

Aunt Mira looked at them, blinked a few times, and said in a cunning voice: 'Can fulfilment be, if egotism persists?' And mockingly: 'Davis Blood, friend of many and friend to none!'

He turned and made for the dining room table. He sat, picked up his pencil, reached for paper. He put them down, stood up, went back into the kitchen. She was right. Her face was turned towards him, she knew he'd be back. You shrewd old thing, he thought.

Before he could say a word, 'She was convicted of Freud, you know,' Aunt Mira said, nodding at Ursula, then looking back at him with her gleaming eyes. 'I prosecuted. Passing herself off as your mother, she was.'

Aunt Ursula left the room in high gear.

'She's scared of my interminable meringues.'

'I didn't know you could cook,' he said drily.

Aunt Mira let loose one of her frightening laughs. It clattered and honked, it screeched like forty fat galahs, enough to scare the living daylights out of you. Until you got used to it. To a stranger it was as big a shock as one of Lillian's sneezes.

'You'll carve out a Nietszche for yourself, you will,' she burbled as the laughter wound down. The tears of laughing had brightened her eyes, which sparkled with a pitiless clarity. 'Didn't know you could cook: Hah! H. Moses and a Jesus crisis! Talk about sons and loners — this boy needs a bit more exposure to the effluents!'

'Don't you mean the elephants?' he said.

'Exposure to affluence would be better. And don't forget when you meet royalty to shine your suit,' she said. 'Now give me music! Songs! Glory, glory, acidosis!' she sang in her screechy voice. 'Music! Viol music! The Poet and Pedant, played pussicato! The Love of Three Colonels! The Three Gonad Hat! Come on, you publicans and singers — This little Respighi went to Market! Some chamber pot music! The Sonata Desperina! The Silent Opera! Coral Symphony — or is it the Chloral Symphony of Ludwig in a Van! The frogmarch in C! Sympathy in A flat! Tomato in B! Symphonie Escargot! Come, You Cannibals, Across the Pubicon! Rally, all humans! The only animals capable of grasping the insignificance of their insignificance!'

She stopped to take a deep breath. She was tired. Soon she would droop and be asleep. He began to go.

In a low voice she said, 'Carmen through the rye. Lay off the last Minstrel. Tiptoe through the dewlaps. Hobo Concerto. Mozart's Seventeenth Piano Sadness.' Her voice stopped. Her head fell. She wasn't quite asleep.

'Ave Moruya,' she said. And, 'Tedium.' Pause. 'Ah. Old age isn't for the weak,' as her voice lowered and stopped. Now she was asleep, and the house quiet again.

He went out into the beginning of darkness, on to the small landing at the head of the back steps, and leaned against the waist-high railing. To the south the distant lights of the city twinkled in the evening air. The various neon signs in red, blue, white, and one or two green, gleamed.

'I'll make —,' he began to say, then edited it. 'I'll be there, someday,' he assured himself, but part of him wondered why he'd said that. When he found what he was meant to do, what did it matter where he was?

Words Rushed Out

The world seemed bigger, time had more space in it: he began to draw in spare time he didn't know he had.

He drew a rubbish tip, with the old tip in mind at the end of Police Court Road. His drawn tip was reserved for the throwing out of paintings, statues, etchings, drawings, sketches: any sort of recognised art that had been rejected. He smiled, looking back over what he had done, thinking, with good humour, that his own things probably belonged there.

In the same vein he drew the noble Parthenon, in this case sadly diminished. Stretching far away on either side of the remnants, people hurried away with blocks of marble; others nearby were dismantling the columns; still others were cutting up the blocks that formed the columns, into manageable size for home building. There were even some houses going up in the distance, with foundations of marble; the structure above the marble was cheap building board and imitation timber.

He drew a party of tourists, bargaining with Greeks to buy packets of marble chips as souvenirs; he had heard stories from Danielle's older friends when they returned from European trips.

There was something grimly amusing about the sad state of the remnants of public art that had survived from the past. It almost seemed such things felt they had no right to be still clinging to existence, but ought to be buried, as most of their contemporaries were. They had an apologetic air. Yes, that was it.

Suddenly his head felt full of words. They rushed out on to paper.

Underneath the run of this day's dogs
Beneath the fission of character,
Explosions of inhumanity,
Above all dreams of rectitude
Warping inward from the bulrushed swamp; or —
From this Sinai of terrible commands
To the olived Mount of paradox
Commit my sins for me and bear the scarred brow of guilt
All suburbs have directed at my hand
Which, working unsteadily at the machine
Of my life, bleeds words
Arrowed at the guts of the world.

He looked at them, and shook his head. Rubbish, was the word that came into his mouth. He wrote at the top right-hand corner: 'Rubbish written off the top of the tongue', and the date, and added it to his pile of papers.

Jesus as Rameses II

As another thingoid he made a statue of Christ at Emmaus, constructing him as Rameses II; mummified, with bandages rotted, teeth brown with age, but walking nevertheless. No wonder the disciples didn't recognise him. He didn't tell his father the idea behind it, just left it in his room with no title. Jackson Blood wouldn't have liked Christ in that form. He made him of clay, burned him in the open fire, diluted his sooted exterior with some biscuit-coloured waterpaint until the colour of the clay was brown, the same brown he'd seen in the open black sarcophagus of an Egyptian official at the Museum. The bandages were real bandages, but coloured a lighter brown, the threads pulled to make it seem they'd rotted.

The teeth he smoothed until with a coating of gloss paint they looked like enamel, the feet were skeleton's feet.

The household took his occasional thingoids for granted, there were hardly ever any comments made.

He wrote the title underneath, into the brittle clay: Christ at Emmaus.

Aunt and the Free Society

Aunt had been going on about things, specifically the Free Society, and having demolished that, got on to money, then profit.

'Profit is a buzz word for folk awed by large sums of money, who don't think of profit as seed-corn but something that goes on caviar, jewels, yachts, works of art; who envy so-called socialist countries where different people do the calculating and planning about what money goes where. Otherwise, as far as the ordinary person goes, they might be the same, whether socialist functionary or capitalist executive, because we don't know one of them, you and I. Banks, financial institutions: the same sorts of people work in them under any sort of government, and they're not us.'

'What do we do?'

'Talk about them. Dig in our gardens. Run down the bush.'

She meant him. She sounded so sure in everything she said. He envied that sureness, but only a little. He didn't feel sure about much at all; he didn't need sureness. He thought perhaps he was adjusted to constant unsureness and wondered if he was nearly right.

'In general, you could call us the poor, under-educated, aimless, the class for whom it's torture to stay home

Saturday night. Well, some of us,' she added with one of her grotesque grins.

'And we who do stay home. What have we got? Television! Escape, entertainment, voices reaching millions and saying nothing.'

'Telly Ho!' screamed Aunt Mira's voice.

'My God, she's awake,' Aunt Ursula said.

'Hadn't you finished?' the boy said solicitously.

'I'll never be finished. I'll be in mid-sentence when I fall off my perch,' said Ursula.

'Perch?' screeched Aunt Mira. 'Perches are no great shakes! Observe the sequins of events. I sleep, I wake, I shake, I fall off. Down among the name-droppings. My birth sign is —.'

'Virago,' said Ursula grimly, wheeling herself out.

'Farrago, yes,' Mira said in a cocky voice, and went back to sleep, happy with herself.

The boy smiled, as he left the kitchen. What was he thinking? Oh yes, Aunt Ursula's sureness about things, and he so attuned to uncertainty.

Running

He took a ball and walked the long way round to the sports oval. Not far from home, going up the steep hill in Country Road, a boy he knew drew up alongside him on his motorbike.

'Race you up the hill,' said Dennis Hart.

For answer, Davis set off uphill, legs pumping. Dennis gunned his bike and drew alongside, contenting himself with keeping alongside, and watching the speedo. After a hundred metres he said excitedly, 'Thirty-five kaypee! That's great!'

'What can you do on the flat?' he asked when the sprint was over. The boy didn't know. They separated at the top of the hill. Dennis went off somewhere to practise the triple-jump. That's what he was good at. He was going to be a great athlete.

Sometimes Davis Blood felt so much like running that he would race every vehicle that came by. He tried to race the odd dog, but dogs got suspicious and dipped out, thinking he was making fun of them.

Mornings, on the way to the station, he ran up Big Hill on to the flat of Anzac Street, and trotted the rest of the way. He liked the way his body responded immediately he gave the order.

Other days he ran steadily the whole way. There were no days when he didn't feel like running.

Nightingale's Song

He'd been reading some nineteenth century regional English poems, and after tea thought he'd do something with the images the poems had left with him. One was on the nightingale's song. He made up some lines, in imitation of the tones of voice of some of the poems he'd liked.

OLD SONG
The white thorn blows against the sky
And brittle sings the bird
So black a bough
So hard a song, the while
Sharp spears of rain do poise upon the hill.

When I did see your sad face carved in dreams
Your quiet breath a song
Then sharply sweet
The bird sang in the tree
The white thorn in my brittle heart.

Fit music of the mind, that never seems
But made for ecstasy and wounding still.

Captives and Free

In the spiritual confines of the Dissenters' Meeting, he'd heard of liberty from desires of the flesh, freedom from sin, even of the individual's freedom to sin, which went hand in hand with penalties spiritual and earthly. He'd heard often enough at home the word 'freedom' used in terms of the lives of ordinary people in the countries of the world.

Briefly in fifth and sixth grades at the special school, when his teachers had been passionate about political liberty, his interest had been awakened, but it wasn't until now that the word took on its greatest importance, attractiveness, emotional power.

Miss Mumford, the social studies teacher, approached the subject from the point of view of those countries in the world where people sat in jails without having committed crimes; who lived under regimes where dissent from government policy and opinion was punished in spite of constitutions and laws framed in glowing, liberal terms. Although a socialist, she had a liberal conscience.

She had set the subject in the context of Captives and

Free. It didn't matter that the exams were finished, and he would soon be gone or that school life for him would soon be over: the subject was alive in him.

The moment he finished his last homework for the year he got all schoolwork cleared away out of sight, and laid out fresh paper, pencils and pastels. The sight of them there made him feel rich: he had all he needed.

People queueing to suicide at the end of unsatisfying lives: was that a form of freedom? He did a drawing. It lacked conviction.

Men called up for military service; men carried back dead from the front; fresh lives sent out to replace the fallen. He drew. This was better; an illustration of Captives. Captives to their country, to political decisions.

He showed a woman constructing her own prison cell. The ambiguity satisfied something in him; but was that no more than the desire to have it both ways? Yes, he thought, it was more. People are free to construct what will confine them: it goes with being alive in a world, but not alone. The woman making her own cell wanted to be free from others, even if it meant confinement.

He worked joyfully on his captive and free series each day after school.

He showed newly hatched turtles struggling over sand toward the sea and seagulls waiting at the water's edge.

He made a picture of a baby snake emerging into the light of a cage at the zoo.

He drew a survivor newly freed from the perils of the ocean, thrown straight into jail on the island where he landed, a suspect in enquiries on drugs, spying, political subversion.

He did a drawing of a woman, the shopping done, carrying among other groceries in her shopping basket, a man subdued and ready for domesticity.

The same woman in another work carried a man in her

string bag into a secondhand shop, trying to get a decent price on him.

In another, a smart woman executive was leading a man along by a chain and an iron collar. The man being led sat on a low four-wheeled platform; man and platform looked like parts of the one toy.

He laid them aside, feeling they were probably cartoons; then, as an afterthought, put them in with his main pile of work. It was too complicated to be dividing them into different types of drawings.

Next afternoon he drew more captives and free; his first of an Australian convict from the early days whose chains were being struck off his ankles. A woman waited, ready to snap the handcuff of matrimony on him.

He illustrated, and knew he was copying, casual remarks he'd heard on the subject: the situation of his own parents' marriage wasn't something he could know.

How could he picture a person captive to an idea? With a net, with suitable surgery, with confining cords or chains. He sketched some ideas.

On the same track, he drew a man helplessly captive in a balloon, which rose, free and unballasted, into the sky. The balloon, too, was helpless, within apparent freedom.

He had another thought: of an idea flowing through human veins, forming inside the body, gradually making captive the host body. He drew it, but the scope of the fullsize body outweighed the details of the veins. He drew a section of veins, much enlarged, with numbers of branches off a large vein, and the little ideas forming, breeding, spreading throughout the internal network. It wasn't satisfactory.

A captive to love! Another facet of the theme. He could show a man carried curled inside a woman's stomach. As a variation, he did three drawings of this: one with the man inside the woman; the second with an unformed shadowy man inside the strongly emphasised body of a woman; the third he changed round into a definite little fully-formed man inside a shadowy woman.

The complementary situation was of a woman in the belly of a man. He drew that, grinning. He drew the woman dressed.

He sat back in the chair, thinking of nothing, his eyes on the glare of the western sun as it illuminated the gum-leaves, shrubs and grass, as it tipped the edges of the thick turpentine leaves in their grove of four trees at the curve in Country Road just west of the house; sunlight reflected from the eucalypt leaves, as if from glass or metal, dancing slowly to the rhythm of a light breeze.

Without knowing he had been thinking, or that something in him had been working on this theme, he began to draw the portrait of a lover. And that's what he titled it. It showed a fine young man, strong, thinking well of himself, with part of his chest exposed and dark, a cavity not outlined, but merging into the texture of his shirt, and showing, just as the religious pictures of the Kellys showed, a gift-wrapped girl where his heart was.

He chuckled, gathered up his work and put it away.

He went down the back, into the bush towards the creek a little way, breathing in the smell of leaves and bush soil and the fragrance of young gums. Then he walked back up to the woodheap and picked up the axe.

As he stood with the axe in his hand he was shaken by a violent, continuous shuddering, that gradually became less, but didn't finally go away: it subsided into a tingling. It was like being made to vibrate to an enormous bell, helpless in the grip of a sympathetic harmony that tingled through every part of him. He half expected to hear it, and to see the world buzzing with the same vibration.

The world? The universe! Wasn't he made from the world, made out of things that made up God? Didn't he consist of what underlay the universe, sharing part of its electro-chemical nature? This harmony stirred him with the realisation.

There was a leaf fallen from the camphor laurel tree; it lay on the grassless area of the woodheap. It was bright red, its veins still a diluted green. It was the most beautiful leaf in the world. In a way the world, and life itself, were in that leaf. Looking at it, knowing God was in that leaf, and that leaf was part of God.

He felt alive and expanded in every part of himself. This larger self knew that he could draw things in a way that would lay bare their innermost parts; he could hold up one word and volumes would pour from it. A world in a word.

He was so happy! He imagined he breathed an air no one had breathed before. It was sweet, full of something better than air, different: it was wonderful. He savoured it a long time, then full of joy still, began to chop wood.

Once he stopped, axe raised, and looked around at the little valley that was home and that he loved. Ah! He thought, if only I'm able always to live a strenuous life.

Then began to swing the axe with more joyous vigour. But he hadn't meant chopping wood.

Twenty minutes later he came in hot from the woodheap, had a drink of water and back to the table, to draw again.

Captives. A rich man, prince of one of the old royal houses of Europe. A tribal king of Africa, weighed down with wealth and jewels. He drew, but remained unconvinced.

A returning heroine from the Olympic Games? Smothered to death under the weight of tonnes of flowers in a parade. Only a cartoon.

A woman of the sort he'd heard his father refer to as a camp-follower came out — in one frame of a drawing — to greet an army. One sequel to show her trampled flat; another, torn in pieces by men hungry to touch female flesh.

He had his shower, and returned to the pile of white paper.

Three more captive and free drawings appeared before he was called for tea. In the first he pictured a sort of freedom. A jailed man's friends pulled, with a bulldozer, at the bars of his cell, hoping to bend the bars and allow the jailed man out. Instead, the whole cell came away, with the man still trapped in it.

The next was a woman in her own house, surrounded by appliances, food, cooking and washing, children and duties: a prisoner.

The third was difficult to draw. He wanted to show that one person might have his own self for a jail, or might be free because his self was free. He tried, but could get no satisfactory image.

Lillian called him for tea.

Last School Day

On this last day of school, which was bored and lifeless since no one wanted to work, he felt he'd come to the end of a section of his life.

Most final day periods were free for individual work; Davis Blood went to the library. He took down a German book, found a Stefan Georg poem he thought he could translate, and went to work on it. When he'd done the best he could, he wrote out a fair copy and put it in his schoolbag, for transfer to his pile of work at home.

> TRANSLATED FROM STEFAN GEORGE
> *Come into the park they thought was dead, and view*
> *The shimmer of distant smiling shores;*
> *The spotless clouds' unimagined blue*
> *Lights up rockpools and coloured paths.*
>
> *There take the soft grey, deep yellow*
> *Of birches and of box; the wind is mellow;*
> *The late roses still are not shrivelled:*
> *Pick them, kiss them, wreathe your laurel.*

> *And the last asters — do not forget them;*
> *The purple twists on tendrils of wild vines*
> *And what is left of green life twines*
> *Lightly round the shaping face of autumn.*

He said 'see you' to some of the boys as school broke up for the Christmas holidays, knowing he'd never see them again. The train journey home was sad.

He said nothing at the dinner table, and after he'd washed up went straight to the big table and picked up his favourite soft lead pencil.

Almost straight out, apart from juggling the four rhymes, he wrote nine lines on a new white sheet of paper, the latest bundle Randal had brought.

> *There is a winter in the life of man*
> *Begins at sunset. Each day the weather*
> *Sharpens and grows cold, the body's pores*
> *Close a little, birds bed down in sleep*
> *And everywhere eyes close their lids like doors*
> *Against the drifts of dread that lie as deep*
> *As darkness round the living heart. Whether*
> *Spring will come and sun rise no man*
> *Can know, only that dying is a lot like sleep.*

He felt better when it was done, but the loneliness of having no schoolfriends stayed with him. Not that any were close friends, but for three years he'd been with them five days a week.

However apart he felt, he did like having others around.

It seemed he'd only just got used to being a boy — he hadn't even learned all a boy needed to know — when whoosh! — he had to start being a man.

Well, he supposed he'd have to keep doing, and working-off, boy-things while he was becoming a man. He felt that he wasn't a coherent person, but an assemblage, even a flux of parts. Perhaps that was the most he could be; perhaps in this he would be most himself.

Would this changing flux of parts travel deeply into the life of humanity? Who could know, at fifteen?

He remembered some words of Uncle Hector:

> *'Some read, some write, some think, and
> some follow sport.'*

How strange we are, seen from various angles, he thought. Systems of articulated bones carrying around a bag of flesh, a few litres of blood. Or, from a different angle, bags of blood carrying around odd collections of desires. The angles were limitless, he felt, so was the strangeness.

Last Sunday at the Meeting

On Sunday night, after going to the Meeting once more, to please his father, he sat on Ashwood Station waiting in the half-dark for a train. His father's wartime Bible, with the brown leather cover that folded right round it and fastened with a press-stud, sat warm in his pocket. Ever since he was a child he had gone to the Meeting either at Bellbird with the Includings, or Ashwood's Occlusives, but why should he keep going? Those Meeting people had never accepted Jackson Blood into their circle. He smoked, therefore lacked the commitment to belong: smoking was an addiction to the pleasures of the world. The Dissenters were in the world, but not of it, they said.

Their religious beliefs held them fixed in that single attitude of attendance on their God. They made no effort to interest those who didn't believe, beyond a small, sober black board on which the times of their Meetings were announced in little white painted letters. They referred to themselves as 'the elect', and to outsiders as being 'without the light'.

Nevertheless on that night he had to admit that he was moved. A creeping shadow of chill travelled up his body, as he listened to an eloquent evocation of how cold Jesus was in the garden of Gethsemane: ice-cold as he went to meet his death.

His father, home from hospital on visits, sometimes got out his New Testament and underlined more passages in red, but not often. He still pondered the future of his Seven States of the South.

Why go back? Why ever go back? There was no reason. Davis decided, then and there, not to. The train came, he looked back once at the Meeting Hall, then he was rocked away into the night on the long journey home.

He sat in the train, allowing his thoughts to go over some of the details that had nagged at him over the years of going to the Meeting.

He wondered that those grave modern men and women, as well as his parents, had as the fountainhead of their religion a God who allowed himself to be crucified. Not only assailable but easily killed, like a sheep. Since Jesus was God, and they said this was the spirit that permeated all things, the ordering spirit of the endless galaxies! Why would such a being bother with the inhabitants of a tiny planet that orbited a minor sun on an arm of one galaxy among millions? What of the possible other life on suitable planets of other suns, in this galaxy, in other galaxies? Did he have to sacrifice himself over and over? In different ways according to the various beliefs of the inhabitants of different planets on which life was possible?

On Sundays they ate him. His flesh and blood, symbolised by bread and wine, was placed in each mouth; after which he was chewed, and swallowed.

It was Jesus who worried him most. He felt a little naughty when he remembered grinning one day at the part about Jesus writing in the sand. Signing the planet, he'd thought then, just as the teacher signs your book and gives you a mark out of ten. Or giving the sand a tick, for attendance. His grin was only for that, not for the circumstances. He had a proper respect for: Let him who is without sin cast the first stone. But even that was only fairness, and could have found a place in any system of moral values.

The teaching, in broad outline, he revered for its humanity, its generosity, its farsightedness, particularly in the case of people with burdens, those in need of immediate help. It was the things and events, surrounding the teaching like a frame, that he baulked at.

Poor man, to have such followers. When, in the Meeting they spoke of Jesus trying to din into the disciples that he must die, not overthrow the Roman occupation, he couldn't help thinking of the fairy story where the wolf said: You must kill me. Or the frog prince. Those disciples, during his life, seemed never to understand that he was travelling towards his death, a death necessary to the whole redemption theory of the sacrificial lamb.

After his death he was seen again, though only two of the four evangelists reported the sighting on the road to Emmaus and on the mountain, and only two reported, between them, the three other sightings. Yet no one knew him. They were a funny lot, to have forgotten so soon. As if he were a stranger in the street. And Thomas, if he had eyes at all, surely didn't need demonstrations: blind Freddy would have noticed scars like those on the hands of Jesus. And how long after the execution was that? Were the wounds healed, or still suppurating? No answer.

Why didn't they recognise him? Where did they go when he died? Not mentioned. Did they scatter in terror? Not reported.

Did they think it was all over? Then later, after he was seen again, did someone rally them and piece together the story, find the Old Testament prophecies, and fit it all into the framework that set their religion on its feet forever, the spiritual edifice which Paul continued and elaborated?

Davis Blood took a deep breath. The accounts left to us are so sketchy, he thought, and leave so many questions without answers. Why did he suffer as man, and refuse to be immune to suffering as a God, if he was both?

Why say he was coming again, if he didn't say when? Why ascend? Why not come back and resume his ministry, to the confusion of the Roman army of occupation, again and again if necessary?

Was he really a beautiful character, with a sublime majesty to him? He seemed to be able to get angry, as in the temple; he loved to win arguments and throw his opponents into confusion; he defended a woman's extravagant gesture towards himself: all very human. And when the Canaanite woman from the coastal districts of Tyre and Sidon kept badgering him for help for her daughter, he wouldn't talk to her, but told his followers: 'I came to call the lost sheep of Israel. It's not fitting that the children's bread be thrown to the dogs.' Pretty testy, that, even if he did relent later, and heal the daughter. Later still he decided that his mission was to the rest of the world, after all.

Davis Blood had to admit that Jesus was a strong character, though he'd like to have known something of his boyhood to age twelve; then, after the episode in the temple, more of the life he lived and the studies he accomplished between then and his appearance as a prophet at age thirty. The lack of information in the Gospels made it appear that he came from nowhere, out of the blue, miraculously.

There was one bright spot for him in that evening's meeting. The text had been Luke 17:21, 'The Kingdom of God is among you'. On a previous night a different address had been based on Luke 10:8, 9. 'The kingdom of God has come near you', and the preacher had referred to various translations, in which the words were 'has come very near to you', and 'is close to you'.

In his father's concordance he'd found the Luke 17:21 passage under 'Kingdom', and after work one day he'd checked out both passages in the translations available in a Bathurst Street religious bookshop.

On the Luke 17:21 text he found six versions which said 'The kingdom of God is among you' or 'with you' or 'in your midst' and one, the King James translation, said 'within you'. The only one. All the versions of the Luke 10:8, 9 passage gave 'the kingdom of God is close to you', or 'near you'.

It looked as if his intuition was original, that he'd come to as a small boy: that God is within the individual, though he found it hard to credit that Jesus wouldn't have seen the significance, for a religion of inwardness, of 'God is in you'.

The train was on the bridge over Eel River. The metal stanchions whished past; blue lights and gold, red flashes and white, shone on the water.

The business of Grandma's resurrection stuck in his throat. The funeral was over a year ago now: he'd tried to push it down into part of his head where he wouldn't think of it, but it surfaced in spite of him. Grandma alive again was still unbelievable. Why should he bend himself, trying to exert the muscles of faith, to believe what his mind shouted was absurd?

Did he doubt God? Surely he didn't doubt that God or some power, some intelligence, some organising force or thing, existed? No, of course not. Even Einstein believed in God, though not in a God who minded day to day human affairs.

For years he'd accepted his beliefs on trust from those he respected, tried his hardest to embrace them and make them part of himself, but some just would not take. They were foreign bodies, to him.

It had begun to seem to young Davis Blood that the various pieces of which Christianity was made do not fit together, and perhaps never could.

As for his elders, his parents and the grown ups he'd heard speak in the Meeting: they needed to believe the whole package.

From the way they spoke, it seemed to him they felt lost in a mysterious universe without any purpose — which seemed to him a fair enough construction to put on it — but they were frightened by this, and he wasn't. Purpose?

Why, that had to be supplied by the individual. If it wasn't, or couldn't be, then that individual was truly lost.

He would supply his own purpose.

Dimly, with occasional feelings that he was reaching out to it but not quite grasping it, he could feel he was working his way towards that purpose: his purpose.

His drawings — his love of solitude and the bush — his jealousy over the use of his time, that often would not allow him to spend time with other boys in boyish pursuits, boyish idleness — these were the intuitive, groping, but finally unstoppable attempts that something in him was making in the struggle to get out of its straitjacket and into a position of control.

As the train climbed towards Bellbird Corner, he summed up his position. The voices spoke to him, and he to them. At such times whom was he addressing? Himself? Well, yes, in a way, but also that part of God that lived in him; that place inside him where he was really himself, where he couldn't deceive himself intentionally because he knew; the place in him where justice lived, and where goodness was a friend.

He believed in more than Einstein's impersonal God, but the physicist didn't have Davis Blood's insight that God was in mankind and mankind in God.

To put the message of the Meeting, of his parents, into his own words, it was like this: mankind can't live as properly realised individuals without God, for God is part of mankind. Mankind is also part of, but separated from, God; and can't be whole until re-united with God, in some way that he couldn't yet see.

The train stopped.

The Future

The effort of thinking made him feel heavy. For once he didn't run home till he got to the top of Big Hill. Then he ran down in the dark, triumphant in the feeling that his feet knew every rut and rock, and arrived home full of energy.

He had turned his back on part of the past. He took his pencil and wrote a few lines in the tone of voice of something he'd recently read.

> *No stone, nor rune, nor tongue long still*
> *Could tell my tale, but one voice only.*
> *I played this game of life as it has pleased another*
> *Who now is gone, without whose voice how shall I know*
> *Who is this lives on.*

But his father wasn't gone. He had certainly tried to please his father, but why had he written those words? He felt suddenly guilty, as if he'd wished his father dead. It was an effort to throw off the feeling and dismiss it from his mind.

He still felt alive with energy. Two doors had shut; he would think of the future.

The soft black pencil seemed to roll towards his fingers. It felt already warm, when he picked it up. It wanted to be used. He began to write, covering the paper with words and lines; writing phrases that seemed good, some over on the margin where they'd wait till he found a place for them. He accumulated three pages of words, phrases, lines and crossings-out, then took fresh paper, and in one run-through, assembed four verses on a clean sheet.

> THE FUTURE
> *Is it to be set in sudden order*
> *by the jangling of a new rhythm*
> *imposing its harsh pattern:*
> *austere, violent?*

> It's in the delicate flowering of empire
> among jungle, money, guns
> and scattered bits of men.
>
> It's in that squat, sunburned painter;
> a careless flicker of an eye
> towards an artificial sky.
>
> It's in the face of a dead soldier;
> a network of bloodstains
> the sum of all lost songs:
> austere, violent.

He turned the paper face down, so he wouldn't see those words while he wrote something else. There would be time for corrections later.

There is a valley, he began, and stopped. Half shutting his eyes, he imagined details of a valley he'd never seen.

In the same way as before, he jotted down words and phrases, filling pages before he was ready to choose and assemble.

> *There is a country where the gold of spring*
> *lies puddled, unregarded all the afternoons.*
> *Light drips from ripening fruit, forever falling;*
> *Insect fingers attack the hairy bud; monstrous tides*
> *lap fiercely resisting mountainsides;*
> *insane colours riot in rich decay.*
> *Wattles brawl in the wind. The land's features grow*
> *sharp with butterflies, and, acquainted with the night*
> *cherry trees in white tap the cool windows.*
> *Where a name is an infinitely sad story.*

It would do as a basis for something better, later.

For a time he sat, thinking of nothing. He felt tired again, and heavy, as he'd felt getting off the train. It was the end of the day for him.

As he got ready for bed he thought: these lines I write are all very well, but they're too general, too loose; too diffuse, perhaps. He felt he'd like to write of actual things, of objects, of what was concretely there, just as he'd like, best of all, to draw things that compelled others to look — images that stayed in the mind, that became part of those drawn to them.

They All Had It

Monday he had some things to fetch for Lillian, and was pleasantly disturbed and shaken by the number of holidaying schoolgirls in Bellbird — how pretty some of them had grown.

He looked at them, one after the other, as they enjoyed their freedom from school uniform. Why was sex so important? How could it come to dominate so much of a person's life? Was he abnormal? He felt sex urges daily; usually several times a day now.

He couldn't forget Orissa. As he walked home through the shopping centre he imagined himself writing a poem to her.

> *You are a dream.*
> *And I shall never reach you.*

Pretty miserable sort of poem, he thought cheerfully. But you are a dream, I think, Orissa.

Why did he see so much that was interesting, even gripping, in girls? In their faces, the line of a neck, the subtle graduation in shape of an arm or a leg? Why was he overwhelmed by their grace, their colouring, their shape, the music of their voices, their healthy joy, the apparent speech of their eyes? Why was it? Why couldn't he see them as ordinary humans? It was more than beauty of line and contour, to him. It was heart-filling beauty that sang within him, that lifted him up, re-arranged him, that coloured the world, strengthened his blood, energised his body, that put courage in him. And all of them had that beauty: it was youth.

Still Life with Flowers

Back home he had something to eat, and went straight to the drawing table. He drew a plant on whose leaves the shape of a vase was printed by nature. The leaves and stems, the imprinted vases, floated in air and threw shadows. The shadows were of shapes different from the leaf-shapes.

He wanted to say something about the shadow of an object being different from the thing itself, but this wasn't saying it. He put it away from him.

He drew a vase of flower stems and arrayed the flower heads themselves around the base of the vase. Were they neatly cut or savagely pulled off? Some of each, he thought, but then found he had destroyed any meaning there might have been, and substituted only ambiguity.

On the next sheet he drew flowers banked high in the sky, and a painter on the ground using the sky-flowers as a model to paint flowers on a grassy bank — not on a canvas, but on the grassy bank itself.

But words wouldn't let him go, and recent sights still filled his head. Orissa, and the images of the girls up the street, rose like solid dreams in his head. He made another poem-thing, as he began to think of them, this time addressed to Orissa, and to the other girls who had emerged like dazzling things from the chrysalis of school uniform. That was puzzling, but words were calling him, and wouldn't let him delay.

Again he covered pages with words and phrases before copying out on a blank sheet the ten lines he salvaged from the mess of possibles.

> *More deeply than the tidal wave of joy*
> *Patterns the tumbling chaos of the heart's events,*
> *Or the extravagant embellished signature of grief*
> *Etches the record of a bereaved mind's tears,*
> *Have you graven on my heart gesture and word*
> *And the delicate thrilling songs your eyes sing.*
> *I am enfolded by your look.*
> *Your slightest movement is a spell cast*
> *Within the ring of enchantment which is your presence;*
> *Your least wish a list of delights.*

Now that he'd put those ten lines together, what did they mean? His first thought was to answer: Mean? Why, it's a poem, that's what it means!

But there was more to it than that. Among many other things it might be, which he didn't yet recognise, it was a tribute, it was reverence. It was almost religious.

Sensibly, he decided to analyse no more at present, but be ready to catch the flood of words next time they pushed to get out.

He sat on the side rail of the verandah looking out over Kookaburra Valley. He felt as if filled with light. All around, instead of the usual border between living and dead things, he perceived everything was alive.

The world was full of life. People, trees, rocks, clouds, air — all alive. He felt in that moment that he understood everything.

Mardi Gras

He'd never seen a Mardi Gras, so he went to the city to see the opening parade of floats, bands and street dancing.
He watched, letting colour, excitement and movement sink in. He didn't allow himself to think about it. When he got home, there would be paper and pencils; the sights and sounds would be safe in his head till then. More than safe: something inside would be working on them.

The Lost Mardi Gras

December rain poured from low clouds. The morning, at least, would be spent at the big table.
By the time he stopped for lunch he had done thirteen drawings, which he called the lost Mardi Gras.
One drawing showed the Mardi Gras procession of people from the rear. The light was at their backs, their shapes and figures diminishing towards the front of the procession until they had faded into the darkness.
On the same idea he showed the procession from the side; the darkness, like a live fog, swallowing them front first.
Another showed the people dancing downhill towards a lake of black water, and disappearing into it.
The fourth and fifth showed them lost in the country. In one they were bright and full-bodied and the country dead and grey; in the other they were dead things walking in a green and cheerful countryside.

Another gave them an overseer with a bull-hide whip. They were slaves to Mardis Gras; the whip lashed them into obedient laughter and frenzied capering.

The next showed the revellers, in their sad bright clothes, shuffling dispiritedly forward, faceless every one.

The eighth had a bright Mardi Gras at the front of the procession, with the surroundings bleak. As the Mardi Gras dulled and faded towards the rear, so the surrounding buildings came up into brightness.

In the next they were lost far out in the hill country; they were slouching in-line on a high western ridge with the moon above. It was bright; they were silhouettes, each with a cold moon-touch striped down one side.

As a variant, this idea was repeated, showing the wan procession to the east on the same high ridge at dawn, the sun just rising.

The Mardi Gras in full flight; once joyful and bright, surrounded by city lights, but now the procession had left the lights and were heading through a run-down street on to a pier jutting into a dark and miserable harbour. The first ranks were toppling like automatons into black water.

In the twelfth they'd lost their way in side streets — still brightly dressed, with music playing — and succeeded only in amazing a few spectators as they tiredly plodded past. Two incredulous dogs looked sideways at them.

In the last he showed spectators lining the streets waiting for the abandon and joy of the Mardi Gras to come to them and lift their spirits. It didn't come. The participants in the festival couldn't match their bright costumes with joyful feelings: they were lifeless.

The Mardi Gras he'd seen was none of these. It marched and laughed still, in his head, where he had access to it at any time.

A Poem-Thing

He came back from a bush run and with the pleasure of habit took up a pencil and the top sheet of paper from the pile. Pencil and paper had become almost as beloved to him as the bush with its trees, shrubs, rock and winding tracks, its contours and scents. As he began to write words and phrases in preparation for one of his poem-things, he reflected with a smile that having his routines was very like having a friend.

In the making, he transferred to paper some of his present feelings about himself and his situation; in the guise of more general comments on the world.

The mistake is,
In looking for paradise.
The modern mister faces a going back
To hopes humbler than he imagined;
Quiet, domesticated, cow-like hopes
That look for nothing from him
But a contribution to living with others
And an expectation
Of much the same state of affairs tomorrow
As in the grey past that inhabits us.

We haven't changed:
We've had some glittering dreams,
Imagining we were round the corner from paradise
Instead of on the edge of our old paddock,
Which has, now you look closely,
The air of a one-time swamp, done up a bit.

Tiny tyrannosaurus on a rock snaps at a fly,
And puts his bird tongue out at a man,
Mindful of his proud descent.

He had an appointment next Monday morning with Pacific Television, to be interviewed for a job. His holiday was nearly over. When he got a job he'd have to confine his trips to the bush to weekends; there would be less time for drawing. His poem-things he regarded as exercises in words, which he'd discovered he loved.

It was raining again. He watched for a while, then began another exercise.

RAIN

Water lay around in pools,
Old defeats reflected
The grim sky
Which partook of boredom, deflecting
Sunrays.
Water gathered at the roots of living earthplants
Wet the feet of moving, dying organisms.
Day removed its hat, water
Like a benediction fell.
The water cannot help itself,
Nor you, nor I.

Welcome the Stranger

Jackson Blood nodded when his son told him he was going for a job first thing Monday. He was, unfortunately, only capable of a rather bitter remark to the effect that a businessman was a father-figure to whom the rest of us apply for a job, money, a home, a pension, food and economic security. He thought of employers as businessmen.

Davis Blood looked at his father as carefully as he could without appearing to examine him. His father often did a sort of thinking aloud that wasn't exploratory, but encapsulated opinions, like putting objects he possessed into little boxes. For instance, a politician was a mediator between business and the public; an advertising man tells you what you want and where to get it; a doctor frightens you then shows you a way he'll be necessary to control your fear; a sportsman is one who can do things we'd all like to do.

His father felt him looking, and took it that the boy was waiting for words from him. He said what was on his mind.

'I feel like John the Baptist,' he said, smiling suddenly. 'Prepare the way!

'Yes, prepare for the kingdom that will be. Prepare the land, prepare Australian hearts, for the kingdom is at hand. It comes!

'If they were my last words to you, Davie, I'd say: Prepare for the wave after wave of welcome visitors who will provide the bulk of the new nation.

'Make no mistake: we must become a nation first, before we can join other nations as an equal, just as the individual has to complete himself before he can attain equality with other individuals!

'Welcome the Stranger! That's the motto I'd give you. They are the gold of our future. Invite them! America did. They were settled two hundred years before they got the idea of inviting the world in, and when they did, they really took off! It's time we did it.'

He said, 'Yes, Dad,' and was puzzled as he went down the backyard to sit on Brown Rock and commune with Orville's tree. It struck him that on his visits home his father still seemed to have turned away from his studies of the Pauline letters, to thoughts of Australia and its future. It was a long time since he'd mentioned the Last Days, which, along with 'Behold, I come quickly', had been taken by people at the Meeting, and his father, to mean pretty soon the world would be finished.

Australia had never done much for Jackson Blood, only recruited him in a lottery-style ballot to be exposed to chemical defoliants in someone else's war; a shortened life and imminent death was the logical consequence. How could a man love a country that played such a big part in killing him? For that matter, how could a fifteen-year-old boy love a country that allowed him to leave school, when he had the ability to go further? Just to provide an extra bit of money for a household.

At least his father wasn't dying scared, running for cover to God when death was near.

Giant's Wings

Davis Blood got the job. He started the day after the interview. He didn't realise it, but he was the sort of person Pacific wanted: someone too bright to be leaving school early, capable of being trained, energetic enough to do a better job than the usual junior, and straight enough to want to.

As for him, he was ashamed. It was humiliating to have to show yourself before all these older work-people. They'd ask themselves: why isn't he still at school? Is he an idiot? A vegetable?

And the work itself: dull, taking no effort to understand, hopelessly simple. And so repetitive. It was wrong: he should be learning new things every day. How would he ever be able to get out of this?

He didn't allow himself to hope. He was stuck there. Invoices, purchasing orders, weekly and monthly deadlines — a life of bondage to trivial things stretched ahead.

On the first pay day, he stopped short of going to the railway station and straight home; he went into the heart of the city to a bookshop.

Several bookshops were open. He went to the biggest.

The feel of being there with thousands of books filled him. The new season covers sparkled in the well-lit shop, a smile came from inside him and fixed itself to his face. His eyes shone. Such books! Even the presence of the cheap thrillers, romances and mystery books, elementary children's books, subject books he had no interest in, didn't disturb the feeling that he was friend to all books, and all these books were citizens of a larger world.

Poetry, the sign said. Near the top left, Baudelaire. Penguin Poets. He lifted the paper volume out, let the pages turn. English translations on the right, French original on the left. *'The Albatross.'* *'Sailors to amuse themselves . . .'* And there, that line. *'His giant's wings will not let him walk.'*

He held the open book on his palm, unseeing the book, the page, the other books, other people, everything.

Giant's wings. On earth, in this case the deck of a ship. Mighty in the air, graceful, beautiful; on the ground helpless, pitiable.

He stood there, not seeing, not looking; eyes open, mind possessed by the image and its extension to himself. He was different. He didn't fit in. Did he have wings? An ability undiscovered that made his present life so awkward, so ill-matching the people and the life around him?

In those moments he felt he had inside him a lifetime of drawings, of paintings, of poem-things, of — what? The expansive emotion lifted him up, his mind swelled with the possibilities inside him. He stayed in it for some minutes, until gradually it let him go.

When it was gone, he knew there was no answer, yet, to his question: a lifetime of what? When would he know?

In the time left to him before the bookshop closed, he read greedily. He hadn't known such a thirst before.

Every night after work he spent there, and all day Saturday, making it a special trip, and sometimes Sunday. He encountered poetry a good deal different from what was in his mother's old poetry anthology.

Poems were compact, summaries of much thought and feeling.

He discovered the art sections of the larger bookshops,

particularly Angus and Robertsons, and pored over everything that wasn't locked away. Paintings often seemed like poems. They, too, were limited by that teasing edge where life goes on beyond the frame.

Sometimes he'd look into a painting, trying to enter it and the life that was what the painter saw. The artist was trying to fix into permanence something that was in motion. Often when he left the art section he felt so elated and full of ideas that it seemed anything his eye lighted on was a subject that deserved the best he could do. Even a corner of the train carriage or the station platform. The humblest object, he felt, ought to be praised for what it was. The best work, perhaps, was a sort of gratitude, even a reverence for the object.

The International Poor

On the first Sunday of his working life he took another trip to the city: he hadn't seen it on Sunday since he'd been on the way to the ferry with his mother some time before.

The quietness interested him. Without the streets full of shoppers and office workers the place was dead. He found his way to the Domain and listened to some of the speakers, until he came to an open space just as a young man carrying a step ladder got there and set the ladder down, climbed a few rungs and rested an elbow on the top of it. He began to declaim. Davis Blood listened. The orator wasn't much older than he was.

> '*There is in existence today*
> *a so-called capitalist world*
> *and a so-called socialist world. A third world*

overlaps them: the undeveloped world.
Running through the lot is a fourth world,
the International Poor. Broadly, the world is divided
into rich and poor, what now is called North and South.
In every land there is a north and south,
rich and poor, have and have-not.
For this south world of international poor
the problems of hunger, in a world
where food must be sold, not given
and scarcity among plenty
are paralysing:
they have paralysed all efforts to solve them.
The thing standing in the way is the social structure
and economic structure of the world of the Haves.
For theirs is the world and all that's in it.
Have-nots are outcast from that world.
If you believe them unworthy to live
by reason of family, race, religion, colour,
intelligence, or any other reason,
then you will act accordingly, and leave them to starve,
and their children after them.
But if you believe, because they are humans
and for no other reason, that they have a place
and their lives are valuable because human life is valuable,
and as worth saving as any forest or beach,
as any part of the environment, as worth treasuring
as any animals, birds, fish, insects,
within the ecological fabric of the world,
then you will think of doing something about
the social arrangements, the financial structures, the economic
walls, the suitability tests, the locked doors
that keep the poor of every nation away
from the life-long feast of plenty that the rest enjoy.
One more thing.
It is perhaps possible that you think of these things
but wish the world to remain the way it is,
not wanting to solve problems, but
to live in and enjoy a world of harshness and conflict.
If so, so be it.

> *But whatever your position or temperament*
> *I ask you to think about what you think!'*

David Blood drank in every word. He stood, letting the words sound again in him, as the young fellow climbed down, folded the ladder, and moved to another part of the Domain, where he repeated the performance. He answered no questions, engaged in no repartee as other Domain speakers did: simply said his piece, folded his ladder, and left.

Davis Blood stood in the shade of a Moreton Bay fig, thinking of the poor. There were many sorts of poverty, therefore many proletariats — the sick, the old, the poor, the uneducated, children; pet animals and food animals.

It wasn't enough to listen. He ran after the young fellow, who had crossed Art Gallery Road and was now carrying his ladder down the concrete steps towards the sea-level road at the bottom.

He caught up halfway down the second flight of steps. The young man looked at him, continued on down to the next landing, and stopped.

'Well?' he said, managing to look down on Davis Blood as if he were an irritation.

'How?' he said. 'How can the problem be solved?'

'Solved?' the young fellow said contemptuously. 'It'll never be solved.'

'But what would it take, to do it?'

'Power, benevolent dictatorship.'

'Power.' He stopped, furiously thinking. The other smiled. Why did it have to be a dictatorship? He didn't believe that.

'Power corrupts,' the orator prompted, as if speaking to a child.

Davis Blood stepped back, away from this disagreeable fellow, who turned and walked on down the steps without another word.

Davis Blood walked by the wharves and up through lanes and byways he'd never seen before, thinking, trying to reconcile a profession of concern for the poorest and the masses with an attitude of abrasiveness and unconcern for the individual: for him, Davis Blood.

Sometimes, in lanes, in alleys, he glimpsed another world, the world mentioned on television and in the news, but which, as far as he knew, didn't exist in Bellbird Corner. Down those alleys people lay in filth, ran away clutching stolen handbags, sat in gutters drinking or lay asleep in the sun, drugged or drunk.

Transactions were done in those dark places. The feel of danger and death hung about them as closely as the garbage, broken glass, and smell of rotting men.

The people who lived like that must be different, he decided.

The young speaker was different, too. Perhaps he was simply speaking another person's lines, and wasn't involved in what he said. How could one have compassion for people in the mass, and be contemptuous and dismissive of them singly, face to face?

He walked till it was dark, noticing again something he'd seen in the city after work many times, that the places of drinking and amusement announced loudly but unconvincingly a weak defiance of night. Trying to keep at bay blackness, the end of daytime, the division of one day from the next. The limits of day were set too narrowly for them.

To Davis Blood, with his years of the Dissenting Brethren at his back, it all seemed empty. Freedom from boundaries, perhaps, but not the sort of freedom he liked, which was freedom to be doing. For him, freedom was empty if there was nothing to add to it.

Aunt Ursula was on the front verandah enjoying the evening air and the moonlight when he'd run to the bottom of Big Hill, across the road and up the front path.

She smiled at him.

'What's been happening with you?'

'Aunt, do you believe power corrupts?'

'Power corrupts, yes. But lack of power can eat like acid into the soul until self-esteem is gone and all that's left is envy and vindictiveness and a need for violence.'

Good old Aunt. You always got an answer bang on the knocker from her.

'It doesn't have to, of course. Not all people are identical,' she added drily.

'No,' he said. 'But they all have a piece of God in them.'

'Perhaps a lot of people don't know that,' she observed.

He went inside to shower and change and wash the city off him.

Under the needling jet of water, the world opened up to him by the compassion of the speech in the Domain brought to the surface his eager feelings and youthful idealism about the as yet mysterious work he was to do. How good it would be to live your life so that, at the end, you had done all you wanted to do, said all you wanted to say: to have worked yourself completely out!

Whatever Happened to be Near

*T*ime spent at work went by unremarked, as if he had no life there. An automatic part of him, once trained, simply did the work with the least possible effort.

He drew at home, thought and read in the train. After work, in bookshops or at the Public Library, he devoured books of painters' works and read poetry; sometimes he had the urge to do another poem-thing. When it was done, he put it on his pile of work.

After looking through many art books, he tried to find,

without quite telling himself why, books that would hold all of a painter's output. He found some: Van Gogh first, Goya, Matisse. Next, some of the French impressionists. He was amused to read, in Van Gogh's letters, of his perspective frame, as the artist taught himself perspective a mere eight years before his death. He remembered his own father's brief lesson, when he was little.

Something bothered him. He leafed through books in which the paintings of numbers of artists were reproduced. He found that although there was a detectable coherence, or so it seemed, in the works of each one, the range of subjects seemed just as random and unplanned and, in spectacular cases extremely limited, in the books of single painters as in books of collections of painters. Why was that?

How did painters choose what to paint? Why did what they chose seem so inconsequential? As if anything else could have done. Was the action of painting more important than the image?

It seemed to him from the books he'd read that if writers wanted to paint pictures, in words, of the society they lived in, they would settle into work and do it. They could start at the bottom, the top or the middle, but there was a range of things they couldn't avoid painting. Painters could avoid anything.

In painters' work, he thought, there was no design, no plan, no direction. Even in Kandinsky's work, which he thought of privately as geometry in Paradise. It was random. Whatever happened to be near was included. There was no guiding theory except: paint! Circumstances could uproot them, set them down elsewhere; wherever they found themselves they looked round and simply painted. In a room they painted the room, a table, a bowl of fruit, flowers, and the view outside it. He thought again of Van Gogh conferring immortality on a postman and a postman's wife, and telling his brother his work consoled him for not being a doctor.

Writers sometimes did much the same, he reflected; except that this observation was accurate only in the broadest sense: painters seemed like magpies, picking up the next thing they came across. Writers had to pick and choose; or was it more accurate to say: pick up everything and throw away most?

Did such accidental work have any value? Could it? Yes, he answered himself, but not much; not as much as if — if what? An answer seemed on the tip of his tongue, but as he grabbed at it, it danced away out of reach.

Perhaps the paint, the brush-strokes, the approach, the method were the permanent things, and the subject didn't matter much. But he couldn't imagine being satisfied with that; perhaps he was too young.

Voices

In another part of the house, his mother's voice, that he'd listened to all his life, that was part of him, sang,

> *'I've found a friend*
> *Oh such a friend*
> *Loved me before I knew him.'*

The music of her voice at that moment seemed almost unbearably beautiful. Together with the words she sang and the absolute sincerity of her love for her heavenly father and the conviction with which she held her knowledge of his closeness, they combined to produce a powerful feeling that he, Davis Blood, although in the old house on Country Road, was at the same time in a place of intense worship. It had the physical effect of making him feel lifted up, high above the rest of his life, on a platform from which he could see a long way in every direction. What it would be to live at this height!

> *'Nothing I have my own I call
> I hold it for the giver'*

his mother sang.

This was where he belonged. To live with this perspective on the so-called realities of the world. To use whatever powers he'd been given, on a lifetime lease, to the extent of his energy. To fill every minute with directed effort.

> *'From him who loves me now so well
> What power my soul shall sever?
> Shall life or death? Shall earth or hell?
> No! I am his for ever.'*

His mother's song ended, but in his head it was a symphony of meaning and dedication. Whatever his work would be, whatever he would be, however fulfilling it was, he knew — he couldn't escape it — it had to be for others, not himself.

From the depths of the valley came the call of the strange bird he'd heard before.

'Caprigel! Caprigel!' came the brilliant tones. 'Caprigel!' Triumphant.

The Proper Study

He was no farther forward. If only everything could be plain and straightforward, he thought, and I knew what I was meant to do. I'd get to work now, I'd work like a demon.

Nevertheless, he was unrepentant enough, or unsubdued, to use his quandary to make a poem-thing.

Self-Knowledge
It is the final voyage
Endured by the strong.
Vultures of mourning
Blacken the wasted
Tracks. Overhead
The sky is a sweet
Bright blue.
The journey to change,
To invulnerable humility,
Is dotted with selves,
Mislaid, rejected,
Unrecognised: and some
Unborn.
Sufficient, in fact,
To lose and dazzle
Those for whom
Wherever is definite
And whenever
Often enough.

As he laid it on his work-pile, he looked back over the words and remembered some of the poets he'd lately been reading.

Where Were the Rest?

*H*e thought further in his spare moments of the painting books he'd looked into, and the idea that had dodged away from his grasp. He'd get it, he knew that — some time when he was thinking of something else, or of nothing — though he knew his confidence was confidence and nothing more: there was no rational basis for it.

Perhaps there were some painters he'd missed in the books available to him, some who did have a method of getting down everything (was that the key to the elusive idea?) or working systematically through their world and displaying in their work the transformation that world underwent as it passed through their vision into their minds, and was expressed by their hands, out where others could see it.

Was such a scope what he judged the painter's duty to be? Getting down everything? Working through the whole world?

Something of the sort seemed to echo in some words of Streeton, writing to Tom Roberts.

> 'I must work more and produce bigger, more serious things.
>
> 'I picture in my head the Murray and all the wonder and glory at its source up towards Kosciusko, and the great gold plains, and all the beautiful inland Australia, and I love the thought of walking into all this and trying to expand and express it in my way
>
> 'I fancy large canvasses all glowing and moving in the happy light.'

He'd read this in one of the art publications he'd come across. But where were all those Streeton paintings? Did he work too slowly, or die too soon? Or, when he and his friends were gathered together in groups for company, did it all run away in talk?

On Saturday he went to Sydney to the Art Gallery and made for the Australian rooms to look for Roberts and Streeton. He found two he wanted to look at closely: Streeton's 'Fire's On At Lapstone Hill' and Roberts' 'Bailed Up'.

'Bailed Up' took his breath away. Not for the artificial scene of horses and coach, but for the recognition of the steep hillside. The dry sandy soil, the rocks, the sandstone colours, the straight gums stuck vertically into the steep flanks of the hill. This was the slope round from the Point, that part of it that stretched back towards Nerida Pass, with its blackboy spears rising out of their clumps of what the kids called 'cut-grass', or 'sword-grass'.

'Fire's On' had similar bush and sandstone colours. He loved those colours, and the parched breathless feel of a hot day.

He knew something else. Among his sister Danielle's holiday photographs were hundreds of bush scenes, of forest, scrub, plains, desert, river, billabong; many just as interesting as Roberts' and Streeton's. Even given that these painters' works were distributed among private and institutional owners, there weren't many. Where were the rest?

The suspicion persisted. There was nothing thorough or systematic about it. Even in the days when painting recorded events, landscapes and localities, there was no method to it. Was it a sort of self-indulgence, a wilfulness? Was it an illustration of how things were inside the painter?

He didn't know, and sometimes longed for a teacher; but knew this was a weakness. Even a casual reading of the art books he'd encountered, a superficial acquaintance with newspaper art reviews, and a few visits to different little galleries showed him there was nothing to be known from teachers if originality was the aim. He would have to do the work of understanding entirely alone; his own attitudes and thoughts were the important ones.

If that were so in this case, then Roberts' and Streeton's attitudes and thoughts — and their various systems — were the important ones in their cases. Danielle's photographs gave little of life, character, mood, poetry; of feeling, or even of sudden impression: they were sodden, loaded and lifeless with detail. Perhaps Roberts and Streeton did all they wanted to do in a few paintings, then when that was done, moved on, with not a thought of being systematic, only of satisfying themselves.

Before he left the gallery he noticed an old painting of a sea shore with a breaking wave. There was his green! Underneath the crest, which was white as the wave began to break, was the thin wall of water, almost a wall of glass, with the light succulent green that ravished him when he saw it at the beach.

He stood before it a long time. He had no thoughts of systematic approaches, only of the light that came through the back of that breaking wave and shone right into him, into his secret places, where he was most himself. He bathed in it.

As at last he backed reluctantly away, then turned and walked out through the foyer into the afternoon sun that shone full on the gallery entrance, he carried with him the green of that wave, the green of the remembered waves on Driftwood Beach, the green of the new camphor laurel leaves outside the kitchen window, and also, as if they couldn't be denied, the caves of silence between the cool green leaves of the crinkly-leaved pittosporum outside his bedroom window, and the quiet mysterious darkness of the Corot trees he had seen in his sister's books of paintings: green darkness that was poetry to him, full of feeling, saying without words things he couldn't yet comprehend.

On his way through the city to the station, he stopped and bought a bottle of toilet water for Aunt Ursula, to help in her lifelong battle to conquer the smell of methylated spirit.

The Starting Point

He began to reflect on that part of the painting process which takes place before the expression: the getting of the idea, the germ of the painting.

How did it happen in his own drawings? He shied away from that angle on the question. It threatened to come too near things he hid from himself. He tried to think how it must be for those artists whose products were reproduced for people like him to pore over.

They must, somehow, settle on an object, and how they did this was the secret he hadn't uncovered. They worked out what they aimed to do with it; tried seeing it in various ways; worked out the material they would use; decided on a palette; a method of attack; had an eye on the boundaries of the whole work; made constant appraisal of the painting as it grew out from their hands. But this was simple common sense.

He didn't think like this when he made a drawing.

What did he do? He knew the answer, but it was dangerous: he didn't want to know it. Nevertheless, it had to be faced.

He started from words. He revered words. Words had power. Words were objects, almost beings in their own right.

Three Sisters

On Sunday he went bush all day, intending a long run and a swim. Past Rising Sun rifle range, down along Wombat Ridge, he came to Water-doctor Pools, a chain of waterholes that looked like Bread and Butter Creek as it became Spectacle Lake, blowing out into bubbles of river with a satisfying wideness, but not quite making it and being pinched off into a narrow stream again; then gaining confidence and breadth again, only to falter and be squeezed off into a stream hardly wider than a trench.

He stripped off, dived in. The water was warm, except for over one or two deep holes, dark with treeshade. There were ledges under the water. He could stand waist deep on them, push off and swim over to other ledges.

He practised floating on his back, but wasn't good at it in the fresh water.

He stayed in a long time. It was pleasant being sixteen and naked and alone. Water-doctors skimmed the surface; dragon flies shimmered, suspended by thin wings in thick air. A soldierbird flew quickly up into a tree in blossom, followed by its mate. A young goanna scratched in the ground-leaves, and clambered a metre or two up a stringy-bark tree, legs spread wide.

He heard dogs in the distance, and sounds nearby, but it wasn't till three women showed themselves that he knew they were there. Two pushed branches of leaves aside and came out into the open, one holding his trousers, another his shoes and shirt.

'Hi,' the biggest one said. 'Come on out, the sun's fine.'

'Let's have a look at you,' the second said. 'See what you've got.'

Big women, they wore shorts and shirts and shoes for walking in the bush. They were brown in all the bare places. He felt funny, treading water there, under their eyes. He found the ledge and stood on it, the brownish water — from the eucalypt generations of leaves that had dropped into it dead — showing just a little white skin from navel down towards his growing black patch. He glanced down to see, but it didn't seem important. Of course they could see it, but they were older; older people had seen everything.

He climbed up the ledge into the shallowest water, and turned to face them.

'Where is it?' called one of their voices, a raucous one.

'Don't be scared, little man,' said the other.

'Another inch less and you'd be one of us,' said the raucous voice.

He looked down. True, Sylvester had shrunk, but cold water always did that. They were rough women, and they had his clothes. It was bush all the way home, if he sheered off down Flying Fox Valley before he got to the sports grounds and ovals, and climbed Bandicoot Hill to Kangaroo Point. From there it was his familiar track back to the end of the street, and all he had to do to be unseen was to go downhill into the bush at the beginning of Country Road, and stay in it until he came to the back of number twenty, then run up the path to the back steps.

For the long run home he put the women out of his mind. Running up the slope under the western side of the Point, he came on several tree-stumps that plainly showed the marks of his axe — a larger and a smaller gap about three centimetres apart gave an axe-print with two raised parallel lines that distance from each other. His marks.

Up on the flat, he ran easily. Those marks, and his presence, would be there until the stumps rotted, at least as long as he lived.

Vermeer

Sunday night he settled down with his new book of Vermeer. As he opened the book and walked by the water at Delft, he was surprised to find the air much the same as in Bellbird Corner, though the light was a world away. What an expression of time and place, of light and mind! He wondered what the same viewpoint would show now, a few hundred years later — and why there was no such thing, as far as he knew.

He turned the page. For a long time he searched the painting of the woman pouring milk from a jug. He looked into the colours trying to enter them; felt the solidity of the woman, the crustiness of the bread, thrilled at the feeling produced in him by the horizontal of the milk level in the jug. He had looked at it as intensely as he could each day since he had bought the thin book of plates from a discount bookshop, and each day he'd seen something new. As he became comfortable with one part, another struck admiration and wonder from him. For days he lived in that picture.

Perhaps a work of art never gives up all its meaning, no matter how long you spend with it.

Would he ever be capable of producing a thing called art? Why was the painting of Vermeer slightly different each time he came to it? Was it because he was different? Whatever it was, something depended on what he brought to it. What he brought to it at each successive time of looking was himself, plus what had happened to him and in him since last time.

He got down some of his Old Masters series of books and looked through them.

There was feeling, there was emotion in these Old Masters. But at least for some of them, it seemed to be true that in their later works there was, perhaps, more of the painter's emotional life spilled over on to the canvas. Sometimes it seemed as if the work was one whole slice of that life. Perhaps they spent a lot of their lives learning to dig into themselves and get on to the canvas what they found there. Then they died, though their work lived on.

Looking over them again quickly, and comparing them mentally with more recent painters, it seemed to him that craftmanship was a means to accuracy of expression, elegance of feeling, but then it began to be reduced to a point where it hardly survived. Surely a painter lost a great deal of joy by this curtailing of the expression of his natural skills.

There was a lot to think about.

Changing

It was peculiar, sitting in the big open office of Pacific Television that took up a whole floor — apart from the directors' and managers' offices along one wall, over the best view — and working at his invoices, purchase orders and delivery dockets, knowing that at that very time the boys he once learned with were still together, still learning, opening up a greater gap between them and him.

Perhaps that feeling was an education in itself, since it taught him he was more alone than ever: solitary and exposed. Whatever he did or failed to do was up to him. He would have no teacher: what he did he would learn to do himself. He would be his teacher, except for the good and great dead whose works were lessons in themselves, waiting to be understood.

He could feel his body changing. He had days and moments when he felt different from anything he had felt before. Things that once hurt — cuts, knocks, falls — he no longer felt.

His shoulders and back had broadened from years of using the axe and carrying home logs to split, and his two tied chaff-bags of split wood for the kitchen fire.

Logs once hard to lift seemed to spring up into the air with little effort. He could run, even, with a log up. One blow with the axe sliced right through a sapling cleanly so the cut tree was still upright, though severed, before it started to fall.

And once, he came down Big Hill so fast, rock to rock, that Jackson Blood, who had watched, said approvingly that he had the makings of a footballer. Did his father see something in him to admire, or was his comment simply a just recognition of a fact, and things were as they'd always been? How could he know?

Jackson Blood laughed when the subject of his will was

raised, and made a joke of it. Preston said seriously that it wasn't the best thing to die intestate, and his father, after a while, agreed; though he still couldn't resist making fun of the solicitors his son recommended, Chorley, Snellgrove and Horton, and persisted in calling them 'Chortle, Snigger and Hoot'.

He put it off, delayed, forgot, and finally did nothing about it.

Sometimes in the Public Library he was overwhelmed by how marvellous the world's *ad hoc* collection of civilisations was. In spite of everything, new things did get invented, new methods of making were found. The records of much that had been thought and discovered were there in that very library building, ready for the next bright person to come along and put together two things no one had thought of putting together before, and coming up with something new, which in turn could be matched with something else by another person later on to produce a further improvement. How could civilisation proceed if all these records were lost; if all these precious things, that no one person actually knew, this fund of thought and recorded experiment, were destroyed all over the world? How horrible destruction was! How terrible, and final, was loss.

Sometimes as he read, his sympathy with suffering humanity, precarious civilisation, the horrors of war, so overpowered him that he sat at a reading desk, tears running down, while he held his head low so others wouldn't notice.

At other times his dream-thoughts were placidly prosaic. He sat at a table in the reading room and looked up at the high ceiling, in which glass panels glowed with concealed lighting. The sound of the air-conditioning was low, pleasant, hypnotic.

He thought of the air between him and those lights; of the air covering the planet like an insulator, a permeable blanket; of its weight; of the winds created by the earth's rotation and by the myriad other influences acting on it.

Just as the ocean is a sea, he thought, and sea-creatures live and eat and sleep in it, defecate in it, breathe its water in and out, with all that is dissolved in it, so the air is a sea. Air creatures defecate in the air-sea, breathe air in and out. There are particles in it from other bodies, other lungs, including animals' lungs. Perhaps some of these particles are hundreds of years old! Perhaps there are still some particles, or bacteria, or whatever else is breathed in and out, that are still in existence from all the bodies — animals, humans, birds, insects, bacteria — that have ever breathed.

In this reading room he, and the other readers, were recycling each other's expelled oxygen, nitrogen and bacteria. He screwed up his mouth at the thought.

Sometimes, again, he imagined he heard his mother singing, in the city, songs she sang at home:

> *'What a friend we have in Jesus',* or
> *'Forever with the Lord'.*

Sitting gazing up at the distant library ceiling he even projected a choir of 500 voices — hers — filling the place with 'Oh, for a thousand tongues to sing!' Five hundred mothers raising the roof.

Moments of Not Being There

Sometimes he seemed to have no feelings — about himself, or those around him, or the work he had to do. Numbed, he did the usual things: went to work, came home, slept and ate. Working life was easy: annoying but simple. Even poverty and the prospect of future joblessness didn't alarm him; all was unreality.

Sometimes his eye fell on a printed word. What was that? It reminded him of something. It was composed of squiggles, stumpy lines and curves. He knew it was intended to mean something to humans, but it baffled him for a minute or two.

Then, it resolved itself into a familiar word, like 'floating' or 'ungrounded': words he knew well. How was it that for a minute they'd meant nothing?

And the cries of children in the primary school near the Pacific Television works; what did they mean? Were they being ill-treated or were they happy? Cries of delight, or screams for help? Here, too, for a minute he was baffled. As if he was enclosed in a capsule and couldn't break out to understanding.

Then, with no warning, everything switched to normal.

Emasculating the Old Masters

At home after work he did a series of drawings which were an excuse to give himself practice in copying Old Masters.

He drew a Cézanne orchard, light green trees and brown trunks, adding a boy in one corner playing with a naked baby on his knee.

A Degas dancer, bending. She, too, was in an orchard in her dancing costume, examining a handful of soil with a magnifying glass. Nearby a working hoe and some tall brown potatoes were up on ballet points, picking oranges.

The 'Mona Lisa' he drew sitting inside a doorway, with an electric heater alight beside her and the room lit with a red lamp, as he'd seen in streets near school.

Rembrandt's gold-helmeted soldier he made into a safecracker, whose operations were lit by a miner's light set in the golden helmet.

Napoleon on a rearing white horse by David he showed as alive at the front end, and in the process of being sprayed into Magritte-like metallic statuary and immobility at the other by two graffiti-artists. One had a spray can of chestnut enamel, the other a glossy blue-black.

He half regretted that familiarity with these popular works from the past allowed him to make fun of them, but didn't destroy the drawings.

This Floating Cell

When he asked at home about how things were in the past, the economic depressions were often brought up, dating from those at the end of the previous century through the thirties calamity, and Ursula never tired of reminding him that there had been other little depressions since, and that even then the world was in the middle of one. The subject came up on one of Uncle Hector's visits.

'Once,' said Aunt, 'I thought the young and energetic would hit back when they were put out on the streets jobless, existing on handouts while their neighbours had jobs, but now I think people will put up with anything. There's no help coming from those still in work. It's heads down and don't look. There's a sort of fire lacking in Australians: no anger. Something hurt us in the past and beat us down and we've lost the idea of getting up and fighting.

> *'This floating cell for felons,'* she orated, *'This sunlit raft,*
> *This ancient soil, democracy of cringe,*
> *This lump of rock set in a peaceful sea,*
> *This land of harmless souls —*
> *This other Europe,*
> *This envious breed of men*
> *Copy of the outside world —*
> *Fortress built against those who live within.'*

'Who said that?' asked Lillian innocently.

'I did,' said Aunt. 'I wrote it when I was just a girl at school.'

'It seems a very poor and depressing picture to me,' said Lillian.

'The boy here will change it all,' said Aunt grandly, changing the subject and pointing to him. 'He's the one. He's going far, this boy.'

His mother looked at him doubtfully. 'He's got a long way to go,' she said. 'And no ego, to speak of.'

Uncle Hector took up the past, as if Aunt had gone away somewhere.

'Cousin Cyril,' he said, taking another slice of fruit cake, and launching himself from the shores of the kitchen on to Lake Reminiscence, 'used to say that he had a vision, a dream, that blood is like a plant that spreads its branches and tendrils and root-shaped capillaries through flesh and bone. He thought of himself as an artist in those days —.' Aunt Ursula glanced at Hector; Lillian returned part of her attention to her brother-in-law, and part to God.

The boy was thinking furiously. No ego? What did that mean? Why did his mother say such a thing? Had she changed her mind about him? Everything wavered: his hold on life, his feeling that he was himself. Surely her life, given up to God and her will resigned in favour of His, were an example of life without ego. Or were they? Had he misunderstood someone so fundamental to him as his mother? With all his life to think and watch and listen, could he still get it wrong?

Or was it approval? He had assumed it to be criticism, since her way of putting it was as a lack. Whatever it was, he knew he didn't understand her.

Aunt Ursula had seen the quick contraction of his attention. She answered Lillian's words.

'Or so much of it, an ego so large, that he doesn't need to play the usual game of parading it,' she said.

Lillian looked back to Ursula, thinking. At last she said, 'Possibly,' and not a word more.

Uncle Hector hadn't noticed. He went on about his cousin's blood-tree.

The boy looked at Aunt Ursula's face. Was she simply being encouraging? He felt insubstantial still. He was in a prison cell so large that it looked empty and free, but it was youth and ignorance, and a prison just the same.

His mother didn't understand him. Or had she turned away from him? If so, he was truly alone. Was she, had she always been, incapable of understanding him?

Fishing Drawings

A letter from Orville to the family told of disappointments with the teachers, triumphs with girl students, and of going fishing in the Murrumbidgee River, not far from the college.

'I've learned something about education,' he wrote.
'Those who can, do.
'Those who can't, teach.
'Those who can't teach, teach teachers.'

But it was the fishing that struck Davis Blood. He thought about it in his dreaming state as he sat at the table. The word 'fishing' set him off. Waterbury the dog barked out in the darkness of the yard at something he thought he'd heard. Maybe he'd been dreaming and had a nightmare: Waterbury was given, lately, to nightmares.

Davis Blood drew the dog fishing from a sandy bank in the shade of a river red gum, his equipment spread out round him. He was fishing for eyes, and there they were, swimming about under the water. He used tiny ladies' legs for bait — the thought of good old Randal probably suggested that, by his liking for ladies, as he called them — and the dog hooked something. What was it? Only an empty can, of canned ladies' legs. Several eyes lay on the grass beside him, his catch. All had hook marks where he'd hooked them and extracted the hook.

He drew a leg fishing, with tiny legs as bait, again, for eyes. Then a leg fishing with eyes as bait, for legs. He got tired of extending the idea, which didn't amount to much, anyway.

He drew a human fishing for people-fish. There they were swimming, with goggle eyes and bubbling mouths — with miniature people for bait. There was the bait tin, squirming with canned people.

A Visit from Preston

Preston visited one Saturday. Without saying anything, it was clear enough that he deeply respected his mother, even if the word love couldn't be used. His being there was, to him, the proof of his feeling. He had a cup of tea with and spoke briefly to Lillian, who then went out into the garden. Preston looked around the old house restlessly. It seemed small, full of pathos.

Aunt Ursula arrived home from a visit with old friends to a number of city art galleries, where she kept up with the work of local artists. She couldn't resist having a friendly dig at Preston.

'How's our revolutionary? Has the big day come yet? The big push started?'

Preston rather liked being thought a revolutionary. It was so far from his world that it gave him a vicarious excitement, rather like a world traveller being asked his opinions on Samarkand, Akademgorok, or Lhasa, though he'd last seen them many years before.

'It's started,' he said. 'The workers won't know what hit them. The universal middle class will swamp them all and drown their feeble cries.'

'The middle class don't complain?'

'They compete. It just sounds like complaint.'

The background of their mild skirmish was Aunt's observations — well in the past by this time — that revolutionaries come most often from the educated and the middle class: those who are annoyed by safety and the tedium of comfort, and lament the lack of comradeship, and the ultimate sterility of individualism: not from the workers he feared.

Preston didn't see that Ursula's target was his own craving of security: he didn't have it in him to despise safety. He agreed with that State Premier of the past who said that the point about being from the working class was to get out of it.

He rattled on, showing his heart was in the right place by — as so many Australians do — attacking himself in the guise of his country.

'We're not a demanding people, you must admit. We still wait patiently for good roads, hotels, resorts, until tourists need them.'

'We're basically a poor-minded people,' his Aunt replied. 'Like the poor, we never taught ourselves to want, or what to want. We do without, and call it virtue. Then, when we have good things, copied from others, we beat our breasts in regret for what we lost by being so lifeless.'

'What does little brother think of all this?' asked Preston heartily, when Davis showed his face.

'Nothing much,' he said.

'How about your rights? You young aware people are always going on about rights.'

Davis Blood didn't hold it against Preston that there had been no offer to help keep him on at school: in Preston's world it was every man for himself, and a brother was just another individual. But he knew Preston cared nothing for the things he was talking about: he regarded time spent on them as a mental holiday.

'Not me,' he answered.

'I tell you,' Preston said, 'the only rights you've got are the ones governments have forgotten, or that they think are not worth taking from you.' Preston regarded taxation and governments as twin evils.

'Don't you have any ideas about changing society?' he persisted.

'No, only keeping hold of one thing.'

'What's that, Boysie?'

'Making sure we hang on to a voter-society, and never letting it become an administrator society.'

Now this was something Davis Blood had thought of, himself, on the daily train journeys. He hadn't meant to let go of it, especially in conversation, for he felt that good thoughts were wasted in talk. More than that, they were somehow worn, as if they'd lost some meaning, some gloss of relevance to him. He was sorry he'd opened his mouth.

In the event, it didn't matter. Preston let it pass as if the difference were hardly more than the merest distinction. What the boy didn't realise was that the business community — and Preston — had as much to fear from an administrator society as did a sixteen-year-old theorist, and one by-product of their activities was a preservation of a number of significant freedoms. Preston made another slighting reference to the people.

'The mob merely want to be comforted, and told that all will be well. They don't care about the fine print.'

'Bourgeois eyes are pitiless when they look at the poor,' said Aunt Ursula, and Preston was pleased, feeling complimented.

'As for the rich, Davis,' she continued, 'the entire population of the country is in a minority, counted against them. Their capital outweighs our bodies. Governments want our votes, but their support. The rich are the enemy, from where we stand, just as the government is.'

'Well,' said Preston, 'government is about money. Democracy itself is taxation of the people by the people for anyone clever enough to get their hands on it.'

'I think you're right,' said Aunt.

'All this talk is making me thirsty,' Davis Blood remarked. He took a fresh glass to the kitchen tap, and quickly tossed down two glasses of water.

'How's the drawing going?' said Preston. In his voice it was plain that drawing was an innocent hobby, no more.

'Plenty to do,' said Davis Blood.

'Keep at it. Strive to be unequal,' he advised with a knowing grin. 'Don't be satisfied to be equal to the mob. What's your ambition?'

It took the boy by surprise. 'To see what everyone sees, to notice what no one notices.' Again he could have kicked himself. Of all things to slip out, that was one of the most revealing.

He needn't have worried. Preston didn't think much of seeing and noticing, and certainly didn't see what they implied.

Banished from Eden

On the Monday morning he was asked at work to go to the University and fetch a book for Mister McPhee, one of the directors. The feeling of being out of the place, legitimately, after months of having to turn up at the same time each day and do much the same things was rather like the way he felt getting out of hospital after his appendix was removed. The sun was brilliant, the world cheerful and new. The life of streets and shops and other workplaces had been going on all the time he'd been shut in; now here it was and he could taste it.

He sat on the grass reading the book when he'd got it. It was Percy Scholes' *Oxford Companion to Music*. Time passed, and as he burrowed into this delightful book, he was taken into a large world of wonderful beings, who did things no one had done before them: inventors; thinkers of new thoughts; makers of new ideas; arrangers of new emotions; composers who opened their minds and hearts and showered them over others who might never invent a thing, but who could perhaps feel. He was one of these.

On the way back to work he walked past council workers digging and putting rock fill into a hole where storm water had collapsed part of a road. He noticed their stone-breaking hammers. In the lunch break he wandered back that way to look.

One of the young men had been breaking stones to dump in the hole. They were now at lunch. He looked at the hammer with its long handle. Davis Blood finished his third sandwich and picked up the hammer.

'Hey! Whattya think you're doing?' he heard, from the workmen's hut.

'Just having a look!' he called back.

'If you want it, take it!' came a young man's voice, probably the one who'd wielded it before lunch.

'Don't forget the bloody shovels! Take them, too!' called

another. He knew they wouldn't leave their lunch hut and their rest.

'Pick out a shovel or two and piss off with 'em, kid! We don't mind!' He lifted the hammer, felt its weight.

'While you're there, break up that pile of rocks, son!' came the first young man's voice.

As if to oblige, he brought it down on a big rock. Some edges came off the rock. That wasn't the way. There was a grain in the stone. He pushed it round with the hammer and hit the rock fair and square. It shattered satisfyingly.

The men called out more things, but he took no notice. He swung and cracked, getting into the swing of it, short grip on the head as he lifted, just as he hefted the axe at home, easy swing and a little extra as the business end was about to connect. He shifted ground, to use the grain of the stone for easy splitting. After a minute or two he found, as with the axe, that he had more strength than when he began.

He swung and swung. Rocks became stones. The joy of it got into him and took over. His speed increased. He loved it. Stones became sand. At one stage the powder glistened with circular patches like large flowers with spokes radiating like petals from their newly flattened centres. A fleeting image of hammering out flowers crossed his vision. But the intentness of his ferocious attack made no room for a smile at the thought.

A man came up and stopped him.

'That's enough, son.' It was the ganger, by the look of him.

He dropped the hammer and walked back to work, stone-dust all over his shoes. How awful it would be to have to do that all day, every day, for years.

He got back to work, feeling great, his arms full of blood, his hands thick and slow and full of strength.

Graveyard of Old Models

*H*e noticed the phrase ('graveyard of old models') in a morning paper; it referred to old model cars. To him it was as natural as breathing to abstract the word 'models' — any models — and to start drawing from there.

He drew a graveyard of old female fashion models: broken, spirits crushed, lamps gone, wings twisted, legs fractured, bumpers crushed, engines stolen; ready for the compacter.

And over there were some already compacted: several dozen intertwined, crushed into blocks. Their previous forms could be seen by lines on the blocks' surface showing where legs, arms, heads and torsos had been reduced in the crusher.

He drew it on soft paper with soft black lead, taking delight from the way the picture came alive at that point just past the end of his hand where two fingers and a thumb held the pencil. In a way, it was like music unwinding from a record at the touch of the stylus.

Revision

*S*aturday morning he took out the little piece of blank verse he'd written Friday night in the library. He'd been going over parts of *Hamlet* for the dozenth time and something bothered him about Hamlet's eulogy of mankind.

Everything about it bothered him.

What a botched work is mankind
How hesitant in reason
How limited in faculties
In form and movement clumsy and laughable
In action how like an ape
In apprehension like a fox:
Ransacker of the world
Tyrant among animals.
And yet to me, what is this future dust?
Material and instrument both — the best we have.

Yes, that was more like it. Hamlet's original words were more suitable for satire.

A Team Defeat

Saturday afternoon he did his duty and went along to watch his team play United. His ear torn in the previous game wasn't healed, but he could have played. The coach and the team manager wouldn't hear of it: it might have a bad effect on the other players, or on kids in lower grades. They weren't specific. Everyone made a fuss about it, but for him it was all over.

When he got home, Aunt wheeled herself into the dining room to talk to him. As usual she started without prologue, but his mind was still back with the team. Something someone said about 'a team defeat is everyone's defeat'. It wasn't till he was on the way home that it struck him: they were talking to him. They wanted him to be cheerful or sad in tandem with the team's wins and losses and the emotions of the other boys.

It reminded him of a previous defeat.

He hadn't particularly noticed his habit of going his own

emotional way until one of the team looked reproachfully at him as he came whistling off the field after an earlier defeat against Wanderers. He felt fine, the game had gone well, he had scored two tries — one from his own quarter, the other from fifty metres out — so he whistled. The other boys looked very down in the mouth; they expected solidarity. But he hadn't been defeated; the team had.

As he showered it came into his head that he had never felt defeated. Neither had he felt much joy when he'd won, certainly not so much as the other boys showed. They jumped around, shouting and laughing and being so emotional about it that he had to smile.

Usually he felt good that he'd played, good that it was over, and good that there was another game next week. Not for one moment had he ever wanted to be captain, thinking for the other boys, telling them what they ought to do. Not for one moment was he going to be deflated, unless after the final game of the season, when it stares you in the face that next week there's nothing. Only cricket, and that's tame and slow by comparison.

First Things and Last Things

Aunt was still talking. He hadn't heard a word. Guiltily, he opened his ears to her and closed them a little to his own thoughts.

'Clues, directions, hints, pointers, can be found in all sacred writings. The ways of God can be seen anywhere, in any teaching. It doesn't matter which. Go from one to another.'

'Clues?' he asked, feeling dopey.

'Clues to your human nature, to what you are, that part of you that you share with God.'

Of course. He'd mentioned his theory of 'In God and God in us' to her. Aunt didn't forget. He sparked up.

'But I thought you had no time for religion.'

'I'm not against religion. The great questions are:

> *Where did we come from?*
> *How should we live?*
> *What should we do with our lives?*
> *What ought we to try to be?*

'Now they're religious matters if anything ever was, because they're about salvation —'

'Salvation?' he asked incredulously. 'Salvation?' He was thinking of repentance, faith and forgiveness of sin, as he'd heard at the Meeting and from his father; and of people — seekers — coming forward and kneeling out the front of the Meeting hall in contrition.

'Salvation, yes, from things we know, and from things we fear but don't know,' said Aunt. 'It's not as simple as sin, you know. In my case, salvation has nothing to do with sin. But forget me, I mean salvation from the trivial, the wasteful, the evil, from irrationality, greed, corruption, cruelty, falsehood, from unreality. I'm all for it. It's foolish not to think of first and last things.

'There's a lot more to religion than is admitted in churches. The demarcation lines are not as clear cut as they say. Love, loyalty, wonder, reverence, even respect, in any setting, I would include in the religious impulse,' she said reflectively.

'Then you believe in a God? You don't reject the whole thing?'

'Not at all. But with this proviso, that the God I can believe in — or imagine, whichever you prefer — didn't create details and isn't concerned with what we do, but instead started the whole system off. This universe and our little galaxy is a consequence of that; and since our tiny planet has temperatures and pressures and elements conducive to life appearing, then life appeared and we're a further consequence. There may be other systems, other universes, apart and away from this one, some with life, some incapable of life. But this was a planet on which life was possible, so eventually it arose. The whole message of physics, as I see it, is that the forces making for being are more powerful than those making for nothingness.'

'What's heaven, then, Aunt?' he said, looking for light relief while he allowed her words to sink in.

'Heaven is where everything is known, nothing is hidden, yet all is forgiven; and nothing can ever change. You wouldn't like that.' There was a long pause.

'Just started the whole thing off?' he asked, still thinking about it.

'Yes, provided the means for life to be. We bring the love and the hate, the good and the evil. He's not responsible for our cruelties. We made the morals, to reduce friction and to let us get on with producing babies and food. Nothing offends against its own nature, until morality comes along.'

'And that came once there was a number of people,' he said.

'I think so.'

'God isn't dead, is he?'

'Not dead, but locked away in each heart. Imprisoned, forced to be silent. You see, I agree with your theory of his presence everywhere.'

'Oh.' That was a surprise. 'Then what is God? Do you know?'

She said in a wry tone, 'I think God may be more complicated than people think. Religions, particularly Western ones, tend to simplify God and complicate religion. The whole God thing has to be re-thought. We need a god that can be accepted by people of the next few centuries. Mind you, I think humans can't ever know God. He'd have to be unknowable, incomprehensible.'

'Why?'

'Because we can't even understand this world, and that's just one thing that comprises God — on your own reasoning, your own theory.'

She was right. From the time when, as a small child, he'd heard God was a spirit that filled space and permeated all things, it had been obvious to him that this wasn't any spirit he could imagine: no one could describe or understand it. Humans referred to it as He rather than It out of a decent respect.

Yes, he thought,

> All things are not God: Though he's in all things.
> We can't know him, but he's in all we can know.
> He isn't entirely life but is in all life.
> He isn't exactly light but is in light.
> He isn't properly love but is in all love.
> He's not the details of the universe, but is in the
> universe, and also outside all things, bigger than all,
> over-arching everything. He is the rational connection,
> the laws governing the behaviour of his universes,
> the way they work, why they work as they do.
> He's there when the talk is of first things
> And last things — of which human minds
> Can say nothing, only guess.

She watched him think. When he looked up, she continued.

'Not only that,' she said, 'but harking back to "unknowable and incomprehensible", if you could get in touch with God, you'd find that he's different from what others find he is. Your God would be your God.' She paused, to let it sink in.

'All things act to their nature, and no one is the same as any other. That's the way I look at it, anyway.'

He thought about that for a while, looking straight at her. Almost she thought she could see him stuffing the new thoughts greedily into himself, as if they might get away. She spoke again.

'There's more. Your theory implies that this Presence is for all beings, all objects, even. The permanent, the transient. Objects and empty space.'

'Yes!' he said eagerly. 'Even space. I believe space is a

physical entity. And words, too. Thoughts. Dreams. Plans, inventions, anything we can think.'

'And in sinners?' she asked in a dry tone. 'Murderers? Victims?'

'Yes.'

'New-born babies?'

'Of course.'

'Accidents? Diseases? Catastrophes?'

'Yes, because he made it possible for all to happen. What I think is that God is in all things already, they don't have to do anything. He's there!'

'Then the cat,' Ursula said. 'And the birds? And so on. In other words, a form of consciousness shared by all things?'

'Yes!'

'How can we let them know? We haven't found a way to talk to them yet.'

He was silent. Perhaps beings without language knew such things without help.

'Perhaps they know?' suggested Ursula. 'That we share this common consciousness?'

'Perhaps,' he said. But God was in all, and when we died, our matter was conserved and went to help other life into existence. Before we were made, our genetic components had been waiting to be assembled, and our physical particles too. We're part of the past, the present, the future; down to our minutest particles. We'd always had eternal life, of a sort. The ancients, though they intuited a kind of continuing, had got it wrong.

So the animals, and other life, whether they knew or not, were part of it. When they came to die, perhaps they knew their brief life was a gift, and their going would make room for other life. Perhaps they knew, and, wiser than we, made death easier by regarding themselves more humbly than we do, who never seem to come to terms with it.

He was lost in contemplation of this further wonder: the conservation of the building materials on the planet, in which particles, atoms and elements are raked over constantly, part of the one inventory, to keep life of all sorts going. That was the mystery that we never seem comfortable with: that we are but one form of life in a larger network. We constantly want to be more than human, to live forever, undeterred by the thought of carrying around with us our animal nature and short-lived bodies. As if it was no great matter to abstract ourselves from the network of other life that formed us, and no strain to exist alone. As if we were gods, and all other life existed to praise and worship humankind, whereas God is part of all.

Ursula had been about to say something querying the need for priests and religions when she saw that she'd answered herself in her remark about one's God being different from other people's Gods, in which case there might need to be as many priests as there were Gods.

But seeing him following his thoughts, she wheeled herself off.

Apart From All That

Now that his daytime hours involved the strict discipline of work, his enjoyment of drawing seemed to increase. It was perhaps helped by his habit of having a pencil always handy and plenty of paper to use. The pile of finished drawings and sketches grew.

Everything he saw offered him ideas. Often a word turned itself round in his head to become the germ of a drawing. Sometimes he had a number of ideas at once. When he attacked the first, he forgot the rest. Never mind, he got so many ideas he would either think of them again, as new ones, or think of others in their place.

When he saw the aftermath of a street accident — he had never seen a dead person: they didn't let him see Grandma — he drew a hospital bed and a patient: the drip machine that fed nourishment into the insulted veins was a tea urn. A variation was an espresso coffee machine, with

Italian curves, and curlicues decorating it. This lacked respect: a cartoon, he decided.

With this step into eating and drinking, he thought of the doughnut-making machine he'd seen in Dohnanyi's Do-nuts window in the shopping town as a bomb and drew it as such, with fins. This was weak, but he kept it.

He drew a meals series. Here plates held incongruous dishes: old boots; raw liver from a corpse; little towns with church spires and people in the streets; buildings again; a crowd of people; horses' hooves raw; an orchestra busily playing; a courtroom scene; the Sydney Opera House; a piece of harbour on which yachts sailed; a football game; a suburban lounge-room scene with snacks and television; an office typing pool; a car sale yard; a cathedral; and so on. He was fond of this series, and added to it regularly.

He drew a cake shop window which displayed unusual cakes: parts of animals; people-cakes made of blocks of compressed people; a barometer cake; a book cake; a cake of leaves; a cake of earth.

He drew a people-muncher, a woman chewing off bits from a long stick of compressed people. This in turn gave him an idea for a people-sculpture, where the intertwined bodies of writhing men, women and children formed a tall columnar piece of sculpture, rather like a totem pole. He set this as a foreground to the Federal Parliament buildings.

He drew shops that contained weird fruit: heads; hands; bowls of fingers; brains growing on stems like flowers; noses on legs; a dish of feet; a jar of pickled ears.

As extensions of these ideas, he drew strange animals queueing up for slaughter: as well, the cooked bodies of unusual animals served up to diners.

Much the same idea involving a number of people showed a welter of people fiercely and energetically enjoying themselves, drinking, talking, playing, kissing, eating. Some distance away, apart from all that, was one person, perhaps a youth, perhaps himself, building a wall of civilisation, which included as parts of the wall: buildings, factories, libraries, parks, statues, galleries, houses, bridges, shopping centres.

Milking Time

It was afternoon in the valley. Challoner's cow was being walked back up the slope towards the bails. Kim Challoner and Katie Thorold were waiting to do the milking. Kim was teaching Kate, he thought as he watched them in the sunpatch that caught the afternoon sun, all yellow-green grass and black silhouetted tree-trunks. He could see them, from the drawing table, through the open french windows.

He drew a horse being milked by a tall woman; a cow milked by Katie Thorold, with the sticking-out bottom; an emu milked by a small boy; a dog milked by a toddler; a cat by a tiny human in top hat and tails; a mouse milked by Tom Thumb.

When he finished, it was time for football training. He ate only a scratch tea on those days. After a shower in the changing rooms he'd be back home well before ten. Time to do another drawing.

The Bridge Goes Nowhere

*I*t was a kilometre-long suspension bridge. It began in a recognisably Australian suburb, across the waters of a bay towards a distant shore, which wasn't defined. The bridge-work stopped, petering out in the misty distance.

He liked this drawing. It would make a painting some day, he thought, but there was too much to get on with right now to be stopping for one idea.

Loss

*H*e went for a Sunday run in the bush, out to Kangaroo Point past all the trees and rocks he knew, the bends in the track, the flats where white sand pooled, the part of Nerida Pass where Big Rock and Indian Head stood, the steep valley sides where the grass was translucent green and the gums stood straight up.

Standing on the overhanging rock at the Point, he could see all the valleys around, some glimpses of the creeks and the river not far away, sliding and pushing to the sea.

He would lose all this one day. Like Preston, Danielle, then Randal and Orville, he would move out of his parents' house. Where would he go? He liked it here.

He loved it. The dips and slopes on the hill sides, the tree in the middle of the track, the low bushes and native shrubs on the ridge flat, the whole book of shapes of this part of the bush had reconstituted themselves inside him. The landscape he knew so well, even to the placement of the trees and rocks, the curves of the hills in the distance, were in him, part of him. It would be no small thing to tear himself from all this that was his.

And when he lost it all, what would he have? It was too big a sadness to bear thinking of.

Divided Aims

He came back from his run and drank a big glass of water. His brothers used to tease him when they lived at home by talking of his run as a jog. They knew he didn't like that word.

He thought about his sensitivity to their little joke as he sat down to his pile of paper. Heaven jogs, he thought. Keep fit in heaven. Enjoy eternity: jog!

He drew it. An endless line of joggers stretched from one horizon of the traditional sky-as-heaven to the other, jogging on fleecy clouds, sweatbands on their foreheads, padded shoes on their feet.

His feeling for economy, his lack of taste for decoration and frivolity — which accorded well with his early years in the ascetic atmosphere of the Meeting halls — made the fleecy clouds prick his conscience a little, along with the ludicrous idea of a heaven in the sky, but not enough to have him tear up the drawing.

On fresh paper he attempted another poem-thing in memory of what he'd seen in the street one day on the way to work. A group of young men were gathered round a digging machine by the side of the main road; their work would come later when the yellow machine had dug the hole. They spent the time watching each female that passed.

The one that interested them most was a well-shaped young girl studying to walk steadily on high heels. The boy thought of hunting animals watching a herd of prey, selecting the one they'd attack. As with lions he'd seen in animal encyclopaedias and on television, the young men's mouths watered most over this young tender flesh that wasn't very mobile. If they had chased her, there was no chance she could have escaped. The awkwardness, the small steps, the near helplessness: all these registered with the watching predators.

He wrote his first verse about hunting animals watching the herd for stragglers, the easy to catch; and sighting a plump young one, which ought to have been buried safely in the mass of the herd. It had wandered to the exposed edge of the mass, and was marked down as prey.

The second verse spoke of a leopard skin dress on a leggy girl, tender, plump, who walked awkwardly in high shoes.

The boy's mouth watered, just as the young men's had. He understood what they felt, but getting it into the right words was another matter.

After an hour of trying, he felt he was no farther forward. He had separated the two narrative images out into fragments, and worked on them one by one.

It was difficult.

He looked back into his memory of the roadside workmen and remembered one of them smoking. Ah! An image of the man's concentration came to him: the cigarette burning down to his fingers, the exclamation, the dropped cigarette, the eyes returning to the girl in spite of the sting of pain.

It was a beginning. It was harder to do than drawing it. Drawing came easy.

Tristram

*H*e picked up his copy of Tristram Shandy, that he'd bought at a book sale — the contents page said it had the Cruickshank drawings in it, but it didn't — and glanced through it before beginning at page one.

In his usual way, he allowed his mind to dream. Back it went, covering years in a second or two, to his father saying, and to him agreeing silently, that nothing was flat, straight, round or smooth, that such things were only words, whose meaning could never be realised in the actual world of objects.

This carried with it, of course, the corollary that the words were invented without benefit of exact physical states preceding them. In other words, the words weren't exact copies of actual states, but rather the embodiment of wishes or perhapses, or nearlys: fairly straight, nearly round, just about smooth.

What did this mean for Tristram Shandy? Did it mean nothing is a word? No, he could see no fruitful way ahead there.

Suddenly he saw! This book was a form, a narrative of part of a life, in which everything was broken up, partial, fractional, and life isn't smooth, round, flat, straight. Life isn't connected strictly: it's in bits, held together only in being loosely constrained within an intermittent consciousness, itself within a time box of indefinite size. In this way the life of a person could be thought of in something of the way you think of time, matter, energy, light, gravity, and so forth, as being in bits, yet recognisably the same person's life.

He had an odd feeling that this would mean a great deal to him later.

The Biology Text

The next special job he was given was again to go to Fisher Library at Sydney, to pick up a biology text for the engineering director, Cameron. In it were beautiful pictures of animal cells, and since he'd been criticised for taking so long the time before, he had little time to pore over it. He cursed the bus on the way back for swerving and overtaking, making it hard to hold the book still.

The text was about the developing embryo of a chick. It told how cells, which appear no different from each other as far as can be seen, seem to move into position alongside other cells, and having done that, turn themselves into a different part of the chick, an adjacent part. As if they knew that the other part needed the next bit further on, and they became that. What told them? Did they know, somehow, what to do? But, he thought, as he looked up from the book — in despair at seeing the factory buildings looming ahead — if cells can interpret their position in developing tissue, might they then have a sort of consciousness?

The thought overwhelmed him. It was his stop. He got off.

But how did they know where to go? The cells pictured were of a chicken's wing, and when cells that were from the corresponding site on the other embryo wing were transplanted alongside the little spur that became the elbow, they grew into another elbow. That would seem to indicate that there was a difference in the cells, never mind that it couldn't be detected. Did the difference consist in what the cells were told to do? Or were the cells all much the same, but did different things because of where they happened to be?

And that other picture of the two sides of a human embryo's nose: the cells in each part of the nose, so far apart, knew they had to come together to make two nostrils joined in a fleshy nose. Were they perhaps as intelligent, on a small scale, as the finished human body?

Did they recognise their neighbours? Did they speak to each other? Remembering that we, living humans, speak to each other with movements, face expressions, blows, kicks, sneers, frowns, just getting out of others' way, or staying silent. They must speak to each other, or they all have a plan to work to and maybe they read it together. Between them they find out and know what they are to become, so this bit knows that that bit fits alongside it, and they proceed. Or do they know the plan, the order they are to be in, beforehand? Is it in them? Is there something else, nearby, that gives the orders? That is a sort of conductor of the whole symphony that is development?

He delivered the book to Cameron, the engineering director, enviously as he took it without expression and threw it on a table. There it lay, closed, no one reading it. What a waste! So many books, at that moment and the next, lying unread, holding in them the results that came after so many brains thought or imagined or guessed, or re-arranged other men's words looking for a new arrangement that might work or might suggest another thing entirely. And no one reading them. He returned to his work, heavy with the thought.

In the train on the way home that night he thought with sadness of the book thrown carelessly on that table, perhaps lying there still. Did the brain grow in some way like those cells of the chicken's wing and the human nose in embryo? He looked out of the window at the blur of the train's speed producing parallel lines as he went with open eyes into the state his mother called dreaming. If only he knew the physics those kids in his old class were learning now. Could it possibly be that the working and construction of the brain in some way reflected the growing or working or even the creation of the universe? Could the universe be an organism? With a development path of its own? Was there communication between all its parts by virtue of their distance relations? Was the relation of their parts to one another a part of their nature? Were they communicating simply by being where they were in relation to the others?

If the physics of the universe, its creation, its workings, was shown somehow in the working and construction of the brain, perhaps the working of human society had such a link with the working and construction of the brain.

And did our human society include the animals and other beings we ate, petted, bred or gambled on, or simply admired? Yes. We must mean all of us, the whole lot together, just as — in his untutored fancy he imagined — the whole body is an extension, an expression of, the head.

Why Not and What If

The time of day had been a subject of some anger at the office. Truck drivers often had a more free and easy attitude to times of delivery than the persistent office workers, who were paid to baulk at little differences in stated time and figures. It was a day of rain, and when he arrived home wet from work, he went straight to the dining table, and drew humans with clock faces. He showed clock-faced people driving trucks and cars; the traffic directed by clock-police; clock-faced shoppers and salespeople; clock-faced pets, diners, entertainers, drinkers, footballers. There was no end to the list, he could see that, but perhaps the most appropriate was the drawing of clock-faced athletes running against time. He noticed himself putting different times on the face-clocks, but found this meaningless, and destroyed the drawing.

He changed and had his shower, then before tea drew a little series of trees: a tree of smiles, tree of cats, tree of teeth; the tree of grunts, a tree of toes. It was pleasant work, but no more than that.

He ate his tea under a cloud. This sort of drawing was so easy, how could it be proper work? All he did was take one of the ordinary subjects that surround all of us, and either alter it or put something with it that altered the usual look of it, but at the same time opened up the questions: Why not? or What if?

He said nothing during the meal and did the washing-up without saying a word.

No one chipped him or commented, apart from a few glances at his face. With true family kindness they let him think his thoughts.

When Lillian passed behind him as he stood at the sink, he heard the half-humming, half-singing, but very softly.

> *'How sweet the name of Jesus sounds,*
> *In a believer's ear.'*

She didn't want even her spiritual life to obtrude on his silence and his thoughts.

> *'It soothes his sorrows, heals his wounds.'*

The sheer consideration she showed him made him smile, in spite of his mood, as he finished the little job, and he gave her a pat on the shoulder as he went out of the kitchen, to show he knew.

> *'And drives away his fear.'*

Objects Without Words

Sunday, he wallked north through the bush, past the waterfall to Slide-grass Hill. He thought he would teach his legs to run faster than he could make them go on the flat. Ten times he ran from the top of the hill, making his legs take short steps to speed their action. Satisfied with that, he began a series of downhill runs, letting his legs take their own time, allowing them to wait for whatever impulses they wanted to obey.

In that relaxed state he felt as if he was flying. His feet seemed to be playing with the grass, hardly touching the ground. His thoughts became detached from what his legs and feet were doing.

It was a gentle walk home through the bush. His legs had forgotten their furious activity; all was quietness in him. The mind that took over when he was drawing was elsewhere. He looked at the trees he loved, the shrubs and bushflowers, the friendly rocks, and not a word came into his head. Everything was itself, as if words hadn't been invented. Grey rock, moist ground, cool trunks of gums, bacon-and-eggs bush, these were shapes and colours, distances and textures, not words. The word had been slipped off each object like a glove and the object stood there naked, to be felt and seen as it was before words came.

Under the Floorboards of the Universe

The winter had been a cold one, made more so by the odd warm days interspersed between cool changes and fierce winds. His pile of drawings had grown so much that he put earlier ones away in a drawer in the old mantelpiece with its cupboards, carved doors and large mirror that Grandfather Blood had made.

Often he came home with his head full of peculiarities. He drew God and angels jacking up the cities of the earth to check on what was beneath them; God's finger lifting the fabric of the earth beneath forests and lakes; the earth as a skin lifted to show floorboards underneath; or the floorboards of the world raised to show a different primal Eden below. On the same theme, one drawing showed the floorboards of the Universe raised to show, underneath that, the surface veneer of another civilisation beneath.

Others were more ordinary: joggers running up the stairway to Paradise; policemen random-breath-testing a cripple in a Rolls Royce wheelchair; a city workman with broom and dustbox sweeping under occupied seats on a railway station, forcing his broom between intending passengers' legs, doing his duty objectionably.

Orissa

On Saturday morning he saw Orissa at the local shops. As she walked he noticed that her feet waved outwards as they left the ground, then swivelled back to a straight forward position as they touched the ground again. He didn't know why he noticed.

She was covered up, so that only her hands and wrists, face and neck were to be seen. He gained on her, coming up behind her as she looked into the Zandra Carlatti dress shop. He watched her face, saw the white neck-skin rising from her blouse and disappearing into the beginnings of her dark shining hair. The graduation from white to pink as his eyes followed her neck up and forward towards her left cheek seemed to him marvellous. Why should this be so? Other girls' cheeks were pink and their necks white, too. He didn't know why it meant something more in her case.

She lifted her right hand up to her bottom lip and smoothed her index finger along that lip from side to side. This gave him a glimpse of her palm. Was it pink? Yes and no. It was a shiny white at the outer edge of the palm, as if something had given it a light polish. Then on several raised parts — the pads of her fingers, the heel of her hand, and in three spots near the base of her fingers, there was a delicate suffusion of pink. Something like the mother of pearl shell on the mantelpiece, where pearly white ran into grey, then to some colour short of blue, and with this shade merging with something less than pink, then pink itself. Or was it? No, for when you looked at it directly, it wasn't. Only when you looked to one side of it, did it show pink.

Her ear was a generous pink at the lobe; he could see it glowing behind tendrils of hair. Blood and life flowed strongly in her.

She moved on, unaware of him.

He stayed, standing near the shop windows so passersby wouldn't disturb him, watching her walk. He tried to get his feelings into her limbs, trying to feel what she felt when her legs swung from the hips, trying to feel the pressure she felt when her feet touched the ground, then rose and swung forward on the ends of her legs.

As she went into the distance he remembered something he hadn't known he saw: the skin below the collar of her shirt as it went down towards her chest. There was a shine to it, of the same sort as that on the side of her hand. Perhaps the skin was fine; perhaps when it touched things it took on a smoothness that pressed the grain of the skin together, and that gave rise to the shine. He thought, with a warm feeling, that even her hands looked as if they had soft brown eyes.

He moved after her when she was at the corner, outside the newsagent's shop. He followed her to the hardware shop, but didn't go in. He'd be too conspicuous. To the butcher's, from which she emerged holding a plastic bag full of bulky parcels in brown paper bags with the shop name in red.

The wide slow curve of her hips, below a small waist, engrossed his eyes. He followed, more slowly than she walked, until she turned the corner into her street. Not once had she looked back.

He went on walking, full of a peculiar emptiness now he could no longer see her.

What if he never saw her again? What if, on the way to work, he stepped off a city footpath without seeing a car in a hurry? He stepped up his pace; found it too slow; walked faster until he was nearly breaking into a trot. Would she have reached her house? He ran.

At the corner stood the big old Illawarra flame tree. He stopped behind its flat trunk and looked along Orissa's street. She was gone. He leaned against the tree, his arms round its bulk. Something tapped the back of his right hand.

Orissa's face came round the tree, her mocking mouth curved, eyes derisive.

'Well?' she said.

He looked at her face. Some of her hardness, her careless way, had gone.

'What's the idea? What do you want?'

He couldn't tell her he feared he might not see her again, and had come running. She knew he'd run.

'Haven't you got anything to say?'

She was here. He was with her. What was there to say?

'Come on. You can walk me home,' she said firmly, setting off. He walked beside her. He felt his hand grasped. They were walking hand in hand, her cool fingers in his warm ones. Would she find his hand too hot? Was his hand sweaty? He was in a swirl of doubt and discomfort. He hadn't wanted to touch her, only see her, to be with her, yes, that was good, but just to see her, to be able to look at her, that was all he could manage now. His fingers felt thick and dull, hot wooden pegs.

Suddenly he felt his hand released.

'You don't have to if you don't want to,' she said with coolness. Was she angry? He looked at her face. She looked straight ahead.

Why am I such a fool? he asked himself. He could feel the air on his fingers and palm where her hand had been. Why did I let her know my silly feelings? he thought. If only he had that little hand again. Why do I make such a mess of things?

Desperately he grabbed her hand, and this time her fingers lay lifeless and unengaged in his. He looked at her face. She glanced at him briefly, then away, as if to say she couldn't stop him looking. She began to talk, looking straight ahead, of war and weapons. She talked of the world, of planet earth, as the better newspapers, magazines and television spoke of it. He noticed this particularly, for in his own mind there was a gulf between that world, and the one he saw round him of rocks and trees, of Country Road emerging from thick bush and petering out in the west, of Spectacle Creek and the Lake, of Driftwood Beach not far away, of the sun setting in beauty on deep stillness in the same way it had set on this little valley as far back as could be imagined. Even the city he knew was weirdly different in newspapers and on television.

She talked of robots and the future, of over-population and pollution. He'd heard it all for so long, at home and at school, that it was no longer necessary to think about it. It was background noise, wallpaper. It was like thoughts of one's death, of how the world will be when we are gone: thoughts everyone has, but from which all must turn in order to live properly and with self-respect in the time remaining.

They reached her front gate. She took her hand away from his, opened the gate and went down the concrete path between the neat border flowers her mother had planted. He said nothing.

On the front step she turned and looked him in the eyes for some time, without speaking.

'You may not agree with me,' she said at last. 'You may not be as horrified by war as I am. I believe young males often welcome war as exciting, heroic, a chance to travel and see the world. I'm not male.' She made as if to go inside, then turned again and said, 'I've given up my diary. I've stopped writing it. Nothing seems to matter any more.' She went quickly inside her house.

When he could no longer see Orissa, he felt something he'd never known before. He felt miserable, out of sorts, alone. He'd always been by himself but this was different: something was torn from his grasp, he was less than he'd been when she was there in front of his eyes. That she was gone seemed like a hard lump of something tangible: she left a shadow and he stood in it and was cold.

It would be natural, he thought, if they were together; natural like a tree growing, a rock providing shelter, birds defending territory.

Davis Blood walked back along Waterloo Street, down Big Hill and home. He couldn't take in what she'd said, her evident misery.

He was aware that this was the first time in his life that he'd thought much about another person. It must be love, or something like that. Whatever it was, it wasn't entirely happy.

    He thought of her at home, at work, in city streets. The lines of her face, her neck, her arms, seemed to say things to him. There seemed to be a meaning in everything she said and did, in everything about her, if only he could make it out. He felt that the many shapes of her outward form were special to her, weren't characteristic of any other, and spoke, in the ways they flexed, changed, and returned to rest, of her alone. The way she placed her feet when she walked, the different little attitudes her fingers struck when she held or manipulated something, consumed his attention. Long after she had gone, he could see them still, could call them to mind at any time, exactly as they had been. The way she sat, turned her head, suddenly looked up, had a significance to him beyond the actions of any other person, a significance that occupied the back of his mind no matter what else he was doing. He entered into those actions, however slight; his own fingers, arms, head, feet, tasted just how those actions were performed by her. He was, in the purest sense, inside those actions, tasting what it must be like to be her, seeing and feeling the world the way she did.

If other females disappeared he wouldn't have noticed much: she was the only female.

He thought of her in the reading room of the Public Library, under that high ceiling, as he came to the end of Faust: *'das ewig Weibliche zieht uns hinan'*.

What did it mean? What was the eternal feminine? Or the everlasting womanly?

He needed more than his elementary German and his youthful mental background to assimilate this. Was it simply that the female component, the other half, was necessary for balance and wholeness?

He didn't know enough about the world.

He didn't know enough about Orissa, either; she was still in process, as he was.

Aunt Ursula, some months later, brought news that she'd joined a Christian group that sang, prayed and gave their message in shopping centres and places by the sea where there were big audiences. She played a musical instrument and was beginning to be known for her fine and passionate commitment to the Crucified God and the process of redemption and salvation; and for the individuality of her presentation.

Aunt seemed taken with two features of Orissa's message. One was her primary insistence, not on sin and repentance, but on beginning a dialogue with God now, and becoming friends. The second was a dismissal of attempts to check first on the truth of this or that article of dogma or waste time with arguments over God's existence. Need is what counts, she urged; help may be instantly obtained.

She preached to those in need, those with problems, the lonely, the lost, the inadequate, the hurt, the shy; those who yearned for a better, more fulfilling life and for good and loving people to be with; for kindness and smiling faces; for forgiveness, tolerance and as many second chances as were necessary.

Davis Blood whistled softly when Ursula had finished. So that was how it had taken her — he'd never have predicted that. It stamped her even more deeply on him.

'Why do you think she'd do that?' he asked his Aunt.

'No idea,' said Aunt imperturbably. 'There'll be a good reason. You know, women usually act logically; more logically than men. Men sidestep logic; sidestep quickly and cleverly. This sidestep possibly explains why the average professional footballer is better at football than the average housewife.'

He looked at her sharply. She was smiling, in her fashion. She'd got him again, his leg neatly pulled and he hadn't felt it happening until it was done.

Later, in the Sunfilled Yard

Later, in the sunfilled yard, he stretched full length and hugged the good green grass. Down past the borders of the yard, in the bush, he put his arms round a cool redgum sapling, and along the valley a little way past the banksias and prickly moses, with the tips of his fingers touched a pale creamy eucalypt whose skin was the colour of Orissa's neck.

As he stood near a cigarette plant with white red-tipped flowers feeling the breath and stillness of the bush round him, a sentence came in to his head. 'Heaven and hell are married together in you.'

Where had that come from? A black-eyed Susan stared up at him. A lizard rustled. He kept still. A honey flower opened a fraction. Minutes passed. A spider moved out of her nest in a twisted gum-leaf suspended above a bacon and eggs bush. Her slim black legs gleamed in the sun.

Was it one of Aunt's phrases? Had Orissa said it? A silver-eye landed briefly in a tree a few metres uphill. There must be fruit trees nearby, he reflected. Heaven and hell? But he was technically without a formal set of religious beliefs, since he couldn't accept at least one major doctrine, resurrection, that was essential to Christianity, the only religion he knew.

Of course there were fruit trees. In his own yard. And a hundred metres or so west, McCarthy's backyard had oranges and soft fruits, plums, loquats, nectarines, as well as their lemon tree and the other citrus. The silver-eye would like them all. It flew off.

He was without specifically Christian belief, but full of God belief. He needed belief and would, he felt, need it more as he grew older. His own spontaneous delight in the world around him, and sometimes in its people, were not enough. He needed the God in him; he needed a way to live. It wasn't enough to be an individual, however splendid and strong. He longed to immerse himself completely, to lose his own self in a larger whole, in his case in that incomprehensible power outside human selves, outside all possible knowledge.

He felt powerfully that the enemies of the person, and of humans as a whole, were cynicism, fear, disillusion, lack of confidence, lack of curiosity.

His own reading, his efforts at thinking, had shown him that people, no matter how separated by distance and language, eventually had registered the successive shudders that signalled the failure of so many optimistic perceptions of the future, made public in the late nineteenth and early twentieth centuries, and were deeply afraid. He had seen how new ways of being, of seeing, of organising, of making, of living, had fallen down one by one, not because of force applied from without, but weakness within. In other words the perceptions, the hopes, the possibilities prophesied, though positive and often encouraging and seeming full of faith in the future and humanity, were wrong-headed, breaking too violently with the traditional bases of people's lives hammered out over centuries; often lacking in humanity; shortsighted; bewildered by new freedoms, as in the arts; sometimes brutal as in art, architecture, politics; in one case genocidal, in politics again.

Some imagination had gone into them, but not enough. In one case history itself was represented as almost a force of nature, and what was plainly not science was said to be science.

They promised more than they could deliver. They were, in fact, lies; based on special interests, hope, and little else.

He shifted position. His hand brushed the prickly leaf-ends of a five-corners bush.

The places where something was happening that could be called improvement, were science, medicine, and technology. No overall progress came about in politics, the arts, philosophy, nor in the goodness of humankind. But humankind had forgotten that simply staying civilised requires a major effort.

The smells of earth, woodchips, of eucalypt leaves, breathed round him and into his thoughts. He stood, relishing them, then switched back to the process of his thinking.

Science itself was no longer a harmless search for knowledge that was occasionally useful. It was in chaos. It had become magic once matter could be transformed and life altered, while at the same time physical and theoretical research pointed to an increasingly incomprehensible cosmos, a universe that could no longer be described in symbols, still less objective words. The more that was uncovered, the stranger it became.

In science, in social and economic arrangements, in politics, humankind had no idea where it was going. Hopelessness was growing, fear was a habit; humankind lived under a sun-occluding cloud while the threat of nuclear war persisted.

He missed the silver-eye. Seeing a little bundle of life like that — so alert, so quick, so full of life — gave a deep pleasure.

A small copper-tailed skink darted from cover, stopped near a three-petalled bush orchid, ran a bit, a bit more, past a wedding bush, then sped under the shade of a brown boronia and on under a rock.

A little more pleasure. If the future was dark, the time to come an abyss, then these were crumbs of pleasure on the edge of that abyss. And there were always trees.

With a sigh that was partly a wry smile, he put aside his gloomy thoughts. How serious they were, yet in a moment they could be dismissed. For his search had a different direction. He had begun to feel, dimly as yet, that the world, and the future, started anew with him. He would turn on the light in him: the first field for the exercise of his will would be within. An inner sea had to be traversed before the seas outside.

Once he was — what was the word? Coherent? Together? Whole! That was it! — Once he was whole he would travel, pursue, conquer, discover, out in that larger world. Prepared by being united with his whole self, he would be equipped to reach for what was now beyond his grasp.

He had been standing still for many minutes. Birds had come and gone, a blue-tongue lizard had ambled fatly from cover, sunned itself a little, then departed for another part of its territory. Territories probably overlapped without end. And why not? It was their planet, too.

He moved, going slowly, deeper into the thick bush. When he'd done thinking, he would run home on one of the bigger tracks. The notes of the pallid cuckoo rose again, in their upward progression, stopping suddenly at the top note as if wanting a confirmation of the tune.

He was different from everyone in the family, he thought as he brushed aside the whippy branches of a hakea and a pink spiderflower; and, indeed, from everyone he'd met. The way belief took him wouldn't be the same as it was with Lillian, or with his father. He skirted a pale drumsticks bush noticing its straight steel-coloured branches.

The God in me is different, he said, echoing Aunt Ursula's, 'Your God would be your God.'

He was in the midst of thick undergrowth near the creek. Lilli pilli and sassafras harmonised with the coolness as if they had created it. Small animals rustled as he pushed his way through, a green tree-snake silently climbed past his shoulder; their movements in alarm or panic; his in impatience at the opposition to his comparatively great strength. He changed direction, making uphill past the red bloodwoods and the casuarina places with the floors of needles, for the big track that would take him quickly home. His hands touched the bushes as he climbed, wax flower, native rose, white spiderflower. How he loved these hardy plants, so tough in their leaves, in their resistance to poor seasons, to fire: so fragile if they were transplanted or their roots disturbed. A bottlebrush branch brushed his cheek, its flower spare and red.

As he stood on the wide track and faced west towards the old house, it hit him with a sharp urgency, that inside him was a great need, a spiritual hunger. He must run towards the future, not dawdle.

The Destroying Angel

There were things he didn't allow himself to do, just as there were things he didn't talk about in front of others.

His conviction that he was out of the ordinary, that the future held great things for him, was so strong that he saw the foolishness of telling others of it, the impossibility of making words and arguments support and justify something that, however strong inside him, however naturally it had grown in him, couldn't be seen and tested by others. Inner convictions and hypotheses aren't visible: only later fruits.

He didn't talk to others about his drawings, or writing exercises. He kept these things hidden. They were precious: he didn't want others' dirty fingermarks or speechmarks on them.

There was something else inside him to be guarded, and confined; something he was deliberately holding in. He had begun to know more of the violence within him. It was there all the time, sometimes small and harmless, resting perhaps, sometimes huge and seething just below the surface. The effort of holding it in check produced many silences, all sorts of unexplainable awkwardnesses. He would back away at times from his own assertions, back away from others' bumptiousness, from the appearance of opposition — just in case the thing in him got out of its cage.

Others thought it shyness, social unease, nervousness, personal troubles.

The common domestic form it took was anger: anger at objects, anger at himself for mistakes, but also an undirected anger that came for no reason he knew of. As if something had lifted the lid on what was seething and swirling inside him, a lid that ought to be battened down tight.

He thought about that anger as he loped down the bush on the big track whose complicated surface his feet knew so well. It was as if the anger was a flood and the banks too small, sometimes, to contain it.

He felt no great changes happening in him beforehand, no special feelings he associated with its onset. He felt, even a second before it erupted, no different from usual.

Sometimes he held in his hands something he valued, and was in the process of looking at it, or putting it away, when the anger struck. Without stopping himself, he would calmly destroy it, no matter what it was. This was a calm, final sort of anger: anger with no afterthought.

He promised himself he would never pick up his drawings in two hands, in case the destroying angel, whose existence he could feel as a presence, struck him then: for he would certainly rip them to shreds. The destroying angel forbade him to regret anything it did through him. It forbade him to feel pain, it prohibited suffering.

He was sufficiently alarmed at these irruptions into his life of destructive feelings — even though he was confident they would never issue in gross violence — to go along to a gym to learn to box. Perhaps there was something in the old folk wisdom of getting things out of one's system.

As he usually did things, he simply went along and joined, then thought about it later. It wasn't until after his first lesson, on the straight left and the way to turn his wrist in delivering a punch, that it occurred to him he might have joined in order to provide himself with more violence, rather than to escape it.

At the Kitchen Sink

He'd fixed himself something to eat in the kitchen, and was at the sink washing up the plate, cup and knife he'd used.

Suddenly he was overtaken by a feeling of helplessness, an overwhelming lack of all the abilities necessary to do the mysterious thing which seemed to be waiting for him a little way off in the future.

He cried out, in panicky anguish: 'Eternal Ones, help me, guide me!'

They were immediately there.

>*We will.*

'Tell me why I am here.'

>*To obey. To build a vision for*
>*those with you and those who come after.*

'Touch me, then! Put strength into me! Help me think! Protect me from the violence inside me.'
In my proper self, my best self,
I don't want to run wild and hurt others.'

Predators in a Food Chain

He didn't hear Ursula come in until her voice cut across his state of attentiveness to the Voices.

'Davie!'

He turned on her, as if control was the one thing absent, then, remembering where he was, forced himself into calmness.

'Yes, Aunt.'

'Who are you talking to?'

He said nothing. Had she guessed?

'I mean, you look as if you are listening. What are you listening to?'

It was on his face, that his attention was taken up with things not visible in the kitchen, he was listening to voices she couldn't hear.

'Voices.'

'Whose?'

'My voices.'

'How many?' As soon as the banal words were out, she cursed herself. Why, she asked herself, am I never equal to moments like these?

'It doesn't matter how many,' he said gently. 'It's just one voice, but it has so many tones it sounds like voices.'

'I'll go. I'll leave you —.' She began to wheel away.

'It's all right, Aunt. No need. And thank you.' He said it as if he were going away. She turned her head.

'What are you thanking me for?'

'Things.'

'Where are you going?'

'I don't know, yet. Things,' he continued, 'years ago. Things you said then.' He owed much to her.

So this was it, she thought. He's beginning to leave us. The journey's there, on his face. Perhaps he knows already where he's going.

He didn't.

Wherever it is he's going, whatever his talent, I pray, she

thought — yes, me — pray! — that he possesses that strength of remorseless persistence, without which the gift of talent is a joke.

'Don't forget,' she said. 'If you're to be an artist, that an artist develops in depth, not outwards towards others.' She was thinking of his natural loneliness.

Thank you, Aunt, as usual, his head replied.

Then she said a funny thing.

'Well, you're still growing up. You must grow up, at least part of you, but keep the child in you alive.' My goodness, she thought, I'm talking as if he's never coming back. 'Keep alive the baby, the youth, the adolescent, the gravel-rash, the skinned knees, the broken saplings, broken glass, the lighted windows in you, the hunger for tomorrow, the zest for doing: all must be kept alive if you are to be a whole man.' Some of the words were familiar. Dimly he saw himself much smaller, looking up as Aunt said: 'keep the child in you'. Another thing, it was the first time she had used the word 'man' to him.

'Aunt,' he said slowly, dragging the words out. 'Do you ever get angry?'

'Sometimes.'

'Very angry?'

She smiled. 'Only at things that are none of my business.'

'For no reason that you can see?'

'Not often. But you do.'

He was startled. 'Have you noticed?'

'Of course.'

'Is it a bad sign?'

'It's a sign of fires banked inside, fires that must be controlled if they're to make a difference to the world. Otherwise destruction and nothing else will follow.'

'I don't want to destroy things!' But even as he said it, he knew he might be required to be violent, ruthless, at times when he was in his calm, sunny state. What would he do then? For it was hard, perhaps impossible, to break out of.

'Much destruction and man-made chaos come from the best motives and liberal humane values, Davie.'

'How can destruction come from liberal values?'

'There's a big hole in our liberal philosophy. The things we believe and act on, the assumptions we rest our lives on, go to make up the daily philosophy of us all, and in sum, of our society. It's what we actually live by but not our stated philosophy. It's necessary for everyone to have a philosophy, whether they know it or not, whether or not they bother to examine it.'

'Does the hole begin with divisions?' he asked. 'With systematisation? Order without freedom? Obedience without judgement? Duty and loyalty in return for safety?'

'Something like that, in that you're talking of values, and values are part of the way we live.'

'Tolerance, and so forth?'

'Yes.'

'Do you mean —' he interrupted with something that had struck him recently ' — the quantities? I mean the amounts of the different values?'

'Exactly. You can't have one hundred per cent tolerance, or you'd end up tolerating those who would destroy tolerance. How much you have can never be settled permanently. But tolerance is only one value. You can't have one hundred per cent honesty, or cruelty comes in the door, or public panic. But there's one example so familiar that I'm sure you'll get the idea.

'Picture this,' Aunt went on. 'A vaunted liberal humanistic culture that is a curtain, a screen, hiding the realities of the way we live.' She paused, to shift her angled body in the wheelchair. 'Horrible realities. Savage, cruel, daily realities on a vast scale.'

'That's grotesque, Aunt. Hypocrisy. What does it mean?'

'This vaunted culture is not our real culture, merely our reputed culture. It ignores, in all its public appearances, the central fact of mankind's existence: how we live from day to day, how we survive. We live in a savage universe. Sublime, yes. Awesome, thrilling, appealing to our love of adventure, danger, of extremes; but cataclysmic, merciless; we're made from it, we're just as savage as it is, though smaller. We're savage events to all sorts of life round us. To stay alive in a world that wasn't made for us, we must find what we can eat, then eat it. If it won't cooperate, we kill it, then eat it. If it's poisonous, it kills our friends, so we avoid it. We're predators, among predators. Humanity itself is inhuman. Each day millions of living beings whose natures and personal lives, hopes and joys and fears we don't know, are led in orderly regimented fashion up to the slaughterman and their lives taken. We eat their bodies. Our philosophy is a lie because it makes no mention of this. No culture that doesn't account for its manner of survival in its description of that culture can be said to represent it truthfully.

'The whole thing is a hotch-potch, a patchwork of values that arose at different times, and don't fit together. But the hole, the need to survive, to eat, is so big that any horror can pass through; for once one sort of killing is allowed, any other can follow if survival is seen to be at stake. Then we'll kill to live, or because it's in the public interest, or simply because we're ordered to kill.

'Tolerance, humanity, love and the perfectible future are ideals, not part of live culture, which is the real life of the community. They're a superstructure; beneath is greed, ruthless competition, pain, fear, loss, death. Killing is part of our lived culture. Whether of animals, plants or other humans. To be fair, of course, we are eaten, too.

'Now, here's my punch line. The hole is in you! In me! The human self has to be adjusted, or can be. Remember Faust!

"Lay first this self in ruins, shattered, blind:
"A new may rise its place to fill."
Apologies to Goethe.'

'Just before the bargain, in Faust, Aunt?'

'Yes, Davie. Just one more thing: mankind needs a desert, at times; the dry air of solitude. Where can he find it? In his work, in his home, in himself if he's lucky.'

She rested, her chest inflating and deflating with the effort of so much talking. He was glad of the pause, and stood by the stove, thinking. The valley quiet was broken by a flurry of laughs from a kookaburra. Another joined in.

'You don't believe I'll be destructive, do you?'

'Of course you will. Whatever you do will have unintended effects. Walk through the bush, or down the backyard, and dozens, even hundreds, of living things will die.'

They both felt stifled in the big kitchen. Aunt wheeled herself out on to the high landing above the little valley.

'Ah, that's better. It's as well, when you're talking of the world, and our place in it, to have a good look at it, and keep referring to it; not just using words, which if used apart from the objects they denote, get tired and limp.'

He was silent, looking out over the loved, familiar, shining, half-seen slopes and trees, knowing how well he knew them and the rocks, shrubs, bush flowers. It was his country, his land. He loved its face, its soil, its flavour; its voice, its moods; its unique life and big skies. I am a white Aboriginal, he thought.

Love of Objects

'Look at it, Davie,' she said warmly. 'Look at it. Air, trees, clouds, rocks, grasses, insects. All things are alive in their own motion.'

'Motion, yes,' said Davis Blood. 'A motion you can't see, but have to believe. It's all so marvellous, Aunt. Made of electrons and protons and so on that to all intents live forever. Made of bits that have been used before, many times; made from past life, past clouds, past rocks, past grasses.'

'And we give those things, those bits, back when the loan's over?'

'Yes. It's the insight primitive people had when they invented the idea of life after death. For there's no end to those bits, only to the borrowers of them,' he said.

'The bits of God?' Aunt asked teasingly.

'Well, I like thinking of it like that,' he said. 'We in God, God in us, all made of bits of God. The universe: part of God.'

'On your showing,' Ursula said, 'God's everywhere, in everything. There's no escape. Not only is science not an enemy, it continually furthers, broadens understanding of God, since it furthers understanding of the world and the universe into which it fits. But I remember the time when some people — scientists, philosophers — couldn't believe in the unseen. They couldn't and didn't.'

'And now,' he said, 'the unseen is what science is about.'

'Yes. Now science routinely shows to every girl and boy eternity in a grain of sand.'

'And therefore God,' he added quickly.

'So it's no use being an atheist?' said Aunt.

'Pointless,' he said with assurance.

'Years ago,' Aunt said, 'there was something I read in a Saturday newspaper. It was about the writer's life and what kept a writer going. And, you know, it sounds silly saying it, but it was objects. The bits out of which the planet is made. This writer loved the bits.' She smiled, with her mouth out of line, but brilliant eyes.

He waited.

'You don't prompt, do you?' she said mockingly, but it passed over his head.

'I wait for you to say it,' he said calmly.

'Never mind. I do remember the part, it was:

> '. . . *beyond words and more full of wonder*
> *is the thing itself*
> *for all things have in them*
> *some thing that is without end.*'

'Was it a poem?'

'No, just five hundred occasional words, in the *Sydney Morning Herald*. But it was as a poem that I remember it.'

'Do you suppose,' he said excitedly, 'that the writer meant what we mean? That he loved objects because God is in them?'

'Perhaps. Maybe not.'
'There's a chance he did?'
'A chance.'

Sincerity

It was an art review article in the Saturday Magazine section of a Sydney newspaper. The reviewer said in one place, *'Absolute sincerity is required of the painter. Its long-term lack is catastrophic, even a momentary lapse leads to disaster.'*

He read the article to the end, then came back to the words on sincerity. What did it mean? How did it apply to painting? To drawing? To what he did?

He sat on the verandah edge on the western side of the house, legs dangling over the side where the ground dropped away sharply down to Bread and Butter Creek. He thought about sincerity.

To me, he thought, sincerity corresponds to exactness; it is to be me, as originality entails being genuinely oneself.

How could anyone detect it or its lack in a painting? How was it he hadn't read about sincerity in writing? If sincerity was detectable anywhere, it had to be detected in words, for they came in thousands, they said something, and what they said was there, on the page forever. He would need to think more about these things.

In a rival Saturday paper he read, *'Whatever else it may be, all great art is about greatness.'* Saul Rosengreen, combative and ambitious, was holding forth. 'All profoundly ugly art looks original at first.'

These pronouncements, though probably indicating a surprising new twist in the erratic flight of art fashion, didn't help his understanding of art matters. They contrasted, however, with the embarrassment he'd felt when he read, while browsing in the city, in the text of a Cézanne book: 'Nature is made up of a series of curves and squares, which interlace.'

How could Cézanne have said that? He hadn't looked closely enough, surely. Nothing was square, or straight, except in the imagination.

He thought of 'Afternoon in Naples', of 'Les Demoiselles d'Avignon' and the paintings that followed, from both Picasso and Braque. Cubism was a nonsense to him. And yet. It wasn't entirely nonsense. Sometimes, when he suddenly looked back to those graceless masonry-like figures, he fancied he could see — what? That they were ghosts of something not altogether present? That around, or behind them, meanings were grouped? Was the artist both interpreting and creating, at the same time?

Sometimes he was persuaded — Ah! But was that it? He had to be persuaded that there was a great deal more there than could be seen at first glance! He had to know, beforehand, what he was looking for, and supply it. He had to come prepared, far more prepared than when he approached Van Eyck, Corot, Constable, Turner, Renoir, Van Gogh, Monet. They, and painters before them, needed some preparation, some background, some groundwork, but not on the scale required here: and they gave more sensual rewards, perhaps because they engaged more of the artist's time and talents.

These, with their hints and overtones, their nuances, reputations, auction prices, publicity, and importances grouped round and behind them, were more like puzzles: their rewards were intellectual recognition, self-congratulation on a successful solution, or an acceptable one. But you had to have the theory first.

There was another, darker thought he had about them. Could it be that the shapes, the grouping, the individual strokes that made them, were in some degree accidental? He knew from his own drawings how a slip, an irregularity, could suddenly be there on the paper and possess an eloquence that he hadn't intended but which he welcomed, and incorporated into what he was doing. He was too experienced in drawing to believe that the artist knew, at the beginning, what the finished painting would be, any more than he knew before starting what a poem-thing would contain: the thinking, the exploration, adding and editing, went on as the work proceeded.

There might be cases where a colleague or critic of these painters had seen something in the artist, in sketches, or in earlier works, and had given a hint that the painter decided to explore. But these were perhapses, he would never know: no one was likely to admit such things.

He thought, more prosaically, of something practical that bothered him from the first time he set foot in a gallery. Why wasn't it possible to see, in every public gallery, books of copies or prints of all the paintings of the past that had survived? In that way, each centre would have a full range so the young could see and get to know all of them.

Not enough trouble taken, too little thought, he decided.

As he sat on the grey verandah boards he saw in his mind's eye the vast sands of the Australian deserts as a thick pollen of spring, and smiled at his wayward thoughts. What could possibly blossom from Simpson's Desert, the Great Sandy Desert, or the stony one of Sturt? Apart, that is, from flowers in the wet season. He smiled at his own earnestness; the smiling part of him acting the part of an onlooker, outside Davis Blood.

A picture came into his mind, of crowds staring fixedly at a sunset; of the sunset breaking up, collapsing under the pressure of so much attention, spoiled by too much viewing. He jumped up and ran inside to jot down the idea; it might make a drawing. In mid-stride some words formed in his head: 'Past experience should be a rudder, not an anchor.' Where did that come from? As he went through the french windows he ran through the words, to remember them, but before he'd gone three steps he heard: 'The aim of the innovator is to set foot on new ground.' There wasn't time to wonder where — he'd be lucky if he got them down on paper before they left him.

He noted down all three, then the idea of desert sand

being pollen. What could be made of that? Was it a drawing? A painting?

'Mankind is born partly free, partly in chains and a baby entirely.' Now where —? But he put it down. He would have to make a separate place to put these little ideas and sentences that now seemed to jump fully formed into his head. Their origin didn't matter, if they were worth noting.

'The future is our conscience.' Another one. Perhaps the books he'd been reading had thrown ideas up like vapour, and they'd settled out in little drops of phrase.

One thing was becoming clear: they weren't all suited for translation into drawings.

The heightened life and restlessness in him wouldn't let go: he took pencil and paper with him to collect whatever new things sprang into his head.

Unfortunately, these prudent preparations seemed to signal the end of that brief period of ferment, and though he carried the pencil everywhere he went for days, nothing more came into his head until he left it behind.

A Boy in the Men's Team

The cricket trials began while the football season was still on, with semi-finals and finals to come. The football team Under 18s had won their semi-final and had a bye while the other semi was being played. He tried out for the local A grade cricket team.

The trouble was, it was one of those days when he didn't really feel like playing. But he'd said he would, and now here he was, bowling in the trials. It didn't matter to him that his rival Mahoney was bowling from the other end, with the wind, and he bowling into it. That was one of those trivial annoyances that were par for the course.

The tall eucalpyts craned their elegant tops just outside the boundary of the cricket field at Bellbird Park. They were his friends, far more than the men and boys around him. He would rather be down below the hilltop, walking on the wide bush track towards Black Snake Corner, smelling the undergrowth and the fallen leaves carpeting the soil, baking in the heat of the early spring sun.

He put all his strength and unease into his bowling. The batsman hardly saw the first ball, merely had time to leave his bat where it was in the block-hole, turning the blade full on to the red leather missile, blocking it. His second ball was so furious that he bowled it too short and outside the stumps on the leg side. It was hooked for six, and deserved to be.

'Bad luck,' Mahoney said. But the boy knew it had nothing to do with luck: it was bad temper. When he batted, he felt so dour and inside-himself that he hit every ball down, sent them whistling along the grass, and made A grade, the only boy to get in the men's team.

Thoughts in the Outfield

They usually put him in the covers to field, since he was quick to the ball, but somehow that day he was out at lonely long-on. He enjoyed the feel of the sun and stooped to pick a spring nut-flower from the short grass. It had no smell.

He ruminated. He'd read in the library about smell, and how only a few molecules of a substance is thought to be necessary for detection by the sensitive patch in the nose. If the way we smell things depends on molecules of the object being loose, and dispersed from it, then molecules of all sorts of things are loose, mingling with other things.

Perhaps trees and beasts, flowers and birds, decaying matter and the fragrant sea, in a small way blur with each other at their borders.

Nothing can be entirely that one thing; it must have on it small depositions of lots of others that have come through the air and settled awhile.

All sorts of things touch us without our knowing it. The breaths breathed out by other humans, by animals and birds, by insects and so on, blown on winds never-endingly round the planet; breathed in again, or dispersing, settling on water or earth; or even held in the air for years. Why not centuries?

He looked up. The men were taking all this cricket seriously. A game, though, that's all it was. He looked round at them, one by one: at the Ugly Duck, at Trunky, the Woolly Dog, Bugle-bone; at Road-metal Williams, the captain, at Hoppy and Stumpy, at the Sad Machine, at Lemon Dog, at the Gentle Bomb, the seam bowler with the misleading change of pace, at the wicket-keeper whose nickname was The Dangerous Friend: he chatted amiably to the opposing batsmen, getting them relaxed and off guard — men of the district with distinct personalities and proclivities, but to his mind all much the same. To him they were foreigners.

They had no thoughts of working for the world until they dropped; they lived a warm life of gentle workdays, card evenings, barbecues, reciprocal visits, beach parties, and in many cases knew each other since they were kids. He didn't belong here, either.

Men worried him; boys too. When they were together in a group they seemed to sink to a common level; anything fine or better was lopped, anything cerebral or thoughtful was out. Among the boys what was good and kind, or generous, was rubbished: the gamest, most daring was worshipped and followed — the one constantly, brutally active and inventive. At work, too, he reflected on the male workmates he had round him: the storemen and packers, drivers, clerical people, supervisors, sales staff, managers, directors.

Why was the atmosphere in the place so grey? Were the men so grey in themselves that they accepted others' rules easily? Why was it brighter when women came, who would ignore any number of company rules, but never their own? Why were they so serious about their work, their hobbies, their games? Those who sailed boats, even when out for a day's fun, had to form a triangle and race someone. They seemed oblivious to joy, unless they overcame a rival; unless they had triumphed or made a joke at another's expense; unless they'd made a gain. They seemed incapable of innocent joy in simply being: life had to be grim. They were such dry things; the moist and happy life of the planet didn't overcome their seriousness; when they conceived a plan of action, they went at it headlong and noticed nothing on the way to the goal, and the goal was always in the future. They didn't live in today, but tomorrow.

Men weren't people of now, it seemed. If ever they felt joy, they would be serious about it.

Were they afraid? Was fear their driving force? Was their bent to action a constant surmounting of constant fear?

All they touched was something to use. Why couldn't they see, feel, honour the wholeness of things as they are in themselves?

The bowler missed a hard-hit return. Davis Blood had a spot of fielding to do. As he threw the ball to the bowler, he reflected that he wasn't being fair to men, his thoughts were too general and his observations limited. Even so, he was convinced he was on the right track, and that in comparison with women men were depleted creatures. By contrast, women seemed warm, approachable, tolerant of all types and conditions of life, and welcoming to living things generally. He didn't want to dry out inside and become like that sort of man, but while working with the future in mind, give each day its proper value. Life here and now was important, too.

Bondi Beach

He went to a city beach to meet Doyle, from Accounts, who surfed through the winter months. A walk round the rocks on the south end of the beach fed many sights into his head, particularly the heavy cliffs undercut at the base by the erosion of whitish-grey rock so soft you could scoop bits out with a fingernail. It was well above the water line, wind eroded.

'The wind is taking from the rock . . .' he said aloud that night as he was getting into bed.

He dreamed, later in the night, of the rocky shores of the world crumbling, the sea encroaching, land ebbing, and flowing out under the sea. In the dream all land was reduced until the planet's surface was sea. It had been a mistake to come on to dry land. Now all life would go back to the sea, to interminable watchfulness, endless violence, to the democracy of terror of the predatory deep.

He woke from the dream, holding it clear, still, in his eyes. He wrote on paper, 'The wind is taking from the rock', and went back to sleep.

At work he added more lines, and after work, in the mechanical hush of the library, made it into a sort of poem.

> *The wind is taking from the rock*
> *the seismic caves are shrill, still*
> *attrition takes no holidays.*
> *The cliffs diminish at the base.*
> *The past is a word, but no door*
> *the future: all remains unspoken.*
> *Heart-cracks probe the stone; time*
> *is brief before its certain end.*
> *The wind-gauge screams into the wind,*
> *grass bends that grows from buried minds.*
> *Pity the human irrelevancies*
> *that cram the world with busy lives,*

> cope with vast unknowns, forget
> the wind is taking from the rock.

He began another pile of papers, separate from his drawings and his idea-sentences, to include word-sketches and stories. On top he placed his little poem, with a mixture of brotherly pride and autocratic tenderness, which he detected, and which made him wonder if they weren't, perhaps, his children.

Certainly they were his thoughts, his work: part of him was alive while they were.

The Biggest Series to Date

In his drawings people appeared, doing and being some of the things he saw and thought about day by day. In one weekend he completed the biggest series he'd ever done.

He drew comments on ego in humans. A large lump of mankind was fed into a funnel at one end of a process, and out the other end came a mass of tiny copies, all of whom marched off in orderly ranks.

A variation of this showed humans coming out neatly packaged.

An extension of the idea had them coming out at the product end shaped for different uses: some as nails, some screws, some as marbles, gambling chips, buttons, tablets for the sick, food: still recognisably human in origin, but shaped for new uses.

He did a small series of drawings on History as something which became an active force; alive, even.

He showed it in successive drawings as: a globe, crushing individuals; a beast eating the human masses; a python swallowing whole columns of people; as a huge baby, rolling and helplessly crushing the tiny figures of differently dressed peoples of the world; as a bomb whose fuse is lit by idiots; a dinner at which the plates are full of those fattened up and about to be swallowed by history.

With a coming Olympic Games in the news, the idea of the podium took his fancy — the little box-like stand on which the winner, second and third place-getters stood to receive medals and applause. In his head was Ego, subject of a previous set of drawings, in which he had deflated the individual.

He drew the winners' stand with its one higher than two, two higher than three; the Olympic five rings bore the five characters of W W I I I; over to one side in the main part of the arena contestants aimed guns at each other, awaiting the starter's gun to begin firing. The winners' stand was empty, waiting for the place-getters.

He drew a cliff suspended above the void. Tiny footholes for climbers were recessed into the cliff; the climbers were, in spite of their own precarious positions, shooting at each other. Those hit, fell.

He showed winners' stands, and instead of the one, two and three he had in successive drawings, variations on My, Me, Mine; such as I am, I will, I shall; and Me, you, Them.

The petty rules and procedures at work frustrated and annoyed him; they were aimed at the slowest, most irresponsible and thoughtless employee and his behaviour.

Thinking of this, he drew a rubber stamp-cum-official seal. He showed it in four attitudes.

The first was a huge threat suspended over the world; the second as a bureaucratic battering ram aimed at the houses of citizens; in the third it was used as a personal weapon, as in a duel, or again a blackjack to flatten an enemy from behind; and last as the Secret Weapon, suitably packaged with propellant, motors and guidance system.

He'd have done more except other ideas beckoned.

At work, in the firm's factory area, rows of machines were attended by rows of assemblers and machinists, putting together electronic components for the retail market.

Davis Blood sometimes walked past a corner of this place, where the busyness of the workers was of a different sort from that in the general office. The lines of seated figures made an impression on him that he welcomed — because of its possibilities as a subject.

The Family Machine was a woman reminiscent of a poker or fruit machine; the man was the operator, and children tumbled out in the money tray.

The Education Machine was a large factory-like building, into which hordes of small children were fed. Large children came out the other end, with uniforms.

The Media Machine showed, under a sign GARBAGE IN GARBAGE OUT, the facade of a big apartment building, one wall removed. In the many rooms were television sets fed from a downpipe that looked remarkably like a sewer pipe. He didn't think of television programs as garbage, he accepted them. In the drawing he showed them as many thought and spoke of them, despite their viewing habits.

The Housing Machine showed groups of people, father, mother and children, who stood at regular intervals on blocks of land with little gardens and fences made, and trees planted; ready-made houses were suspended over their heads, ready to be lowered once the mortgage chains were in place.

The Conformity Machine I showed people going off in all directions, straining against cables attached to collars, held back like dogs in leashes.

Conformity Machine II was a large piece of equipment which churned out people in different groups. Out of one spout came military people, out of another public servants;

out of others managers, teachers, bankers, sportspeople, painters, musicians.

The Uniform Dress machines showed some people fitted into their uniform dress comfortably, some struggling, and others whom nothing fitted. He thought this drawing too weak, and crumpled it into a ball to throw away, then had second thoughts. Later he might think of a better treatment. He smoothed out the paper. It was now a network of wrinkles in a wonderful random pattern, and the sheet of paper smaller than it had been. It went on the pile, a reminder to him not to be hasty.

Dream of Orville's Death

He sat at the big table, the afternoon was outside. The sound made when he put his elbows on the table was the only sound. Head in hands, he dreamed.

Much older, he hurried along the narrow corridor of a hospital, which he now recognised: it was Happy Valley Hospital, where his appendix had been removed on his fourteenth birthday. He'd just visited Orville, pale and weak. On the way out past an open double-door, he snagged his leather jacket on the tongue of a Yale lock, but didn't stop. He made for his car.

A few days later, he was there again. A sign read: 'James Ward'. Orville was breathing shallowly for a time, then missed a breath. His hand lay cool and bloodless in Davis Blood's hand. Ten seconds passed, then with an indrawn sigh, Orville breathed again — quickly at first, as if to catch up. Gradually his breathing slowed again, and once more came to a halt. Next thing, he was dead, his last breath taken and expelled. His bottom lip and chin dropped a fraction and remained slightly open.

Davis Blood drew paper and pencil towards him, and made a poem-thing starting from his observation that some of the willow's summer leaves were still on the tree past mid-winter.

Orville's Tree
How faithful in summer are leaves of the willow tree
But the smallest are most faithful, clinging
Till the last memory of warmer days is gone.

This is the tree my brother planted, who now is gone.
Its leaves, veined as my flesh is veined,
Bear traces of days I can never forget.

Dead days litter the ground, forget
The branch they grew on. Numb in memory's net,
My days are lost in the fall of the last leaf.

Come back, sun, show me your first new leaf,
Another spring will grow from last year's death.
Life itself will outlive us all, my brother's tree!

He put this on the orderly pile in the cupboard in the mantelpiece, to work on later. He'd gone as far with it as he could go for the moment. When he looked back at its infelicities he could feel a tangle in his head.

Fresh from Gazing at Plants

Fresh from gazing at plants in the garden and his mother's new green curtains, he made a pastel of an interior looking outwards to the exterior. It showed green curtains and a large brown bottle, and, through the transparent windows, green plants growing in brown soil. He arranged the two greens and the two browns for a strong-weak effect: bottle and curtains strong, natural soil and plant-flesh softer; yet to him the softer colours were stronger.

He regarded this as an exercise. If he'd been asked why, he would have said the picture said nothing. He wanted to argue, to assert.

The sight he'd so often seen on the long journey to work, the four chimneys of the Old Power Station, he put into a pencil drawing, coloured it with colouring pencils, showing the four chimneys canted over, pointed like four howitzers with barrels smoking. All round was devastation.

Choosing what he thought of as a random method, he turned the pages of his mother's women's magazine. A pretty woman in a pool. He made her naked, reclining on nothing but the water. She was pneumatic, inflated and buoyant, sinking into the water only as far as inflated rubber would.

His daily work came into his head. The factory, where the assembly of parts was done. No, another factory, one he'd seen near where he worked, was better. He drew that: heavy machines stamping, milling, drilling, rolling steel, brass sheet, and other metals. Over on one side of the factory space, against the wall, he drew a line of four confessionals for the workforce. Industrial cathedral, he called it.

From his poetry anthology, he took Leda and the swan. Leda became a man; the great Auk had him in her talons, carrying him high in the air to her mountain eyrie, where chicks bigger than the captured man waited with open and terrible beaks.

Another bird came into his head, this time with human face; falling from the sky, wings trailing upwards as it fell. A case of wing failure. The human face showed panic in the face of certain death.

Back to that idea of confession which among the Dissenting Brethren was a personal thing, without priestly intermediary. He drew a series of four pictures of confessional booths. One was a laundry, one a betting shop, the third a sweet shop, the fourth a real confessional: a priest's head could be glimpsed inside it.

Birds again, a large bird swooping. Its friends, a large cloud of them diving down the air after it. This near bird, though, had a granny's face.

Things in animal shapes; animals and birds in human shapes. Why not other things with human shape? The curtains of the dining room, for example. He drew them, fabric falling in shapes that became graceful legs, an arm on the opposite curtains. The cushions on the sofa extended into the shapes of thighs. There was a face in the top ruffled part of the curtain. He called it the living house.

A Laborious Death

While he was at work in the city one day, his father was brought home from the Waratah War Veterans' convalescent hospital where he'd been for six months. Jackson Blood was put by himself into the boy's pale-blue room, that he'd inherited from Randal and Orville. Davis Blood slept on the verandah again.

The sick man sat in the kitchen a little each day for three days then stayed in the bedroom, making some effort to go back to his study of the New Testament, but unable to stick at it. Once he said to Davis Blood, 'I used to believe we were in the last days. Now I know it's just my last days.' He needed a lot of rest, but sometimes sat up in a chair, warmed by heavy woollen clothes, or wrapped in a blanket. He had no warmth of his own. Once, he remarked to his youngest son, 'This is just the beginning for this country. I was wrong. Thinking of last days is a mistake.'

Next morning, when the boy went in to say goodbye before running up the hill to the station, Jackson Blood was sitting up staring out of the window. He turned his head a little as his hefty sixteen-year-old son came in, then looked again out of the window at the little slice of world there.

'You know something, son? I'm Old Australia. On the way out,' he said with a smile, as if to say: don't worry about it.

'You're New Australia, my Seven States. You're full of vitality, with the capacity to be a great nation. You are liberty; you are the land; you are flood, drought, desert; you will welcome the visitors, the newcomers, the next Australians; you will love them all.

'You are star and child, harvest and open road, ocean and tree, city and pioneer, home and travel, Adam and democracy, song and sex, husband and baby. You are all nations in one.

'Do you understand any of what I'm saying?'

'Yes, Dad.'

'Good.' Pausing for breath.

'You're hope working like a spider repairing its web every day, fragile but never defeated.'

His voice came with difficulty, yet he sounded light-hearted as well as strangely passionate. Where were his usual spiritual thoughts? Were these concerns about his homeland in a sense religious? Or was he so confident in his God that he needed no sadness at the end of life?

He went on, less passionately, but more impressively, as if he wanted the boy to forget nothing of what he said.

'We are becoming an individual people. The powers inherent in us are forming. We have a future among the nations.

'The day will dawn when the true Australian — unassuming, direct, honest, tolerant, servant of no one — will be known most of all, as the brother and sister of all mankind: that sea of peoples, all different, all valued members of a family.'

He stopped, breathing hard. 'Now, off you go to work. The future's for you, not me. Get a move on. The years will pass like houses flashing past your train window.'

As the boy ran up Big Hill he remembered how his father said cheerfully, 'I'm on the way out.' He was dying game. They'd let him come home to be with his family a bit before he died. He remembered all the rest when he sat in the train, with trees, houses, shopping centres, factories, cuttings, flashing past the window.

Absurdly, it occurred to him that the family dogs and cats ought to be told, but perhaps the animals knew already.

Lillian sang aloud now, unless the man was sleeping. The boy went to work as usual Monday to Friday, and heard her voice before he went and when he came home. Often she was in there with him, Jackson Blood, singing.

> *Brief life is here our portion*
> *Brief sorrow, short-lived care.*

On Friday, the eighth day, his father lay down for the last time. When the boy arrived after having run down Big Hill, he found his mother on her knees beside his father's bed, her head on his chest.

As he stood watching, there came into his head the thought that perhaps if there were no structure to his parents' beliefs, no blood, no sacrifice, no atonement or resurrection, the process and its benefits would still be potent, given their basic faith and given a God that was part of what was outside, the non-self, exterior to the individual, part of the mystery of otherness. For the process resulted in love of others, kindness, forgiveness, doing as little harm as possible, absence of revenge, belief in change and newness, a measure of renunciation of material things and a prizing of things of the spirit.

His mother certainly loved everyone and everything, as far as he could see, except cruelty and hatred. She lived in harmony with others, without trying to dominate; she returned good for evil; she was content, kind, compassionate, forgiving, self-disciplined. He had never known her to be greedy, unsympathetic, to show hate, and rarely to lose her equanimity. Maybe selfless love comes easy to a mother, he thought wryly, for the catalogue of his mother's goodness seemed a formidable barrier of difference between her and a boy of sixteen.

How alert she must be, he thought, to jump on the bad things that arise from within, for he was aware of many such things in himself that rose up first and had to be battered down: in her they didn't seem to surface.

She must be more conscious of her inner workings than I am, he thought; she must be listening to her self all the time, and judging.

Part of her religion must be to try to be perfect, however impossible that was to achieve.

He stood in the doorway as she knelt over the dying man's bed. She didn't look up, but sang softly.

> 'When this passing world is done
> And has gone this glaring sun.'

The boy didn't go in. His father's breathing was laboured and loud, his eyes shut.

In the morning, Jackson Blood didn't wake, though he wasn't dead, but strenuously unconscious.

Aunt Olivine came on the Saturday. She prayed, and sang to her dying brother.

> 'And with the morn, those angel faces smile
> Which I have loved long since, but lost awhile.'

She joined Lillian in reading some of Jackson Blood's favourite passages from the Epistles to the Romans, and the Hebrews. They knew which they were, for he'd underlined them in red in his Dissenters' testament. Then they sang together,

> 'I heard the voice of Jesus say:
> Come here to me and rest
> Lay down, O weary one, lay down
> Your head upon my breast.
> I came to Jesus as I was,
> Weary, and worn, and sad.'

but by that time both were full of tears and couldn't go on.

The dying husband and brother breathed on, laboriously, dying hard. Next day an ambulance took him away to the War Veteran's Hospital.

A Cartoonist's Talent

It came into his head, after picking up a book of cartoons in his favourite city bookshop, to spend the weekend doing a series of mock-serious captioned drawings; starting off with the captions, then doing drawings to fit them.

'*It was a perfectly ordinary bear-trap,*' he wrote at the bottom of a fresh sheet. Where was it? In the spirit of the English-style description, he put the bear-trap on the croquet lawn.

'*It was the first earthquake he had ever witnessed.*' A golfer about to putt stood in amazement as the earth opened between him and the hole.

'*It was a large spider.*' It climbed drunkenly out of the punch bowl as members of the party clustered round with empty glasses and the hostess had a dipper at the ready.

'*His feet had grown.*' A mother looked in dismay at her baby's elongated feet poking well beyond the neat baby clothes. Amused and malicious neighbours looked on.

'*He was absolutely full of guts.*' An operating table; a team of surgeons held long strings of intestines up at arms' length above their heads. Still more were coming as one of their number pulled.

'*She wore her hair long.*' It streamed behind her for about five metres as she drove along in her red sports car.

'*She had lost a finger.*' She looked for it in the salad bowl.

'*Underneath it all, they were unbearably sad.*' They threw themselves around in a frenzy of mirth and merriment, party hats on, full and empty bottles and glasses everywhere.

'*Their spirits needed a lift.*' He drew a ring of old and sad people, dry and cobwebby with neglect, starved and skinny.

'*They were dead, quite dead.*' They were skeletons.

'*No one seemed to be home.*' Workmen had battered in the door, a crane lifted the whole house off its foundations.

'*But there was a house here.*' A party of bewildered visitors scratched their heads and looked vainly round for the house. All that remained was a series of raised marks in the plot of grass where the lines of house walls could be expected to be. A path of concrete led to where a front gate might once have been.

'*He attended to the washing-up.*' With a fire hose.

'*It was the most attention he'd had in years.*' It was his autopsy.

'*Only the bones were left.*' The skeletons of a child and a bullock lay on the ground. A fat and satisfied cat sat on a stump, regarding them sleekly as she attended to her toilette.

Of all the exercises he had given himself, this was the easiest. Illustrating a sentence or a phrase, he could see, was a limitless field for drawing, but it was a cartoonist's talent. He didn't think it would satisfy him for long.

Visiting Your Dying Father

The bus bound for the War Veterans' Hospital pulled up at a large intersection just outside the city. There, waiting for a different bus, was the brilliant Kulakovsky. Davis Blood's face opened in a silent gesture of admiring recognition of this boy who was so bright, so obviously marked out for big things, so fortunate in his well-off parents and his introduction at an early age to brilliant men and women among his family's intellectual friends.

His bus pulled away. The boy felt the quick gladness of seeing someone he admired, shame at having so openly been seen to be glad — it made him feel for a moment servile — and the feeling that endured as the bus went on towards his failed and dying father, that yes, of course, Kulakovsky would be waiting for a different bus, that was the way things were.

The rest of the journey he spent thinking of financial headlines he'd seen at the station:

IS CAPITAL UN-AUSTRALIAN?

DISASTROUS OUTFLOW.

Why not have a capital register, to record each citizen's holdings and dealings, in and out of the country? A capital register would show those who moved capital out and could be made public, he thought.

He was aware, though, that there were many shadowy rules, customs, agreements, and principals that neither he nor the public would ever know of: such important matters were arranged by those so powerful that no governments could oversee them. His little amateur ideas weren't likely ever to be adopted, no matter how sensible they seemed to him.

He sighed. He hated hospitals, though he was very curious about their inhabitants. He would soon know more.

Jackson Blood, one-time boxer, horse-breaker, soldier, circus trainer and insurance salesman, was dying in a white world where he knew nothing. He looked serene and untroubled. What he could see was in his head. He had no problems, nothing was in a bad way. He could now look on poverty, wealth, new life, disappointment and death with equanimity. All was beautiful and satisfying; he needed nothing outside himself. They tried to feed him and he did take some food at first, but very little. Davis Blood touched the right hand of Jackson Blood. It was cold. The once-tanned skin was white, the big fierce veins blue and shrunken. What was terrible was that he would never again feel the sun.

After the limits of pain, a white untroubled silence wrapped him round. The job that started in a jungle clearing full of fine spray, then of gasping, choking, and burning, was finished. At the end, Jackson Blood's version of the family's recurring dream — a tidal wave of blood —

was echoed in a large, free haemorrhage, after which he was empty of life.

They told the boy it would be better not to go and see.

What did his father feel? What was it like to die? Would he have a chance to grow to be a man before he, too, died? His father was a man, but would he ever be? Would he ever destroy the coward that he carried within himself? Would he ever traverse successfully the labyrinth in himself? Would he be condemned to the hell of beginning over and over again the acts he failed to complete? Was there a lesson to be learned from his father's death? He didn't know. There was no one he would have asked. Even if he could, one day, have been able to talk to Jackson Blood, he was now deaf forever.

He didn't like dwelling much on how he felt, and why he reacted as he did; it seemed like playing with himself, unnecessarily. There was nothing he could do but go home and tell the family. He went out into the street to catch a bus back to the station.

You Don't Have To

As he approached the steps that led down to the underground railway, an abandoned drink carton lay in his way. It had held strawberry-flavoured milk — a drink he detested for its sweetness. He aimed a kick at it, a kick that would carry it off the footpath into the gutter.

Unfortunately it was nearly full. His foot lifted the thing into the air and onto the street, where it smacked into the hubcap of a car and splashed its pink liquid generously around.

A little girl waiting for the traffic lights spoke to him, forcing him to stop and listen.

'You didn't have to do that,' she said.

He said, amused, 'It was asking to be kicked. What else could I do?'

'I don't know, but you didn't have to do that,' she said firmly. 'You could have done lots of things, I suppose,' she added wistfully, as if looking at a landscape of things he might have done. 'But you didn't think of them, did you?' she said in a forgiving tone.

'Guess not,' he said, and made for the down steps.

In the train he rested his elbow on a window ledge and the side of his face on his hand. This very railway carriage was designed by Verbruggen's father. Another reason to be proud. Roy would be a great engineer some day.

The little girl's words returned. You didn't have to, she said. Might it not equally be the case that he didn't have to be, or do, all sorts of other things?

His angers! What if he said to himself, simply: You don't have to be angry! — and the anger left him? What if he said to himself: Come on, now, you don't need to be unhappy! — and unhappiness went away? And if he said: You don't need to be uncertain! — and there was no uncertainty any more!

The rhythmic sound of the train wheels hitting the joints in the rails, that sound that had become so familiar over the years, was a perfect accompaniment to his thoughts.

What if he said to himself: You don't have to be poor, you don't have to be second, you don't have to be unknown and unnoticed, don't have to be obedient, don't have to be satisfied, or nice, or greedy, or easy on yourself, or sick, weak, scared or tired?

He could see that if, by admonishing himself like this, and accepting it, believing it, he could make these things work for him, he would be able to write his own ticket, to do anything. Equally, he'd be able to refuse anything. It was a discovery.

You don't-have-to, don't-have-to, don't-have-to sounded in his head in time with the noise of the train wheels.

He said to himself: You don't have to be angry. Straight away he felt a silent pacifying warmth spread within him, and a cheerfulness that, although it was his, was not always present lately. A burden had lifted.

He sat, amazed, in the train, as the familiar pattern of houses, parks, bridges, factories, cuttings rolled on past. He owed it to a chance remark, from a bossy little girl.

What if he never accepted the verdicts of others? What if he set his mind on the highest goal he could imagine?

At Bellbird Corner he ran home faster than ever before and arrived at the open front door puffing a little and bright-eyed. Thank you, little girl, he said silently.

Then stopped, still as a tree. It occurred to him, for the first time, that perhaps it wasn't the smoking of cigarettes that stopped his father from entering the circle of fellowship within the Independent Dissenters. What if it was a deep distaste for getting close to the people themselves?

He was probably close to God, Davis Blood thought, but he'd never known him seek to be close to the Independent Brethren. It was as if, while he respected their spirituality, he had little time for them as people. As if the people he respected were in the past, in the Army, on the road, in the ring: not those tame and careful people at the Meeting.

Or was it something better than that? Was it that he, in his own heart, would never, could never, consider himself worthy? That always he must remain at a distance, and never approach closer than the outer circle?

Perhaps that was it.

He brushed his hair back out of his eyes with his left hand, and went into the house.

'Hullo there!' shouted Aunt Mira. 'Here's Syndrome the Sailor back from the Sea. He's been having a faith lift! Quick! Take down his decretals and hit him in the genials! That'll sober him up!'

'Quiet, Mira,' said Lillian, and went to meet her youngest son.

It was all he could do to come back down from his thoughts in which he walked among mountains, to remember his father was dead.

'Dad's dead,' Mum.' Davis Blood said. His mother

nodded. The tears were for later. She went back into the kitchen and sat down at the big table. Just sat looking out of the window like he used to do.

'In the midst of life we are in Perth!' sang out Aunt Mira. 'That's your real Surfer's Paradox! As for this boy, the world is his cloister! Hullo, young larva! What's your midas operandi now? Are you still going to set the world aright? At the moment it's slop-shape and Borstal fashion! Go for it! You'll be famous in the anals of the time!'

'Shh!' said Ursula, annoyed. 'Be quiet!'

'Pax,' said Aunt. 'Pax contraceptive.' She revered no man, nor his memory, nor death. Death had taken from her all she had.

Such an Ordinary Thing

No one spoke for a while. The funeral was two days later. Forty-nine people turned up. Jackson Blood was forty-nine years old, plus one hundred and seventy-nine days. Davis Blood worked it out while Mister Gardiner spoke over the open and still empty grave. It was a hot day; the lumps of clay that had been turned up looked hard as bricks. Perhaps his father would stay dry, down there in that box, until heavy rain fell. It was January twenty-eight. He died on Australia Day.

The friends and relatives bunched around the open grave were, from above, a round cake of people, stuck solid in the unmoved afternoon. It was such an ordinary thing, that edge of earth dropping vertically out of sight, so trivial, so terrible that it was final.

The Burial of Jackson Blood

'That Jesus our Lord and Saviour of our poor brother, rose triumphant from the grave, is our surety that he defeated death and waits for each of those who will be saved. Our sins are gone, no charges ever to arise from them, since all are washed away in the flood of his blood. None can accuse those God has justified by faith in his son, none can condemn. Christ paid the ranson, the work of redemption is done, the victory over sin and death is won.

'Captivity itself is captive led since Jesus lives who once was dead.'

After a long, and, to the boy, awkward pause, Mister Gardiner began to sing. Most of the gathering joined in: Preston, Randal and Orville didn't. They hated the Meeting people.

> *Just as I am, without one plea*
> *But that your blood was shed for me.'*

They sang all the verses, the last ending with:

> *'Here for a season, then above*
> *O Lamb of God, I come!'*

Prayers followed, first by Mister Gardiner, then it was left open for any brother to pray who felt moved to do so. Two did, Mister Lichfield and Mister Rokeby. As they went on, it seemed, from the way their voices rose and fell, that they were over the next hill, the wind now carrying the sound back, now hiding it. They stopped.

The ensuing pause dragged on. The older Blood boys fidgeted; they'd never been back to the Meeting since they were tiny. They kept their heads bent a little, in respect, and eyes open, looking at the trodden grass and the indomitable ants.

The boy could feel the silence was about to be broken by

Mister Gardiner, when a familiar voice said, 'I'm going to sing now.'

It was Lillian. Mister Gardiner and the other active members of the Independent Dissenting Brethren looked alarmed, as if a blasphemy had been proposed.

'The sister —' he commenced unevenly.

'The sister will sing to her husband,' Lillian stated with that gentle insistence that Davis Blood knew concealed her steely determination.

'Sisters must not be heard!' Mister Gardiner said urgently. He looked round, panicky. Others supported his distress with worried looks and agitated, but curtailed motion of hands, or shifted feet. They didn't know what to do. Hadn't St Paul given clear directions to Timothy in the first century AD?

'It's not permitted for sisters to speak in public. Especially sisters not admitted to the circle of fellowship,' Mister Lichfield said in a low, urgent voice.

'Nevertheless,' said Lillian. 'I will sing. Now!'

> 'Are you weary, weak, exhausted,
> Are you sore distressed?
> Come to me, says One, and coming
> Be at rest.'

The Meeting people, with bowed heads, prayed urgently. This was the most serious breach of protocol, of spiritual order, they had encountered. Discipline had always been easy, among this serious, timid flock.

> 'Are there signs to lead me to him
> If he is my guide?
> In his hands and feet are wound prints
> And his side.'

The Meeting sisters looked at her in horror, the relatives, young and old, with interest. Lillian held her head up, as if Jackson Blood was no longer down there on the ground, waiting for his coffin to be lowered in the clay hole.

*'If I find him, if I follow
What's my reward down here?
Many a heartbreak, many a sorrow
Many a tear.'*

Mister Gardiner, face red with anxiety, signed to his fellows to help him lower the coffin into the ground, to get it over quickly. They began. Randal, Preston and Orville pushed in. They were determined to do the honours. The Meeting elders wouldn't shift.

*'If I ask him to accept me
Will he turn away?
Not till earth and not till heaven
Pass away.'*

Randal began to shift them. He got hold of one rope, and Preston grabbed the other, handing an end to Orville.

*'If I hold to him forever
What will be at last?
Sorrows vanquished! Labours ended
All tears past.'*

Lillian sang, steadfastly. Randal and Mister Gardiner at one end, Preston and Orville at the other, lowered Jackson Blood's used and now useless human clay into the clay hole. Lillian sang to his spirit, which had separated from that decaying shell. Davis Blood watched, fascinated, gripped by the thought that some of God was in that coffin, to be buried in wood and clay which also contained God.

*'Finding, following, striving, keeping,
Is he sure to bless?
Saints, apostles, martyrs, Christians,
Answer: Yes!'*

Lillian's voice ceased. The silent, furious battle over the grave had ended. Jackson Blood's body lay in the shiny maple coffin at the bottom of his neat machine-dug grave. Lillian still had her head in the air, as if she expected a reply, an echo.

No echo came. Mister Gardiner and the rest of the Meeting people left quickly. Family and friends remained.

Davis Blood didn't take his eyes from his mother's face. He was proud of her. He wasn't surprised at her inner strength, he knew how strong she was. All those years of talking and listening to God; those long years of holding up her family to God in prayer, for his infusion of strength and blessing; years of being so close to him that often she didn't need to kneel to speak to him, though the boy knew that, in the privacy of her room, she did kneel: all those years of strengthening herself in God had given her a spiritual force no humans could shake.

Watching her, it came to him that though, deep inside, he felt he was much the same person as he'd been when he was a little boy — yet he'd changed, changed a lot — Lillian had never changed, as far as he could see. His father was dead, though some of his teaching remained with the boy. His mother was alive, and more than her teaching was alive in him. Something of her self, her wise example, her love, her patience, her steadfastness and, he hoped, her sheer strength, lived in him, and would stay alive in him all his life, perhaps to be passed on to others he would help create, perhaps also to live in the work he would do for the world, whatever that would be.

Premonitions

He climbed the wooden stairs to Donleavy's Gym, changed into his boxing gear, and came out onto the wooden floor of the gym, amid the smell of sweat and stale air. Pictures of old Jock, fading newspaper clippings, creased posters of fights and fighters of long ago were stuck round the walls. He loosened up, skipped, and went through set punches and blocks with McNamara, his regular partner, then worked on the heavy bag. He practised his jab and hook, then concentrated on the hook, getting the left hand to the bag at his best speed — he was southpaw — and taking it back into position as quickly as he knew how. He was getting a real snap into that punch.

Next he did the same with his jab — speed up and speed back. Until he had to yield the bag to one of the other boys waiting.

He skipped for fifteen minutes, then went over by a window to cool down. Even the smell of traffic was a relief after the gym's much-breathed air. He stood, arms relaxed by his side, watching two boys sparring in the ring.

On the journey home he saw himself, much older and bigger, at Lillian's bedside. It was a nursing home on the North Shore, his mother dying after several strokes. Orissa visited, standing quietly. He bent by the dying woman as her breathing stopped awhile, resumed with a sigh, stopped again.

Danielle, a married woman and looking annoyed, said: 'Do you want to catch her very last breath?'

She didn't understand. He had to be there when his mother left. She had none to sing for her, whose life was filled with song.

He took pencil and paper from his boxing bag, and began a poem-thing, finishing it at home before he had tea.

It was an attempt to convey what he felt as Lillian's breathing stopped for the last time.

> HEARTSEA
> *The air is a sea, and the sea is all*
> *Around me. Branches of trees move,*
> *Expand then blow in on themselves*
> *In currents that spin me and press my thought*
> *Into strange shapes. Like clutching hands,*
> *Brown sea fronds grow small*
> *Then fill with an undersea wind.*
> *The strange sea flowers are quite still,*
> *Unable to move in the thick*
> *Coldness beating at my heart.*

He put the sheet in the cupboard. Lillian was sitting in the kitchen, her face turned towards the slice of world seen through the leaves of the camphor laurel. He said:
How will I know myself
When you are gone?

Random Impulses

In the yard at home he picked a dandelion seed-head that was intact, its fluffy ends spherical. He held it up and blew. Most of the seeds scattered. The light breeze blew them east; he turned in that direction and was fascinated to see, as he had seen so many times but never tired of marvelling at, that they fell to earth seed-first, the fluffy parts like parachutes, letting them down slowly, gracefully. The seed would perhaps spear into soft earth, one in a thousand might drop into a crack in the soil, the crack close with a shower of rain, and there would be another dandelion plant on the way. Most, he knew, were lost and came to nothing.

Back at the drawing table, he drew a sky full of raining animals, each with a dandelion seed held aloft like an umbrella, to make a soft landing.

When he was done, and putting out more paper for the next drawings, his thoughts travelled back into the yard where he'd picked the dandelion seed-head. The long grass, the ground sloping away in successive stages to the lowest part of the valley, the steep roads out of the valley bottom, the wooded ridge on Gunsight Hill, the few rooftops, the afternoon sun glancing off the shiny, hard-skinned gum leaves — there were bits of the world all round him, so beautiful it was hard to imagine the greatest of artists painting pictures worth comparing.

He followed the random impulses that came into his head, this time in the form of words: each time a phrase caught his attention, he found there was a picture in it.

It was October, the dynamo of spring was powerful in him: it seemed to bring a great energy.

In a burst of activity between the second and the twelfth of October he produced things which he knew were brash and arrogant, that epitomised the seething state of his imagination.

He drew street scenes. A leg appeared round a corner ahead of a body; he showed just the leg. And so, with other parts of the body.

He drew a girl with a mirror, examining every line of her face, each spot, each crack and crevice. The same with her shoulder, hunting for pimples.

He depicted a fowl in the luxury of white sheets and flowered pillowcases; a giraffe with the breasts of a woman; a man suspended by hooks in his skin; a horde of huge insects devastating a human city and consuming its people. This last was divided into two sections: in one the insects ate the meat of the inhabitants and left the bones, in the other it was reversed, with piles of loose meat left, and the bones eaten.

Also in this series he had a human baby roasted to a fine brown colour, with a small flower in its cooked mouth. He did pictures of humans with objects protruding from their bodies: knives, arrows, lizards; a person with two skulls painted on his contact lenses; a breathing tree, the tree of life; sketches of trees such as the carnation tree, the petunia tree; a picture called The Enraged Bride, the cause of her rage not being shown; a human built of building blocks layered upwards in a way that looked as if he was a city being constructed, with a network of scaffolding spidered round him; a calm green garden, formally laid out, with a scene of ferocity taking place in it. He drew the sea coming up Pitt Street in Sydney; the heads of two people cut off and stitched, one to the sofa, the other to the owner's stomach; a savage human brutally biting into the brain of a child; a collage of buildings; a horse with a stream of clay leaking from its hind leg and gathering to a pool by its hoof.

There was a life in these drawings, charcoals and pastels that hadn't been in his work before. He worked more quickly.

Still he was dissatisfied. Everything seemed easy. But in the back of his mind the conviction was growing that these things were beside the point, somehow. Was it that they weren't serious in an artistic sense? Was it that he felt no idea could be pictured, or realised in physical form? For instance, how many pictures, or words, for that matter, were necessary to show war, or love, hatred or peace? Such words were voids into which millions of words and pictures could be poured, yet they would never be filled.

Synovitis

At the gym for several weeks, his instructors had been away, and he'd taken as much time as he pleased on the heavy bag, working on his combination punches, getting his hands back into position immediately, but in those punches really letting himself go, planting his fists into the bag as if into a torso, putting all his weight behind the work.

At the office he noticed his left arm made a noise when he flexed the wrist. For a while it amused him, then in a lunch hour he took himself off to the outpatients department of the nearest hospital. The young doctors there — not much older than he was — told him he'd pulled the muscle on top of his forearm out of its synovial sheath. They bound an aluminium splint to his arm and told him to keep the wrist straight and still for a month.

For the time being, boxing was out. He'd like to have asked his father about this sort of accident, but his father was dead. None of his brothers boxed; they wouldn't know.

Doors had opened; he had looked several times into a larger brilliant world inside him, a vivid, clear world that he felt was made from his perceptions, and therefore ideally suited to him. Understanding was there. All that was needed was to live close to that world and to visit it often. In there, his capacities were extended to the full: big things were demanded of him. It was far from the simplicities of earning enough to feed himself. Soon, when his Voice chose, he would know how he was to live his life.

To be doing something valuable, something necessary: that was it!

He took the splint off in order to draw, and after three weeks abandoned it.

The New Testament

His dead father's New Testament lay with Davis Blood's books on the table in his room. Lillian had portioned out some small momentoes of her husband among the children: Davis Blood asked for the Testament, with its red-edged pages, black leather binding, gold letters.

Last thing at night he picked up the slim book, turning it over in his hands. It hadn't been noticed before, but inside the back cover were some folded sheets of thin paper. Davis Blood took them out, unfolded them, and read his father's small, precise handwriting with its long flourishes and large capital letters:

'We are ready to receive a new vision
Of what we are
What Australia will be
Into the future.
Australia is a beginning
A new song, a poem, a sculpture
The latest volume in the book of life
A new-born work of art, a new dream
A fresh start in the life of mankind.

'Australians are a fresh start, too, in the personality of mankind with their decency, good nature, common sense, fair play, good humour, lack of pretence, equal respect for poor and rich, their casual attitude to themselves and comfort, lack of taste for pomp, lack of time for the past, lack of a paralysing aristocratic tradition: with their generosity, ingenuity, resourcefulness, their ability to make do.

'A new dream is waiting for the world.
A new life waiting for mankind,
In which each person will be usual and unusual,
Average and extraordinary, democrat and king,
Worker and thinker, lover and breeder,
Commanding and diligent, active and contemplative
Serving and served, Adam and Einstein.
Each will welcome strangers,
Cherish all that is varied,
Different, marked out strangely,
Wayward, independent;
Tolerant of all but intolerance
And cruelty; fond of faint paths
That lead off into wilderness.
Each will be part of a family.
Each will know kindness, show kindness,
Extend a hand to raise all that fall,
Feed the hungry,
Forgive all but forget nothing;
Remember all living things are persons,
All active systems are alive.

'Australians,
to you is given the job of transforming yourselves.
You are to make yourselves into what your land can use.
In transforming yourselves, you will create Australia.

'The desert, fragile emptiness
Is your first test:
That tense silence, full of things unseen
And dark ghosts walking soft-footed over the land.
You are to cross the blue ridge
You are to go west to that land
You will watch and listen to it
Let it talk to you
Write what it says.

That land says: Here I am. Use me.
What will you do?
What you do with the land, desert, silence,
And those dark ghosts: that is your test.
You will stand or fall by that.

'Australia is the self in which you live.
The desert is in you.
The silence, the emptiness, the dark ghosts
Of the aboriginal past
The mountains to cross
The points of the compass:
All are in you.'

A smaller sheet contained only a few lines.

'There's a secret within our land, but we can't unlock it yet. Something's there, so plentiful that when we can open it, rearrange and transform it, one human need will be met for ages to come. It will transform the inventory of human needs. I pray my youngest son sees it happen.'

As he'd been reading his father's words he was aware that Lillian, not wanting to distract his attention, had silenced her song. Instead, even, of humming, she sang within her head, two fingers of her right hand tapping on the timber table top in time to the tune.

He looked away as he finished, and watched her. She gazed out of the windows, through the branches of the tree, just as Jack had done. Davis Blood followed the rhythm of the two fingers, and worked it out. He smiled.

As if she felt the smile in the air between them, she turned her head. When she saw the smile she smiled in return.

'Well?' she asked.
'I know what you're singing, Mum!'
'Do you, Davis?' The fingers didn't stop.

' "I need you every hour",' he quoted.
'Yes! How did you know?'
'Your fingers tapped it out.'
She looked down at them. They were still going. Then they stopped, and prevented there, the words of the last verse came out of her mouth:

> *I need you every hour*
> *Teach me your will*
> *And your rich promises*
> *In me fulfil.*

He got up and turned away, annoyed by the tears that welled in his eyes. How many times had he heard that loved voice sing those words? He gathered up the papers in a businesslike way.

Lillian began the final chorus, and resumed her watch.

Why did Jackson Blood feel so strongly about his seven states and its deserts? To his son it seemed reasonable enough that people who came from Britain, and never more than 100 miles from the sea, should settle on the coasts of Australia, which had no great broad-river system capable of navigation into its heartlands, as America, Russia, China and Europe had. The continent itself was the most eroded of the inhabited continents, with little good land. What was his father driving at? Perhaps it was the image in his words: Australia is the self in which you live.

Sour Dream

Davis Blood put his father's testament back
inside the cover of the book, and went to bed. Towards
dawn he dreamed a bad dream in which the future had
turned sour:
Australians became mean-spirited,
good nature turned to passivity, apathy;
vaunted fairness was confined to friends;
casualness became indifference,
making-do became carelessness;
good humour had become black, then malicious.
Equal respect was gone, they grovelled to the rich
and famous in the name of success and envy;
used their ingenuity in the service of sloth;
cut short the labour of invention for a little comfort.
The young spoke of ease, travel, holidays.
Luxuries became necessities; giving was replaced
by taking, need became greed.
Their most miserable trait permeated every part of
the life of the country: they were serious
about nothing but being trivial — and ensuring
others were trivial too.

The Promise

He woke, threshing about in a tangle of bed-clothes. Was this the reality? It was bad enough to be true. A dark cloud of fear came down on him.

But the Voice said:

> Detach yourself, and listen to me —
> You are chosen, you are necessary.
> Leave your soft self; abandon normal comfortable life:
> Death lies that way. Follow me,
> Into loneliness cold as mountain tops,
> Embrace the whole world.
> For you freedom lies in obedience.
> Come where I lead you.
> I will make you into a great idea.
> I will sustain you and spread your mind
> Over the earth.
> I will make your name known,
> The mention of it will lift people up.
> All your life you will know I am with you.
> You will trust me, and I will protect you.
> You will have implicit faith in me
> And that will be your great virtue,
> That faith will be your morality,
> Your most valuable possession
> And always, what I tell you to do, you will do.

He settled back on the pillow. Loneliness. So he was to be an outsider still. Through the years something had pushed those boyhood friends and potential friends away. Whatever he was meant to do, he would never have what Kulakovsky, Verbruggen, Peters and King, Pye, Petersen and Yeo, would have: a normal settled existence with comfort, holidays, friends, superannuation, promotion within a career structure, and the rest of that packaged, predictable life.

As he went to sleep it occurred to him that he had no envy and no thought of anything but obeying his Voice.

Death in the Afternoon

It was his last Friday at work before he went on his first annual holidays from Pacific Television. In the lunch break he'd had an idea for another poem-thing. This one was so much on his mind that he went straight to the library after work, and began it there in the crowded anonymity of the studious.

He was much older than when he dreamed Lillian's death; he was a heavy-set man in a large suburban backyard. It was his own death.

> *The little dog with silver silky hair*
> *Waits for me to chase him.*
> *I cannot.*
>
> *The misconnected pump gabbles*
> *Draining the sunken swimming pool.*
> *Water spreads in a wide circle*
> *Wasting on the grass.*
> *I cannot move.*
>
> *The sun stands low, almost gone,*
> *I am greedy for that last bit of warmth.*
> *My daughters with the brown eyes call*
> *To me to catch, return, their many-coloured ball.*
> *They throw, the ball is in the air.*
> *I cannot move an inch.*

Little dog, someone else will chase you,
The sun my life will wait no longer.
The sputtering electric pump is draining me,
My transparent blood wastes on the grass,
The daughters of my heart stretch out their hands, but I,
I cannot move an inch to say goodbye.

He put the poem-thing on its own small pile of papers, and on an impulse, measured the height of his treasured pile of drawings. 166 millimetres.

The Exhibition

He chose a public holiday to go to the Sydney Art Gallery for an exhibition of paintings. He arrived early, but even so there was a queue. He hated queues. To stop himself getting angry, he half-closed his eyes and held his head down to shut out the miserable sight of people in a line. In that attitude he reflected on his own drawings, on the coming sights in the gallery, and on his future, which often seemed to stretch only as far as the end of the next working week, after which — darkness.

He soon tired of thinking about his own concerns, and began to wonder about the mainly French paintings he was to see, the pleasure of looking right at the very canvases the artists had worked on, and how they set about finding subjects to paint, the question that had bothered him for some time. He'd looked through all the books of prints he could find in the city bookshops, and had no answer.

How did they choose? How did they select what to paint next? He didn't know; but now he suspected they didn't know either. Something occurred to them, came into their heads out of the blue, and they called it inspiration, and of course it was. But where was their control, their volition? Was their sheer ability all they cared about, the ability to do anything that presented itself?

Why did it matter? he challenged himself. Because how they chose the next work showed their grasp of what they were doing, showed they were doing something they'd thought about and had to do.

Perhaps one could be a painter, and have life push one here and there, and helplessly paint whatever was near, whatever one could see, but he thought there ought to be more to it than that. If a painter had a new vision, a new technique, it seemed all right to test it on the nearest objects; or if there was one subject that obsessed the painter, then the subject choice was made: the next treatment of it was then the important choice. But after that, surely there were some things in the world so important they had to be painted.

If, as Mr Cummings once said, the world was living in a golden age of mathematics, where was the reflection of it in painting, in sculpture? Where were the artistic echoes of astronomy, the new biology? Where was the artistic vision large enough to pass from atoms to stars, elementary particles to galaxies? Where were the artists able to stand back from the world and see it as a whole, to grasp in their hands and minds the range of human knowledge and experience? Why did they seem not to share his own awe, his wonder at the world?

On a more domestic level, where were the continuing artistic treatments of sports? Certainly there were some, notably horse-racing and hunting. But there were many sports played by the people as well as the rich. Was art the servant of wealth?

Where was youth, with all its glowing emotions, its many colours and moods? Where were the varieties of children, where the sick, the poor, the spendthrifts, the workhorses of the world? Where were the world's varieties of work, and workplaces?

What he'd seen of the output of venerated artists was casual, too casual in its treatment of the world, almost indulgent. Where was a thorough examination of joy? Of happiness? Of old age? The misery of unrequited caring? Where were the faces of guilt, of violence, of shame and defeat? It was all so random, so accidental. There was no exploration of the world.

Perhaps that was the thing that ate at him: he wanted system, thoroughness. Yes, he said to himself, shuffling forward in the queue, art should approach the condition of science — that part of science that discovered and explored, as well as that which catalogued — rather than the fecklessness of holiday snapshots. There should be research, development; the same seriousness with which humans approached mining, biology, particle physics, investment, games. Yes, if he were a painter, that's how he'd approach painting. He'd turn it upside down and shake it: he'd rub their noses in the trick of the new.

The queue had moved him up the steps and into the gallery, cutting short his reflections. It hadn't taken so long, after all. It was silly to get angry about such things. He'd forgotten to say, 'I don't need to get angry,' and kicked himself for the omission. He paid his money and went in.

He took a quick look round the exhibition gallery. He'd never seen these works face to face, though some he'd seen in reproductions. He stopped before the first painting, a small still life: part of a table, a carafe, a bowl, and three pieces of fruit.

Why were they painted in this way?

The richness of the colours; the thick, uneven, but oddly poetic outlines: what had the painter seen, what happened inside him, that he made this harmony from those few common objects? Was this an interpretation of matters inside him? Or, and this was a new thought, did this painting contain the wider feelings of the painter about the world, when confronted by those things? Perhaps so.

There was no question here of lack of sincerity, he thought, with the newspaper article in mind. Then he smiled, remembering Van Gogh and his perspective frame, teaching himself perspective only eight years before he died. Perspective wasn't the point in this painting, at least not that sort of perspective. There was an emotional perspective; it was of warmth and love for these objects.

He looked at the carafe, the fruit, the bowl, his eyes going constantly from one part of the painting to another. Crowds of people swirled around him. He saw no one. He tried to get into that painting, to enter that scene, to swim in it, to breathe its air, to be part of it and to make it part of himself.

Slowly, creeping into his mind, a light began to spread over all his thoughts; a clarity illuminated him from within his own head. The painting of the carafe, bowl and fruit was being transformed. Then — he saw it! He could see! The painter had put something else into it. This painting wasn't just an imitation: it was much more. It was its own world. It could all be different, unusual, wrong, unacceptable, one might not agree with it; yet this was a world, with its own laws. It wasn't a world he'd like to live in, but in that painting everything cohered; it was right, within itself.

If he, Davis Blood, had drawn those objects, he knew what they'd look like. Yes, they'd look like faithfully rendered objects, clearly outlined, correctly proportioned, but that was all.

The objects in the painting seemed to rely on each other; the table depended on the fruit, the bowl, carafe, and so on in an interlocking dependency. There was a wholeness about it that didn't leave you thinking about the rest of the table or the other objects in the room. This was the whole of it, no more was needed.

In a powerful sense, this was the artist and this painting was a work of art, not because a gallery director said so, not because people queued to see it like sheep waiting to be dipped or crutched, but because this table, this carafe, this bowl, this fruit were another world. They'd been created, not imitated; a new world had been begun by the painter, a new world that had come out of the artist. It was part of the artist, not merely a hand-painted photograph. It was as if that artist had built a house of a kind that had never existed before, and made the bricks himself. Having made it with himself in it, with much that was new and hadn't existed before, the artist was, in a way, on show, up for inspection: fully responsible for what he'd done. If he'd merely copied, or imitated, his responsibility would be less, and some of it shared by the objects.

Yes, he thought, this painting was a step into a new world, where objects existed in that form, with those colours. Yet once seen, and taken into him for assimilation, those forms, those colours were immediately part of that growing world in his, Davis Blood's, head, formed by the accretion of all he had seen and taken into himself up to that point. What's more, it now seemed a natural part of his inner world.

He'd never thought this way before about a painting; nor had he ever seen fruit, furniture and crockery in this way. In future he would see these things differently. His way of seeing had been changed.

But what was that thing that the painter had put into the painting that made it so different from an imitation of the objects, or a photograph? He guessed that somehow the painter had pulled something out of himself — some element of feeling, of insight, of love — and soaked the painting in it. Or perhaps the painting came from within him already impregnated with it, whatever it was, a kind of essence of the artist.

He closed his eyes, alone in the whirlpool of excited people, and dredged deeply into himself for a way of putting it clearly. Back he went, in time, to geometry and his humiliation over axioms. In a sense, the painter's axioms — the flat planes, straight lines, the points with position but no magnitude — on which his geometry, the painting, was built, were the collection of qualities: understanding, insight, love for the objects of the world, feeling for harmony, that were contained in the painter; products of his experience, ability and innermost nature; the world in his head. But what that was, in detail, Davis Blood couldn't tell.

How much would he have to see, to experience, before he was able to put the essence of himself into a painting? How much would he have to paint before he, too, saw ordinary things in a way no one had seen them before? Or at least, before he painted and presented them in a way no one had painted them before? For he was not so simple as to imagine that any finished work was necessarily how those objects had been seen. Maybe it was, but only maybe. He'd been drawing long enough to know how the accidental, the missdrawn line, with its unforeseen emotional impact, the misplaced emphasis, awkward curve, can be seen suddenly to be something new or to lead to something new. It was an opportunity, and at such a moment the hand and eye are opportunist and don't blush to take credit for a lucky outcome and build on it.

Yet, it seemed to him that he lacked something this painter had: a spring, a source he didn't understand, an ability to translate his own feelings and emotions into colour and the harmony of design this painting showed, an ability to be original in paint.

He stood concentrating, trying to imagine himself making the same step the artist had made, in making this from objects like those, in a world in which they'd never been seen before like that.

He went further, gathering himself up into a ball of intense concentration: he tried to imagine what he would make of the same subject that was as different from this painting as this painting was from the original table, carafe, bowl and fruit.

Long he tried, forcing himself, until sweat stood out on his face; until his body, under the clothes, was wet.

He couldn't.

Again, he pictured to himself the way he'd have painted these objects. They'd be dead, he decided, objects in a waxworks, corpses mimicking life, for he had nothing to bring to them but an eye and an accurate hand. The painter's truth about those things was in this painting, not in Davis Blood's accurate lines. Here was warmth, understanding, harmony, richness, unity.

He knew in that instant, with terrible force, just how much he lacked. He had nothing in him to bring to that carafe, that bowl, those pieces of fruit, that portion of table, to transform them in the way this artist had done, to make of them a whole in colour, design, and newness.

Painting was not for him.

The Central Statement

Time passed. He stood in the same spot. His thoughts ran ahead. His questions of the past few years had been answered. It was no longer a matter of how painting got from Corot and Constable to Cézanne, from Renoir to Picasso: it was a question of differing personalities, of the creativeness of different painters. The times were different, the world different, but the central fact was the creative urge and its expression.

Perhaps it didn't matter that the painters seemed to lack system, it might be a necessary lack, but the ones that survived from the past didn't lack creativity. It seemed to him that once the creativeness of the artist had formed a new world, even in such a simple thing as a picture of part of a table, a carafe, a bowl and three pieces of fruit, that was all that was needed. The central statement was not fruit or furniture or crockery, but the artist and creativeness itself, and the new world that resulted from them. One painting would do.

His earlier concern about the apparent randomness of painters' subjects vanished. It no longer mattered that not every corner of the world was systematically explored. If all you wanted was copies, representations, you'd need the entire world represented, but if it was the spirit of the painter, the special gift, the creativeness, all you needed was that one painting. Once a painting was done that way, anything else could be seen in that light. The first one to that vision was a model for the rest to follow, and for the next artist to build on or shy away from.

The painter's reaction to and comment on the varieties of earthly experiences, on the world's objects, on social and political matters, was within the work, but not necessarily in its subject matter: it was in the fact of that person's creativeness that shone out from it. Creativity, intellectual insight and love of the world, was the message.

It meant, he thought as his thoughts raced ahead again, that the world was open to all, given the urge and effort and imagination that went to make creativeness; open to be changed: new worlds were waiting to be created. Ideally perhaps, each person was capable of producing his own art; perhaps this was the democracy of opportunity that he'd heard behind the words of his idealistic teachers at Archerfield. Whether they did so was up to the individuals who had this life-giving, life-extending urge.

He shook his head.

'It's not for me,' he said aloud, and wasn't embarrassed. 'I haven't got that sort of originality.'

But how did he know it might not flower in the future? Was there something else in him that wanted to see his first love dead, so that it, the late comer, might force itself on his attention and take over his energies?

The Forking Paths of Fashion

He made himself move round the gallery and see the rest of the exhibition. He stood before paintings that moved him, that gave him delightful feelings of pleasure, that filled him with admiration, and, one or two, with wonder; paintings that he liked much more than his carafe and fruit. He brought his new eyes to each, but his attention was no longer so fierce, so tenacious, so hungry. He was gorged.

Some of the conversations around him left stray words and phrases with him, where before he'd heard nothing but noise.

Some were 'theory', 'figuration', 'selling their souls to commerce', 'arts bureaucracy', 'decline of the individual', 'curators create artists', and, the one that struck Davis Blood with force: 'each new fashion changes faster than preceding ones'.

Fashion changes. Fashion. Yes.

At that point he stopped listening and began thinking. That was one thing he'd thought about, but he'd been hindered by thinking of the 'steps' from the older painters to the more recent, in the way those transitions had been presented to him. He hadn't considered that that very point might be full of nothing, worthless. He'd tried to see some progress, some superiority, in later work because that's how it was presented in books, reviews, histories. Later was better, more advanced; progress was being made merely by time passing; the past was stale and second-rate.

But that way of thinking was wrong! Each new movement or fashion wasn't a step forward, it was a new fashion.

This later body of work wasn't superior to that earlier one: it was a different fashion, that's all. Why were these sequences represented as progress, as some sort of journey towards something? Each fashion was simply a spur road leading off the main highway and coming to a natural end.

The main highway, of course, was the core of individuals with new approaches, fresh feelings for the world and the material, new insights into the work of the artist. And that work wasn't going anywhere! Like its creators it was drifting in time towards something called the future, for want of a better word.

The only place it was going was along its natural line of development in the hands of the artists who developed it, to its natural death when they died, or lost interest, or the idea seemed drained of energy.

And was highway the right word? It seemed to him that

not only was there no vanguard: there couldn't be. The people doing the daily work of art were fragmented off from others, separate: with separate aims, different methods; a mass of people flying apart in all directions — oblique, tangential, opposite — making their own paths or travelling on paths others had made. There was no coherent front to such a mass, therefore no vanguard.

Why had the adult world used the word 'progress'? Because dealers, galleries, teachers, makers of books, historians, needed to believe that since this came before that, this led to that. All in the cause of neatness, so they and the public had something simple to grasp. All nice and tidy, so proles and buyers of art could feel there was a meaning; so students could write essays on it, lumping the inchoate mass of art works together as a subject.

And there was no meaning. That mass of work, that historic record, was an aggregation of individual sensibilities, of highly personal work, of private geometries built on axioms made, not found.

Each new fashion wasn't a step forward at all, just a branch road which might peter out, or carry on, or be added to later. It might even hark back to a previous fashion, and itself be a further few steps down a spur road begun before: a road at an angle to all other roads.

A Head Full to Bursting

The hubbub in the gallery became deafening as the intensity of his thinking passed and he looked round at the people, the paintings. He felt dizzy. The throng was too much for him; their excitement, together with the colours, the shapes, the variety of the paintings, overwhelmed him. He left the gallery.

His head was full, almost to hurting, with the mass of things he had seen, but more, with words and feelings that teemed and barged about inside him, colliding and quarrelling and calling attention to themselves; all shouting at once. Words, words! — a chaos of words.

He walked in the Botanic Gardens, but got no relief. He hurried out of the Gardens. The cliff of business buildings across Macquarie Street seemed more like the boundary of a stockade than ever. He ran downhill through the half-empty streets, to the station, to get away from the city quickly. Perhaps the train noises would overcome the noises in his head.

In the train he sat back. The carriage was nearly empty. What was he doing here? Why was he alive, a person with his mixture of traits and talents? Did others have their heads full to bursting sometimes? With words of all shapes and sizes, words with labels and without, heavy words, light words, brilliant fire-cracker words.

He tried to set out his thoughts on the long train journey, but by the time he got to Bellbird all that had happened was that the noises and feelings filling his head had quietened a little.

What was he? What would his life be? He got off the train ready for the run home. He didn't think his life would be concerned with having power over others in any obvious way. He felt he didn't have enough practical goodness, enough wisdom in him, enough concern for what they did, to be over others. Until today he'd thought he might be a painter. His mother had once hoped that he'd become a singer, because of his beautiful boyhood voice, but now he knew that to be just a mother's fond hope. He ran up the overhead steps. Maybe his life would consist of watching and listening — he was good at those things — but there had to be more to it. Why couldn't he see what it was? How could he force back the darkness hiding what he had to know? When would he discover it?

Yet. The light he needed was in him. Already there. All he had to do was enter, search, discover.

He ran lightly down the steps and all the way home.

On the last leg of the run down Big Hill, with its ruts and rocks, a funny thing happened in his head. He was once more that little self of seven, vowing to get even with the Papworths and Downies; then, without noticeable transition, was fourteen and coming home from sports day looking forward to a meeting with Ginger Lip in a ruck in a return match, so he'd have a chance at face-stamping. And all the time he was his larger self of sixteen running headlong down Big Hill, surefootedly from rock to rock, ridge to ridge.

He laughed a short, explosive 'Ha!' He would probably never see any of them again. But they would see him.

Was Lillian right? Did he have no ego? Certainly not for trivial things like revenge. Perhaps his ego was so big it didn't notice pinpricks, as Ursula suggested. More likely, he thought, he had no ego for the present moment: his ego was for the future, the same fault he'd noticed in men he'd observed. But now the question was meaningless. He didn't need ego: ego had been replaced by obedience to his Voice, faith in that Voice of the God within, which had spoken to mankind since mankind began.

Obedience

At the front gate he was stopped. Something locked his arms and legs so that he had to stand still. It was like one of those moments in a dream where urgent action is required, but arms and legs are held in the vice-grip of sleep, and no amount of struggle can achieve anything, except perhaps wake the dreamer. He knew what it was that had stopped him.

Yes? he asked.

His Voice said,

'You will go in the house,
You will take your drawings
All your drawings done over the years,
Since you were seven.
You will burn them.'

Yes, Davis Blood said. He walked into the house, saying nothing to anybody and went straight to the cupboard in the carved sideboard that grandfather Blood had made, and took out the whole pile of drawings. He held the pile, 166 millimetres thick, in both hands, found matches in the kitchen, and carried them down the fourteen steps to the laundry. Under the copper he made a fire and got ready to feed the sheets in, a few at a time, and burn the lot. Last, he would put the rest of the matches in the flames, since they were part of it. His hands would be empty.

He set the fire and touched a match to the paper under the kindling. The fire caught. He reached for the drawings, peeled off a few at a time to feed them into the flames.

Stop! his Voice commanded. He stopped still.

'There's no need to burn the things you've made.
Now I know you will do as I say,
Because you were ready to destroy your drawings
Which are like children to you
And substitutes for friends you will never have.
I will see to it that your words
Will be a blessing to all who read them
Because you have faith in me, and obeyed.

Words! 'Your words.' So that was it: a writer! Was this what was meant on that third day of October forty days after his fifteenth birthday, when the Voices said, 'When will we hear from you?'

Davis Blood took the drawings, tied them in a secure bundle with twine, put them back in the sideboard, and left them.

The Voice wasn't finished with him. Between the sideboard and the bathroom he was stopped again and made to listen.

> *Study to fit yourself*
> *To make your exodus from the comfortable coasts of youth*
> *To cross the Blue Ridge that's in you*
> *To enter the wide plains of your life*
> *And approach its deserts,*
> *My testing grounds.*

Lillian and Ursula watched silently. They saw the mute drama with the drawings, the matches. They saw the stops, when he seemed to be listening to something they didn't hear. They were outside his field of action now. Their work was done. Both knew they would never know what went on in him; he was closed off from them and on his way into the future.

His Voice was in him, sounding in his head. As he stood there, he thought how much like silent prayer his actions, his way of standing and listening must seem. But it was so natural, so clear. God is everywhere, therefore in us; in our heads, since that is where we hear God's voice.

He'd arrived, with help, at those thoughts when he was a little boy, and was proud of them then: they were his very own thoughts. Now it was all obvious, elementary, part of the ground of his being. Now their time had come. They'd risen out of the processes within him, followed by other thoughts they had given rise to, which he hadn't, so far, expressed.

The Point

He was too restless to feel easy round the house. If he could have cleared them all out and sat at the big table with the place to himself, that would have been different. It wasn't possible. He grabbed shorts, shoes to run in, and the axe, and set off down the bush. The sun wouldn't be gone for several hours yet. He ran at an easy pace. The axe in his right hand felt almost weightless.

He slowed to a walk at Black Snake Corner, and followed the ridge track through thick, shoulder-high brush round to Kangaroo Point, place of peppermints, white gums with their divided branches, and scribbly gums; where he stood on the flat shelf of Point Rock. The sun shone full on him, the quiet of the bush cocooned him. The nearby scribbly gums seemed to sleep.

At first he thought of nothing. Then, as a gesture towards the violence of his renunciation of years of drawing, he allowed gentle thoughts of gratitude to flow through that place in him where he was really himself, gratitude that he was free of the inner friction and nervous waste that might in another person have stayed his hand with caution or indecision; that he was able to feel joy at personal desolation, sacrifice of himself; that he was willing to live with pain, with severity; that he could trample on things once precious to him in the service of what lay ahead.

He sat on the outermost edge of Point Rock, his hand round the neck of the axe-handle. How he loved that timber feel, the hickory handle, and the Kelly axe-head that he'd known for so many years. How long before he would be compelled to leave it, too, without regret but with a stern joy?

He looked at it and ran his left hand up and down the handle smoothed by use.

It was good to be alone. He looked out over the place where the creeks met and began to flow together to the sea, the junction where the waterloving trees gathered; casuarinas, paperbarks, scented satinwoods. The hill slopes, where the blue gums and grey gums grew tall, regarded him benignly as they cooled slightly, ready for night.

The afternoon sun had been shining along the valley below and to his right. Now a shadow pooled at the junction of the creeks.

The boy was silent a long time. The shadow where the valleys met crept higher. The light thinned. There was something incomplete in what had happened so far. Being given directions for his life work was one thing, but where was the provision for what *he* might have to say, day by day? He needed more than a God; he needed a friend.

For a while he sat then, jumping to his feet, axe in hand, he shouted at the top of his voice into the deep valleys: 'Tell me more! It's not enough to be given orders and to obey. What about me, when you have nothing to say? There must be more! Tell me the next step!'

The brittle echoes bounced back and forth as he stood there looking fiercely at the rising shadow, at time and light passing, shaking the axe with the impatience of his demand.

His Voice came.

'All is in you.'

the grave deep voice pronounced.

'You need nothing, but to open up.
Don't adjust the world, alter yourself;
After that, the world will change.

'How am I to alter myself?' Davis Blood asked.

'I am within you: release me.
Stop trying to be your own God:
Alone, independent, self-sufficient.

> *Be opposite to me in your weakness*
> *Not competitive with me in my strength.*
> *Be complementary: allow my positive*
> *To flow through and suffuse your negative,*
> *And I will be liberated within you*
> *To reach into, and flood, every cranny of your self.*
> *No longer is the unaided self the centre*
> *For God displaces the self and becomes the centre:*
> *That is the key to wholeness.'*

The Voice ceased. Davis Blood's grip on the axe-handle relaxed a little. Only then was he conscious of having choked the axe with his fierce grip on the neck of the handle.

He said, 'But how do I begin? How do I get in touch?'

> *Talk to me! Question! Report to the inner God.*
> *Speak to me! Engage me in conversation.*
> *Then, once you've begun, continue*
> *The conversation for the rest of your life.*
> *If you stop talking, I retreat.*
> *Determine to reach within and find me.*
> *Begin your talkwork and its discipline now,*
> *The initiative is yours.*
> *You have been preserved, protected, given all you need,*
> *When will I hear your voice?*

Shadow darkened the valley. Only the ridges were sun-covered. Davis Blood stood, took a long look round at his loved and familiar bush and at an easy pace began the run back home. In the scribbly gum nearest Kangaroo Point Rock a large grey bird watched him go, then resumed its meditations on the consciousness shared by all living things.

At the big table he took paper and wrote down everything that had been said.

The Male Imperative

*H*e stood and stretched, arching his back, flexing his arms and shoulders. Now, if he was to settle down to sleep on this night of nights he needed something quite different to do for a while.

He playfully decided, since he now was a writer, to begin a book. He held up a small pile of good old Randal's white paper in both hands and brought it down on the table edgewise to get the sheets all square. As the paper flexed, he noticed a brief resemblance to a sail-shape.

Sails for merchant ships were in the news. If you had a sail, he reflected, that didn't need hauling down, that could stay in position in any weather, accommodate any wind, any change in wind direction, you would have a valuable fuel substitute. What would such a sail look like?

Well, he thought, in light air it would look like this sheet of paper, a continuous surface. What would it look like in a gale?

It would be a skeleton of a sail. And for winds of intermediate force the spaces between the ribs of the skeleton would be more or less filled in to suit the wind. Such sails could be made of metal or carbon fibre. The masts would be central to the sail so the sail could turn in any direction. But how to fill the spaces in the sail, in the small squares when needed, and open them when the wind was stronger? That was the design problem.

He visualised the small movable sail-bits within the ribbed structure as small squares, rather like sheets of paper; perhaps a trellis-shape, an expanding lattice, was the answer.

He put the paper down and laughed at himself. Here he was, on the most crowded day in his life so far, inventing, when he was supposed to be writing a book. Perhaps the activities had a lot in common. He contented himself with a last look at his mental picture of a ship at sea with its half-dozen masts, its metal sails filled with a heart-satisfying wind, as it ploughed on heroically towards its destination. In the engine room, the sensing and controlling equipment monitored wind-speed and load on its sails, the little page-shaped spaces in the sails opening a fraction and closing, controlled ultimately by the wind pressure itself.

What would he do? It had been easy, with drawing pencils and paper. Objects and situations surrounded him wherever he was: he needed only pick up a pencil and sketches flowed. What did he know, to cover the chasm of ignorance within himself? How could he use words to talk to others, when he himself was empty?

He had nothing. He would have to supply what he needed. As he wrote he would teach himself, he would learn about the world, about others, about himself.

One day it would all be true, and he would have the capacity and assurance to pour out the godlike suggestions that then would be pressing for birth within him.

What would he write? How about the story of a young person like himself, coming to a decision about what he would do with his life? Such a youth might have several courses open, but would choose one and launch himself singlemindedly on that.

It could be called 'The Male Imperative'. He printed this in big letters on the first sheet of paper.

Why that title? He knew of no specifically male imperative, unless you counted sex and the perennial male vice of living in the future, and the usual perception that males craved to succeed, desired to defeat others, and hoped against hope that they feared nothing. Wanting to be better, to be best, was for anyone; all you needed was to want it enough.

To be different, original, interesting, were common compulsions among men he had observed, whether in their behaviour to each other or to women, and certainly in their efforts to succeed in their various enterprises. Maybe there was a male imperative of sorts.

Nevertheless, it was too much like a special case. He crossed out that title and replaced it with:

'Portrait of a Young Artist.'

The Liberated God

Writers often wrote a dedication for their books. He would do that, too. Smiling, he set out on the second sheet:

'To Aunt Mira, the most literate old bird in history,' and enjoyed the family joke for a minute before crumpling that sheet of paper and getting another.

No, he thought. When I become the parent of a book, I'll make a proper dedication. He wrote:

'To the Liberation of God.'

For he knew now that God is everywhere in chains.

Beginning

At the big table, he pushed the papers aside and sat still, pencil in his fingers. He looked out into the night. Slowly, and with concentration, he said the two words that had been in his head for a long time, that he had craved to say: Internal God.

He felt the warm tide first in his stomach, then his legs and feet, then it was all through him. The world was full of peace, its vibrations sang with gladness. Every irritation was gone, every rough place in him smooth. A weight he'd never noticed before lifted from him. His whole body felt loose and easy, completely at home in the world.

He understood why it was good that he was different.

He was reconciled to the world around him, the past he'd come from and the world towards which he travelled. He was reconciled to a life of laborious effort; reconciled to death, too, since whatever happened, he or his parts would be with God.

He felt he was being filled with light. The myriad diversity of the planet and the worlds beyond sparkled and shone in his head with the brilliance of God. It was marvellous.

He got ready for bed, and lay down, unaware that his fingers still held the pencil, in that pale-blue room where his brothers had slept and where his sick father had stayed, like a boarder, until carted away to die. The room was dark with the fragrant air of night. He looked out the window, where high in the north Orion swaggered across the sky. He had a new text:

> *The internal God is my refuge and strength.*
> *I am unassailable. I can do all things.*

He said the words again. Internal God. Again the mysterious stress-dissolving peace ran through him as he lay there, remembering.

Remembering the time when as a child he encountered the belief that God, a spirit, permeates all things. That belief permeated him. It was his starting point, his axiom.

Remembering the related discovery of his mother's silent talking and listening to that spirit that went on in her head, and only God knew what was said and heard in there; and how he went on to elaborate his own picture of the presence and accessibility of God in himself.

Until this very afternoon, when in one continuous burst, insight after insight poured out from him as realisation, and back into him to be stabilised as new knowledge; insights which had grown in him, worked on by processes of which he was unaware, that gradually had compiled a picture of all that was in him, then proceeded to build a structure that provided motive power, sustenance and support; a structure in which and by which he would live his life to the fullest extent. And this was his geometry.

Simply to live — to breathe, eat, sleep, play, work — used only part of his energy. With the balance he'd done what countless generations before him had done: he had constructed his world. He needed a God; he needed a way to live; he needed a work to do. He had them all.

What would happen when, obeying his Voice, the spirit of life was liberated in him?

Internal God, he said silently, though inside his head the words resounded as if proclaimed in a cathedral.

Internal God. Internal One.

Confidence filled him. He feared nothing. He smiled, and fell asleep, the pencil still in his hand.

FOR THE BEST IN PAPERBACKS, LOOK FOR THE
PENGUIN

ALSO BY DAVID IRELAND

A Woman of the Future

Alethea Hunt is a child apart, a singular young woman, and an exceptional personality striving to come to terms with herself in a haunted world. Often a victim, more often a survivor, she is buoyed by those things her society has labelled as obsolete: an unfailing sense of self, of love, of vulnerability; her authentic and original voice stands as a lone outpost amidst the vanishing complex of feelings and meanings.

In *A Woman of the Future* David Ireland has written one of the most striking novels of our time – and one that is disquietingly familiar in its implications.

Winner of the Miles Franklin Award.

The Glass Canoe

The Southern Cross is a pub, an old, battered and experienced place, somewhere in the centre of Sydney. Meat Man is a regular, a very regular regular, who views his world – the world of the pub and its clientele – through his beer glass, his glass canoe which transports them all to other worlds, worlds of fighting and loving and, above all, drinking.

The grand saga of the Southern Cross or the tragic futility of humanity at a watering hole? Perhaps it's all to be taken on a bent elbow with another swallow.

FOR THE BEST IN PAPERBACKS, LOOK FOR THE

PENGUIN

City of Women

The city of women is love, Billie Shockley says. But in the city of women that is her world, love takes strange forms.

The city is Sydney; from its familiar streets and gardens men have been banished. Their existence still threatens its precincts and Old Man Death moves rapaciously and relentlessly among its citizens. Billie observes them – their hedonism, rivalry, passions, cruelty, power, fragility. Reflecting her own anguish at the loss of love and youth, they suffer brutality and decay.

Archimedes and the Seagle

'I have to listen to all sorts of crackpot remarks from humans with little knowledge, and be thought to agree. They – the humans – think it's worship when I look up with my mouth open; or at least respect, since I don't answer back. Sometimes, I can't help it and let out a short howl if they've said something unusually stupid.'

So says Archimedes, from his dog's eye view of the world. Of humans with their vulnerability, and of their tyrannies over things, creatures, themselves, over language and knowledge.

With compassion, generous delight and simple wisdom, he observes life's complexities, from the petty, squabbling greed of the gulls to the not-so-different patterns in human nature.

As he marvels at the soaring, solitary flight of the seagle, he recognises how much of his own joy and energy are social. And that even the earthbound can dream of the sky.

FOR THE BEST IN PAPERBACKS, LOOK FOR THE

PENGUIN

The Flesheaters

A novelist who lives up in a tree; a child who likes to paint dead bodies; a granny who lives in a kennel and bites . . . these are some of the characters of this extraordinary novel set in a dilapidated stone mansion in Sydney.

Bizarre, bitingly satirical, richly ambiguous, it is an image of the modern world which the author sees as 'a madhouse without walls'.

Double Agent: David Ireland and his Work   Helen Daniel

David Ireland's novels have won Australia's most prestigious literary prizes and have been damned as literary 'sewage'; they have been prescribed for some literature courses and banned from others.

But they cannot be ignored. Ireland lurks under cover to ambush the reader. His novels – from the grim energy of *The Unknown Industrial Prisoner* to the optimism of *A Woman of the Future* – take apart contemporary society, enjoying a pungent delight in exposing its absurdities.

What is David Ireland: master of 'literary subterfuge' or writer of 'blasphemous hogwash'? Helen Daniel has pursued this evasive, reticent writer in search of the inspiration behind his work. And, paradoxically, she has discovered much of the private man in his very public writings.

FOR THE BEST IN PAPERBACKS, LOOK FOR THE PENGUIN

BOOKS BY THEA ASTLEY IN PENGUIN

Hunting the Wild Pineapple

Leverson the narrator, at the centre of these stories, calls himself a 'people freak'. Seduced by north Queensland's sultry beauty and unique strangeness, he is as fascinated by the invading hordes of misfits from the south as by the old established Queenslanders.

Leverson's ironical yet compassionate view makes every story, every incident, a pointed example of human weakness – or strength.

Beachmasters

The central government in Trinitas can't control the outer island. But then neither can the British and French masters.

The natives of Kristi, supported and abetted by some of the *hapkas* and *colons* of two nationalities, make a grab for independence from the rest of their Pacific island group. On their tiny island, where blood and tradition are as mixed as loyalties and interests, their revolution is short-lived. Yet it swallows the lives of a number of inhabitants – from the old-time planters Salway and Duchard, to the opportunist Bonser, and the once mighty *yeremanu*, Tommy Narota himself.

Salway's grandson Gavi unwittingly gets caught up in Bonser's plans and, in a test of identity too risky for one so young, forfeits his own peace.